# IMAGININGS
# OF SAND

*André Brink*

Minerva

**A Minerva Paperback**
IMAGININGS OF SAND

First published in Great Britain 1996
by Martin Secker & Warburg Limited
This Minerva edition published 1997
by Mandarin Paperbacks
an imprint of Reed International Books Ltd
Michelin House, 81 Fulham Road, London sw3 6rb
and Auckland, Melbourne, Singapore and Toronto

Copyright © 1996 by André Brink
The author has asserted his moral rights

A CIP catalogue record for this title
is available from the British Library

ISBN 0 7493 9587 7

www.minervabooks.com

Printed and bound in Great Britain
by BPC Paperbacks Ltd, Aylesbury, Bucks

*For Mazisi*

dear friend, who knows about exile,
and returning, and stories,
and ancestors

# Author's Note

I am indebted to Abraham de Vries who first recorded the legend of the idiots of the Little Karoo in *Die Uur van die Idiote* ('The Hour of the Idiots'), and to V C Malherbe's *Krotoa, Called 'Eva': A Woman Between*, for the raw material of my Kamma/Maria in Part Three, while for Wilhelmina's story in Part Five I have drawn on the Great Trek diaries of Susanna Smit.

The epigraph by Octavio Paz has been translated from the poem *Blanco*.

On the map of South Africa the site of my Outeniqua would roughly coincide with that of the ostrich town of Oudtshoorn; but Outeniqua is not Oudtshoorn, nor should the inhabitants of the one be mistaken for those of the other.

More than anything I have written before, this story needed a woman's hand; and the help of my wife Marésa has been inestimable. Where I have failed to follow her advice the blame is squarely mine.

*you fall from your body to your shadow* not there but in my eyes
*in a motionless fall of cascade* sky and earth join
*you fall from your shadow to your name* untouchable horizon
*you rush through your likenesses* I am your remoteness
*you fall from your name to your body* the furthest reach of seeing
*in a present that never ends* imaginings of sand
*you fall to your beginning* scattered fables of the wind
*spilling on my body* I am the column of your erosions . . .
      *The unreality of the seen*
      *lends reality to the seeing*

                                   OCTAVIO PAZ

## An attempted reconstruction
## of Ouma Kristina's family line

KAMMA/MARIA birth unknown – became a tree in c. 1770
[married ADAM OOSTHUIZEN]

LOTTIE birth unknown – vanished in search of her shadow c. 1790
(other siblings unrecorded) [married BART GROBLER]

SAMUEL born c. 1776 – disappeared, presumed drowned 1831
(+ 17 other SAMUELS) [married HARM MAREE]

WILHELMINA 1805–1862 [married LEENDERT PRETORIUS, 1829;
HANSIE NEL, 1841; BERTUS LINGENFELD, 1845]

PETRONELLA 1839–1921 (+ BENJAMIN and 14 other siblings)
[married HERMANUS JOHANNES WEPENER, 1863]

RACHEL 1874–c. 1891 (+ EULALIE 1865–1902, WILLEM 1867–1901,
BAREND 1871–1900, MARTIENS 1871–1901)

KRISTINA (OUMA) 1891–1994 [married, for what it was worth, CORNELIS
BASSON, 1921]

LOUISA 1921–1990 (+ 8 other siblings)
[married LUDWIG MÜLLER, 1949]

KRISTIEN born 1961 (+ ANNA b. 1952:
married CASPER LOUW, 1977)

# Contents

# Contents

# ONE

---

## *The Return*

# I

*A big girl now*; the stupid phrase careering through my head from the moment the plane took off from Heathrow. The great return. All these years of wondering how it would be; so many others have risked it, some to tumultuous crowds, toyi-toying, shouting, singing; others slinking home along back ways. Not I. The day I'd left the country I'd sworn it would be for good. And I'd held out, unyielding to all natural appeals. Then this phone call, and what else was to be done? I did not even stop to think. Only after I've already been assigned to a narrow fate on the plane, squeezed between two bulging businessmen – the one on my left, on the aisle, in textiles; the other a civil engineer; both drinking steadily, each intent on outwitting the other in setting up dates with me (the one on the aisle even suggesting moistly in my ear, at three in the morning, as the window-man, feigning sleep, attempts to slide his hand in under my blanket, that we decamp to a toilet) – it dawns on me that I am actually on my way home. Or whatever is now to pass for home. But this is how it has to be. Ouma Kristina is, has always been, different. And I have no choice but to obey, not just because I bear her name. (Had I obliged my father and entered the world a boy – he was convinced it would be second time lucky – I would have been, in honour of an array of his ancestors, Ludwig Maximilian Joseph Heinrich Schwarzenau an der Glon; seeing me born, like my predecessor, without the distinguishing appendage of the right sex, he retreated in disgust and pretended I hadn't happened. Left to my mother, I would have been stuck with an operatic name, Aida or Lucia or Elvira or, who knows, Butterfly; thank God Ouma's practical sense prevailed, as it had with my older sister, and I became a no-nonsense Kristien.)

Death has this way (Dr Johnson's words in the narrow attic above Gough Square where I went with Michael, the insipid light spilled on the floor like too-weak tea, on the day we became lovers) of concentrating the mind. But it isn't death as such that hurls me headlong home. I have survived Father's death, and Mother's. Not 'hardening my heart', merely accepting inevitability. Then why succumb, now, to Ouma? Is it the shocking nature of the event, the gratuitous violence of it, coming at a time when everything is supposed to be returning to whatever in that remote place is regarded as normal? Or is it the fact that she wasn't, when Anna's call came, dead, but dying, which left me with a choice, a possibly fatal choice?

It is the kind of experience that provokes memory. Fending off the encroaching hand from my right thigh as I become aware of another on my left, moving with Tarquin's ravishing strides towards his design, I escape to memories of Ouma, to memories of memories.

'How come you remember so much?' I asked her once, years ago, interrupting the flood of stories.

She merely smiled, her mouth a deeper fold among so many others (even when I was a small girl she was already incalculably old). And said, 'I am a very ordinary person in most respects, Kristien.' A lie, and she knew it as well as I. 'But in one respect I know I am extraordinary. My memory. You're right. I have an amazing memory. At times I even surprise myself. I can remember things that never happened.'

The two male hands, resolute, mindless, are converging across my separate thighs: the predator on my left adorned with a carbuncle of a ring, the other sprouting small tufts of black bristles between the stubby joints (I'd checked on them, before, over dinner: I always notice hands). These little piggies going to market. Abandoning myself to Ouma, reclined, head leant back, in what they must interpret as the sign of ultimate surrender (I am female flesh, I may be invaded), I take the two advancing hands in mine and place them on each other in my lap.

I count to three before the message reaches the two sets of intertwined fingers which then withdraw in unseemly haste. One of my neighbours hisses venomously in my ear. 'Bitch' is, as far as I can make out, the word used. Afterwards I am allowed to rest in peace.

Hurtling through the night, Africa invisible below but omnipresent. How easily eleven years can be peeled from one, a shift stripped smoothly from an unresisting body, leaving me naked, approaching death. The loss of innocence. Now; here. Not that faraway day – twenty years ago? I was not yet thirteen – when I ran indoors from my hideout in the great loquat tree to raise my dress and show Ouma my

4

soaked panties, the only grown-up I would ever dare to share it with: 'Ouma Kristina! I'm bleeding inside, am I going to die?' Calmly, efficiently, she took charge. Sent me to the bathroom with firm instructions, then ordered the handyman Jeremiah to drive her all the way to town, to the chemist, returned with the brownpaper parcel and withdrew with me into her own bedroom, sacrosanct to all but me, to 'fit me out' in bouts of giggles interspersed with solemn and amazing confidences. *You're a big girl now.*

On her dressing table the small oil painting in its frame, no bigger than an envelope, of the naked man gazing untroubled at the spectator ('Mother, for God's sake, you should put that thing away, the children are growing up'). We'd never dared to ask her about it. Not even I. Although we'd made, whenever we spent the summer holidays with her, furtive incursions into that all-but-forbidden half-dark room, simply to stare, and simper, and scuttle out again. On that afternoon amid the clutter of her shaded room deep inside the towering incongruous house that sat like a mirage on the white, hot plains, somehow the provocative picture on her dressing table witnessing the mystery of my bleeding became involved with my feeling for her; and if the riddle remained it was not because the naked man had no name or history but because *she* chose to keep the secret.

She drew his body, not his identity, into her explanation of what was happening inside mine – not as a graphic lesson in sex, but as a story. Her stories always resolved everything, without disturbing the miraculous nature of the world. Which was why I could never have enough of them.

– Ouma Kristina, tell me about the woman with the hair as long as a river – the girl who killed herself in the cellar – the woman who built the palace – the one who was as strong as a buffalo – the one whose tongue was cut out – the one who came from the water – the one who wrote in sand –

If it won't senselessly prolong your agony, please stay alive until I'm home. I'm on my way back, after these many years. I haven't forgotten, you'll see. I'll listen to every single story you wish to tell me: don't let them die with you. I'm coming home, to whatever remains of that improbable castle in the desert. I'm coming, you'll see. I am a big girl now.

The house originally came from a mail-order catalogue, chosen by Ouma Kristina's mother Petronella about three-quarters through the nineteenth century, at the time the ostrich-feather boom lured most farmers in the Little Karoo into investing all their worldly wealth in birds. As it happened, my ancestors had something of a head start over everybody else as they had eradicated every vine on their near-limitless farm and changed to ostriches, prompted not by visions of wealth but by misplaced piety. In one of her legendary nocturnal conversations with God Petronella had been instructed by this Highest Authority (seated astride her ample bosom, which aggravated the poor woman's asthma) to get rid of the sinful vines that had assured the family's prosperity, and start anew. The climate ruled out wheat; it was a bad year for watermelons and there was no demand as yet for lucerne; it was the wrong kind of grazing for cattle or sheep; and after a number of ever more desperate trials and spectacular errors her husband Hermanus Johannes Wepener hit, from sheer audacity if not perversity, upon the idea of ostriches. Never one to tackle anything on a small scale, and more to 'show' his wife than for any rational reason, he covered his thousands of newly barren hectares with birds. And then came the boom.

Not really knowing what to do with all their new-found wealth, they decided, well before any of their neighbours, to invest in the kind of palace only the Queen of Sheba or the builder of the Taj Mahal could dream up; in the aforementioned catalogue an illustration of just such an abode was spotted and recklessly ordered, and in due course all the parts and materials arrived on a long line of ox-wagons from Port Elizabeth. The problem (to Ouma Kristina's glee in the retelling) was that the original plan had somehow been lost in transit; Petronella refused to wait another year for a replacement to be sent and proceeded to supervise the building herself. It took five years to construct, undergoing countless additions and modifications along the way; a seemingly unending succession of caravans from Cape Town and Port Elizabeth continued to bring in new materials from the most unlikely places on the globe – glass and wood and stone and sheets of iron, candelabras and chimney pots and sculpted shapes – as Petronella's fancy took her on ever bolder flights. Her sizeable army of builders and handymen were driven more by enthusiasm than by proven skill or experience: crude practical men used to hammering a recalcitrant tin roof into shape or stacking a kraal wall or roughcasting a structure designed to withstand a hundred years of hellfire, tornadoes, hurricanes, and the occasional summer deluge. As a result the finished house resembled nothing else on this planet. Coleridge or Ludwig of Bavaria would undoubtedly have approved. Three storeys high, topped with turrets, minarets, flèches, campaniles, domes, what had started off as a High Victorian folly turned out as Boer Baroque. Sandstone and redbrick, delicate fluted iron pillars and broekie lace, interspersed with balustrades of finely turned Burmese teak, flashes of Doric and Corinthian inspiration and even a Cape-Dutch gable on the south façade, contributed by a homesick Malay team carted into the interior after a mixed gang of shady Italian and Austro-Hungarian bandits had had to be deported for wreaking havoc on the site.

The interior, to us children, in the blaze of summer holidays, was an exhilarating maze of archways and branching corridors, magnificent marble or teak staircases and unexpected other, dingier, flights of steps leading to dead-ends or upstairs doors opening on the void; attics and rooms and closets and cubicles with no obvious or imaginable purpose, hidden among halls and chambers more comprehensible, even ostentatious, in the proclamation of their functions. Each family visit brought to light new spaces, whose existence we had never before suspected; at the same time we invariably lost track of others, hideouts of secret delights for all the cousins who converged there every impossible summer. During any given holidays there might well have been thirty or more of us.

Our games and explorations took us all over the place – from staid never-used sitting-rooms behind closed shutters, with mysterious bulky shapes shrouded in sheets; to kitchens and sculleries and shiver-cold coolrooms with the carcasses of slaughtered animals suspended from hooks; to bedrooms never slept in; up to the sprawling attic with its lingering smells of dust and dried fruit and feathers. In one corner we even discovered a stack of coffins, one chillingly described by Ouma, when we enquired, but without any attempt to offer an explanation, as 'second-hand'; all of them filled with raisins and dried figs, bundles of faded plumes, and the empty shells of old ostrich eggs, some of them decorated with weird faces.

But our favourite haunt was the basement, tall enough to stand upright in, and replicating with disconcerting exactness the plan of the ground floor, in the same way as, many years later, I discovered in

Paris the warren of subterranean sewers repeating the street plan above. Each room and lobby and passage had its corresponding space down here, like a subconscious mind, a memory of the house above, in which each event and gesture, each coming and going from the official world could be echoed and mimed, in minor key or mirror-image, all clad in shadows and redolent of must and dry rot and mouse droppings and dust; a space frequented by the spirits of the dead – the Girl, and the two unknown men whose skeletons had once been found there, and God knows how many others – but as real to us as the strange but very tangible objects our treasure-hunts brought to light.

Some parts of the underground cavern showed signs of earlier occupation: mouldy tables and chairs with the remnants of cloths and cutlery and crockery and cushions, two narrow rickety iron beds with the filthy remains of blankets and pillows and embroidered sheets and coir-stuffed mattresses, decayed cupboards and chests of drawers, tarnished brass or painted porcelain lamps, lanterns, candlesticks. Most intriguing of all were the markings on the walls – all the more fascinating as they were in such a state of decay that it was impossible any longer to make out what they had once been. Some of the unscarred patches suggested images of tantalising obscenity, a cavorting of fantastic sexual creatures, just enough to fire our dirty little minds without confirming anything. But who had made them? Who had lived here? We all presumed it must have been the Girl, whispered rumours of whom had haunted all the ramifications of the family for years. Ouma Kristina refused to divulge anything. Not even I was let in on the secret. 'Later,' she would say, 'one day when you're ready.' 'But when will that be?' 'Perhaps when you're sixteen.' And when I turned sixteen, 'No, wait until you're eighteen.' Then, 'Twenty-one.' In the end I had to resign myself to waiting. Sooner or later, I believed with an unshakeable faith, she *would* tell me, when she felt the time was right. Ouma Kristina wouldn't, ever, let me down. I was not only her favourite grandchild, but the one elected to take over, from her, the burden – or the delight, depending on how one looked at it – of the family's memories, recollections, fantasies. The whole house was a living treasury of stories, unto each room its own, but all culminating in the ghostly presences and imaginings of that lugubrious cellar, inhabited – still – by the long-dead Girl, its walls bearing the Rorschach stains of those indecipherable paintings, her memory now stained and splotched by the markings of time and the droppings of rodents and of the odd bird that has blundered in there through crevices and broken airvents.

8

The house was a veritable ark for a vast variety of bird-life. Under the eaves or in the immediate surroundings nested all manner of birds, swallows and finches, yellowtails and red-eyed wood-pigeons, even – at the back – a couple of small falcons; some left in autumn to return again in spring, others stayed; on one of the many chimneys a pair of blue cranes nested, on another a couple of storks; in the attic lived an extended family of barn owls that never failed to scare us stiff whenever we dared to venture into their smelly dark domain. And outside, the tangled shrubs and massive trees – pepper and conifer, monkey-puzzle and hardy palm, ash, cedar, bluegum, syringa, wild fig, oak, and one incredible loquat tree as ancient as the earth – was home to flocks of starlings, sparrows, mousebirds and yellow or scarlet weavers (one summer lightning struck the great loquat and afterwards we collected one thousand two hundred and seventy three birds among the broken branches on the soggy ground); there were even, from time to time, a few bedraggled vultures whose mere presence would frighten the hell out of us; around the muddy green farm dam geese cackled and approached with spread wings and outstretched necks to scare off intruders as if it were the Capitol they were defending; while on the patchy drought-parched lawns strutted fantastic peacocks that stained the surroundings with their brilliant blues and greens and purples; and at night their cries sent ecstatic tinglings of fear down our spines where we all lay wriggling and giggling together in the great communal bed the grownups had made for us on the floor of a cavernous hall well out of their way.

The farm, for some obscure and no doubt fanciful reason, was called Sinai; but to us it was always known as 'The Bird Place', and it seemed only natural that in the midst of such ornithological excess Ouma Kristina herself should gradually come to resemble her surroundings, as dogs are said to resemble their masters; smaller and frailer she shrank into a delicately boned birdlike body, her nose beaked, her wispy grey hair for all the world like scraggly feathers in the moulting season. Beside her, old Lizzie, one-time family servant turned lifelong companion, resembled more and more an angry brooding hen.

Seen from a distance, surrounded by a dark dense mass of trees and shrubs, the palace with its turrets, spires, domes, and chimneys, looked like the wreck of a great ghost ship perched on a submerged rock or sandbank in a sea of petrified undulating plains, windswept and sun-scorched. A place where anything or everything was possible, might happen, did happen. At night it was visited by ghosts and ancestral spirits – I know, I've heard them, felt them, seen them, believe me –

9

but even in the daytime, in the stark God-eye of the sun, it appeared mysterious, improbable, dream or nightmare, wishful thought or guilt-ridden vision, desperate and exuberant proof of the extremes the human mind, let loose, is capable of.

'Aren't you afraid of ghosts?' I once asked Ouma Kristina.

'Of course not.' She seemed amused at the mere idea. 'I know them all.'

'But what do you do when they come at night?'

'I just brush them aside.' Like cobwebs, I imagined, both horrified and reassured.

Over the years I've seen the place change, not just bleached and eroded like the surrounding landscape, but a sadder and more subtle kind of change, as the swarms of summer visitors slowly dwindled; fewer and fewer of the relatives turned up for Christmas as the young grew up and discovered other attractions, devising ever more ingenious excuses and explanations for not coming; as the old grew older and more disinclined to exert themselves, or became incapacitated in one way or another, or died, gradually using up the coffins stacked in the attic. Grandpa expired (not a day too soon, Ouma Kristina commented, dry-eyed) and with that his – considerable – side of the family subsided into obscurity. Father and Mother still honoured, with grim determination, the old tradition: once a year, then every other year, every third; then they too stopped visiting. (The delight of those journeys, especially by train, all the way from the remote Transvaal where we lived, the tic-a-tac, tic-a-tac of the wheels on the rails embedded in my memory. The car journeys were less pleasurable. Anna and I used to quarrel so much on the back seat that a set routine developed: every two hundred kilometres, on the dot, Father would stop the car, and get out, and remove his belt, and give us each a hiding, and then drive on.)

As the stream of visitors diminished to a trickle and then dried up, Ouma Kristina remained alone with old Lizzie in the sprawling surreal palace, until Lizzie too was gathered unto her mothers, leaving only Ouma behind, smaller every time I saw her, beginning slowly to stoop and shrink under the weight of time, seventy, eighty, ninety . . . moving soundlessly through that home of many mansions, a thin grey shadow with wispy hair and knuckled hands, fingers bedecked with rings, a glittering array of jewels on her ears and round her scrawny neck, enormous brooches on her concave chest, as ancient and in her own way as redoubtable as God. A shadow among the shades inhabiting the house, enveloped in emptiness, a silence disturbed only by the sounds of owls and bats and peacock-screams at night, the crying of a lost child, the whisperings of the dead. The outside world fell away from her. She was surrounded only by trusted labourers from earlier days, mainly the members of old Lizzie's substantial family, and they lived some distance away from the palace. No relatives arrived on her doorstep any more, no visitors at all. Only I persisted, once a year, at least until I was almost twenty-two and left the country. Never to return, I swore.

'You'll be back,' said Ouma Kristina, unperturbed. She should know. She, too, had left once, for good; and returned. (She, at least, had the small painting of a naked man to show for it.)

And here I am on my way back to her. But will she still be there? And what has remained of the house itself?

# 3

Anna's call came at the most mundane of times, just past noon on Saturday. Bad news is supposed to come at night, when one is vulnerable and unprepared; not in the middle of an early spring day when life seems bountiful and to die absurd. I was sitting on the toilet reading the paper; Michael took the call as he was within reaching distance, being in what passes for a kitchen, rustling up lunch – he is much more adept at it than I am, which may be one of the reasons I have put up with him for longer than with any of his predecessors. (That, and the fact that he's Michael, not Mike; I'm allergic to Mikes and Nicks and Dicks. Not, I should add, that marriage, for me at least, is on the cards, not even after three years of sharing a fair amount of our waking and most of our sleeping hours. Michael has no axes to grind, no cause to espouse – his predecessors used at least to be into Anti-apartheid; his only passion, except for me I hope, is Shakespeare.)

'Somebody called Anna on the phone,' he announced from the door. 'She said "Ah-na", frightful Afrikaans accent. I told her you were involved in a matter which requires your undivided attention but she says it's important.'

'My sister!'

'I didn't know you had a sister.' He sounded hurt.

'She's part of a past I've written off.'

'And now it's catching up with you.'

'No,' I said, 'I won't let it.' But I felt more apprehensive than I dared let on. I picked up the telephone. 'Anna? It's Ouma, isn't it?'

Because this was the one thing I'd always feared; this was the phantom limb which one day would begin to ache again.

A gasp at the other end. 'How did you know?'

'She was here last night. She came on the back of a big bird.' The memory was startlingly vivid. I'd looked at my watch, it was just past one; Michael was snoring. She'd come with the memories of sunsets and thunderstorms and dust-devils swirling on the plains, and of birds, and of silences deeper than earth or water.

Anna's voice cut across the recollection. 'Kristien, what are you saying? You mean you dreamt about Ouma?'

'No. I couldn't sleep. And I saw her, but she wouldn't talk to me.' Hearing an unintelligible sound in my ear I sighed. 'All right, then. Let's say it was a dream. Now *tell* me.'

'Something terrible has happened.'

'Is she dead?' I whispered.

'No.' A catch in her voice. 'At least, not yet. She . . . They burned down the house. Last night. And now she's . . . she keeps on quarrelling with the doctors and the nurses. She thinks you're with her and she keeps on talking to you.' A choked laugh. 'She says she has stories to tell you.'

'For God's sake get to the point,' I snapped, aware of Michael lending an ironical ear to the conversation. 'Tell me what happened,' I insisted.

'I'm trying to. It was after midnight. Someone threw a bomb or something through her window. No one knows for sure yet. But they say the place is burnt down, you can imagine, all that woodwork. Somehow she managed to get to the phone before she collapsed, but even so – it was hours before they could put out the fire – and now she's in hospital in Intensive Care. She's in a bad shape, Kristien, you know she's over a hundred.' It was some time before she could go on. 'Casper says I must hurry up, it costs money. But it's so awful. There's police all over the place, and the farmers are calling up a commando, and Heaven knows what's going to happen.' Followed by a muffled remark, presumably addressed to Casper. I could imagine him remonstrating authoritatively; the whine in her responding voice unnerved me. How old was she? Thirty-three plus nine, forty-two. About the age Mother was when I was born, the *laatlammetjie*, the afterthought, that put paid (as she never oh never failed to remind me) to her 'singing career'. Now Anna. Was I supposed to pity her? But this, after all, was the destiny she'd chosen, knowingly, my once bright-eyed brilliant exemplary sister, straight As, first tennis team, top of the Bible class,

Jacaranda Queen, all the right things at the right times, including married bliss, for better or for worse, happily ever after. Unlike this obstreperous youngest sibling who'd spurned commitment and, backed only by Ouma Kristina, had left behind family, friends, lovers and job security to emigrate when, as they say, the going got tough. Which earned me, from Father, the moment I had my first address in London, the solemn reminder from, I think, Jeremiah, *The heart is deceitful above all things and desperately wicked*. It tickled me so much, I copied it out in the italic script I was then so proud of, and stuck it on my pinboard on the kitchen among the unanswered letters, the cards, the cuttings, the cartoons, the photographs, including the nude one Jean-Claude had taken of me and which I found a useful conversation piece, or conversation stopper as the case might be, with would-be new suitors.

'What do the doctors say?'

'They don't seem to think there's much chance. She – '

'But she's still talking, you said?'

'On and off. I told you she keeps on speaking to you as if you were here. But she's very weak. A few days perhaps, no one can tell. Kristien, please – '

'But it's ridiculous! Why would anyone want to throw a bomb at her?'

Scandal had been the key to Ouma's life; even her death, it now seemed, would be scandalous.

'The whole country is a madhouse,' sobbed Anna. 'Everybody is killing everybody else – ' More muffled conversation. 'Casper says – '

'Fuck Casper!'

'Kristien! At a time like this – '

Of course she didn't know, had never known, about Casper and me. And if she had *I* would have been the one to blame; I'm the wicked female. Ouma's bad blood, presumably.

'Anna, I'll see what I can do. It's the middle of term and everything. I'll phone you back.'

'You can stay with us if – '

Casper's voice growling in the background.

'Just give me time to think.'

Yet the moment I replaced the telephone, even before I turned to face Michael, I knew I would go back. What swayed me, ridiculous as it might seem, was what Anna had said about the stories. Michael would hold the fort. Surely it would not have to be for long. I could rely on his charm to placate Mr Saunders at my Hampstead school. As for the kids – I felt a momentary twinge of conscience, one never quite escapes the Calvinist background, but they'd survive; and I could do with a respite from my habitual casting of false pearls to real swine.

'What's up, love?'

'My gran's dying.' I gave him a brief summary of Anna's garbled message. 'I have to go back.'

'What's the point?'

Only last night we'd spoken about it in bed (not much of a bed, just a heap of tangled sheets and blankets on the floor in the corner of my room, the mattress salvaged years before, in my more obviously indigent days, from a pavement off Russell Square): what a relief it was at this time, more than ever before, not to be in that benighted country. At the very moment, 'democratic' elections in sight, when one would be expecting to see the unresolved rage of centuries temporarily settling, however uneasily, into the tense calm of anticipation, wave upon wave of violence was racking the place. We didn't even feel like turning on the television any more; it was all so nauseatingly predictable. And so last night, too, it had surfaced in our conversation, just enough to turn us resentfully – not against each other but against the world – from the bliss and oblivion of love.

Now here I was, a mere twelve hours on, contemplating return.

'I have no choice, Michael. I have to go.'

'It's madness, Kristien! You took your leave of her long ago. She probably won't even recognise you. If it's really as bad as this Anna person says – And with the whole country going to the dogs.'

'I know. But it's Ouma. And if she really needs me – Michael, while I pack, will you please phone Heathrow and find out about planes?'

'When?'

'Tonight.'

'But it's – '

Less than three hours later we went out into the unwavering sunshine; an April more translucent and balmy than any I had seen in the years of my chosen exile. It was with a strange feeling of resignation that I drew the front door shut behind me: the bright red door which, seven years before, had first drawn me to the gentle graceful curve of Sussex Gardens, its deceptive green-thought tranquillity. Now I was leaving – only for a week, a fortnight at most, I reminded myself; yet with a feeling of facing something much more unpredictable than death.

(If I were to have known in that instant what I was heading for – not that single death but so many; and my role and responsibility in all of

14

it – would I have pressed on regardless? It seems inconceivable. And yet – )

There was a moment when Michael, carrying my single hastily-packed scuffed suitcase, stopped, asking in a strained voice, 'Kristien, do you realise what this thing – at this time – could do to us?'

I said, 'I don't know what it can do to us. I know what it may do for me.' Looking at him – we were mere feet apart – it felt as if I was, already, very far away.

He winced. He looked strained and pale; this was the last thing we could or would have foreseen, wished.

'You are being incredibly selfish,' he said.

'Yes,' I said. 'I know. If I were not I'd probably fall apart.'

What I thought, but did not say, was, Can't you see that I'm not going just to have my way? This is something I have to face myself, something I do not understand and need to understand. I'm sick of being, if not all things to all people, at least many things to many people; it is time to return to older kinds of knowing, to withdraw again to that desert where Ouma and her spirits have roamed and where they are now in danger of extinction. This is *my* call of the wild.

'South Africa brings out the worst in you,' he said tartly, but still quietly. Michael is not one to raise a voice. 'Even melodrama.'

'If that's all it means to you – ' I said. And took the suitcase from him and hailed the cab that was providentially passing, leaving Michael with his car keys already in his half-outstretched hand. (A totally unwarranted expense, and I regretted it a minute later; impulsive action has been the bane of my life.) I looked back once, as we curved towards Bayswater. He was still standing there, tall and slightly stooped, with his unkempt hair and grave spectacles, angry and not-so-young, something vulnerably boyish in his attitude; and for a moment I felt like turning back. Was I not making a dreadful mistake – not in going home to Ouma, but in leaving him behind? Three years. When I'd first met him, when we'd first made love behind that scarlet door, on our return from Dr Johnson's house, so curiously excited by notions of death, he'd seemed such an elegant solution, even if it were to a problem not yet identified. Three years of propinquity, too much or not enough? Where, how, had the shift occurred that turned solution into problem? Or had I been the problem all along?

I telephoned later from Heathrow to apologise, but Michael wasn't home, or didn't want to answer. Unfinished business. God, how much of it have I accumulated in my life. But I have to face it. I'm a big girl now.

# 4

If you are to spend a few more hundred pages with me I suppose I should have gone all out from the beginning to make a better impression. You may already have taken a dislike to me. *Mea culpa.* I am in many respects not a pleasant person. I can be nasty, prejudiced, petulant, vindictive, unreliable, you name it. My father undoubtedly thought of me as a witch. (Perhaps that was what the man on the plane said, 'Witch'? That is, if he ever took the time to reflect on me. One learns to deal with many things; others return to haunt you, or to take revenge on you at unguarded moments. It is all the more difficult to cope if one tries, as I am doing, to work through it in what remains something of a strange language. At the same time it offers the kind of distance useful for the soul-searchings I'm indulging in. During my years in London I became quite fluent in English, of course; I've been told that I have a 'flair'. But it can never be my native tongue. And I have delusions of grandiloquence. I tend to say 'impetuous' when 'wilful' would do, or 'proceed' rather than a simple 'go'. So be warned. You'll have to take me as I am. Also, I'm left-handed.

# 5

Anna is there to meet me at the pretentious little airport outside George. In Johannesburg I was swiftly deserted by my two surly companions. One was swept up in the crowd; the other, the textile man with the ring, Mr Tarquin, I happened to see again as we emerged from Customs and he stepped into the enthusiastic collective embrace of a woman and two teenage daughters. I could not restrain myself from sidling up to him and taking him by the arm. 'Thanks again,' I said. 'For everything.' I patted his hand. 'Do keep in touch. You've got my number.' I walked off with my scruffy suitcase, followed by their silence. In a dingy cubicle I positioned myself under a shower head that haphazardly and intermittently squirted three thin, well-separated jets of water, two cold, one scalding, in the general direction of my lathered body below, and dried myself with the towel an inattentive attendant had handed me between bouts of shouted conversation with an invisible person presumably at the far end of the airport building. I had a cup of tea, and a sandwich draped over a plate – the persistence of memory – and paged through a lurid Sunday paper. There was something on page three. Centenarian attacked on remote farm. Seventh elderly victim in past three weeks. Massive manhunt launched by police. Commando of farmers scouring district. Minister warns not to take law in own hands. Security to be stepped up in country districts. Mrs Kristina Basson, who celebrated her hundred-and-third birthday two months ago, reported to be in a critical condition. At that stage, mercifully, my connecting flight was called. For three more hours I've lolled and dozed, open-mouthed for all I know, this time undisturbed by prospective ravishers. And here, at last, I am; here she is.

At first I do not even recognise her and walk right past her, stopping to turn only when I hear her voice behind me. Can eleven years make such a difference? This tired, shapeless person surrounded by what seems like innumerable children: is this the sister once held up to me as the model of all I should but never possibly could be? She engulfs me, wetly kisses me, then hands me over to her swarming brood to be pummelled and mauled and drooled upon ('Auntie, Auntie, did you bring me something?')

I fend them off. Ever since what happened in London I'm intimidated by children. I know I'll have to work on it, but I'm simply not up to it now.

Emerging at last from the ruck I gasp at her, 'Anna, is she all right?'

Her face contorts. But she nods furiously. 'She's alive. That's about all.'

'Can you take me to her straight away?'

'Don't you want to rest first?'

'No, everything else can wait.'

I grab my battered suitcase from the conveyor.

'Is that all you have?' asks Anna; but whether I should read envy or disparagement into her voice is difficult to tell.

'I don't need much,' I say, as neutrally as possible. 'It's only for a few days.'

She darts a calculating look at my hand. 'No ring yet?'

'No ring.'

'But there was one, once?'

I shrug. Before the inquisition can proceed the children descend on me, pulling and tugging, to wrench the suitcase from me. Anna makes no attempt at all to impose even the semblance of discipline on their tumultuous ranks; it is clear that she has given up. She seems bedraggled and confused, her make-up has been applied half-heartedly, her clothes are nondescript, hanging limply from a body in need of care. How different from the elder sister I remember in her prime, erect and tall and beautiful, with ample breasts and a predilection for dresses and blouses with necklines practically down to her clitoris. The recollection brings a new warmth of sympathy for my sister. But it is tinged with anger too, at the dissipation of all that early energy and exuberance. Look at you now, I feel like saying; but I cannot hurt her so.

Amid vociferous protests the children are bundled into the back of Anna's bakkie parked outside; only the youngest, an unpleasant little boy, is allowed inside the front compartment with us.

'Not very comfortable,' I say, as always putting my foot in it. 'You should get a car.'

'I used to have one,' says Anna, with what I take to be a touch of resentment. 'But Casper thought this would be more practical.'

'For you or for him?'

She blushes briefly, grates the gears, then explains emphatically, 'Oh, I have a lot of deliveries to do, you know. Also, it's easier with the children.'

'Where is Casper?'

'He's out with his commando. I thought I told you? The farmers are up in arms about this whole business, you can imagine.'

'Isn't it better left to the police?'

'They don't trust the police any more. With the elections coming up next week, I tell you, the whole country is in a mess.' She turns her head to study me. 'I can't believe you're really here. You look so – smart.'

'You look good too,' I say perfunctorily.

'Please!' A sudden edge to her voice. 'I know what you're really thinking. I must look like a country bumpkin. But when you live the kind of life we have there's no time to think of appearances.'

'And you think I – ' I'll have to change the subject; why have we never been able to spend ten minutes together without getting into each other's hair? I restrain myself to say as neutrally as possible, 'I want to know about Ouma. How come she was all by herself?'

'Have you forgotten what she's like? We've tried time and time again to get her into an old-age home. She's as stubborn as always. Worse. And anyway, who would have thought – ' She's on the verge of tears again. 'I mean, other people die when they're seventy or eighty, perhaps ninety. Couldn't they just have left her to die in peace? For a thing like this to happen when you're over a hundred – '

'She's incredibly strong.'

'She won't survive this. No one else would have come out of it alive. I told you, I think she's hanging on only to see you.' Adding with a new touch of reproach, 'You've always been her favourite. Casper says she – '

'I suppose Casper can't wait to lay his hands on Ouma's farm.'

Her face flushes a very deep red. But instead of reacting aggressively, as I'd rather hoped she would, she resorts to the long-suffering whining tone again. 'It *is* the family farm,' she says. 'And I'm the oldest. Casper is my husband, so it's only fair – '

'Ouma isn't dead yet,' I interrupt her with a flash of anger. Then I let it go: what is the use? I love a good fight; but attacking Anna is like pummelling a pillow. 'Anyway, I haven't come to deprive anyone of anything. My life is elsewhere.'

'When we spoke yesterday – ' she says impulsively, a brief brightness in her voice. 'I wish you weren't quite so far away. We used to be so close when we were kids.'

'Not really,' I say, not to offend her, merely to remind her. 'You had your own crowd, you did everything together. I was much too young for you. I cramped your style. By the time you were having boyfriends, I suppose I was a real pest.' I stop to let the memory find its way. 'You were quite a hit in those days, remember? You could pick and choose. I still don't understand why – ' I stopped, contrite. 'Sorry, Anna. I've done it again.'

She gives a small grimace; both her hands are tight on the wheel. She drives like an old woman, staring grimly ahead. The town falls away behind us as we enter the dark mountains. There is a sharp fragrance of pine. I turn down the window; a gust from the sea, far below, comes washing over us. The child shouts in angry protest. I close the window again.

It has been so many years since I last drove along this pass, but it all comes back as forcefully as that reminder from the sea. The sensation, not of following the contours of the mountains but of moving right into them, enfolded by their moist immediacy, the rich darkness of their colours, the many greens, the blacks and browns and near-reds, the intimation of secret bird and animal life, clusters of virgin forest in deep folds, glimpses of thin white cataracts. Even the child between us falls, temporarily, silent.

Already I anticipate the next stage. This I will never get used to: the suddenness with which the mountains drop back as one is thrust out on the high plateau beyond. I almost gasp as the high light breaks over us, with a ferocity my eyes are no longer used to. Nothing gentle or attenuated here: all is brutally immediate. A rough and tumbling landscape, ochre and burnt umber (it is too early for the aloes); as if the earth heaved and tossed, and then froze in mid-motion. And then the restlessness subsides, the landscape opens up, the plains unscroll around us to expose its still indecipherable hieroglyphics of scrub and stones, erosion ditches, clumps of brittle grass, clusters of blue-grey sisal plants or prickly pears, rows upon rows of blue hills in the distance. And we, too, become part of this ancient writing, a story whispered among the others in the wind.

Touches of desert: not as stark as in most of the seasons I remember (the rains must have been recent, and abundant), but emphatic both in its outlines and its detail. Configurations of rock. Patterns of earth and sand. Minimal and bare, the clear lines strip away whatever is mere ornament or fancy, challenging the imagination. A space in which mirage becomes a condition and a starting point. This has always been Ouma Kristina's landscape. If one looks hard, and for long enough, they will appear, I know: the woman who had her tongue torn out; the one who wrote – because no one would give her pen or paper – on the bark of trees, on rocks, on sand; the one who disappeared, whose footprints simply stopped; the one who tended sheep she turned to stones to prevent their wandering away; the ostrich woman; the tree woman; the child who bore a child; Ouma Kristina herself. 'Look around you, my child. This is where you'll find out about what lasts and what the wind will blow away. Once upon a time – '

'Did Ouma ever tell you the story of the woman who came from the desert?' I ask Anna.

She glances at me, frowns, shakes her head. 'Can't say that she did. She can be such a bore.'

'Well, this woman lived in the desert. No one knew anything about her. And only three times in her life did she ever leave the desert to come into the city. Every time she asked the same question.'

'Which was?' She stops at a traffic light; we have reached the town. Outeniqua: the name itself lets in a new flood of memories. Awareness of the desert is temporarily suspended, but its intimation lingers.

'She asked the people, "Do you know what I am going to say to you?"'

'A rather stupid question, I must say.'

'The first time she came, the people said No, they had no idea. "You are ignorant," said the woman, and returned to the desert. Then, many years later, she came back and asked the same question. Remembering the first time, the people slyly said Yes, they knew. "In that case you don't need me," said the woman, and she went away to the desert again. For years and years the people kept on talking about her. And then, one day, the woman was back. "Do you know what I am going to say to you?" she asked, as before. This time the people were ready for her. Half of them answered Yes, the other half No. The woman gave a tired little smile and said, "In that case the ones who know can tell those who don't." Then she returned to the desert and no one ever saw her again.'

Anna laboriously turns into a side street. 'Is that it?' she says.

'What more do you want?'

'Really, Kristien.' She stops. 'We're here.'

# 6

The amazing thing about the hospital is the birds. The whole red roof of the building, the surrounding bluegum trees, all the lamp posts as far as the eye can see, are covered in birds, all kinds of them, swallows and sparrows and weavers and mousebirds, long-tailed birds of paradise and hoopoes, and even larger ones, hadedas and guineafowl and partridges.

'What's going on here?' I ask Anna.

'Where? What do you mean?' It is obvious that she hasn't even noticed.

'The birds. Look at them. They're going crazy.'

'Well, it's autumn. I suppose they're getting ready to migrate.'

'The swallows perhaps. Not the others. You ever seen guineafowl or hoopoes migrate?'

'How must I know?'

'They're Ouma Kristina's birds,' I exclaim in a moment of illumination.

'Don't be ridiculous. Why should they . . .' Her voice trails off as she notices a pair of barn owls stirring, eyes at half-mast, under an awning near the entrance. 'Better go inside,' she says hurriedly and turns back to the bakkie.

'Aren't you coming?'

'No. This is your turn.'

There is a flurry of activity at the reception desk when I announce myself. From the deeper recesses of the building a doctor is fetched by a squall of nurses. Hands behind his back, glasses perched on the tip of his fleshy nose, looking for all the world like a benign marabou – is this a hospital or an aviary? – he emits, in several small bursts of chattering, a series of random comments among which I recognise phrases like, 'Stabilised, thank heavens' – 'thirty per cent burns' – 'receding danger of lung failure' – 'heavy sedation most of the time' – 'incredible resources' – 'intensive care' – 'swelling beginning to subside' – 'breathing more easily' – 'at her age' . . . The rest is submerged in the twittering of his white-starched underlings, one of whom finally escorts me to the end of a very long bile-green corridor.

A small bundle which I take to be Ouma Kristina lies on a high narrow bed against the wall opposite a large closed window. A tangle of tubes and leads connect her to futuristic machines and drips on tall stands: she seems wired up for an electric chair.

With showy eagerness the nurse pushes past me and starts chattering, pointing at the objects surrounding us as if I'm a late-comer at a party to be introduced to the other guests. 'Plasma – antibiotics – glucose – morphine . . .' Pleased to meet you all. The introductions are interrupted by a thud against the window opposite, followed by a screeching sound. A starling has hurled itself against the closed pane and now lies dazed, with fluttering feathers, on the outside sill.

The nurse seems curiously unperturbed, if not wholly unaware of the racket. But I cannot prevent myself from going over to the window. A number of small dead birds are scattered across the path and the threadbare lawn immediately outside the room; it looks like Ouma's littered yard after that thunderstorm.

She looks like an ancient withered embryo peeled from a shell. The few wispy hairs on her head resemble the scraggly baby-feathers of a young pigeon; her closed eyes look like a dead chicken's, the pink lids veined, thin as rice paper. One single talon lies, knobbly and twisted, on the edge of the sheet, with the needles of various drips taped to the wrist; the other, like most of the rest of her, is swathed in bandages. Her face is blotched. There is no sign of life at all in the withered bundle. Bone, I think, everything reduced to bone, as the landscape beyond is cast in stone. How terribly small she is. A little scattering of *dolosse*, a witch-doctor's clutter of bones. But what can it still foretell of a future, remember of a too-distant past? Only this insignificant hard knuckle, a joint on which the familiar world hinges on another.

Another bird flings itself against the pane and falls, flapping, yellow beak gawking in surprise and pain, to the sill below, from where it turns a round, baffled, accusing eye towards us.

'Is she dead?' I whisper. But the nurse has left already.

The transparent eyelids flutter. Two pale milky eyes gaze at me from their deep hollows. She whispers something. The talon unfolds, then closes again.

I bend over with my ear against her mouth. There is the merest sigh of breath.

'Open the window,' she whispers.

'But – '

A weak, impatient twitch of her knuckled hand.

Casting a cautious look at the door I hurry to the window and open it. Almost instantaneously the whole room is invaded by birds. I huddle in a corner as they come sweeping past in a great rush of sound, wings fluttering, tail-feathers spread, delicate long toes outstretched for the landing; it is like one of the wild pillow fights we sometimes had as children in Ouma Kristina's house, when a whole room would be turned into a blizzard of swirling feathers. It takes quite a while for them to settle on whatever perches they can find, most of them on the bed, turning it into a living, undulating, multicoloured quilt.

What next? The re-entry of the nurse; two nurses. This must be the worst possible moment, and of course I shall get the blame for it. Yet to my surprise they altogether ignore my presence, as if I'm no more than a picture awkwardly suspended in the corner. What is rather more astonishing is that they pay no attention to the birds either but go about their swift efficient business of changing one of the many drips beside the bed, though at least twenty of the brightest-hued birds are perched on the stainless steel frame. Minutes later the nurses leave again. I follow them on tiptoe to the door to peer through the glass pane, making sure the coast is now clear. When I turn round again to face the room the birds have gone. I can make out the shadow of a smile on Ouma Kristina's face.

Her free hand invites me with a tentative gesture to approach. Once again I bend over with my ear close to her. She has great difficulty mouthing her words.

'You're back,' she says. 'I told you years ago, didn't I?' I have to guess most of the words; the rest of what she says is a mixture of sighs and mumblings. But she persists. 'I knew you'd come. I went to look for you last night.'

'I know,' I say. 'I saw you.' I put out my hand and touch hers. 'I didn't want something like this to bring me back.' I feel an urge to cry, but it is more from helpless rage, I think, than sorrow. 'How could anyone have done this to you?'

'I don't think they meant it. They just did it.'

'Is the pain very bad?'

'Most of the time they make me sleep.' A slow shake of her head. 'You know, there's only one thing that helps for burns. A man's seed. I told the doctor, but he wouldn't listen. I suppose he thought I was expecting him to provide it. Now they're making do with what they have.'

'How *are* you, Ouma?' I demand urgently.

'I'm afraid I'm going to die,' she says very calmly.

'Don't say such a thing. Please. We'll nurse you back to life, I promise.'

'Who says I want to live any longer? I've just waited for you to come. You're a good girl.'

'I'm not a good girl!' Guilt and anger flare up in me. A good girl is one who stays, who cares, who assumes responsibilities, not one who is headstrong and runs away and chooses her own life and believes the future is more important than the past.

'It will be better now. Like the old days when you and I – '

'Don't talk so much, Ouma, it'll wear you out.'

'I've waited long enough. Just one thing . . .' There follows such a long pause that I begin to think she has lost track of her thoughts. But then, after another feeble gesture to demand my close attention, she continues, 'I want to go home.'

'But you need the care. You have to be here.'

'If I'm going to die anyway, what's the difference?' Her pale almost-not-seeing eyes stare at me with the milky innocence the very old have in common with the very young.

'If I stay here that wily old undertaker will get me. Old Piet Malan. He's been lying in wait for me all these years. I've seen him at the door every time I woke up. Can't wait to get his hands on my body, the randy old goat.'

'Ouma, please – '

'Promise me you won't let him get me.'

'Of course he won't.'

'Then you must take me away from here. Take me home. It's the only safe place.'

'Anna says the whole house was burnt down,' I say gently.

'She always exaggerates. She's like your mother. I want you to go there. I'm afraid I rather neglected it these last few years.' She brightens briefly. 'But there are still peacocks in the garden.' A faint but resolute nod. 'Go and see if the place is still standing. Then come and fetch me.'

'What if something happens to you while I'm away? I've come all this way to be with you.'

'Then make yourself useful. I have no intention of dying in this place.'

That's not for you to decide, I want to say; but of course I check myself. Ouma Kristina is quite capable of taking control, as she has always done; even over death.

# 7

'What do you think?' asks Anna on our way home.

'I never thought I'd one day see her like this. A little dry twig. She was always so active.' I cannot restrain a smile. 'The first image I have whenever I think of Ouma is of her marching up and down through her palace with a transistor pressed to her ear, listening to rugby, commenting at the top of her voice, egging on her team, which was always Western Province, calling down fire and brimstone on the enemy. She never missed a match. I often saw her get so excited she'd hurl the transistor to the floor or against a wall. She must have gone through two or three sets every season.'

'She always went overboard with everything,' Anna says with unmasked disapproval. 'The last few years she became quite impossible.'

'She just didn't believe in half measures.' And now the memories start flooding back. I remind her of the family legend that soon after the Second World War an agricultural inspector visited Sinai and condemned Ouma's small flock of goats. Infested with scab, he said. The whole flock – which in Ouma's eyes was the prime flock in the district, of course – had to be slaughtered forthwith. There had been a long history of animosity between her and the inspector, and this was his moment of triumph. But he hadn't reckoned with the length she was prepared to go. Ouma personally cut the throat of her best billy, stuffed the head into a burlap bag and, ignoring all poor Oupa's feeble remonstrations, took the train to Cape Town with the head as her only baggage. Parliament was in session. Ouma brushed aside the guards at the entrance to the Assembly – that was long before Verwoerd was assassinated, and security was slack, to say the least – marched right past all the honourable members and took up position at the desk of the Minister of Agriculture. She upended the bag, shook out the gory head which by then had begun to smell something awful, and said, 'Now *you* tell me, Mr Minister, whether this goat has got scab.'

'But the goats were slaughtered after all, weren't they?' asks Anna.

'That's the sting in the tail. Don't you remember? After the uproar in parliament, there was an investigation, and the following week Ouma's whole flock was reprieved. Only then did she send Oupa to the abattoir to have them all slaughtered.'

'Poor Oupa. She was never easy to live with.'

'I know. Sometimes she drove me up the wall too. But life was never dull. When I was at varsity she would come down all the way to Stellenbosch three or four times a year to visit me. If there was a rugby match at Newlands, she'd haul me there no matter how much I protested. I could never stomach rugby, not even for the short while I had a boyfriend in the first team. But she always managed, by hook or mostly by crook, to get tickets, and I was given no choice. She was spectacular. She had everybody around us in stitches. And after the match came her great finale: she'd take me by the arm and rush out ahead of everybody else until we were a hundred yards or so clear of the crowd. Then she'd turn round and hurry back, head down, right into that surging mass and stop chosen individuals to ask them with an air of total innocence, "What are all these people doing here? Is it Communion?" Or to feign shock at seeing the match ended already, pretending we'd just arrived from some godforsaken little place on the map.'

'That's just plain childish,' says Anna, unamused.

'Not when one was there with her. She got such pleasure out of it. Just as she did, when we went shopping in some department store, to walk down the up escalators and up the down ones. Grinning at all the foul or disapproving stares that met us.'

Best of all, I remember wryly, were our visits to restaurants. Ouma wouldn't take me to any but the very poshest places in the city and encourage me to order the most expensive dishes. She could be terribly stingy at home, but on these outings she really let go. Not that it cost anything: that was the point. Towards the end of the meal she'd draw from her scuffed old ostrich skin handbag a beautifully carved and inlaid little box, all mother-of-pearl and semiprecious stones. It came from Baghdad, she'd tell me every time, with undiminished glee. My stomach would contract in sheer mortification when I saw that box.

26

For inside it was a startling collection of quite revolting items. A couple of dead flies or bluebottles. Worms of the most obnoxious hairy or juicy kind. A half-alive cockroach or two. A few thin jagged crescents of toenails hacked off without finesse. She would select whatever in the particular circumstances appealed most to her, and after a quick check to make sure no one was looking, she'd deposit one of her prizes on her plate, slip the box back into her bag, and call a waiter to complain. By the time the matter reached the management, Ouma's voiced threatening to penetrate the most distant nooks of the restaurant, they were usually only too happy to scrap the bill in exchange for a reluctantly given undertaking not to prosecute. We never went to the same restaurant twice, of course. We often had stand-up fights about it afterwards. Every time she would solemnly promise never again to subject me to such a scene. Perhaps she even meant it sincerely. But she simply couldn't resist the temptation.

Impossible, now, to reconcile these memories with the wretched little creature on the high bed. She was right: to die in that hospital would be the final indignity.

'Can we go to The Bird Place straight away?' I ask Anna.

'One shock is enough for today.'

'I *must* see for myself.'

'It's dangerous. For all we know the terrorists who blew it up are still around somewhere.'

'I've promised Ouma.'

'Let's find out from Casper first. And anyway, you need a rest.'

8

And now, a full day later, we're driving through the tall gates, absurdly ostentatious on the naked plain; they are guarded by two policemen armed with automatic guns, to whom we first have to identify ourselves. From well over a kilometre away, under the sky which even on this late April day is still smouldering with sullen heat, the oasis of exotic trees surges as from a dream. Ouma has never allowed anyone, ever, to fell a tree, matter how unruly it became. 'Cut down a tree,' she used to say, 'and it will become a ghost to haunt you to the day of your own death.'

We pull in under the great loquat tree in the front garden, once inhabited by birds, now somehow not quite as enormous as it seemed long ago. But its shadow is still impenetrable and reassuring; and as we get out of the bakkie, Anna and I, I involuntarily stop to stare up into the tangle of branches above where so many years ago, on Sunday afternoons when we were supposed to sleep in the oppressive heat, I would entice one of my more intrepid male cousins (not always the same one) to clamber about, vying with the darting birds for the highest brightest berries; and in the top branches, protected by the foliage, giggling and deftly balancing, we'd strip off our clothes and indulge in the daring, immemorial experimentations and explorations of the precocious, hands and bodies sticky and slippery with the secretions of the fruit of that wise old tree; and if, as it invariably happened, sooner or later, someone emerged from the front door and passed underneath, we'd try to pee on them from on high, a precarious undertaking for which the cousin's equipment proved decidedly more precise in its aim than mine.

Anna refuses to get out with me and remains sulking in the bakkie. (The children have stayed at home, already thoroughly disillusioned with their intractable aunt.) She has remained dead against the ideaa of this visit. And Casper supported her, during those disturbing few minutes last night when he was home between two sorties of his commando that behaved more like a gang of boisterous boys preparing for a picnic or a hunt than grown men bent on the business of death. 'If you absolutely *must*, then wait till I can send a couple of my men with you. The bastards that blew up your grandmother's place – we have reason to believe they're disaffected MK terrorists. They're not to be toyed with, I tell you. A woman on her own' – a knowing wink – 'and such a woman too.'

That was yesterday. This morning Anna pretended to have forgotten about my request, and it was only when I threatened to drive here on my own that she brought me, making it very clear that she disapproved.

'There's no need at all for you to come,' I reasoned with her. 'As a matter of fact I'd much prefer to go on my own.'

'It's not safe,' she said curtly. To my dismay she put a pistol and a small box of cartridges in the cubbyhole.

'What's that for?' I asked.

She looked at me as if I were daft: 'You can't even think of driving without a gun these days.'

'Is that what Casper says?'

She glanced at me, on the defensive. 'Why do you ask?'

'Just wondered.'

'I tell you it's dangerous,' she insisted.

'Do you really know how to use it?'

28

'Of course. I've been taking lessons for almost a year now.' A touch of pride: 'Actually I'm quite good.' For a brief moment there was more life in her voice. 'Would you like me to teach you?'

'Most certainly not,' I said. 'Can we go now, please?'

And here we are.

What disturbs me is the silence, as if all this enormity of space surrounding us is holding its breath. At first I cannot explain it, but then it strikes me. Of course: the birds. This whole place used to ring with their presence, their twitterings and screeches and squawks and calls a never-ceasing din in one's ears, as if the sky above were a vast upturned bowl amplifying all sound below. And now it has fallen silent; the birds have fled, leaving only emptiness in their wake.

Unnerved, but unwilling to show Anna how it has affected me, I muster up some courage to proceed. As I approach through the trees, stooping below the branches which have clearly not been trimmed for years, I see the palace looming. In the excitement of the first sight it seems unscathed. And even if it appears, somehow, less outrageous in its proportions than I have remembered it, the rediscovery of that splendid façade with its towers and turrets, its architectural excesses, makes my heart jump. It is true after all! This is no dream or memory, but something all too real. As real as the shocking damage the place has suffered. For now, from closer by, I have a full view of the scarred wing to the right of the front entrance: these must be the rooms into which Ouma Kristina moved some years ago, after my departure, as her increasing frailty made it more difficult to continue climbing the stairs to the top floor she used to inhabit. The new room presumably overlooked the stoep where the worst damage has been done: the vcrandah lies collapsed in a heap of rubble; above it gape the blackened skeletal openings of doors and windows; one balustrade hangs at an angle from high above; the whole façade is covered in soot and grime.

The strange thing is that it makes *me* feel guilty, as if in some inexplicable way I am to blame; as if I'm an intruder in the one placc that used to be my sanctuary from a world with which all too often I felt at odds. And the guilt gives rise to fear; Anna's dire warnings about lurking terrorists no longer seem quite as far-fetched as before. What if there really are intruders inside, ready to follow up the senselessness of their outrage with still more violence? Yet the very fear makes it necessary to investigate. It is, I suspect, the same urge that once provoked me into leading midnight excursions with as many cousins as could be mustered down into the cellar with its ghosts or up into the attic where the coffins stood on their trestles. Do the thing you dread.

So I follow the trail of destruction round the ruin of the right wing to the back.

The outbuildings – sheds, barns, stables, dairy, garage – appear unscathed, though in a sad state of disrepair. Through a missing plank in the garage door I can see a glint of black and chrome. My God, the hearse. I've forgotten about it. Oupa used to drive a Pontiac as big as the Titanic, also black, but when he died, in the hospital in Cape Town, she bought this Chrysler hearse, second-hand, to transport the body back home. She could never stand trains. 'They don't stop where you want to be, and they make you get off where you don't want to be,' was her cryptic explanation. That was the only time in her life she drove a car; she'd never had a licence. And she enjoyed the 'feel' of the grand old Chrysler so much that after the funeral she sold the car and kept the hearse. She didn't drive again, though, but instructed the farm's foreman and factotum, Jeremiah, to bedeck himself in white dust coat and leather gloves and drive her when necessary, whether to town, or to friends in the district, or upon occasion even the four hundred or so kilometres to Cape Town.

Amused, and somehow reassured as well, I move on. In the dairy the separator still stands; in my mind I can hear the clinging of its rhythmic bell. It is comforting to find these signs of continuing life. But the back of the house itself looks terrible. It is hard to believe that anyone has lived here in recent years. The scullery door hangs from its hinges, an oversized charred slice of Melba toast. Inside, I find the kitchen flooded in black water, testifying to the eager incompetence of the fire brigade. I take off my shoes and turn up my jeans. Gingerly I step into that dark space, hesitate for a while, almost hoping to hear Anna's voice calling me back, then venture into the nearest passage. At that moment a scream reverberates through the place, so loudly, and so close, that I exclaim in fear. And a flash of electric blue and green comes fluttering past me into the blinding daylight outside. A peacock. A burst of hysterical laughter racks me. It takes several minutes for the shock to subside. I take a cigarette from my shirt pocket; for a moment the flare blinds me. At last, my eyes now more accustomed to the gloom, I set out on my exploration, reclaiming from memory one room after the other, along what remains of the ground floor, then down a crumbling staircase to the sprawling cellar (there is no electricity left, but I have the ludicrously brave little flare of my lighter to guide me down); then upstairs again, from floor to floor, expecting at every moment the scurrying movement or the warning sound that will, if I am lucky, precede attack, the proverbial fate worse than death. But it doesn't come, and from one improbable room or hall or landing or nook to the next I proceed, stopping frequently to retrace some steps with the hope of surprising a pursuer; until I reach the attic where a single premonitory coffin still waits patiently in the cobwebbed light from the narrow dust-covered windows. Ghosts? I giggle like the girl I used to be: if one were to confront me now or try to sidle past I'll brush it aside and Ouma will be proud of me.

About a third of the house has been destroyed, it seems. One wooden staircase has subsided altogether, leaving a gaping black hole half-blocked with rubble; another has been reduced to eerie scaffolding draped with charred tapestries which pulverise into ashes as I touch them. But the main staircase, of stone and marble, is intact, and the whole left wing of the house appears largely unscathed. Windows still stare blankly outside, interrogating the view. This is what is most disconcerting: the way the sky obtrudes, the invasion of the house by outside space. It appropriates walls and floors, pours through gutted windows, leaks from above, stares through broken frames. The usual demarcations are no longer adequate.

Also, it interrupts the very process of return, the tensing forward, as it were, to reassume an identity suspended when I left this place, recovering the self that remained behind.

On a purely practical level, this is not the kind of habitation to receive a centenarian wishing to prepare for death; but there are more important considerations and a move seems feasible. I can imagine what Anna will have to say; and Casper. But I think I can handle them. If the hospital staff can be persuaded, Ouma Kristina can come home to die in peace. I am resolute.

# 9

At any rate, I cannot return to stay indefinitely with Anna and Casper. Difficult enough at the best of times, it is impossible after the new glimpse I caught last night of a world I'd thought – hoped – I had left for good. Coming home from the hospital Anna insisted that I take a nap. It was hopeless, of course. The transition from London to the Little Karoo was too sudden and too drastic; too much had happened, too fast; too much was still unresolved. Ouma Kristina's minimal features on the pillows, the feeble urgent motion of her hand, the breathy whispers; that hallucinatory scene with the birds. The still-unfulfilled need to return to Sinai. The enervating memories of the previous night's flight and the prolonged battle to fend off the attentions of Tarquin & Co. But even if it were possible to dispel all of this and simply succumb to the accumulated fatigue, there was the disturbing proximity of the children in the house all around me. Anna had done her best to instil the fear of God in them should anyone dare to make a noise (which must have put the seal on their already manifest dislike of the obnoxious aunt who had so unexpectedly materialised in their small loud world, turning several of them out of the room assigned to me and creating a domino effect of congestion in all the adjoining rooms): even so their mere presence wreaked a silent havoc throughout the place. This kind of inaudible throb, more than the blaring of trumpets, must have been what caused the walls of Jericho to fall. So what rest I had was neither long nor untroubled; and the bath which followed, in a tub bearing the growth rings of grit and grime from children's bodies, did little to restore my spirits.

I was all for setting out to Ouma Kristina's palace as soon as possible, before nightfall. It was, after all, a mere fifteen or twenty minutes' drive away, Casper having judiciously and calculatingly bought this adjacent farm when it came on the market only a few years after he'd married Anna. But such a visit, no matter how important it was for Ouma, was immediately ruled out.

'We have to wait for Casper,' Anna explained. 'He'll be home for supper.'

'But I'm sure I've seen at least eight or ten women in the kitchen working on the meal,' I objected.

'There are only four, really,' she said. 'The others are just relatives or hangers-on. You know how it is on the farms these days. But anyway, it's not that. It's that I can't let Casper wait.'

The retort, tart of taste, was already on my tongue, waiting to be spat out. But I restrained myself.

The taste was familiar, even though it came from a good sixteen years back. Their wedding day; the reception at the Bird House. A huge marquee on the front lawn – not so much, I suspected, to keep the sun out as to protect the guests from bird droppings. I was seventeen. In spite of my foul-mouthed protestations that put everyone but Ouma Kristina to shame, I was roped in as a bridesmaid. Swathed, of all colours, in what Lizzie called 'chocking pink'. Fit, I assured Mother, for a Mimi to expire in. Of constipation, I said, meaning consumption; but she showed no sympathy. She didn't even seem to catch the vicious side-swipe at her choice of 'Che gelida manina' to entertain the guests on the lawn on a ferociously hot sixteenth of December – not anticipating that her once splendid coloratura would be more or less drowned out by the cat-calls and hoots and shrieks of the birds. How sad. This was what she'd forsaken all her dreams of the Wiener Staatsoper and La Scala for, the one day that was supposed to be the culmination of a career that never was (*Exsultate jubilate* in the church; Puccini's tiny frozen hand and one fine day on the lawn); and she really had had a beautiful voice, once – before my untimely birth had spoiled all hope of it ever receiving the training it had merited and she had aspired to; now to be shat on by birds. Really.

Having temporarily forsaken the bride I became one of a pandemonium of waitresses shuttling between house and marquee to ply the sweating, glistening, purpling guests with enough food and drink to feed most of famished Africa for three days. We took turns to take small breaks, retiring with iced drinks into some of the deeper, cooler recesses of the gothic palace. On one of my turns I filched a crystal pitcher of iced water from one of the fridges in the kitchen, and slipped down to the basement, into the shadow-room of the main dining-room above, where I knew it would be cooler than anywhere else. Also, content that this was the one place where I could count on being alone, I kicked off the silver shoes and stripped off the disgusting pink dress and layered petticoats in which I'd been constrained since before sunrise to dance attendance on the frantic bride. In the light of the single dusty low-watt bulb I draped the clothes over a rickety chair to keep them from gathering too much dust. Then, recklessly, exasperated, I gulped down a fair amount of water before splashing the the rest of the contents of the pitcher over my face from where it streamed down over my breasts and body. And I was still standing there, head thrown back, eyes closed, the pitcher raised above me, when I was interrupted. It was a scene so offensive in its banality it still makes me cringe.

In brief, Casper had followed me (accusing me afterwards of having 'invited' him), and now began to paw me – the whole heavy-breathing act, while mouthing imbecile phrases like 'kiss for the bridegroom' and 'Come on, we're family now' and 'I love a bitch with some spirit.' I could have screamed, I suppose; nothing wrong with my lungs, and I have Mother's operatic voice, an effortless high C. But I was too angry, and screaming was too humiliating a way out. No one had had occasion to teach me about a knee in the groin, it just happened by itself, and hard. And as he bent forward I struck him a solid blow with the pitcher

33

on the head. And grabbed my clothes, and ran, turning off the light at the top of the stairs as I came past, and slamming the door behind me.

There were people at the far end of the passage, the kitchen end; but I had the advantage of knowing the terrain, and ducked into a side passage and from there into a purposeless cubicle attached to it like an appendix to the intestine, and pulled on the petticoats and the dress again. The shoes had remained behind. Too bad.

I resumed my waitress duties, ignoring the pointed glances and nods in the direction of my bare feet. ('Not *again!*' said Father.) It was at least half an hour before I saw Casper emerging from the house, really not looking very spruce at all. 'Must have been something I ate,' I heard him mumble when he got back to the bridal table where his absence had been only too noticeable; and I made a point of being especially obsequious to him every time I passed the happy couple in the course of that long hot afternoon.

During the four or five years that followed, before I left the country, I took care to avoid every occasion of being alone with him; and as his rage and rancour subsided, together with – I suppose – the fear that I might spill the beans, his attitude became one of suspicious tolerance. Even so I did not exactly relish the prospect of meeting him again, now, under his own roof, and of being in any way beholden to him for his hospitality. But it was not to be avoided. At any rate the atmosphere was so thick by the time he did come home, two hours late for supper, the children weepy and crotchety with hunger, Anna uptight with the reproach she dared not utter openly, that the tension between the two of us went almost unnoticed.

In the circumstances he was unexpectedly amicable, to the point of overdoing it. 'My, haven't we grown beautiful?'

It touched a raw nerve but I kept my cool. For Anna's sake I swallowed the resentment I'd been nurturing ever since that early encounter. At the same time it was unsettling to discover that he had in fact mellowed with the onset of middle age; far from the repulsive image I'd built up inside me, I had to acknowledge that he was not unhandsome, exuding a kind of sturdy animal charm. Not that I allowed it to fool me; and God knows there was enough in the ensuing conversation – a brief ten minutes before he rushed off again to join his gang of vigilantes, without bothering to touch the supper we had all postponed on his account – to confirm my worst suspicions.

What had happened, as far as we could make out, was that one of his commando members, on patrol duty, had come across a white Toyota bakkie, Transvaal registration, with four black occupants, all heavily armed, speeding along a dirt road towards an outlying farm, belonging to one Abel Joubert, at the foot of the Swartberge. The rest of the commando had promptly been informed on the elaborate radio network that linked all their members, and Casper and his band had valiantly given chase. It had taken over an hour along all the byways of the district – 'It's clear the bastards are from this area, they knew it like their own backyard, which proves their number plates were false' – before they'd cornered their quarry in a sandy patch. The occupants of the Toyota jumped out and scattered into the dense bushes marking the course of a dried river-bed. Casper and company started firing with all the weaponry they disposed of; but by that time the sun had already set and with the swiftness that characterises the African dusk the night had come down. It was asking for trouble to pursue the terrorists in the dark. At least they had the satisfaction of discovering that one of the four fugitives had been wounded. They'd seen the blood. At first light they would resume the pursuit; but with such bandits around one couldn't take risks, so the whole commando had to keep watch on all the neighbouring farms overnight.

This also put paid to our intention of visiting Ouma Kristina in hospital last night. And although it made me feel both resentful and guilty, it came as a relief too.

Not that it was the end of the day's excitement. Barely an hour after Casper had driven off again, the engine of his Land Cruiser roaring and its tyres skidding and spinning, the police arrived in a yellow van and a bleary-eyed officer appeared on the doorstep. Anna had opened the door with a gun in one hand; there was relief all round – except among some of the boys who, I suspect, had hoped for more action – and she invited him in. He turned down the offer of coffee. His business was not with us but with Casper. And when he learned what we could tell him he was clearly annoyed. 'If only you people would stop interfering and leave it to us – !' Then, making an effort to calm himself, he filled in the blanks in Casper's story. The four blacks, he assured us, had not been armed at all. They'd gone to Abel Joubert's farm to deposit a relative, one of Joubert's labourers, who'd been away for a few weeks to visit his sick mother in Soweto. This was what Abel Joubert personally told the police when they responded to his call about several cars and bakkies descending on his farm, firing in all directions as they went.

'But didn't they check with Joubert first?' asked Anna.

'They phoned the farm and Mrs Joubert told them, but I got the impression they didn't believe her. You must realise the people in the district are up in arms because Abel Joubert has allowed a lot of squatters to settle on his farm and they're causing problems all over the place. So you can imagine the men were suspicious about what Winnie Joubert told them.'

'Of course they would be,' I couldn't help saying, making no effort to mask my viciousness. 'A woman's word doesn't count, does it? This is still a country ruled by men. Nothing has changed.'

Both the officer and Anna were staring at me, uncomprehending.

'Never mind,' I said frostily. 'I'm also just a woman.'

The officer uttered a small strained chuckle; Anna merely looked irritated.

'So what are you going to do?' I asked the policeman.

'We're trying to track down the commando members to send them home,' he said, wiping his soaked brow. 'And if you happen to see your husband before we do, Mrs Louw, then for God's sake tell him to stay home. Our job is hard enough as it is.'

'They're only trying to help,' she said, flaring up. 'How can anyone be safe with those murderers who attacked my grandmother still scot free to terrorise the district? *You* haven't caught them yet, have you?'

'Mrs Louw – ' I could guess what he was going to say, but then he thought better of it and took his leave. I locked the front door after him.

'Sounds like a bloody mess to me,' I said when I came back. 'Suppose Casper's crowd killed that black man?'

'What difference would that make?' she asked, more aggressive than she'd been all day. 'Jesus, Kristien, you don't seem to realise what's going on in this place. It's them or us.'

'Now come on, Anna.'

'Look, you've been away for God knows how many years. Please don't try to tell *us* what to do. We *belong* here.'

'And I don't?'

'No, you don't. You made your choice years ago.'

'I'm not here for you,' I reminded her. 'I came for Ouma. In case you've forgotten.'

She sat looking at her spread fingers on the kitchen table, toying absently with her wedding ring. After a long time she pushed herself to her feet. 'Tea?' she asked dully.

'No, thanks. It's time I got to bed.'

'You must be exhausted.'

'You look tired too.'

She ignored the remark. 'You sure you have everything you need?'

'Of course.'

'Perhaps a . . .' She hesitated. 'Can I lend you a black nightie?'

'A black nightie? What on earth for?'

'Well, Casper has asked me to make black nightclothes for myself and the children. In case the house is attacked and we have to flee in the dark, you know.'

'You must be joking?'

'This *is* serious, Kristien. I wish you would realise it.'

'I'll be all right. Black sheep aren't visible in the dark either.'

She was stung; her first impulse, I could see, was to attack. But taking a deep breath she controlled herself. A moment later, to my surprise, there were tears in her eyes. 'You really don't understand the first thing about us, do you? This time, this place – '

How maddeningly she had manoeuvred me into having to say, 'I'm sorry.' She didn't react, didn't look at me either. And after a brief battle with myself I offered the olive branch, 'You coming to bed too?'

'No, I – ' An awkward pause. 'I think I'll sit up for a while still.'

'Good night then.'

'Good night.'

In the passage, on my way to the bedroom assigned to me, I stopped at the telephone, pressed my hand on it, then returned to the kitchen. She looked up. I said, 'Would you mind if I telephoned Michael?'

'Michael?'

'He's a . . .' I suddenly felt at a loss. As if it would expose something private to explain.

'In London?' she asked. She might as well have said, 'On the moon?'

'Yes, of course.'

'It's terribly expensive.' She appeared embarrassed.

'It's all right,' I said quickly. And turned again to go.

'Please!' she said behind me. 'Honestly, if you want to . . . It's just, well, Casper might – But by all means go ahead.'

'It's not important, really,' I said, not succeeding very well in keeping my voice neutral.

She said something more, in a weary, cajoling tone; but I wasn't listening. I passed the telephone without looking at it. God, how perversely I missed him now! – an aching, burning, physical need more intense than anything I'd felt for a long time.

I should have slept like a log. But I didn't. For hours I lay awake in one of the two forlorn little beds that smelled of baby-powder and sunlight and grass and pee, my whole body tense, unable to procure any release on my own. I caught myself straining to listen: but what was it I could possibly expect to hear? The Land Cruiser returning in the night? Ouma's remembered voice? The cry of a peacock or some nameless night bird? There was nothing but the occasional sound of a child coughing, or moaning in its sleep; once, from the kitchen, a kettle boiling; outside, nothing. Nothing at all.

## IO

As I leave through the surreal back door of Ouma's palace, screwing up my eyes against the sudden violence of the sun, I can make out, among the farthest trees, a smudge of colour that stains the drab surroundings. It is the peacock, presumably the same one that scared me so, now strutting with its tail fanned out in lurid defiance. There is something both sad and funny about it. A generic thing. Each male who sprouts an erection acts as if he is the first of his kind to achieve it, the prototype of the species.

Its brilliance lures me. At first I move slowly, then more resolutely as I come closer, relishing – like so many times when I was a child – the spectacle of the peacock's growing concern as it tries to strut off in stiff little steps, bent on maintaining its dignity; until I am too close, and it turns and trots, its pride now drooping. Seeing me still in pursuit it spreads its wings in a series of jerking motions as if swimming against a too-strong current, and clumsily takes off to land on the wall, once whitewashed, of the family graveyard beyond the trees.

The gate has rusted from its hinges. The single grave that lies outside the walls, at the far corner, unmarked by a headstone, distinguished only by a bush of rosemary, is unkempt. But inside the walls, among the almost black cypresses, the small square patch appears trim and weeded, the grass cut, the gravel paths raked evenly, the headstones and severe rectangles of the graves well tidied. There are several of them. My great-grandparents share one: HERMANUS JOHANNES WEPENER 1838–1919; PETRONELLA WEPENER 1839–1921 (in our family the women tend to outlive the men). To the left and right of them, a number of their brothers and sisters, with spouses where applicable. In a second row, Oupa's: CORNELIS FREDERIK BASSON 1889–1974. Beside the granite slab covering only one-half of his double plot is a hole, dug – we have always been told – simultaneously with his, covered with sheets of corrugated iron, awaiting Ouma's arrival. On the stone she will one day share with Oupa, her name is already engraved: KRISTINA BASSON *née* WEPENER 1891–. Only the final date remains to be added.

The grave itself has been in readiness, like the coffin in the attic; it serves, she used to say (and the good Dr Johnson would have concurred), a useful purpose, and every Sunday we spent on the farm, for as long as I can remember, the whole family was required, just before sunset, to accompany Ouma on a solemn little pilgrimage to that waiting hole.

On her own, apart from weekly or fortnightly daytime visits to do whatever spadework, cleaning, planting or tidying was required, she would go to the graveyard every evening after the nine o'clock news on the radio (she never succumbed to TV). The length of the visit depended on how much she had to discuss with the dead. It was the one moment of her day when she could be wholly uninterrupted, at peace with herself and the world, to carry on, in a normal tone of voice (I know; I followed her whenever I could, and shamelessly eaves-dropped), a quiet chat to bring them up to date with events on this side of the grave. Seated on the headstone of whoever she was talking to, she would enquire after the welfare of the dear departed concerned, convey her regards, and communicate all the events of her day. And invariably she would be refreshed and in high spirits when she returned. That is, except for the evenings she spent at the unmarked grave outside the walls; those visits tended alternately to depress her or enervate her.

I would hurry home ahead of her and wait for her in the kitchen to share, depending on the season, the late-night mug of cocoa or lemon syrup that was my special privilege. I was already eighteen or thereabouts – it was certainly after Anna's wedding – when one evening she casually asked, as she dredged the remains of her cocoa from the mug with a forefinger, whether I wouldn't prefer to accompany her to the graveyard in future instead of skulking about in the dark to peep from a distance. 'Perhaps it is time,' she said with a straight face, 'you met the rest of the family.' I felt my throat tighten, but I nodded. I waited with trepidation, hoping she might forget, or change her mind. But that was unlike Ouma. And the next evening after the news when she prepared to go out, she waited at the back door and said, 'Kristien!' We went through the backyard together, followed the footpath through the trees, and reached the churchyard; the walls were opalescent in the moonlight. Ouma opened the gate. I stood for a moment, then said, 'Ouma . . . I think . . . you should go alone.' She said nothing. I turned and went home. It wasn't only fear. That I could overcome. It was a belief, sensed only confusedly, that this was her territory, that even if she'd invited me I was not meant to intrude. I never followed her again. And since then I've often thought that that had really been the purpose of the whole exercise.

## I I

In the immediate vicinity of Ouma's empty grave her single sister and several brothers have already taken their places. My parents lie here too. LUDWIG WOLFGANG MÜLLER 1920–1988, LOUISA MÜLLER *née* BASSON 1921–1990. This is the first time I have seen their graves, twin-bed style, in keeping with the mores of their generation. It is unnerving to see their lives reduced to these spare facts; perhaps that is why I find it so hard to relate to them. When it happened – six years ago, four years ago; Father of a coronary without prior warning, Mother in a car accident – I was so far away it seemed unreal; and to return home, whatever 'home' still meant, merely to attend a funeral and parade for the benefit of others a grief that came too late, seemed, in both cases, pointless. It is only now, here, standing at the foot of their graves as once, very small and very scared of the dark, I would stand at the foot of their beds, after a nightmare, and plead to be taken in and comforted, only to be ordered back to my own room – it is only now that it begins to seem real. But even as it edges towards reality, the stern headstones with their unimaginative legends keep me at a distance. I stare and stare, urgently wishing I could *feel* something, perhaps even break down and cry; but I can't. I remain unmoved. They lived, they died; they never really were part of my life, or I, I think, of theirs.

Desperate, I try to remember something real about them, something to redeem this moment. But the memories only confirm distance, instead of bridging it. Father: the magistrate, into whose courtroom I would sometimes slip during a trial, to crouch in a back seat, trying to relate to the stranger up there on the high bench, in his ample black gown, remote and stern, dispensing justice. However strange he seemed, I was proud, immensely proud. This is my father, I wanted everyone to know, this man who can listen to all these people and then decide, just like that, what is right, what wrong. *He* knows. Then, one Saturday while he was playing golf a man came to the back door to ask for him, a black man in such rags and tatters one could see parts of his bare body right through them, his baggy trousers tied to his thin waist with string, the front fastened with an inadequate safety pin; but what shocked me was that his whole face was covered in dried blood. He was unsteady on his legs, but whether he was drunk or whether it was from pain I couldn't tell, I was too young, and certainly too terrified. Mother was inside, practising arpeggios, the door closed, which meant *Keep out*; Anna was in the bath preparing for an evening out. So I had to deal with him. He wouldn't go away. When I told him Father was out, he said he'd wait, he *had* to see him. Why? Because his baas, he said, had beaten him – 'Look at me!', and he began to cry, it was the first time I'd seen a man cry – and he wanted justice. Those were his words. 'I want justice.'

I offered him water from one of the tin mugs Mother kept under the sink for the servants, or for blacks like this one who came to the back door. He gulped it down thirstily. 'Why don't you go the police?' I asked, all stupid innocence. He just shook his head and sat down on the back step. From time to time he moaned in pain. I stood there all the time, watching in horror and misery. Until Father came home. I ran to the garage to tell him about the man. He tried to shake me off. 'This is not the time, Kristien. I have to shower first.' And he walked right past the man into the house. It must have been almost an hour before Father emerged from their bedroom again; he was pouring his whisky when I entered and reminded him. He was ready to dismiss me, I could see; but I stood my ground. 'If you don't come out to see him,' I said, 'I'm going to bring him in here.' 'Don't use that tone of voice with me,' he warned. 'The man is in pain,' I said, 'he's been beaten, he has come to you for help.' Making no attempt to hide his displeasure he came past me, the glass still in his hand. 'Yes? What do you want?' he brusquely asked at the back door. The man staggered to his feet. The front of his trousers was all wet. He began to tell his story. Even before he'd finished, Father curtly interrupted him: 'Go to the police. This is their business, not mine. If it comes to court I can deal with it, but not here.' 'But Baas,' said the man, 'I already gone to the police. They just beat me some more and chase me away.' 'Then I'm sorry,' said Father, 'but I can't interfere. It would be highly improper. Now go away. Look how you've messed up the place.' And he went inside. I fled. I couldn't look the man in the face again. I stopped at the door to the lounge. 'I don't understand you!' I shouted, tears streaming down my face. '*I don't understand you!*' And then I ran to our bathroom – it was still steamed up with Anna's fragrant ablutions – and vomited in the toilet.

I still don't understand.

Staring at the grave, I think of other exiles – those, perhaps, who deserved the name of 'exile' much more than I ever did, even at the beginning when I was still in my 'fermenting, passionate youth' as Michael loves to call it – who have written to me over the last year or two about *their* experience of visiting the graves of their dead. How deeply and urgently did they react to this moment. Enough to make my guts contract in guilt. But I cannot even properly suffer guilt. All I feel is – outside; beyond. I don't want to. How I'd love to feel the burning ache of loss, of *something*. Have I become wholly immune to pain? Am I really beyond the pale? Perhaps, if I could truly feel that I belonged here, it might be different. But I don't. Throughout my childhood, Father's career imposed on us the need to move every three or four years to another place – new house, new school, new friends, new everything – so that I soon learned, in an instinct of self-preservation, never to put down roots, never to get fond enough of any one place to think of it as 'mine'; as a result, this farm, Ouma's place, Sinai, The Bird Place, became the only fixed point of reference in my youth. Even so, it was only once a year – in exceptional years, twice – that we came here. And today the rapture of being here again is mixed with the shock of seeing the palace half-demolished. And I look on it as alien territory.

Which doesn't mean that I belong where I have come from. Michael may represent the closest I've come to 'belonging' over the last eleven years, but even he feels like a surrogate; I remain at one remove. And it will need a miracle, or an act of faith (perhaps they mean the same thing?), to make me part of the – a – real world again.

Years ago a lover told me with all the assurance that was his trade mark that there are basically two kinds of people in the world (an opening gambit that is guaranteed to get my back up: was that why he said it?), those who believe, and those who don't. He classified me among the latter, mainly because I wouldn't believe in *him*. In the strict religious sense he may have been right: when I was ten or thereabouts, Mother sent me to an athletics meeting in my tennis clothes while I'd *told* her everybody else would be wearing special new team outfits for which she refused to see any need; engulfed by the shame and anger of it I asked God to kill her with a single well-aimed thunderbolt, which I'd been led to believe was one of his specialities. But it didn't materialise, and I've been an agnostic ever since. But in the larger sense of the word I have a hunch that the lover in question had it wrong. I am a believer. I know there is in me a small hard core of unresolved belief. My problem is that I have not yet found – or not yet recognised – an object for it.

As I go through the rusty gate (the peacock is still perched on the wall, pretending not to look at me, tail primly folded in), I suddenly remember Ouma Kristina's firm belief that before leaving a graveyard one should always sit down for a while inside the wall, so that the spirits disturbed by the visit could return to their rest; otherwise, she used to say, they would follow one. Too bad. There is nothing I can do now to redeem myself.

In the distance I notice two people watching me – an elderly woman with a bright blue kopdoek round her small head, and a young man in faded jeans and a short-sleeved shirt of indeterminate colour; both are barefoot. There is something wary in their attitude, as if they are ready to turn and run if I approach too closely.

A short distance away from them I stop in surprise, believing for a moment that the woman is Lizzie, Ouma's old companion; then I remember that she, too, has died. Not that, in this place, I would put it past the dead to wander about in broad daylight. This must be her daughter Trui, the one married to the handyman Jeremiah, but the resemblance is eerie. Trui has aged unbelievably since I last saw her, the dark face deeply furrowed, grizzled wisps protruding from the doek.

'Trui?' I ask.

'Morning, Missus,' she says, quizzical, suspicious.

'Don't you know me any more?' I prod her.

Another laden moment; then she exclaims, 'My God, Miss Kristien! What is Miss Kristien doing here?'

'You must know what happened to Ouma . . . ?' I go up to them and offer my hand. Trui takes it cautiously as if it might suddenly change into something else; then lets go precipitately. The young man stays out of reach, glowering.

'Ai, Miss Kristien.' She clicks her tongue. 'It was a terrible thing. The whole place up in flames. And then after they took the Old Missus away it was almost worse, when the pollies came to make us tell them who did it. And how must we now know? It's bad, Miss Kristien, this is very bad.'

'Please don't call me "Miss Kristien",' I say, helpless, like so many times before.

'Yes, Miss Kristien.'

'And you – ?' I ask, turning to the young man.

'But this is mos Jonnie, Miss Kristien,' she says, pronouncing the *j* to sound like a *y*. 'He's my son, doesn't Miss Kristien remember him? But he was only a little boytjie when Miss Kristien left.' Without stopping to catch her breath she asks, 'And is the Old Missus now dead?'

'She's very weak, but she's still alive,' I assure her. 'She wants to come back here.'

'Ag shame,' she commiserates, then turns a stricken face to me, 'But this is no place for her any more, Miss Kristien. Look at it.'

Her son tugs at her arm. 'Let her be, Ma,' he says in a low, furious voice. 'We're not mixing with these white people any more.'

Greatly agitated, she looks at me for help. 'You must please forgive him, Miss Kristien. It's this pollies business. They gave him a bad time, look at that face.' (It is indeed swollen almost beyond recognition.) 'But Miss Kristien mustn't think this is how I brought him up.'

'Ag shaddap, Ma!' he grumbles.

'And now the poor Old Missus – ?' she tries to bring the conversation back on track.

'I've been inside the house, Trui. I know it looks awful, but Ouma wants to come home. If you and your family could give us a hand I'm sure we can make it habitable again. We'll only need a few rooms.'

'You stay out of their business, Ma,' says her son.

She pretends not to hear. 'It's a bad place now, after what's happened,' she says. 'It's spooky.'

'It's always been spooky. And if it will make Ouma feel better – even if it's only to come and die in peace – '

'Yes, Miss Kristien.'

'Please, Trui, I told you, don't – '

'Yes, Miss Kristien.'

At that moment a distraught Anna appears round the nearest corner of the grotesque building in the background, brandishing her pistol, Annie-get-your-gun Hollywood style.

Trui and her son both look round, startled, when they realise there is somebody behind them; when she notices the gun, Trui cowers behind Jonnie, uttering a plaintive moan.

'Put that thing away!' I shout at Anna.

She lowers her hand in obvious embarrassment. 'You were gone so long,' she says. 'I was getting worried. And then there was a message on the radio – '

'God, Miss Anna, you mustn't give one such a fright,' complains Trui, holding a thin hand to her bosom.

'What message?' I ask brusquely. I know by now that the bakkie is equipped with CB radio, to facilitate the farmers' eager games and keep the adrenaline flowing.

'I can't talk in front of them,' she says, gesturing towards Trui and her son.

'I'm sorry, Miss Anna,' the woman says hurriedly, bobbing her mealie-stalk legs in a curtsey. 'We just stopped to say hello to Miss Kristien. We're going now.'

Jonnie pulls her away. 'I told you not to have nothing to do with these fokking Boere,' he says; and as they pass Anna he clears his throat and spits a gob of phlegm at her feet.

She flushes a deep red, but waits until they are out of earshot before she hisses, 'The little shit!' The hand holding the gun twitches. 'Now you can see for yourself what things have come to. And these used to be the people Ouma trusted with her life – '

'You should be ashamed of yourself,' I lash out at her.

'What on earth are you talking about?' She seems genuinely perplexed.

'Oh for God's sake – !' I take a deep breath. 'Well? What was your precious message?'

It was Casper. Of course. Calling from town, I learn, to tell her that one of the band of terrorists, or at least someone closely connected to them, had been nailed. Brazenly walked into a chemist's to buy bandages, ointment and pain-killing tablets, just like that, obviously intended for the thug wounded in last night's shoot-out. But the bastard didn't get far. As it happened, one of the chemist's assistants was married to a man in Casper's commando, and she had the presence of mind, brave woman, to telephone her husband, and when the suspect stepped out on the pavement four or five bakkies with armed farmers converged on him, nearly crashing right into the shop and sowing pandemonium among the passers-by, and set on the luckless man with fists, boots and the butts of their guns. They would have killed him right there, but unfortunately the police arrived and took him off in their van.

'So what do you say now?' asks Anna, a tone of triumph in her quavering voice.

# 13

Not so easy. The town, we find when we get there, is indeed agog with the news; but as it turns out, the poor man who was so nearly lynched, and who is now recovering in hospital, had nothing to do with the attack on Ouma's place. Following up his story to the chemist, the police have found at his home a child bitten by a dog and in need of the bandages, ointment and pain-killers the father had gone to buy.

# 14

Anna avoids my eyes and drives off on her own to do some shopping while I spend time with Ouma. Not a very profitable visit, as I find her in a sleep so deep that if the matron hadn't warned me that she's sedated by a constant dosage of morphine I would be convinced she has quietly expired. Her breath is too light even to ruffle a feather or cloud a mirror; but after some time there is a brief twitching of the hand on the folded sheet. For minutes on end I stand hunched over her, the way an archaeologist might study a dubious relic dug up from a disconnected past.

Is this what I have come back for? What have I really been expecting from my precipitate return? All I know is that this – her lying here so still, so insignificant that there is hardly a fold in the bedclothes to indicate the presence of a body below – is something that eludes my grasp. Not because it is too profound or too complicated, but because it is too simple. Death is too easy for a mind used to anxious or sceptical burrowings. This: to lie here, and to die. I can understand everything, but not this. I can accept anything, but not this. A small sound makes me look up. There is a single sunbird fluttering against the window. The others, the myriads of others, are still perched – I saw them as I came in – on the roof of the hospital, in all the trees, on all the wires surrounding it. But this single, miraculous little feathered creature, not trying to come in like yesterday's kamikaze daredevils, but content merely to flutter and to stare at what, most certainly, it cannot see, moves me more deeply than those others did. I know it is not really a bird. It is the breath of the dying old woman. This urgent

46

whirr of bright wings, this little feather, is the perverse fluttering of hope that keeps one going, the hope of *not* dying, of yet finding something, believing something, salvaging something, redeeming something: a fluttering, light as it is, that outweighs the confusion of history, the futility of time, the heaviness of the world.

I sit down on the straight-backed chair beside the bed. And I'm still sitting there when a plump young plover of a nurse comes rushing in to call me.

'Miss Müller, your sister is here to fetch you.'

'Isn't she coming in?'

'No, she's waiting in front.'

'You can tell her I'm coming.'

'Yes, Miss.' Mechanically, she first checks the pulse, then charges out again.

I bend over Ouma to whisper in her ear. 'I don't want you to die, you hear? I'll be back. I'm taking you home.'

The sunbird thrills against the window.

'Why didn't you come in?' I ask Anna as we get into the bakkie.

'I couldn't leave the bakkie with all the stuff in the back.' She sounds on the verge of tears. 'You know what happened while I was in the supermarket? They broke in' – for the first time I notice the smashed side-window – 'and they stole the radio. Casper's radio.' She swallows back a sob. 'So I had to go to the police. He'll just *kill* me.' I cannot make out whether it would be for the missing radio or going to the police. 'It just never stops. All the time, all the time. I can't *take* it any more, Kristien. And this whole thing with Ouma too – '

This is an opening, I decide. 'She must go home,' I announce as calmly as I can.

'What d'you mean, home?' she asks, flabbergasted.

'To The Bird Place.'

'It'll kill her!'

'She's dying, Anna. And she wants to go in peace. I've taken a good look at the place and I'm sure we can make it comfortable enough for her. She may not last for long.'

'Do you still not realise how dangerous it is? For heaven's sake, they've already fire-bombed the place once!'

'Lightning never strikes twice.'

'You're out of your mind, Kristien. Besides, Casper will never allow it.'

'I wasn't planning to ask his permission.'

A furious intake of breath. But she says nothing. And I strike while the iron is hot, assuming it will be a relief to her to be rid of me for a while anyway: as there is no car rental agency in town, I persuade her to drop me off at Sinai again so that I can commandeer Ouma's vehicle, that glorious old hearse, from a meek if wary Jeremiah.

Anna roars off, wildly indignant, in a cloud of dust. I stay behind to make arrangements with Jeremiah and Trui; then drive back to town to confer and argue, exhaustingly, with Ouma's doctor and the hospital superintendent (when we look in on her, she is still in the same deep sleep, beyond our reach). Out of the question, they say. Neither will give permission. She is their responsibility now. They appeal to the Hippocratic oath. They treat me like an importunate child. But I am resolute. What if her condition improves, I ask them. We can arrange for a nurse to attend to her. No, they cannot possibly take that responsibility: at her age, in her condition. What if *I* take responsibility, I demand. They'll first have to see. This is much too early. At best it remains inconclusive: if – if – if . . . But I'm confident that once she wakes up, and provided they don't deliberately and maliciously keep her asleep, between the two of us we shall prevail.

# 15

Back in Anna's home, once I've parked the shiny black monster (immediately set upon by a horde of savage children who rapidly cover it entirely like a swarm of bees moving into a new habitat), I find her in the large pantry where she is still toiling away, trying – valiantly, but more or less in vain – to stow the veritable mountain of provisions she has brought back.

I gape in unbelief. 'You've bought enough for a year!' I exclaim, in trying my best to sound jocular.

But she takes it seriously. Almost apologetically she says, 'One never knows – '

'What on earth do you mean?'

'Well, there have been so many rumours about the election. Once the blacks take over – I mean, anything can happen. And one has to provide for the children.'

And in the evening, after the servants have gone home to their hovels and the children have been packed off to bed, Anna and Casper (who surprisingly arrives in time for supper, and is kept in ignorance, for the time being, about the theft of the car radio) roll up the carpet in the lounge, raise a trapdoor below and proceed – solemnly and without saying a word – to stack in a cavity under the floor an astounding amount of provisions: candles and small gas cylinders, cartons of long-life milk, tinned food, powdered milk, an assortment of Tupperware containers filled with flour, sugar, tea-bags and instant coffee, bottles of mineral water, a multitude of toilet rolls, spare blankets, dog food, boxes of vitamin pills and basic medicines, and even – honest to God – a spare Bible. Afterwards Anna and I are laconically instructed to accompany Casper to a far corner of the backyard, where by the light of gas lamps held aloft by the two of us he laboriously digs a trench in which he subsequently buries, carefully wrapped in black plastic refuse bags, another hoard of tins containing all manner of meat and vegetables.

'Can you think of anything else?' Casper asks when all is done, wiping his brow in evident satisfaction.

'What about condoms?' I suggest with a straight face. 'You wouldn't want to produce a few more children in a state of siege, would you?'

'You just watch out!' Anna suddenly erupts. 'You come back here for a few days to help Ouma into her grave and then you buzz off again, leaving us to pick up the pieces – '

'I was only joking, Anna,' I answer limply, unnerved by the vehemence of her outburst.

'Oh no,' she storms. 'From the moment you arrived you've been criticising and attacking everything that's important to us. Shit, it's so easy! When things became too hard to handle you turned tail and ran away, expecting us to sort out the mess. And now that you're safe and far away you think you can gloat. But to us it's life or death, in case you haven't noticed.'

'I never ran away,' I say, restraining the fury that is leaping up in me, a dog straining at the leash. 'Do you think it was easy for me to leave everything behind, to start again from scratch, to build a new life, to try and deny what I was?'

'Don't fool yourself, little sister,' she says viciously. 'You've taken the easy way out every time. When you didn't like it here, you cleared out. When you felt cramped with a man who loved you, you just dumped him. When you couldn't face being a mother, you killed the child – '

'Jesus, that's below the belt, Anna,' I say mechanically, feeling the needles in my face. 'I had an abortion. It was perfectly legal.'

'Call it any fancy name you want, in my book it's murder.'

I'm tempted to hit back in anger: Don't you think I call it murder too, and wake up in a sweat at night? But this I dare not share with her, not here, not now. To defend myself I must be vicious too. 'You should have murdered a few of *your* litter,' I hit out blindly, even as I desperately think: For God's sake, cut it out before it's too late. 'You might have been a woman still, not just an incubator and a slave.'

'Now stop it, both of you,' Casper intervenes peremptorily. Stung to the quick, I am ready to turn on him; but I'm held back by the look of abject guilt on Anna's face. 'How about some coffee?' he says breezily. 'We can all do with some refreshment.'

Almost automatically Anna turns to go. I cannot bear the thought of being left alone with him; but to follow her to the kitchen and obediently make his coffee will be worse. So I stay.

'That wasn't a very nice thing to say to your sister,' he says when she is out of earshot; but his tone is amused rather than reprimanding.

'We'll sort it out between us,' I answer curtly. 'We don't need you to tell us off.' I start walking towards the house.

He follows on my heels. 'As hot-headed as ever!'

'And you like that, don't you?' I ask as we reach the lounge. 'That's what you told me on your wedding day.'

For a moment he looks nonplussed; then, evidently, he remembers. 'So you haven't forgotten.'

'Damn sure I haven't.'

'Good.' Now he's turning on the male charm, his tanned face crinkling in a smile. 'I've been thinking quite a lot about you too over the years.'

The extent of his audacity stuns me. 'If I've been thinking about *you*,' I say, 'it's been with relief at how far away you were.'

'You're not serious,' he says. There is nothing quizzical about it: for him it's a simple statement. 'Come on, Kristien, you're much too beautiful to have so much venom in you.'

'And you, I'm afraid, are even dumber than I remember.'

'You may be in for a surprise.' He winks.

I walk away from him, then stop to turn again. 'One day, when you've finished playing games, we can sit down and have a proper discussion.'

'I'm not playing games, Kristien.' Suddenly he is very serious; and hurt, I imagine.

'What else do you call your commando, your driving up and down through the district, your CB radio, your schoolboy fights with anybody that's smaller or weaker than you?'

50

'You don't seem to realise what is at stake.'

'If there is so much at stake, why don't you try to find a solution rather than just fuck it all up?'

'If you're referring to that kaffir – '

'What you need is to have your mouth washed out with soap.'

'Oh I see. We're finicky about language now, are we?'

'I just hoped we could have an adult conversation. In adult language.'

He flushes. For a moment I wonder whether he's going to strike me: it is in that same moment that I know, quite illogically, but without any doubt at all, and with the taste of bile in my mouth, how he must be with Anna. Then, unexpectedly, he changes tactics. 'All right,' he says. 'So we overreacted. But can you blame us? Haven't you seen what they did to your own grandmother? Do you realise she's the fourth elderly person attacked in this district in the last three weeks? The others were not so lucky.'

'And you think violence can be solved with violence?'

'What other language do they understand?' he asks in quiet anger. And then turns on the noble rhetoric. 'This is a bloody tough land to survive in. But we've managed, for over three centuries, even if it meant we had to be tough too. Not because we liked it, but because we were driven to it. And why? Because we love this bloody place, that's why. We've paid for it in blood and shit. It's the only place in the world we can call our own. Now they want to take it away from us. But we won't let them. We have nowhere else to go, Kristien, damn it!'

My first thought is: Please, not again. How many times have I heard all this pious ranting before? But the strange thing – and this is what hits me like a boot in the stomach – is that I know he means it; he really means it desperately. And I try to reason with him. 'Who wants to take it away from you, Casper?'

'The kaf – ' – he checks himself, somewhat to my surprise – 'the blacks. The communists. They've failed everywhere else in the world, so now they've got to make it work for them here. But I tell you, we won't let them. And we're prepared to die for it if we have to.'

I cannot restrain a sigh. And I say, as much in resentment against the weakness in myself as against his passion, 'Don't you think it is better to live for a cause than to die for it?' (This, too, I know, is a cliché, but having waded in so far, why not go all the way? They wouldn't have been clichés if they hadn't been pronounced – and believed – by so many.)

'Not if living means sacrificing everything that matters to us.'

'Like what?'

'Like – our whole way of life, man!'

'And you're absolutely sure your "whole way of life", whatever in God's name that may mean, will change if "they" take over?'

'Haven't you seen what happened in the rest of Africa?'

'I've seen millions of people left to rot because the West turned its back on them.'

'And corruption, genocide, violence, famine? Is all of that caused by the West too?'

'Much of the famine and the genocide, yes. As for corruption and violence, Africa has simply followed the example of its colonial masters.'

He makes an irritable gesture. 'You're too clever by half. You're trying to argue like a man. It doesn't suit you.'

'That's the last-ditch argument of a loser, Casper. And I won't fall for it. You can't send *me* to the kitchen, you know.'

Anna comes in with the tray.

'We'll talk again later,' he says.

'You bet.' I meet his gaze without flinching.

'All I want you to remember,' he says, 'is that we *are* serious.'

'Not serious,' I say. 'Desperate, yes.'

'What are you talking about?' asks Anna, without looking at us. Her eyes are red and puffy. I feel a pang of guilt.

'Man-talk,' says Casper, helping himself to three teaspoons of sugar.

As soon as he has finished his coffee he gets up from the sofa where he has sprawled. 'Well, duty calls.'

'You're not staying out all night again, are you?' Anna asks apprehensively.

'No.' He gives her a perfunctory kiss. 'Just a short round. To make sure everything is quiet.'

'Please be careful,' she says.

Then we're left alone. But it is too soon to face each other; and after I've helped her wash up I go to the passage, quite deliberately, and dial Michael's number in London.

It rings and rings, but there is no answer. And suddenly, unreasonably, I feel weepy and let down. As I reluctantly put down the receiver, she comes past me, hesitates, briefly presses my hand, then moves on towards the master bedroom. The gloom of a failed, miserable evening settles in me. I'll have a bath, I decide: the easy way out again?

# 16

I am just stepping out of the tub when there is a knock on the door, so hesitant that for a moment I'm not sure whether I have imagined it. Then Anna calls softly, 'It's me. May I come in?'

'I suppose so.'

I start drying myself. It is only when after several minutes of vigorous rubbing I hang the towel over the rail again that I realise she is scrutinising me like a buyer at an auction. Involuntarily I reach for Michael's old T-shirt which I wear to bed.

'Sorry,' she says. 'I didn't mean to stare. But you're – you're rather good to look at, you know.'

'You think so?' I strike an exaggerated show-off pose to hide the embarrassment I feel. 'Don't be silly, Anna. *You* used to be the swan in the family.'

'Used to be,' she says quietly. Then, 'I'm sorry I was so bitchy tonight.'

'I was too. I didn't mean to say what I did.'

'It's a bad time for us, you know.'

I close the toilet lid and sit down on it, the T-shirt draped over a shoulder. 'You mean Ouma? The mess in the country?'

'I mean Casper and I.' She starts fidgeting with her dress. 'Mind if I have a bath too? I'll use the same water.'

The economies of a harsh climate? Or a transparent attempt at sisterly bonding? But I gesture grandly. 'Be my guest.' And watch her, even though it makes me feel like an intruder, as she undresses and lowers herself into the still warm water. Varicose veins at the backs of her knees, lemon-peel cellulite, stretch marks on buttocks and belly, the once stunning breasts now sagging, the unkempt beard of her sex. And I feel my throat contract in pity. I would rather have spared her this. What a long way we have come since the time when I was small and she would come, uninvited and often to my spitting anger, into the bathroom when I was there; her snide comments on how skinny I was, my knobbly knees, my lank hair, and worst of all, the likelihood of never growing breasts. I, in turn, snooping little mouse, had strict orders to keep out when she was having her bath. But once, when I was only five or six, I had to use the toilet and barged in, and surprised her shaving her bikini line. Pubic hair was a phenomenon of which until that moment I had been oblivious. I still remember how I stood and stared, and pointed, and asked in awe, 'What's that thing with the feathers?'

Anna must have become aware of my scrutiny. She sits up and hugs her knees in an awkward attempt to cover up. 'Not exactly Miss World, am I?' she asks with a strained laugh. After a moment she adds in a smothered voice, 'Can you blame Casper for losing interest?'

'This old grey mare ain't what she used to be either,' I say, knowing just how unconvincing it must sound.

'You're no good at patronising, Kristien.' But there is no spark of resistance in her voice. And she leans back again, resigned.

'Is it really important for you to keep him?'

'What about the children?'

'Do they need him?'

'He's a good father!' This time I detect a flare of fire.

I look hard at her, but her eyes are averted. The bathwater moves in rapid wavelets across her body.

'Are you sure it's worth it, Anna?'

'I have a family to think of.'

'You have yourself to think of too.'

She shakes her head. 'I suppose it looks different from outside. You're free to come and go. You have the whole of London, of Europe, of the world, within your reach. You needn't ever lie awake at night wondering when someone is going to break in and kill you all and burn the place down – '

'It's just this thing with Ouma that's shot your nerves.'

'No, it isn't. It's been going on for years, and getting worse all the time. When this happened it just confirmed what we'd always feared. I'm so frightened. There isn't an hour of the day or night that I'm not frightened. I can't take it any more. If only I could run away, and run and run to where no one will ever find me again. But how can I leave the children? I'm not so old. Forty-two isn't old, is it? But what have I got to show for it? This isn't life. It's worse than a prison. You know' – there is a brief hesitation, then she plunges in – 'more than once I've almost' – she avoids my eyes – 'put an end to it all.'

'Don't say that, Anna.'

'It's true. What *is* there to live for? Except duties, obligations, responsibilities? And Casper doesn't understand. He doesn't understand anything. When I try to talk to him about it he puts on a bored face and says it'll be all right. That is if he doesn't just get up and walk away. Or else he loses his temper and – ' Her tears are running down her face into the bath. Angrily she sits up and turns on the tap again.

'I had no idea – '

'Of course you didn't. That's what is so unbearable about living here. Millions and millions of people, we're all in it together, yet no one bothers about the rest. We're all alone. So bloody alone.'

I am shocked by the desperation in her voice.

'Do you have a cigarette for me?' she asks unexpectedly.

'I didn't know you smoked.'

'I don't. Casper would kill me if he . . .' She sits up. 'Well, let him.'

'I'll fetch you one.' Wrapping a damp towel around me I open the door and go down the passage to my room. A small child emerges from one of the doors along the way, and stops to stare at me, thumb in mouth, and begins to whimper. I feel, briefly, a perverse urge to flash at him – 'Ever seen a thing with feathers before?' – then cover up with a forced smile and sidle past. In this house, as in my parents', nakedness is not the order of the day. (How unlike The Bird Place, in the rage of summer, when a swarm of us, out on a dare, would rampage naked up and down secret stairways, through basement and attic, and even into the moonlit yard.) Meekly the child returns to the darkness it has emerged from. I retrieve the cigarettes from my room. Through the window I see the veld outside awash in moonlight. Fascinated, I remain standing there, aware of the sensual touch of the night breeze; my nipples become taut. Endless, endless, the plains unfold into the dark, pure space unencumbered by tree or rock. Above, the unnatural brightness of the stars – God, I've forgotten how close and graspable they can be here – the glinting dust of the Milky Way, the confident markers of the Southern Cross. I feel duly cut down to size, and duly alien. Chastened, I turn away and go back to Anna who is still lolling in her amniotic sanctuary.

'I can't tell you how happy I was when you told me on the phone you'd be coming,' she says after the first deep breath, looking at me through the light whorl she has exhaled. 'It was like – I don't know, like the answer to everything.'

'And now it's all evaporated again.'

'Don't say that.' Another slow exhalation. 'Please. You *are* here. It does make a difference. I don't know how, but it does. I wish you could stay.' With a candour she has seldom shown, she says, 'I need you.'

We have stopped talking. For an all too fleeting instant, as if we're outside time, outside history, the two of us are together, sisters, in an intimacy more lucid than I can recall us as ever having known together, contained in the frankness of our naked bodies, our shared femininity. And from this knowledge spreads a subliminal awareness – surfacing only now in the telling of it – of the many circles of the night spreading from this centre where we are: of plains and darkness and beyondness, of moonlight and stars, a free and female universe.

Then there is a distant rumbling sound, soon definable as a vehicle approaching. Anna tenses briefly before she rises in an agitated smacking and swirling of water and reaches for a towel. 'Casper,' she says.

When his keys start turning in the several locks of the front door we are already in the kitchen, running water for tea. Anna is wearing her black emergency nightdress. I have put on her gown over the T-shirt. There is, I notice with pleasurable surprise, a freshness and a new lightness about her.

He seems to sense it too. Going to her, he lifts her hair and kisses her nape. 'Smells good,' he says. 'Missed me?'

'No,' she says. 'Kristien is good company.'

He turns to me, takes in – I see at a glance – my bare feet, my damp hair, the flimsy gown.

'Any news?' I ask to forestall further exploration.

'No. It's quiet tonight.'

'Good. I haven't told you yet, but I'm going to take Ouma home.'

'What?'

'It's by far the best for her,' says Anna quietly.

'But how can you – '

'I'll be taking care of everything,' I say. 'With the police, and with the doctors. Now let's have our tea and go to bed.'

'And by the way,' says Anna as she pours, 'the radio was stolen from the bakkie this afternoon.'

Much later, when the house is dark, invaded by the night outside as if the very walls have become penetrable, I hear the sounds of their coupling from the master bedroom next door. He is taking, I tell myself, in his own way, his revenge. I have a brief image of her in the black flannelette nightdress, pushed up or torn away, her white limbs. Impossible to tell from the sounds she utters whether what she derives from it is pleasure or pain, ecstasy or revulsion. And this is what most disturbs me: not the fact of the event, but the impossibility of discovering what it means.

# 18

This, at last, is the confirmation of return. To be in this fantastic house again. It has taken several days longer than I anticipated. Ouma's condition first had to improve sufficiently; only when it was clear that a collapse of her lungs had been averted and that most of the drips could be dispensed with, the doctors became more willing to consider the move. Even so, several additional opinions from their brotherhood had to be solicited, and in the end a whole rainbow of forms had to be signed to absolve them from all responsibility. At the same time a small army of labourers was set to work on the house: before we could move in, electricity had to be restored and the telephone reconnected, outside doors replaced, burglar bars fixed to accessible windows; the police insisted on completing their search for clues in the rubble; Trui and I, several members of her family, even Anna and a couple of inquisitive neighbours – clicking and clucking, prophesying doom and impending apocalypse – have worked round the clock to clear away the worst of the mess, restock the pantry and the linen-cupboards, replace the most indispensable utensils and implements, clean up and sweep and wash and dust the few rooms provisionally chosen for our habitation in the wing least damaged by the explosion and the over-zealous efforts of the fire brigade. Now we have moved in. It is night, and very quiet.

Ouma Kristina has drifted off into a sleep induced, against her will, by the energetic young nurse seconded to us for the day shift (I am brave, or reckless, enough to assume, for the time being, and against the indignant remonstrations of the doctors, the night watch with Trui.) Before Ouma succumbed to the morphine we spoke for a while; she still had trouble to mouth the words, to make herself audible. But she seemed at last relaxed, at peace with the world.

'Yes. We've showed them, haven't we? The two of us.' Clutching my wrist limply in her single useful hand.

'Now you'll get well again.'

'No. Of course not. I've come home to die. But we have a lot to talk about.'

'You can tell me all about what happened.'

'That's not important, Kristien. There are other things. I think you've forgotten most of what you knew, you were away too long. But I'll give you back your memory.'

'You know I won't forget you. Not ever.'

'It isn't me, Kristien. It's all the others, the ones before us. You dare not forget them now. This land – these – you know . . .' Her voice trailed off. The injection was beginning to take effect.

'Don't wear yourself out. We have time – '

'We'll talk, won't we? We'll talk. There are many stories to tell you again.'

'Yes, yes,' I said soothingly. 'But first you must sleep. You need the rest. Otherwise they'll send you back to hospital.'

'You won't let them, will you?'

'No, of course not.'

'I don't want that Piet Malan to cart me off to his undertaker's and abuse my body among all those skeletons of old cars in his backyard.'

'Nobody will lay a hand on you, Ouma. I promise.'

Then she slid off, returning once or twice, fighting against the drug, mumbling words I couldn't make out, and fell silent, her mouth still open.

Seated beside her bed, in a deep easy chair salvaged from the ruin below and laboriously lugged upstairs by Trui and myself, I have at last the leisure to savour the sensation of being home again.

An impressive and improbable procession has brought us here. A yellow police van in front, followed by Casper in his Land Cruiser, the ambulance with Ouma and two nurses in the back, then Anna and I and a number of her children (stunned into silence, for once, by the solemnity of the occasion) in the huge black hearse, while a doctor in a new metallic-grey Mercedes brought up the rear. It felt like a State visit, and along the way everybody stopped to stare; all that was missing was a contingent of outriders. The day was hot and bright, yet we travelled in deep shadow as we progressed under a moving cloud of birds overhead, accompanying us all the way from the hospital to the farm. There they descended on the incongruous mass of trees that mark Ouma's place on the expanse of the veld; many swept in through open windows to perch on what remained of the balustrade of the marble staircase we ascended to Ouma's new room, leaving only, in a whirr and flutter of wings, after she had been comfortably installed with drips and tubes and monitors and other gadgets supplied by the hospital staff (even an oxygen cylinder in case of emergency). And now we are left, I trust, in peace.

58

Scared? I cannot deny that I am uneasy, much more so than I would have expected back in the turbulent security of Anna's house; even though I know that there are two policemen at the distant ostentatious gate, that Casper or some of his eager commando will undoubtedly visit the place on regular patrols, and that in spite of my protestations he has left me a gun and a revolver, neither of which I have any intention – or capability – of using. A room or two away, beyond my own, which is next to Ouma's, Trui and Jeremiah are sleeping (on the floor, on their own insistence), to be 'available' if required. There is even a CB radio in a corner of the room, connected to a mast rigged up outside; from time to time, always unexpectedly, it bursts into a muted distant cackle of conversation before subsiding again into what seems to be its natural state, a steady crackling superimposed on a low contented hum. So it is not a feeling of being unsafe that makes me feel ill at ease; if anything, I am overprotected. The pioneer women of our family made do with incomparably less, and they certainly survived, one way or another. The uneasiness comes rather, I think, from the simple fact of being here, at last, alone, with her, with all the memories contained and defined by that meagre little bundle of skin and bones and tendrils of hair. I know now the extent of my responsibility, and what it means to be exposed here to past and future alike, conscious of origins and possible endings.

For an hour or two I remain by her side, my whole body tensed up in the attempt to follow her breathing or the occasional flickering of her eyelids as she dreams; once she utters a dry chuckle which trails off into a moan. I have kicked off my shoes to be more comfortable. I feel claustrophobic in shoes. As I invariably do when I have time to kill, I inspect my feet, toe by toe, each nail, each knuckle, checking the cuticles, loose skin, chafe marks, signs of calluses. I have a fascination with feet. There is a sense of easy communication about them. The touch, in bed, of toe and instep, heel and pad, a prelude or accompaniment to love, sign of forgiveness or sharing, confirmation of being together. And I tend to judge men in terms of their reaction to feet. (Some find them sexy, some embarrassing; Michael mildly amusing.)

After a while, to keep the circulation flowing, I get up and pace up and down for a while, stopping in front of the window every time I pass it, to peer into the incredibly peaceful night. At last, armed with one of the several large torches Casper and Anna have insisted on leaving behind, I venture out on to the landing and down the old-worldly staircase to the regions below, acting the child again. I am still barefoot, not just to move as quietly as possible in order not to disturb

Ouma, but because it lends a different kind of meaning to motion, to the feel of surfaces beneath my soles, a sensual form of knowledge, a reassurance of somehow being in touch with what matters.

Aimlessly, relishing the almost-forgotten tinglings of dread down my spine, I wander from room to room. It is a journey that confirms memory, yet allows space for new discovery. Once or twice I am stopped by what from the corner of the eye seems like a moving figure. But it must be myself, caught in the glass of a picture or the mottled, dusty, cobwebbed surface of one of the many mirrors on the wall. Even from childhood I have been aware of Ouma's fascination with mirrors – unlike that ancestor of hers (which one? I'll have to ask her again) who lived in fear or hatred of them and never allowed a single reflecting surface in her house. After each false sighting I move on again, only to be stopped in my tracks, at every turn, by what may or may not be sounds: rustling, sliding, gliding sounds, barely liminal, like sheets or curtains trailing. Mice perhaps, bats up in the attic? But would they have come back so soon after the fire? There are cold and sudden draughts, barely perceptible currents of air wafting along the corridors. They may be ghosts, I tell myself. The ones who followed me from the cemetery. Ouma Kristina has always lived among the dead. They mean no harm. They belong here.

In the preserved wing I find the large dining-room with its long table and high-backed chairs below the moulded ceiling with its two exorbitant candelabras imported from the island of Murano. We have not yet had time to clean up here, and the table is covered with a film of dust and fine black ash which invites me to write my name on it. Many rooms in this house must bear the inscription of my name and those of cousins, traced in dust, scribbled in pencil or coloured crayons, even incised in beams and floorboards. As if it makes a difference.

On an impulse I kneel in front of the huge ornate sideboard – Flemish or Spanish, centuries old – and open my favourite remembered door, the one on the right, carved with the faces of putti and jesters and monsters. Inside, the bright dusty beam of the torch picks out what I have hoped to find: the hundreds upon hundreds of white damask serviettes, each fastidiously rolled and tied up with a piece of string, a small square of cardboard with a handwritten name attached. *Hendrik. Olga. Marthinus. Philip. Cecilia. Mr Jansen. Mrs Colyn. Dr Leriche.* If I take my time, as I used to do so often in the past, there will be exotic ones too: Princess This, The Hon. That, Countess So-and-So. Foreigners, dignitaries, relatives, humble peasants. Every person who has ever sat down to a meal in this room has had a serviette assigned to her or him; and no matter how long one stayed away, weeks or months, years, decades, if ever you returned you would be sure to have your personal serviette awaiting you. Even the tags of the dead have been left untouched, and whenever as a child I asked Ouma about those she would say in her inscrutable way, 'Who knows, they may still come back.'

The real pleasure used to lie in sorting them, in holding up one after the other and asking, 'Who was Henrietta, Ouma?' 'What's happened to Princess Véronique?' 'Has this General Marmaduke ever come back?' I start unpacking them; I have all night. Rows upon rows, some yellowed with age. Until at long last, several rows down, yes, I come upon mine. *Kristien*.

My stomach contracts.

I bundle the serviettes back into their musty hollow, replacing mine on top; tomorrow I'll use it.

For a long time, trying to sort out my feelings, I remain sitting in front of the sideboard, before I finally close the heavy door again, change my grip on the handle of the torch, and return to the passage and the gracious curve of the staircase. A few steps up I suddenly stop dead. There is a sound somewhere. Bird or beast? It is undoubtedly human. A moan. Ouma must be in pain. Only, when I reach the first landing, I realise it is not coming from her room but from the opposite side, the damaged wing.

Now I feel fear.

The telephone, the radio, the guns are in her room. But instead of doing the obvious and reasonable thing I find myself, as so often in my life, turning perversely towards the danger, if danger it is. Soundlessly, on my bare feet, I move across the landing. The torch casts a narrow beam into the darkness ahead. Something moves. A man emerges from an open door. He looks at me. He has a knife in his hand. There is dried blood on his face. It is like that man who came for Father, long ago. A ghost? But he seems all too real.

I must deal with this. I am a big girl now.

# T W O

---

## *The House of Usher*

This, always, in Ouma Kristina's stories: the impossible escapes. The classical scene of the heroine – Ouma had little interest in heroes – finding herself at the edge of the precipice, the foaming river with crocodiles below, the enemy closing in from behind. 'And then, Ouma? And then – ?' 'I don't know. Let's see if we can think of something by tomorrow night.' My own eager solutions would invariably involve the deus ex machina in its multifarious possibilities: a helicopter, the discovery of a subterranean passage under a flat rock, a crocodile that turns out to be a submarine, a powerful friend in disguise among the host of enemies. When Ouma was in a mischievous mood she would resolve it by saying, 'And then an elephant came and blew the story away.' But usually she disdainfully refused external intervention. That was part of the game. 'No help from outside, lovey. She's got to do it on her own.' In the end, exasperated, I would give up. 'Now *what* then, Ouma?' And triumphantly, but calmly, without the flicker of an eyelid, Ouma Kristina would proffer some variation on the immemorial formula: 'With one mighty bound she leaped free.' Leaving me, in spite of indignation and disappointment, with a strange sense of reassurance after all.

This time I find myself saying, 'Stay where you are. Don't move. Don't you dare use that thing.' And instantly, as if it were a magic incantation, help arrives. In the form of an owl. Two owls. They appear, whooping, from the cavern of the stairwell and sweep down on the unfortunate man who, terrified, and desperately trying to hide his face from their flailing wings and clawing talons, drops the knife and crouches down. I pick up the knife. As if that is what they have been waiting for, the great birds hurl themselves into the dark again. Perhaps they have never been there at all. The man still cowers in front of me, moaning in fear or pain or both. One shoulder is drooping, the arm held close to his body, and as I now have time to study him more closely I can see that there is a lot of blood on his shirt.

'It's all right,' I say, shaking my head at the unreality of the scene, the weirdness of my own behaviour. (How can I be so calm? I've never been the cool and collected type.) 'They're gone now.'

He goes on whimpering, his usable arm over his head.

'What are you doing here?' I ask.

'I'm sorry, Madam, I'm sorry. I didn't know there was people here. I just wanted a place to stay.'

'What has happened to you?'

'I'm sorry, Madam. I'll go now.'

'You can't go away in this state. Tell me what happened?'

'They shot me, Madam.'

'Who shot you? Where?'

'At Mr Joubert's farm, Madam. Sunday night. We went there to drop off a friend of ours who works on the farm with me, Madam. Then a lot of farmers chased us in their bakkies and made a roadblock, and we drove off into the veld, and they shot at us, and they hit me up here in the arm, but we got away. I'm sorry, but the pain is very bad now, Madam.'

Casper's fun and games. The man may be lying, but I am, perhaps perversely, inclined to believe his story. He is elderly and pathetic, undoubtedly harmless, and I feel foolish for having been so frightened in the first place.

'What happened to the others?'

He makes a gesture that may mean anything.

'Is Madam going to phone the police now?'

'Of course not.' I hand him the knife. 'Put away this thing before someone gets hurt. Let's see what we can do.'

Trui, I think, in a surge of relief. She'll know what to do. Yet even as I go down the passage towards the room where she and Jeremiah have bedded down, I feel a guilty turn in my stomach. Am I already falling into the South African trap of assuming that simply because Trui is there, she is automatically available to be called upon? I try to persuade myself that I'm appealing to her as a woman, as a mother figure, as a wise and practical person, not as a servant; but when I tiptoe into the room and look down on the two bodies under the grey blanket, set out like bread-dough to rise overnight, the feeling of guilt quickens to a stab. The meekness, the docility of the long-suffering serf. But the word *serf* does not say what I mean. The Afrikaans *lyfeiene* goes to the heart of it: an 'owned-body'. Always there, to be used, to be disposed of at will.

'Miss Kristien?' Trui sits up, rubbing her eyes. She has awakened on her own. Ready to be of service. No need to blame myself.

Together – I still in my clothes, Trui with Anna's dressing gown over the white petticoat in which she has been sleeping – we examine the stranger's arm in the bathroom. Trui is suspicious about the whole business, I can see; but I try to avoid a discussion by concentrating on the wound. It looks ugly, angry, inflamed; we have to cut away the shirt. He flinches when we wash the arm in lukewarm water, but meekly submits to our nursing as we apply disinfectant filched from the vast supply upstairs, and pat it dry.

'What do you think, Trui?' I ask her as we start wrapping the arm in Betadine bandages also retrieved from Ouma's room. I round off the ministrations with a morphine injection, following closely the instructions given me by the doctor. At the very least this is good practice.

'Looks worse than it is, Miss Kristien. It's just the flesh. I think the bone is all right. What happened then?'

'An accident,' I say hurriedly. No need to explain further. She may be less credulous than I. News of the shooting is all over the district, and I cannot be sure which version she has heard. If she gets it into her head that this man is a terrorist we may be in for more trouble than I can face right now.

'Like how?' Trui persists.

'They were hunting. He got in the way.'

'You know him?'

'I know about him. Anna told me.'

She hesitates, clearly unconvinced, but doubtful about countering me.

'Please, Trui,' I change my tactic. 'I need you. We have two patients now and I can't do it on my own.'

'Where we going to keep him?' she asks. She is still resentful but her resistance has caved in.

'In the basement. No one will think of looking for him there.'

'Why must they not find him?' she asks pointedly.

I have a sudden inspiration. 'Casper doesn't like him. You know how difficult he can be. If we women don't stand together – '

The shadow of an understanding smile on her wizened face. 'I'll go and make him a bed down there.'

'No, I'll see to him. You sit with Ouma for a while.'

'May one ask what his name is?' she says as we go out.

'Jacob,' the man answers meekly. 'Jacob Bonthuys.'

'You behave yourself, Jacob Bonthuys,' says Trui. 'It's decent people that live here.'

## 2

Casper arrives at first light. I am in the chair next to Ouma's bed. I have turned down the intrusive CB radio and, after a loud and aggravating check-up call at some ungodly hour, unplugged the telephone; and in the silence, broken only by the old woman's uneven breathing, I must have drifted off. I am awakened, first, by the furious cackling of the geese unleashing a flood of memories: our excursions among their aggressive flappings and rushings with outstretched wings and beaks, to plunder nests; cavortings in the pond; convoys of yellow goslings bobbing on the dark green water; the squelchiness of goose shit between one's toes, its unique colour, which with childish ingenuity we used to call 'shreen'. The cackling is followed by an eruption of other bird sounds. And seconds later I hear the approaching drone of the Land Cruiser, coming as usual to an absurdly demonstrative screeching halt on the gravel in front of the house.

Even before I am fully awake I am already on my feet and thrusting my arms into a gown, running downstairs, conscious only of the need to keep Casper from discovering our lodger. Down in the basement I find a bewildered Jacob Bonthuys pressed against a wall.

'Who's out there?' he asks.

'Visitors,' I tell him. 'Just stay here. Don't make a sound. They'll go away again.'

'They come for me.'

'No, Mr Bonthuys. Nobody knows about you. Nobody will find out if you keep quiet. Okay?'

Upstairs, in a passage, I can hear Casper's 'loud voice calling. 'Kristien! Kristien, are you all right? Where the hell are you?'

Swiftly, silently, I run up the basement stairs again and close the door behind me, remembering briefly my early encounter with him in this place. Then, following the sound of his voice, I return upstairs. Outside Ouma Kristina's door I say behind him, 'Casper! What is all this fuss about?'

He swings round. He has a rifle in his hands. There is uncomplicated fear in his eyes.

'Jesus, Kristien. You shouldn't creep up behind me like that. I could have – '

'Has anything happened?'

'No. But we were dead worried about you. Why didn't you call us?'

'There was no reason to.'

'But I told you – every hour – and we've been calling you since five, but you never answered.'

'I unplugged the telephone after you woke us up at two or three or whatever time it was. And I've turned down the radio. It was making too much noise. Ouma needs her sleep.' And I pointedly add, 'So do I.'

'But dammit, don't you realise – '

'No. *You* are the one who doesn't realise that I am perfectly capable of looking after myself. There are guards at the gate. And *if* anything goes wrong, which I doubt, I can call for help. Unless you start behaving like a grownup I'll tell the guards to keep *you* out.'

'Now come on,' he cajoles, in a predictable change of approach. 'Aren't you going to offer me some coffee?'

'You can make some in the kitchen. I'm getting dressed first.'

'You look good as you are, Kristien.'

'I'll look even better once I've washed my face.'

His eyes wander over my body like two tourists checking landmarks, pleased at finding everything exactly where the guide-book said. 'Shall I wait for you downstairs then?' He winks.

'You may have to wait a long time. I have a lot to do.'

'Kristien.' Now he's stung again, and deadly serious, and I suppose dangerous. 'Why are you so vicious with me? What have you got against me?'

'You really don't know?'

'You're blaming me because Anna – well, because she isn't what she used to be. Is that it?'

'I'm afraid it's not as simple as that, Casper,' I say. 'Of course I'm sad about Anna, but she's not my responsibility. She's the one who's got to sort it out, not me.'

His face is very close to mine now; I can feel his breath. It is stale. 'You sure you're not jealous?'

'Jealous?' I ask, amazed. 'What on earth of?'

'From the first day,' he says, 'you couldn't stand it that Anna was the woman I married.'

'Thanks for telling me.'

'Now, Kristien – '

'What I have against you has nothing to do with sex, Casper. In fact, I'm sure you're a lousy lover.'

'Is that what Anna told you?' he asks aggressively.

'There was no need for her to tell me. She's too loyal, anyway. But that's not even the point, Casper. What gets me is your pathetic need to prove yourself.'

'Look, my girlie, I can show you a thing or two – '

'You already have, Casper. Have you forgotten? But I'm afraid I've seen better than that since then.'

'Cow!'

How unoriginal, I think; and I suppose he can read it on my face, judging from the way he turns round and stomps down the stairs. I wait on the landing until I hear his footsteps crunching on the gravel outside, and the car door slamming, the engine revving. Then I go back into Ouma Kristina's room, but she is still, thank God, asleep – although it takes an anxious minute to establish that she is indeed breathing.

From my room next door I collect my clothes and go to the bathroom. The cold water of the shower makes me gasp, but I throw my head back and abandon myself to the spray, washing the brief pungent memory of Casper right out of me. I work up a lather and rinse myself energetically. And slowly I draw reassurance from this abandon, a sense of rediscovery, of being restored to myself, as if my body is shaped and moulded anew by the stream that washes over me, whole, intact and vigorous and alive. In water I acknowledge myself. *This is me.*

# 3

Ouma Kristina is awake, and in pain, when I return to her. Trui is trying to comfort her. Working from the notes I made of the doctor's instructions yesterday, I change the drip, and between the two of us we do our best to ease the pain; she is very brave, hardly utters a sound, but it is clear that she is in agony. Even overnight the frail body seems to have wasted away further, seared by suffering. Though her eyes are open and she watches us she seems very far away, beyond our reach. I'm beginning to reproach myself for obeying her and bringing her home. I've never been able to endure the pain of others; running away from wounded birds or animals, a cousin's severed toenail, Anna's cupped hands filled with blood after a fall on broken glass, the man with the bleeding face who came to see Father; I passed out once when we found an ostrich with its neck caught in a fence, contorted, its beautiful large eyes panic-stricken, dying.

But fortunately the day-nurse, an active gawky praying mantis all knees and elbows, arrives on time, at eight, and after changing the bandages – which is almost more than I can watch – her syringe brings ease and drowsiness.

Before she drifts away Ouma beckons me weakly. I bring my ear close to her sunken mouth. 'Today we must start working,' she whispers resolutely.

'Yes, yes, of course,' I say, merely to soothe her, for her mind must surely be wandering as she slides across the threshold of sleep.

'I'm serious,' she says, with a surprising mustering of energy.

'What work, Ouma?'

'I have a lot to tell you. You must write it all down before I go. You have a notebook?'

'No, Ouma, but – '

'Then go get one. Soon. This afternoon we'll . . .' Her voice trails off.

'There will be enough time later.'

'No. It's running out. And it's my testament.'

'But Anna told me you already have a testament.'

'This is another kind. And it's important.'

'Will you be all right if I go now?'

'Yes. Just leave the window open for the birds.'

She relaxes into sleep; her mouth falls open. The face I know so well becomes a stranger's face. It is horrible. It is also fascinating, and I find it hard to turn away.

'She'll be okay, Miss,' says the nurse. She scuttles in ungainly insect fashion this way and that before settling at last, to my immense relief, into the armchair beside the bed and takes a garish magazine from her large bag.

In the kitchen I find Trui at breakfast – mugs of coffee, thick slices of bread and apricot jam – with Jeremiah and their son Jonnie. The father scrambles rheumatically to his feet. The son just glowers at me, but has his hands on the edge of the table, ready, it seems, to scamper off, or perhaps to rise and shout abuse.

'Please sit down,' I tell Jeremiah.

He remains standing awkwardly.

I put on the kettle and cut a single slice of bread; we brought some basic provisions yesterday. When the water boils I make a cup of instant coffee and pull out a chair next to Trui. 'Mind if I join you?'

She laughs nervously; the men stare at me, Jeremiah bewildered, Jonnie with suspicion and resentment.

'Please sit down,' I say once again.

But he just grins blankly and mumbles something about having finished anyway, and then Trui gathers both his plate and hers and gets up too and goes to the sink.

Embarrassed, I try to invent conversation, which just makes matters worse. 'Are you looking forward to the elections, Jeremiah?'

'I don't know, Missus.'

Jonnie snorts. He doesn't look up.

'I'm sure life will be different after next week,' I persist awkwardly. 'There will be a new government.'

'We'll still be taking orders, Missus.'

'But it will be a different kind of government.'

He shakes his head, clearly unconvinced. 'We'll just see, Missus.'

'Please – ' But what's the use?

Jonnie goes on stuffing bread into his mouth and gulping down coffee, head down, scowling.

'Jonnie,' I say, pronouncing his name the proper, English, way, which may or may not be a mistake, 'have you finished school?'

He merely grunts, but Trui answers on his behalf, 'He finished, Miss Kristien, two years ago already, and he got good marks too, but now there's no jobs.'

'Have you thought about university?' I ask.

'Ai, Miss Kristien,' says Trui, 'and where must the money then come from?'

'Ma,' he says in a warning tone of voice, without looking up.

'Things may change after the elections,' I say brightly.

'Like how?' Hostility burns in his tone, but at least he has answered.

'I don't know. But I'm sure there'll be more opportunities, openings, possibilities. We can find out if you like.'

'*We?*' It is an open sneer. The puffiness of his face has subsided but it still looks bruised; his eyes, one bloodshot, glare at me in defiance.

It comes close to unnerving me, but I press on. 'Well, I can try to speak to some people – ' Suddenly it sounds such a 'white' thing to say that it makes me feel sick.

He says nothing, merely sits there waiting heavily, challenging, smouldering.

There is no backing out now. 'I used to work for the ANC when I

72

first went overseas,' I say, fixing my eyes on Jonnie. Jeremiah hasn't moved. Trui has stopped drying the plate she has just rinsed.

He still remains silent, but something in his look has changed. Trui is the one who says, 'Haai, Miss Kristien, but they're mos a lot of terrorists.'

'You're behind the times, Ma,' Jonnie snaps at her.

'Hey, you watch your tongue!' says Jeremiah. 'You don't say things like that to your mother.' Then, meekly, helplessly, at me, 'I'm sorry, Miss Kristien.'

I give up. 'Look,' I say, pushing back my chair, 'let's not get into an argument about it. All I'm saying is that I'd like to help Jonnie if we can think of something. Right now there are other things to be done.' I get up, avoiding the young man's eyes. 'I have to go to town. Trui, can you help me make a list of things we need for the house?'

Without pausing to take a breath, as if she has been waiting for this moment all along, Trui starts reeling off in a monotone voice, marking each item with a flick of her cloth, 'Jik, Handy Andy, Omo, Sunlight Liquid, Bisto, more milk, juice, oats, flour, salt, black pepper, rice, mealie meal, and then we'll need some meat and vegetables – '

'Wait!' I stop her, overwhelmed. 'I must get my pen and some paper, it's upstairs – '

'It's all here,' she says, turning to pick up a sheet of notepaper from the window-sill behind her.

'Miss Kristien.' This time it is Jeremiah. 'We must get other wheels. It is not a good thing to drive to town in that death wagon.' He makes a motion with his grizzled head.

'But you've been doing it all these years.'

'This is not the right time.'

'I'm afraid we have no choice.'

'I tell you this is not the right time.' Below his humble demeanour I sense the bedrock of his will.

'I'm sorry.' This is exasperating. 'You really must try to understand.'

'There is the old horse-cart in the shed.'

'No!' I say emphatically. 'It's more than twenty kilometres in to town. We don't have all day. And anyway' – triumphantly – 'we don't have horses any more.'

'But there are ostriches,' he says, unperturbed.

I gawk at him. For a moment, for the sheer hell of it, I am tempted. But – regrettably, perhaps? – sanity prevails. 'Out of the question,' I tell him.

'I don't drive that death wagon.'

'I've been driving it for the last few days, I'll drive it again.'

'That was different. Now you're living here. I cannot give you the keys, Miss Kristien. The old Missus say it's my job to drive, so I drive.'

'Dammit, Pa, give her the keys!' says Jonnie suddenly.

We all stare at him in surprise.

After a long silence Jeremiah turns to me again with all the dignity he can muster. 'You get your things,' he tells me. 'I shall drive you.'

# 4

On my own, under less pressure than on my previous visits, I rediscover, below the garish veneer of new affluence and the overall tastelessness of the modernised sprawling town, the village of my youth. Some buildings have indeed disappeared, but in most cases façades have simply been 'renovated', traffic lights installed, garages updated and streamlined, signboards enlarged, to resemble an American frontier town. Below the surface an old-fashioned world, at an old-fashioned pace, is still going about its business. Bank, grocery store, chemist, butcher's, bakery, home industry, Shapiro's Fashions, church.

The bank has been jazzed up inside, but the customers still look familiar: messengers, housewives, some coloured women with their hair in large multicoloured curlers visible under a doek, a large group of farmers talking shop in the corner, the younger ones in shorts and checkered cowboy shirts and long socks, with bulging calves and biceps, the older ones in khaki, the tops of their foreheads ringed with the white shadow left by their hats. My business takes quite a while; they are not used to transactions in foreign currency, and in the end I'm told to come back tomorrow.

In the supermarket which has replaced the grocery store of my youth, I work diligently through Trui's list before I go to the stationery section to select a sturdy black hardcover notebook, not the type in which deathless prose usually comes to life, but it will do, I guess. From darker corners at the back come memories of Saturdays when the whole flock of cousins were carted in to town on the back of Oupa's lorry; and of the pathetic old man behind the counter, whose young wife had run away with a Brylcreemed lover. My other visits are made purely to indulge my curiosity: the chemist's shop that used to belong to Mr MacGregor, whose eldest son electrocuted himself in my matric year when he tried to rewire his father's house, which inspired me afterwards to tell everybody he'd been driven to it by his unrequited love for me; the butchery, run in my early childhood by a hairy giant who beat the shit out of his wife and five children every Friday night, the bloody results of which could still be witnessed on Saturdays; the bakery next door, once renowned far and wide for the lightness and airiness of its loaves, until the baker's son, a mean-faced bastard, was caught redhanded, in a manner of speaking, wanking off into the dough (which probably, the district knowingly whispered, accounted for the self-raising qualities of his flour); the Home Industries where Aunt Mavis rose to fame with her inimitable green-fig preserve, until it was discovered that she used blue vitriol to heighten the colour.

I am still browsing among the shelves where once the figs glowed like green thoughts in a green shade when I am accosted by one of the busybody women crowding the place – 'My goodness me, but aren't you one of the Müller girls?' insisting, when momentarily I feign innocence, 'Anna's sister, Ludwig and Louisa's daughter?' – the kind of invasion of my own space that immediately gets my back up. But before I can reply, reprieve comes in the form of a new arrival, a woman of formidable proportions, in purple and green, who starts gushing even as she crosses the threshold. 'Jenny! Hannie! Freda! Have you heard the news – ?' In the black township, not an hour ago, now, now, now, she tells us, a farmer delivering mealie meal to one of the shops was stopped by a mob of demonstrators. What happened to the farmer, no one knows; there is little hope that he could have escaped. Where would a white man turn to in a black township, in these times? All that is known right now is that his bakkie was destroyed, totally burnt out, a smoking black skeleton. Honestly, these people. And what's going to happen now? All hell is going to be let loose, of that we can be sure. Mercifully, in the cackle that follows – it's like the night a jackal broke into Ouma's chicken run – I manage to make my escape.

Outside, the streets still appear calm and untroubled; the stillness of the sun is reassuring even if the lump in the pit of my stomach persists like undigested cold porridge. The brightness has gone from the morning. Unnerved by the news I wander on, split between today and yesterday.

Half a block further, squeezed in between two gaudy shop windows, is the entrance to Issie Shapiro's long, narrow shop which once represented the town's notion of haute couture, defined by the Shapiro family – Issie, Miriam, and their five beautiful daughters. Yet in public they were shunned by all the Afrikaners in the district because they were Jews; except before the mayor's annual 'do', when everybody would flock there to splurge on the latest imported fashions. Mother steadfastly refused ever to set foot in the place; Father was a member of the Broederbond, the fierce Brotherhood which ensured that racial purity was seen to be enforced, and under no circumstances could people like us be seen to enter the property of a family who, when all was said and done, had to bear personal responsibility for the death of Jesus Christ. Only once did I pay a visit to the shop, and that was the year when I finally managed to persuade my closest relatives that I was in dire need of my first bra. Mother, as usual, wasn't impressed, even when I assured her she would have to bear the blame if my back became permanently hunched from the sheer weight it was expected to carry. Anna found it hilarious and chose the most inopportune moments to comment on what she disparagingly referred to as my pimples. Only Ouma took it seriously, and one fine morning commanded Jeremiah to drive her and me to town in state in the black Chrysler hearse. And she boldly marched me into Shapiro's den of iniquity. Ouma never shared the family's qualms about Jews. In fact, as in many of the other ostrich palaces, there has always been a special enclosure on the front stoep known as 'the Jew's room', where since the feather boom any itinerant Jewish trader could move in, night or day, unbidden, to stay over until his mission on the farm was accomplished. So there was no hesitation at all in Ouma, once the matter had been decided, to accompany me boldly into Shapiro's emporium, where we were welcomed by a flutter of ancient women exuding a heavy, heady smell of exotic powders and colognes in the dusk. I was taken into a dingy little cubicle behind a curtain and offered the choice of six or seven bras, most of them hopelessly too big. In retrospect I think Ouma, too, had trouble keeping a straight face at the sight of my nipples, which must then have been the shape, size and colour of the snouts of baby mice; but true to form she went through the whole solemn procedure, fitting and adjusting and shifting and fidgeting until I found what I thought I needed. I remember heaving a deep and demonstrative sigh as we left that measly little cubicle, and saying, 'Ah, what a relief'; and Ouma Kristina seemed at least as proud as I was. Ever since then the place has remained in my memory the Mecca of fashion, an Aladdin's cave of incomparable splendour. How disconcerting now, as I venture inside more from curiosity than defiance or need, to find it reduced to this narrow, ill-lit, musty, old-fashioned little hole; and still presided over by members of the same family – the likeness is unmistakable, the black, black eyes, the skin whiter-than-white, like skimmed milk, especially when compared to the recklessly sun-spoilt skins of *our* family – even if the recollection of yesterday's beauties turns out to be rather less than trustworthy. Hoping that the women clustered around the counter have not recognised me, I turn back into the unsympathetic glare of the street outside.

And then the sandstone church with its white finish and tall steeple. Here I make no attempt to go closer than the gate. Those summer Sundays, relentlessly forced into scratchy show-off dresses with ribbons and bows and layers of frills, each mother striving to outdo the others with her brood; my hair drawn back so tightly into plaits that my eyes were narrowed into tearful slits. Those hot, interminable services, desultory singing (only Mother intoning at the top of her formidable soprano voice, causing the rest of us to cringe as the other cousins jostled and giggled and whispered around us), long-winded prayers, the dominee's voice rising and falling, crescendo and diminuendo, as he spoke of fire and brimstone, wailing and gnashing of teeth, for ever and ever, fucking amen. Jesus, how I hated those Sundays! And no escape possible (except on the rarest of occasions, when I could prevail on Ouma to persuade Mother that I was sick unto death). Invariably it ended in family fights, in furious whispered threats and admonitions, often in smacks, sometimes in full-scale thrashings back home. The only diversion came on Communion Sunday when children were normally not allowed into the church but herded into the hall for a special service. But sometimes we gave that a miss and infiltrated the back of the church, to follow with awe the theatrical unfolding of the Communion, the passing of the cup, the silver platter with small cubes of dry white bread. Once or twice, usually the result of a dare, we risked (we were thoroughly convinced) our lives by tiptoeing into the vestry, afterwards, while our parents and their peers were still milling around outside to catch up with news and gossip; and we tasted some of the dregs and crumbs, curious to find out whether it would actually turn into flesh and blood; and on one memorable occasion we espied a mouse scurrying off with a morsel, and some of the smallest fry in our heathen horde stampeded round the church to the grownups shouting that the mouse had eaten Jesus, the mouse had eaten Jesus. Ever since, I have been fascinated by the problem of leftovers.

# 5

I must know what has happened to that man whose bakkie has been burned out. I could go to the police, I suppose, but after being conditioned for so many years to see the police as the enemy it would seem like an act of betrayal. (But, my God, of whom? of what?) I could go into any shop, the news should be all over the town by now; but I cannot face those eager gossips. Not only because it is unlikely anyone will really know the full story, but because I shrink from the vivisection that must accompany it. *My goodness me, but aren't you one of the Müller girls? Anna's sister, Ludwig and Louisa's daughter – ?* A simple matter of information becomes a major undertaking.

I collect my carrier bags and parcels from the supermarket and lug them to the hearse which Jeremiah has parked, judiciously, below the pepper trees behind the church. He approaches from half a block away where he has been standing on a stoep, smoking his pipe, his attitude disclaiming all relationship with the shining Chrysler; and he helps me to load in my wares, but his heart isn't in it.

'Can you stop at Anna's place first?' I ask.

Jeremiah grunts and moves in behind the wheel, perched on the small worn velvet cushion he has to sit on to see over the dashboard. As we drive through the streets the many people clustered on corners and sidewalks stare apprehensively at us; we are like a black omen, a shudder of conscience moving through the town, and Jeremiah is mortified by it. Once we have left the town behind he accelerates. I'm sure he has never driven so fast before and I get the impression that he is just waiting for me to comment on it; but I deprive him of that satisfaction. Now our progress is monitored by ostriches. Along all the fences that line the long straight road they are gathered, necks outstretched, their long-lashed fashion model's eyes blinking, the white-tipped wings of the males lightly spread, ruffled by the wind of our passing. *We know*, those eyes proclaim, *oh yes, we know, we know, but we're not going to tell.*

Casper, as I should have anticipated, isn't home; and Anna hasn't heard anything yet. But she insists I must come in for lunch. Jeremiah wanders off on his own, and as Anna and I go into the house I see him squatting down on his haunches near the chicken run, making it quite clear that human contact, which I suspect he regards at the best of

78

times with less than enthusiasm, is the last of his needs right now.

It is an unusually subdued Casper who comes in just after Anna and I have sat down at the table (the children, commendably obedient for once, are eating in the kitchen); I have not even heard him arrive. I suspect he hasn't noticed the hearse under the bluegums behind the house, because he stops when he sees me, his attitude more diffident than hostile.

'What are you doing here?' he asks.

'Just sharing some women's secrets.'

His eyes have a guarded, warning look. 'Like what?'

'Nothing,' says Anna, raising her face to be kissed, but he doesn't notice. 'It's not important.'

'Of course it's important,' I cut in, annoyed at her meekness; then look him in the eyes. 'Only it's not your business.'

His eyes narrow slightly. 'I see.'

Anna hastily changes the subject. 'What happened in the township, Casper? Kristien told me – '

'Where did you hear about it?' he asks accusingly.

'I was in town. What became of the farmer? Who was he? Did he get away?'

'It's war now,' he says in a strained voice; there is a whiteness round his mouth. I find his stillness more frightening than his explosions.

'Did they kill him?' I insist.

'No.' He shakes his head and pulls out the chair at the head of the table, sits down heavily. 'No, he got away all right.' He looks at Anna. 'It's Victor Henning. Wouldn't hurt a fly. Now they've gone and done this. Bloody savages. I wanted to take my men in. But can you believe it? The army has drawn a cordon round the township, won't let anybody near. When it comes to protecting *us*, they look the other way. But I warned them. I told them – '

'How did the man escape?' I interrupt him; he's been talking more to himself than to us.

For a moment he looks at me, uncomprehending.

'The man – what did you say his name was? – Henning – you said he got away. How? I thought it happened in the middle of the township?'

'It did. At the little supermarket they've got there. Burnt the whole place down.'

'The shop too?'

'Yes. What else do you expect?'

'But I thought it was a black shop?'

79

'Probably suspected the owner of being an informer or a sell-out or something.'

'What would *you* do if you found an informer in your gang?'

'Kristien, please.' From Anna.

I take a deep breath. 'Just asking. Now tell us how Henning got away.'

He pulls up his heavy shoulders, avoiding my eyes.

'Did the police come in?' asks Anna.

'Of course not. They're too shit-scared to risk it in there.' At last he faces me. 'They say a black family took him in. Hid him till it was all over.'

Anna looks down at her hands. For a long time no one says anything.

'Why do you keep on talking of war, Casper?' I ask at last.

'If we let them get away with this – '

'Some attacked him. Others helped him. Are you going to distinguish between them when your war breaks out?'

He is ready, I can see, to let fly at me again; somewhat to my surprise he doesn't. With unnerving directness he asks, 'What do you expect us to do?'

'If you ask me, those people attacked him because your commando nearly killed one of them.'

'A terrorist.'

'No. Just a man who walked into a pharmacy to buy medicine.'

'How can you be sure?'

'Must you always believe the worst?' I challenge him.

'Look, my girl, I've been around much longer than you.'

'More's the pity you can't see what's happening. You're acting as if the world hasn't changed at all.'

'Kristien.' There is a suggestion of pleading in his voice now. 'A week from now will be the end of the world as we know it. Do you have any idea of what's going to become of us?'

'You think your little war games can make a difference?'

'We're fighting for our *lives*, for God's sake!'

'Nothing is threatening your life, Casper. You're fighting for your ego, that's all. And it's a battle you have already lost.'

'I'm fighting to stop what's going to happen next week.'

'You know,' I say, 'at the very least I used to think of you as a practical man. Now I'm beginning to doubt it.'

'What do you mean?' he asks, offended, aggressive.

'Can't you see? No matter what you do, no matter how much

violence you and your squad perpetrate, you can't stop the world. In a week, in ten more days, you'll have a new government in this country.'

'And you think I'm going to accept that?'

'That's the point I'm trying to make, Casper. Whether you accept it or not, *it's going to happen*. The only choice you really have is whether you're going to break your shins and perhaps kill a number of people – or whether you're going to help things run smoothly and make sure your family survives. So instead of being plain stupid, why don't you rather try to make it *work*?'

He glares at me from a place far behind his eyes, behind this moment, this time, this place.

'You think you understand everything?' he snarls at last, rising from his chair. 'Well, you don't. You have no idea what you're talking about. How could you? You're just – '

'A woman? Is that why you're angry? But shouting at me isn't going to change anything. And it certainly isn't going to make you win.'

He stalks off, his shoulders hunched defensively. Anna sits biting the knuckle of her forefinger, giving me a quick nervous smile when she finds my eyes on her.

'You shouldn't upset him so,' she says.

'It's bloody well time he heard the truth.'

'He'll just take it out on me,' she says quietly, looking down.

I draw my breath in sharply. I don't *want* to know what she is telling me. I feel sick.

'I probably deserve it,' she says hurriedly, almost eagerly.

'Don't be damn stupid!' I check myself, confused and guilty: now I'm the one who's taking it out on her. 'Anna, please, listen to me. You've got to start standing up to him.'

She shakes her head, her eyes still averted.

'Are you scared?' I push on.

'Of course I'm scared.'

'It's only because you make it so easy for him to bully you.'

'Do you think it's what I *want*?' This time there is a flash of anger in her voice; and it gives me an unexpected sense of relief. All is not lost yet.

'That's exactly what I've been wondering.'

# 6

Ouma is still asleep when I come back. The nurse is working her way through a photo romance, progressing relentlessly like a silkworm on a mulberry leaf. I offer to relieve her for a while, which she accepts with alacrity, taking the magazine with her.

For the first time since I left London I get through to Michael, on the cordless telephone (another of Casper's security gadgets) which I've taken through to my room; even so I speak with my hand folded round the mouthpiece, not to disturb Ouma.

'I can't believe it,' he says, his voice dry and clipped, reproachful. 'It's been almost a week.'

'I've been trying every day. You're never there.' Why, now that I'm finally through, is there no joy, only this pent-up frustration, this urge to accuse and wound? My mind is saying one thing, my voice another.

'I was here all the time,' he says in his *I'm right, you're wrong* tone of voice.

'No, you were not. Where *were* you?'

'You don't believe me? And where were *you?*'

Oh God, this is not how I wanted it to be at all.

'Be reasonable, Michael.'

'What about you?'

I can strangle him when he's like that. (And he me – ?) I make an effort to return to normal.

'It's been a demented week.'

'I can imagine.'

Is he making an effort too? But I'm still too upset to let him get away with it. 'No, you can't,' I tell him. 'This is beyond imagination.'

'You almost sound proud of it. Possessive.' A small pause. Then, his voice less pinched than before, he says, 'From here it looks as if the boat is sinking fast.' For the first time I detect what seems like genuine concern. 'When are you coming back?'

'I don't know.'

'How's your gran?'

'Bad.' I sigh. 'But she's holding out.' I change my tone. 'Are you all right?'

'Working away on the paper.'

This civility is almost worse than the irritation that preceded it.

He's saying something. I'm not even listening. Halfway through, I interrupt, 'Michael, please – ' Then stop, annoyed, confused.

'What were you going to say?'

'Nothing.'

'Nothing? That's a fair thought.'

'What on earth do you mean?'

'I was quoting.'

'Shit, Michael, can't you drop the literary tone for once?'

'Did you know,' he says, 'that in Elizabethan English "nothing" was a euphemism for "cunt"?'

'Oh please!'

He chuckles, and plunges into a quote. *'Lady, shall I lie in your lap? – No, my lord. – I mean, my head upon your lap. – Ay, my lord. – Do you think I meant country matters? – I think nothing, my lord. – That's a fair thought to lie between maid's legs. – What is, my lord? – Nothing – '* I can almost hear him smiling. 'See what I mean? And don't you agree it's a fair thought?'

'Aye, my lord.' Suddenly, all distance is foreshortened, time suspended; I see him, feel him, smell him the way he was – four? – five? – six days ago, on my floor-bed, the slanting light from the high window over his face, his unruly hair, his shoulder. I suddenly find myself drymouthed with desire. 'It's not thoughts I want, I want *you*.'

'My love, my love.'

'We mustn't let this happen again, Michael.'

'I need you,' he says.

'Michael, I don't *want* to be here. I'm here because I have no choice. I promise you I'll be home as soon as I can.'

'I'll be waiting.'

'Have you spoken to my school?'

'Yes. Saunders was a bit snooty at first, but I did some soft-soaping and he's all right now.'

'You're a star.'

'For you, anything. Just come home soon.'

'As soon as I can.' I try to contain the ache of missing him. 'But you must understand, it may still be a while. Ouma – ' Now I can tell him about all that has happened – the gathering storm in the district, Casper, Anna, Trui and her family, even our house guest – and the unfinished business, and Ouma's preposterous idea about what is yet to be done.

'Stay as long as you have to,' Michael says when at last I have finished. 'But no longer. And look after yourself. For God's sake.'

'I'll be all right. I promise.'

A pause; a chuckle.

'And Lady, it *is* a fair thought, isn't it?'

'Sweet nothing, my lord.'

# 7

Some time in the afternoon I go down to the basement again. I don't want to, but I go. I cannot stay away. I almost wish to find that the man has absconded, but I know it won't be so easy to get rid of him again. And when I open the door at the bottom of the stairs he is there, in the dull yellow glare of the dirty bare bulb, waiting, crouching against the far wall. Behind him are the amorphous colour patches of the peeled paintings the Girl once splashed there to brighten the walls of her dungeon. I wonder who supplied her with paint and brushes? She was no Goya, no Michelangelo. But it must have taken months, not of patient but of furious activity. Not an inch to spare, from stone floor to cobwebbed ceiling, on any of the stained and mouldy walls. Impossible, now, to make out most of the shapes, yet they have a way of teasing one's fantasy with lurid suggestions. Poor girl. What a cesspool of emotions must have been kept hidden away in this dark place.

It takes quite a while before the cowering man shows any sign of relaxing. His eyes are red, his face swollen; he looks feverish.

'Don't be scared,' I tell him, impatient with his cringing. 'Can't you see it's me? I won't harm you.'

'I just heard the footsteps coming. I didn't know it was you,' he mumbles.

'Who else would come down here?'

'I don't know. But perhaps they come for me.'

'Who are "they"?'

'You know,' he says. 'Those people.'

I approach him. 'How is your arm?'

He turns sideways so that I can inspect the bandage. The wound has been bleeding again. Is that a good sign, or bad? If it isn't better by tomorrow I may have to bring the doctor down here. Swear him to silence. There is a Hippocratic oath, for whatever it's worth. But I wouldn't like to run the risk unless it's a crisis.

How do I know it isn't a crisis yet?

'Have you had something to eat?'

'The woman brought me food,' he says. 'Trui.'

'I shall bring you some pills.'

'Thank you, Madam.'

'Don't call me madam, please.'

He just looks at me.

I leave him to himself again, reproaching myself without knowing why; ten minutes later I bring down a syringe with another dose of Ouma's morphine, and a couple of the magazines the nurse has discarded after reading every square centimetre of them and filling in every crossword. A little bit more at ease I go out again. I wander through the house, room after room, trying in vain to pick up some thread from years ago; but today it holds no challenge, no adventure, only gloom and emptiness, a sense of redundancy. It has outlived its time.

Is it the house or is it me?

Wherever I roam in the house, or even outside in the yard, among the trees, in the unkempt rose garden, among the outbuildings, I am haunted by the knowledge of the wounded stranger in the basement. No matter what I'm doing, he is there. I have taken him at his word, yet I have no way of knowing who he is and why he is here. His sole power lies in the fact that I have no choice in deciding whether he should be there to face me, or not. And that power is daunting. I have taken responsibility for him and yet I don't have the foggiest idea of what to do about it. I don't want him here, but I cannot throw him out. And I'm terrified. Not because he is there but because he may die. And his possible death calls me into question.

# 8

And now I'm sitting here, writing. There is a deep comfort in being here. I have turned out all the lights except the small reading lamp at the bed, trained on the new notebook on my lap. I must write, she has said, while she speaks, a small whispery voice, like the rustling of paper, but curiously persistent. The house is silent, except for an occasional creaking of old timber, now here, then there, downstairs or aloft. Trui and Jeremiah are asleep next door, one of them snoring lightly. The stranger, I presume, is down in the basement. In a corner of Ouma's room, when from time to time I look up, I see three owls huddled on a mahogany whatnot, baleful eyes staring. Outside, from time to time, is the screeching of bats, the call of a nightjar, sometimes even a turtle dove half-awakening, then dozing off again.

Ouma Kristina has begun to fidget so restlessly that I'm wondering whether she is delirious. Her unscathed hand keeps groping about in the air, but her eyes remain closed.

'What's the matter, Ouma?'

'The picture,' she says irritably without opening her eyes.

'The house is full of pictures. Which one are you looking for?'

'You know the one. It's always been here on the dressing table.'

Then it must be the small male nude, the one that used to be the object of so much annoyance among the grownups over the years, and of so much surreptitious fascination among those of us still growing up: the slender strong body in a David pose, the mane of wild black curls, the prominent circumcised sex. The style was Victorian, in the Pre-Raphaelite mould, and for that very reason its directness was all the more startling. We all knew that it was one of Ouma's treasures, and that it was forbidden to ask questions about it. But why would she be looking for it now?

'Where is it?' she demands, her thin voice rasping like sandpaper.

'But Ouma – ' I try to be as tactful as possible. 'Have you forgotten about the fire then?'

The hazy eyes flutter open, startled, before a film of resignation settles on them.

'Burnt out?'

I press her hand. 'I'm sorry, Ouma. There was nothing left of the room. It's a miracle you were saved.'

'I should have gone too. But I had to talk to you first.'

'I'm here, Ouma.'

It's like my childhood days again, sitting here with her in the night. For as long as I can remember Ouma Kristina has claimed to have recognised 'something' in me that marked me as the one chosen to receive all her accumulated stories. There always must be one, she used to explain, to hand them on, to prevent their getting lost along the way. I never took it very seriously, although I was proud, of course, of being the chosen one. But beyond the sheer enjoyment I derived from them I must confess I never saw any special significance in her jumble of stories. And being chosen came at a price too: sometimes when she was unable to sleep she'd suddenly appear in her long nightgown, carrying a paraffin lamp (even though the flick of a switch could turn on the electricity), to haul me from the wall-to-wall bed

86

shared by all the children and instruct me to listen. She would either take me into her bed or lead me to the kitchen where we'd seat ourselves at the long scrubbed table, with mugs of milk or lemon syrup, and she would start telling stories and I would listen until I dropped off. I remember that gentle yellow light, the shadows on the walls, the awareness of the secret dark recesses of the house around us. Just like tonight.

'Burnt out,' she repeats after some time, opening her eyes again to stare at me, as if intent on not missing the slightest flicker of expression on my face. 'Poor child. Now you have nothing left of your grandfather.'

'My grandfather?' Involuntarily I shake my head. 'But that couldn't have been Oupa. He would never – ' I stop, feeling guilty. 'I thought Oupa was blond before his hair turned grey?'

An amused grin. 'I'm not talking about the man I married, Kristien. I'm talking about your grandfather.'

It is hard to control the thoughts she has unleashed in me. We've always known Ouma Kristina's inveterate outlawry, especially after old age had conferred on her a liberty even she could not have imagined earlier; but surely there must have been – in those times – limits.

'Such a good likeness too,' she resumes, still refusing to look away. 'The best I've ever done, I'm sure.'

'But you never painted, did you?'

'Not since you've known me. Not since that picture. But what do you really know about me?'

'Then it's time you told me.'

'Yes. It's time I let loose my idiots.'

'Your idiots?'

'Don't you remember the story they tell all over the Little Karoo? About the ostrich times. The few top families of the district amassing all the wealth. Quite staggering. Vain people, who wouldn't mix with the hoi polloi. So they started intermarrying, and in due course there were a couple of little idiots in every family. Kept locked up in the cellar, looked after by orphan girls from the cities. The shame of the great families, never allowed outside in God's sun. Except for one hour a week, from two to three on Sundays, when everybody would be asleep, stupefied by the huge Sunday dinner. The hour of the idiots, they called it.' A deep sigh; her eyelids droop again. 'I think the time has now come for my own idiots.' Another sudden change of tone. 'I wish this whole damned place had burned down, Kristien. I hate it. I can't bear it any longer.'

'But I've always thought you loved the house?'

'Of course I did. The way one learns to love one's cell in prison, I suppose. And this *was* a prison, make no mistake. My own mother was locked up here.'

'You mean she was – ?'

'Not an idiot, if that is what you're thinking. Not like the others, at least. I mean, as our people see it, an idiot needn't necessarily be retarded or a waterhead. It's anyone who deviates from the norm. Anyone who dares to be different.'

'I don't understand. I thought your mother was Petronella Wepener, the one who built this place, one of the leading women in the district.'

'She brought me up, yes. They told everybody she was my mother. How could they otherwise bear the disgrace? But she really was my grandmother. My mother was Rachel. I suppose many people guessed as much, but no one could ever be sure. They were given to understand that Rachel had run away.'

'Then she was the one who made the paintings in the basement?'

She doesn't bother to confirm or deny it. 'That's not all,' she says. 'I only hope we'll have enough time. There is so much to tell. All the stories. The whole history.'

'Stories or history?'

'Not much difference, is there? When you were a child you thought they were stories. But one way or another they all fit in.' Another long silence. Then, without any discernible link, she adds, 'We've always had this yearning for the impossible. Me, you, your mother, all the others before us.'

'Tell me.'

And she does.

'I was very lonely as a child,' her papery voice rustles in the dark, matched by the scratching of my pen as I write. 'All the other Wepeners were already grown up, Eulalie and Willem and Barend and Martiens. Of course they were really my aunt and uncles, although I had no inkling of it then; I'd been brought up to think of them as my elder sister and brothers. Eulalie must have been twenty-six when I was born, Willem about twenty-four, and the twins, Barend and Martiens, twenty. Those two were still around to give a hand with the farming but they'd moved into our townhouse. Willem was running his in-laws' farm in the district, and Eulalie had moved to the Free State, married to a farmer, three children. So you can understand that I was left largely to my own devices. My grandmother, Petronella, who of course I then still thought of as my mother, must have been sixty by the time I was ten, her husband Hermanus Johannes even older, so they couldn't be bothered much with a small girl around. Which suited me in a way, because as you know this house can keep a child occupied almost indefinitely. The only place forbidden to me was the basement. The doors at the top and bottom of the stone staircase were always kept locked, and with dire warnings they tried to instil the fear of God in me to keep out. But that only fired my imagination.

'I can no longer remember precisely how it finally came about, but one Sunday I found the key. The grownups had gone to church and I was left behind in bed with some obscure illness; I often had such Sunday fevers. It is possible that Lizzie aided and abetted me, the little coloured girl who was my only close friend, the foreman's daughter, and as unmanageable as I.

'I won't ever forget the anticipation with which I crept down those cold stairs, holding a lantern that sent the most frightful shadows scurrying across the walls. And then those paintings, totally shocking to one brought up as strictly as I was. You know, I was even expected to keep my shift on when I had a bath. I can still remember the feel of that heavy wet thing clinging to my limbs. Some nights I had dreams about drowning in deep dark water, unable to move arms or legs in that long dress that kept dragging me down, down, down to the bottom. Of course, that had made me all the more curious about my body. You were the same when you were small. Don't think I didn't notice. And when it rained, perhaps because it happened so seldom, I'd take off all my clothes and creep up into the attic and from there on to the roof where I'd sit for hours in a huddle, feeling tragic.

'Now you can imagine the kind of explosion those paintings set off in my mind. Seeing them in the dark, by lantern light, in those deep colours, the reds and greens and blues glowing at me like strange exotic fishes swimming up from some deep underwater world. Men with staggering erections, women spreadeagled, exposing their things like gaping wounds, and all kinds of copulations involving people and animals and birds and monsters, even trees and stones. I was both horrified and fascinated, and from that day on I could not stay away, lured back like a moth to the fatal glare of a flame.

'In the end they found out, of course, and I was given the thrashing of my life. And when I crept downstairs again a week or so later, because obviously that was the first thing I did as soon as I'd recovered, I was stunned to find the walls blank, whitewashed from top to bottom to obliterate all signs of the paintings. I was so shocked that I ran to my father and attacked him, with fists and feet, kicking his shins and butting my head into his huge belly, screaming and shouting abuse in language I didn't even consciously realise I knew. It was a long time before he learned the reason for this sudden attack from me, and then of course it meant another hiding. But in the end they gave up. They had no choice, really, as they knew by then that once I'd put my mind to something I'd cling to it like an octopus. Even when they hid the key in the most unlikely places I was bound to find it; and by the time they finally mislaid it as a result of hiding it so well that they themselves could no longer retrieve it, I'd already discovered another key in the attic that fitted the basement lock.

'Now can you believe it? Not quite a month later the paintings were back in all their blatant glory. Only much later did I learn that they'd tried to whitewash the walls many times before, but that the same thing had happened. To me it was a miracle. But to them, too, if you ask me, judging from their expressions every time they went down there to retrieve me and found the paintings resurrected from the dead.'

'But what happened to the paintings then? Today there are only blotches left.'

'That happened after the Wepeners died. I suppose they served no further purpose then. Another miracle, or just the ravages of time? We'll never know.'

'But how did you eventually find out about the artist?'

'As you can imagine, I never gave the Wepeners any peace of mind about the origins of those sinful images. But not once did they give away the smallest hint. The closest they ever came, at least until I was almost twenty-eight, was to say that the Devil had painted them. Presumably they thought that might scare me off. But it had the opposite effect. I didn't have much truck with God, I'm afraid. I'd had an overdose of religion in the Wepener household; moreover, he sounded suspiciously like a sterner version of Hermanus Johannes to me. I much preferred the Devil, he seemed a lot more interesting; and I would have changed places with Doctor Faust any time, had I known about him then.'

'Why didn't they just send you away? It would have made everything so much easier, for all of you.'

'I think they needed to be reminded of their guilt every day. *And* take it out on me. They probably saw it as their personal responsibility before God to keep an eye on me, even when they were persuaded I was a rotten egg. And from time to time, especially when I was ill and could not run away, they would invite the dominee, or elders of the church, to pray over me and try to exorcise the evil they believed had taken up permanent residence in me. What some of those fervent old men, all of them resembling in one way or another my image of God Almighty, did to tease the Devil out of me, once they had arranged to be alone with me, I need not dwell on. But they certainly gave me a singularly warped idea of our religion.

'The one good thing to come out of all this was that I was once again left to myself. Except that from the time I had my first period I was virtually imprisoned on the farm. No further schooling, except that they hired a governess. My only companion was Lizzie. She'd lost her mother at birth and was living with her grandparents, Salie and Nenna. You remember her, I'm sure. She was almost exactly my age, only a few days' difference, and we remained inseparable for life. Not that the old people approved. Both my father and hers did their level best to discourage our closeness, without ever giving a cogent reason for it. It was only many years later that I discovered what was behind it, and by then it couldn't make a difference any more. We remained like this' – she holds up two knobbly fingers – 'and it lasted for almost ninety years, until she died thirteen years ago. If it hadn't been for Lizzie, my childhood would have been desperately unhappy. Of course, there were also the birds. Wherever the two of us went there used to be birds; usually they were the ones who warned us if Lizzie's parents or mine were approaching.

'I don't know how it came about, but from the time I was very small there was a special understanding between us and the birds. Petronella told me once how they'd flutter about my pram when I was pushed outside in the shade to sleep in the mornings. At first she'd tried to scare them off, afraid that they'd mess on my blankets, but they never did that; and in the end I was left alone with them. They actually looked after me. Once, I was told, they started screeching and twittering when a snake approached the pram; and when it persisted they actually began to attack the intruder. Even the small finches and weavers and bobtails joined in, and that attracted larger birds, and just as Petronella came outside to see what was causing the racket, a hawk swooped down and carried the geelslang off.

'But I did crave human company apart from Lizzie's, and that was largely denied me, as Hermanus Johannes and Petronella became unbearably jealous and possessive of me whenever people arrived on the farm, even if they were close friends or neighbours. It was a life of awful deprivation.

'What made it even harder for me was the family's experience in the

Boer War. Here in the Cape Colony, of course, we were largely out of it, and my father-grandfather was much too old to think of getting involved; but my three uncle-brothers were all swallowed up by the war: Willem was killed on the battlefield, Barend was executed as a Cape rebel, and Martiens died of dysentery in Bermuda.'

'What about Eulalie?' I ask.

'Died in the concentration camp at Bethulie, with her children. The family firmly believed the English had force-fed her on ground glass. We were sent a small finely embroidered cloth she'd made, with her name on it, and the dates of her birth and death. You tell me how she knew that.'

'The Wepeners must have been shattered,' I say.

'They grew old overnight, I can tell you. All of a sudden the future had swung shut in their faces. No sons to take over, and of course only sons counted. All they had left was me. No wonder they became so unbearably possessive.

'Thank God I had by then made friends with an old Jewish pedlar who regularly came to the farm twice a year; he'd discovered my love of reading and, knowing from experience how my parents would react (in our house only the Bible and Petronella's encyclopedia were allowed – I'll tell you more about that later), he soon began surreptitiously to ply me with books. Lizzie hid them in their house for me, knowing my people would never stoop so low as to visit there, and as I read voraciously whatever old Moishe could lay his hands on, life became a little more bearable.

'He was a wonderful old man. He looked, I always thought, like a prophet from the Old Testament. His family had drifted down to Africa all the way from Lithuania, surviving the most incredible hardships. Two things had helped him, he used to say. Laughter and stories. If you have those, he maintained, nothing can kill your spirit. It said in the Talmud, he told me, that God had created people to tell Him stories; but later, sadly, they forgot about Him, they even forgot that they themselves were stories first told by God. And ever since, if old Moishe was to be believed, men and women have been telling each other stories. To fill the gap after the Great Storyteller had fallen asleep. He could tell the most marvellous stories about his own life, and each time it was different. Life, to him, was one long celebration. He used to tell me how, when he was a child, and dirt poor, he used to earn money by crying at funerals. For a perfunctory performance he was paid a shilling, for a good loud weeping he earned five bob. And if he cried so inconsolably that he fell into the grave, it might be a pound.

Needless to say, he invariably ended up in the grave and had to be hauled out. That set him on the road to prosperity. No wonder old Moishe and his stories and his books, even if he came only twice a year, saved me from loneliness.

'From the time I was sixteen or seventeen young men began to visit over weekends, but they were invariably discouraged by the Wepeners. It was only after the collapse of the feather market when the Great War broke out that they came round to the idea that I should get married. We'd been spared the worst thanks to Petronella's encyclopedia which prompted her to start diversifying well before the crash came. But the better prospects in the Little Karoo were beginning to dwindle as one ostrich farm after the other folded. I wasn't getting any younger either. I couldn't care less, I wasn't interested in settling into matrimony merely to satisfy others. I'd always been dreaming about something else, something more, something different, even though I couldn't find the words to explain it. Hermanus Johannes Wepener thought I was a witch. Perhaps he had good reason to.

'Anyway, something had to be done, and after considering all the prospective candidates Petronella settled on Francois Basson, who stood to inherit one of the biggest farms in the Little Karoo. What was more, it was adjacent to Sinai. It was all arranged between the families: first the men got together, then the women were let into it. They believed they were saving me from spinsterhood, a fate clearly worse than death. No one consulted me. Marriage, after all, for them, had little to do with personal feelings. It was simply a form of barter to strengthen alliances or consolidate wealth or ensure the heritage. And a young woman like me was the unit of currency.'

'So you refused?'

'Naturally I felt like sending them all to hell. But the stupid fact was that I'd actually fallen for Francois Basson's charm. There was a wild streak in the man I couldn't resist. Once the marriage had been agreed to the Wepeners turned a blind eye. This freedom was delirious. For the first time I had an inkling of what life could be like away from Sinai. Francois and I would go riding for hours, galloping across the plains, right through the remaining flocks of ostriches, sending the plumes flying. Some evenings he would carry me off to the dam on their farm, and we would cavort naked in the water. For the first time I discovered for myself the passions the Girl had so glaringly exhibited on the walls of the cellar. It wasn't love. It was lust.

'But a mere month before the wedding it was called off. The mayor's daughter, Letitia Meyer, announced that she was expecting Francois's child. If it had been anybody else I'm sure the Bassons would have bought them off. But the mayor was a different matter. And on the date set for our wedding the two of them were married.

'I was devastated. Only much later did I appreciate what a lucky escape it had been for me. Because Francois turned out to be a rotter. He had no real interest in farming and after his parents' death he started spending all their accumulated money. Letitia died in child-birth, and the child didn't make it either. Francois started going downhill. It was a long and painful thing to watch, it took years. They say in the end he would sit on his front stoep in the afternoon, drinking straight from the bottle, watching the baboons from the Swartberg invading his vineyards – the family was one of the few who'd reverted to vines soon after the phylloxera had come and gone; which means that by the time the feather market crashed they were among the most notable survivors. But it made no difference. In the early thirties, the time of the Great Depression, he reached his limit. Watching the baboons plundering his vineyards and destroying his pumpkin and sweet potato crops, Francois would burst into maniacal laughter, waving his bottle, and shouting at them, "You bastards, enjoy it while you can! I'm going to drink this whole farm from under your blistered backsides!" And in the end he doused the house with paraffin and set it alight, then blew out what brains he had left with his shotgun, right there on the stoep, while the baboons looked on.

'The farm was sold, it changed hands once or twice again, a new house was built, and in the end, of course, Casper bought it. He wanted to get as close to Sinai as he could. But that's another story.

'Long, long before Francois came to grief my own fate had been decided. At least the Wepeners and the Bassons had tried their damnedest. If I couldn't marry the elder Basson brother, then what about the second, Cornelis Frederik? Once again the patriarchs met, the wives were called in, and a decision was made. This time I was stubborn. Francois had turned my head with his wildness. But young Cornelis Frederik was different. Not that there was anything wrong with him: there were two idiots in the family by then, but he was not one of them. The problem was quite simply that I found him boring. Cornelis was too good, too solid, too decent to be true.

'Yet what could I do? What other hope was there for me but marriage? I was already twenty-seven. Still I resisted and resisted. I was pleaded with, and reprimanded, and thrashed. The effort nearly caused poor old Hermanus Johannes Wepener to have a stroke; he had to stay in bed for days. I refused to give in. Once again the parade of old men trooped through this house. Dominee Hechter. All the elders, first singly, then in one grim, impressive, black-clad conclave. Then the sourpuss sisters of the congregation. Why? Why? Why? they wanted to know. Because he brings no wetness to my cunt, I told them. I wish you could have seen them.

'I left them, not in triumph but in despair. Even if it might not have seemed like that, I was close to giving up. I promised myself that if I could strike the slightest smallest spark from Cornelis I would accept. But it was impossible. Our parents would arrange ostentatiously to leave us together – left? we were thrust together – to encourage some kind, any kind, of bond. I teased him, and flirted with him. I showed him my ankle, my knee, a flash of thigh. I had rather beautiful legs in those days, I'll have you know. He spoke about the will of God and the temptations of the flesh. One night out here in the garden I took what I thought was the final step. Look, I told him, if you want me, then for God's sake *take* me. Take me now, or leave it forever. He renounced. It was then a kind of madness invaded me. Without warning, I stripped off my clothes and began to dance for him, a fantastic, extravagant, bacchanalian dance. It must have been a frightening experience for him, I realise now, as I rushed about like a creature possessed, flinging myself into the shrubs and bushes, crashing into tree trunks and the fence of the fowl run, whirling up dust and treading in chicken shit. Finally, gasping for breath, limp, exhausted, I flopped into his arms. He made a manful effort to thrust me back into my discarded clothes, uttering gentle and cajoling words, things like, "My dear little child, my poor little girl," although he wasn't much older than myself, and when at last through our joint fumbling efforts I was more or less decent again, he offered to pray for me. Poor man. I grabbed him where it evidently caused excruciating pain, and twisted with all the energy I could still muster; had there been more of it I would have tied a knot, but there was a sad insufficiency.'

'And then you sent him packing?'

'No. The following week I accepted his offer,' she says.

'You accepted?'

'I did. You see, it occurred to me that there were still five more Basson brothers, not counting the idiots. And the thought of going through the same rigmarole with all of them – because the family was set on having Sinai, and the only way of possessing it was by getting me first – that was too much for me. Even if it felt like signing my death warrant. In fact, I secretly vowed to commit suicide before the wedding day. Fortunately, as it turned out, such a drastic step wasn't necessary.'

'What happened then?'

'An act of God. On one of his visits old Moishe brought not only merchandise and contraband books, but his nephew. And the first moment I set eyes on Jethro the wetness came. He was twenty-five, he had studied in Paris, he had the voice of an angel: not that I've ever seen or heard one, but I just knew. He was the first man I'd ever met who was made to my own measure, the only one who could save me from marriage. A man I could love, and fight with, and set the world on fire with. He could make music on his guitar that caused the stars to dance and the moon to tilt. He had the most exquisite hands I've ever seen on a man, and the whitest skin, the blackest eyes, the wonderfullest mouth. He'd come back to spend a year with his great-uncle (his parents, it seemed, were dead) and earn some money; then he would be leaving for Europe again. To do what? To sing and dance and write and live.' Her eyes, closed all along, flicker open and a smile tugs at her lips.

I breathe in slowly, deeply. 'Jethro was the man in your picture?' I ask with a sense of illumination.

'Of course.'

'You ran away?'

'Yes, and no. I first tried to do the decent thing. On the last day before old Moishe and Jethro were to leave, I spoke to the Wepeners. They couldn't believe their ears, as you can well imagine. And in spite of all the resentment I'd built up against them all my life, I couldn't help feeling sorry for them. Everything they'd tried to achieve over the years, for themselves and for me, was brought down crashing on their heads. Then Hermanus Johannes, my father-grandfather, said something which changed it all. His face was twitching as if he was on the verge of having a stroke. (It was, in fact, a stroke that killed him only a month or so after I'd left.) He turned to Petronella and with a viciousness such as I've seldom heard in my long life he spat at her, "Bad blood will out. This is Rachel's doing. It comes from you. There has never been anything like this on my side of the family."

'"What are you talking about?" I asked.

'He grabbed Petronella by the shoulders. "You tell her," he shouted.

'And that was when I first learned about my mother.'

# 9

The old house sighs and turns in its sleep, like an ancient derelict ship creaking on a dark sea, destination unknown. Its silence is replete with all its concealed life: birds and rodents, rustling insects, Trui and Jeremiah in their room, the stranger down in the basement.

Sometimes her voice fades away altogether. I cannot even be sure that what she says is what I write. And what I hear her whisper merges with what I remember, or seem to remember, from earlier times when she told similar stories. Yet I have the impression that our communication is not dependent on something as extraneous as a voice. There is a more immediate insinuation of what she says into my consciousness; she articulates my writing hand.

I have the feeling, both unsettling and reassuring, of recovering something: not the story as such, snatched from what may or may not have been my history, but this strange urge of the real towards the unreal, as if it must find its only possible justification there.

Father, I know, and Mother too, would have been shocked by this; their stark Calvinism did not allow for such invention. But have they not denied, in the process, precisely this surge of the imagination which links us to Africa, these images from a space inside ourselves which once surfaced in ghost stories and the tales and jokes and imaginings of travellers and trekkers and itinerant traders beside their wagons at night, when the fantastic was never more than a stone's throw or an outburst of sparks away? How sad – no, how dangerous – to have suppressed all this for so long.

# 10

'You shouldn't talk any more, Ouma,' I tell her. 'You're tired. We can go on later.'

'No. We don't know how much time we have. And I want you to understand about my mother.'

'Later,' I plead with her.

But she is adamant, and I offer a compromise: first a few sips of glucose water, then oxygen. Thank God, the apparatus works smoothly.

From now on, I instruct her, she must punctuate her narration with deep inhalations from the small tight-fitting mask. Her voice remains weak, but she seems less exhausted.

'To understand something about my mother,' whispers Ouma, her eyes closed again, as if she's talking in her sleep, 'you should first know more about Petronella. What brought her here, how she shaped, or desperately tried to shape, her life, why she married Hermanus Johannes Wepener. Her mother was known as the Fat Woman of the Transvaal. Throughout the violent years of the Great Trek, in a world shaped by men, she had survived by outmanning them all; but in the end she was sidelined by history. I'll tell you about her later. Now it is Petronella's turn.'

Petronella was born at the mouth of the Umgeni in Natal, a year or two after the Boers and the Zulus had their final, fatal encounter at Blood River, just at the time when the English started planning to annex the new land the Voortrekkers had finally conquered. For the first few years of her life the girl lived on the family farm at the edge of the sea. She used to spend whole days on the beach, surrounded by the crocodiles that slithered from the river to the high sandbanks: living in dread of Wilhelmina, they became more trusted child-minders than any dog. Sometimes, when Wilhelmina had business elsewhere, little Petronella could be left almost entirely to their care, building castles on the long clean stretch of beach, or tracing intricate patterns in the sand, then sitting back as the tide came in to watch with fascination as a whole day's dedicated work was obliterated; she knew she could always start again the following day. At other times she would simply sit there on a dune, hugging her knees to her body, staring at the immensity of the Indian Ocean.

On one of those occasions, when her mother had deposited her on the beach with the crocodiles before going on her own business, Petronella saw a ship come past in the direction of Port Natal, in full sail. It was a sight such as she had never beheld before, and it was to obsess her dreams for years to come, even when in old age she began to lose her mind. At the same time it seemed to her the solution to all her mother's worries. They should build their own ship, she proposed that evening, and simply sail away across the sea until they found a place where the English would never find them again. But Wilhelmina dismissed the thought: wherever there's sea, she said, sooner or later there's English. And if Natal were to be annexed, which now seemed more inevitable by the day, the only solution would be to turn their backs on the sea and move inland again, into the deepest interior, where their tribe could at last establish a homeland and be free.

Petronella was inconsolable. But deep in her heart a resolve had taken root that nothing would ever eradicate again. She was, profoundly and almost fatally, in love with the sea – not an infatuation such as one might feel for an idea or a cause or a landscape, but a burning, urgent and almost sensual attachment. She would have run away at the first opportunity, back to the sea, but her mother, who must have expected such a move, kept her tied down in the wagon until they were hopelessly far away.

Their trek finally came to rest beside an insignificant little stream that wound its way through the subtropical vegetation of the Northern Transvaal, a region recently invaded by a group of quite terrifying religious fundamentalists who, confident that they had traversed the length of Africa, took it to be the Nile. The Promised Land was near. Unfortunately the area, for all its stunning beauty and fertility, also turned out to be a valley of death infested by tsetse fly that decimated the cattle, and by malaria that killed off the people.

Here Wilhelmina buried her third husband (she always despised weak men, yet could not resist marrying them) and most of her remaining children; her whole world caved in under her. And just before Petronella's twentieth birthday, her mother finally expired – true to form, though, not with a whimper but a bang.

Among the young girl's siblings two brothers, who had remained with their mother out of loyalty, reinforced perhaps by trepidation at what she might do if they dared voice discontent, decided to return to the Eastern Cape where, who knows, it might be possible to reclaim the family's old farms. Petronella's remaining sister got married within a month of her mother's death and moved to Potchefstroom, at that time the capital of the Transvaal. Petronella was left behind with a single brother, Benjamin, reputed to suffer permanently from brain damage as the result of a blow to the head his mother had once dealt him with a plough after he'd inadvertently broken the blade. Brother and sister were by now living in a shack near the ruin of the house in which their mother lay buried, on the outskirts of the village of Nylstroom.

Petronella, who'd had a streak of religious fervour since a very early age, conferred for several nights with the quiescent Benjamin and decided on a course of action for themselves. It was really very predictable. In the time they had been living there she had already more than once attempted the building of a boat to take them back to the sea, but every time an act of God had intervened. A thunderstorm, once, in which the weird framework was struck by lightning and burnt to a cinder; on another occasion a passing group of blacks uprooted by the trekkers from their ancestral territories set upon a half-built boat and carried off the laboriously sawn beams and planks for firewood; in the end her mother had put an end to it by forbidding all further attempts – and once Wilhelmina had spoken no one, they knew from terrible experience, dared disobey.

Now at last Petronella was free to pursue the dream that obsessed her life. They would build a new ship, she told her halfwitted brother, right there on the banks of the Nile, and then float downstream, due north, until they reached the capital of Egypt; there they would obtain from the ruling pharaoh the wherewithal to cross the Red Sea and rejoin the people of Israel from whom the Boers had descended. And so they would attain the happiness in search of which her formidable mother had so fruitlessly sacrificed her whole life. After her long exposure to the reminiscences of her mother and the demented prophets among their neighbours, there was an understandable confusion in Petronella's mind between the Promised Land and that stretch of beach along the sea that had shaped her consciousness in her earliest years and which was the only freedom she'd ever been allowed in her life. But it was no whimsy, she assured Benjamin. God had personally revealed to her, in a nightly visitation, that a new Flood was imminent; and unless they were prepared they would be swept away like the sinners of the Old Testament, the touchstone of her devout life. These visitations had been a feature of her life ever since the family had joined the trek from the threatened shore of Natal; and as Petronella ripened into adolescence God appeared to become more and more enthusiastic about these increasingly urgent communions with his maidservant. And she, too, it must be said, appeared to derive from this intercourse some quite extravagant and suspect physical pleasures.

It should be interpolated here that Petronella was surprisingly skilled in the art of reading and writing, thanks mainly to the instruction of the leading prophetess of the tribe, Tante Mieta Gous, who had seen in the girl a possible successor. This crazy old creature had two prize pupils, Petronella and a boy called Petrus Landman. (The only reason he deserves to be mentioned here is that it was he, most likely, who imprinted on Petronella the image of an ark: this Petrus told her about some remote ancestor of his who'd built a ship and sailed away into the desert, and this must have given shape to the urge she'd always had to sail away.) What was interesting, as far as Petronella was concerned, was that throughout her life she drew her inspiration from only two books – the Bible, of course, and an illustrated Dutch encyclopedia of obscure origins – both salvaged from the house in which her mother had died. The encyclopedia she would use for what to her was prophesying, while others called it fortune telling. Petronella's method was disarmingly straightforward. She would look hard at her visitor, then close her eyes and enter into some kind of trance, whereupon she would put the huge book on its spine and allow it to fall open wherever it chose to. There she would scan the columns and take the first phrase or illustration that struck her as a starting point, allowing her guardian spirit or whatever to prompt the rest. This was a practice she indulged in to her dying day. The only curious thing about the whole business was that her predictions invariably turned out to be right.

The first time she had resorted to it was when at the age of twelve or thirteen she'd provoked her mother into threatening to beat her to a pulp with a cast-iron frying pan: in her haste to get away Petronella had caused the encyclopedia to fall from the tambotie dining table, and seeing the picture of a lion where the pages had fallen open she'd invented the prediction of a predator destroying their flocks should her mother proceed with the beating. The mother wasn't impressed but as the two of them erupted from the house one of the boys came running from the river shouting that a whole pride of lions was stalking the flock and that someone had to get a gun and come quickly, quickly, for God's sake.

Since that day Petronella's reputation had spread steadily through most of the Northern Transvaal, to the extent that she herself started believing her prophesies (and why shouldn't she, since everything came true?). Small wonder that her vision of a coming Flood caused a considerable stir in that far-flung Godfearing community. And so she and her brother Benjamin started building, aided by what casual help they could afford from blacks in the surrounding countryside and from neighbours either generous enough to offer their services or credulous enough to heed the prophecy of another impending Flood. The boat was, to say the least, huge, its dimensions gleaned from close readings of Genesis: three hundred cubits in length, fifty cubits in breadth, and thirty in height, with the odd door and window in accordance with the instructions the Lord God had once given unto his faithful servant Noah.

One problem was that there was no gopher wood in the vicinity, as stipulated by Noah's instructions for assembly, nor teak as recommended by the Dutch encyclopedia; but in the end they made do with tambotie and wild olive; and the boat turned out very handsome indeed, if rather large and unwieldy (all the more so since they had no inkling of how to measure a cubit) for the trickle of the Nile in those parts. In fact, the vessel effectively stemmed the flow of the little river, causing mild flooding in the area and a total stoppage of water lower down, resulting in outbreaks of hostilities among the affected farmers. But it didn't last too long as the very night after the completion of the ark, and only hours after Petronella and Benjamin had moved in below deck and hoisted the great sails copied from her memory of the splendid sight beheld years before from the beach of Port Natal, the flood did come, washing away everything in its wake and carrying the boat with it, all the way to Egypt.

That, at least, was what Petronella solemnly swore through all the years to come. There were, inevitably, those who ridiculed the story, insisting that the ark came to grief in the storm barely a hundred yards from where the flood first shouldered it, and that both the occupants were so grievously injured that by the time they set out, on foot, for the Promised Land their hold on the real world was, to say the least, tenuous. This might explain why, when they surfaced in the civilised world again, completely off course, in Algoa Bay, almost two years after the flood, Petronella mistook the wide tract of sand and dunes along the Eastern Cape coast for the Sahara or the Sinai desert or the shore of the Red Sea; whatever the case may be, she believed to the day of her death that she had reached Egypt, after travelling the last several hundred miles on foot, the ark having disintegrated along the way. There is no point in splitting hairs. In Africa a few thousand miles south or north isn't worth quibbling about.

What matters is that soon after arriving at what she regarded as her first destination, and while she was still waiting for an audience with the pharaoh to be arranged (she was quite confident that a terse reminder of the circumstances surrounding the original exodus would suffice to persuade him to assist her in all possible ways in crossing the sea into Palestine), a very presentable man made his appearance. He was called Hermanus Johannes Wepener, and he'd come to sell some produce in the Bay. When she told him she was waiting for a lift to Canaan he was most happy to oblige. There may have been some misunderstanding along the way as it is barely credible that he should have deceived her outright; but whatever the specific circumstances, which surely are of little consequence in a story, he told her – or she came to understand – that he could take her to the land of Canaan along a short cut, overland rather than across the sea. She was distressed at having to leave the sea behind – she'd dreamed so much about it and travelled so far to reach it – but found the man's company agreeable enough to consent, provided her brother accompany them. And in due course they arrived here in the Little Karoo which, Hermanus Johannes Wepener assured her, was every bit as good, if not better, than the land of Canaan. My own guess is that she secretly suspected they were still in Egypt, which would explain why this farm was given the outlandish name of Sinai.

Hermanus Johannes Wepener was eager to get married and start a family, but Petronella wanted to make quite sure he could be depended upon. One must understand the situation in which she found herself, even apart from that disturbing religious streak in her. All her life, like the rest of the vast brood in whose midst she'd grown up, she had been dominated by the looming figure of her mother. Whatever differences there might have been between them, that great mother was always there, not just in the background but surrounding her family, as the ultimate arbiter of the permissible and the forbidden, of right and wrong, good and evil. But this was a role her mother could play only because she was exceptional, in every sense larger than life. Petronella on her own, a young woman literally stranded on the beach of an unknown ocean, amounted to nothing, nothing at all. And Benjamin, as loyal as any large floppy-eared dog but soft in the head, was useless.

No wonder she retreated, when it suited her, into the asylum her excessive religiousness had provided; but it would be misguided, I'm sure, to think her mad. Shrewd she was, canny, at times uncanny; but no, not mad. I knew her too intimately, saw too much of her real vulnerability. At the same time there was nothing planned or contrived about the way she grasped at what Hermanus Johannes Wepener appeared to offer. What she did was probably to consult the Dutch encyclopedia which had so amazingly survived the flood with her. And then to read into it whatever best suited her, which was to attach herself to this big-boned, well-to-do, seemingly respectable man who could guarantee her some standing in the world. 'Standing', after all, was what her mother had always had, because of her physical prowess and her ferocious temper in her younger years, her sheer size in older age. On her own Petronella could not attain this; nor would she have wanted to, I suspect, if she could. But with Hermanus Johannes Wepener at her side she might enter whatever Promised Land she had elected.

Even so she wanted to be quite sure, before the knot was tied, that he could be trusted in every respect to do her bidding, while offering her the security and standing she sensed she needed. She proceeded very methodically to put her intended to the test with a series of Herculean labours, the last of which was the uprooting of all the vines, which had been the pride of his farm. Hermanus Johannes Wepener complied. And at last they were married and embarked with commendable dedication to the raising of a family. Eulalie, Willem, Barend and Martiens, and then the fateful girl, Rachel.

Somewhere along the way Benjamin disappeared. God alone knows what happened to him. A poor weakling for most of his life, ever since that plough dashed his hopes of a normal future, he may well have died what in the circumstances would have been a natural death. Or, as some people have suggested over the years, he may have become the first inhabitant of the basement after the construction of this house. Or, as another theory has it, he may have been inadvertently bricked up in one of the thick walls. A more malicious rumour has it that he was the father of the child Rachel came to be pregnant with soon after her fourteenth birthday. Or worse, that he was Rachel's father, standing in for Hermanus Johannes Wepener on one of the latter's journeys to Algoa Bay or the more distant Cape. But there are flaws in each of these suggestions; so why opt for any one? He may simply have flown away with the birds one day, or crawled into an aardvark hole never to emerge again: is this really more fanciful than any other explanation? The story doesn't need him any more, so we'll drop him here, yet another skeleton in yet another cupboard.

In one respect – unfortunately the only respect that ultimately mattered – Hermanus Johannes Wepener did fail her. He never took her back to the sea. That meant that, even after the ordeals she'd put him through, she regarded him as a traitor to the last, unworthy of her trust. Consequently their marriage was a running battle of epic proportions. On the surface, especially in the company of others, they were the perfect couple; but below that veneer all hell was seething. I suspect that for Hermanus Johannes religion was the surest means of advancement in the community; Petronella resigned herself to the rages and disappointments of matrimony because suffering was God's way of proving his unfathomable love. And also because – of this both her Bible and her encyclopedia assured her – it was certain not to last.

Even after forty years of marriage she still regarded this farm as a place of temporary sojourn, a watering place in the desert from which they would eventually set forth to their true destination. And this, I guess, explains the house. She never thought of it as a house. It was her ultimate boat, her ship, her ark, to redeem her from the corrupted world; the vessel in which, one day, when it behoved the Lord God, she would sail forth to the sea that nightly washed the shores of her dreams.

## I I

And then Rachel was born. From the first stirrings in her womb Petronella felt different about this child. The older ones, Eulalie and Willem and Martiens and Barend, were no more than the inevitable consequence and proof of her unremitting war with her husband. They were cared for and, I suppose, loved according to the Bible's requirements for parenthood. Rachel was different.

For one thing, the child was born during one of Hermanus Johannes Wepener's prolonged absences from home which grew both longer and more frequent as the matrimonial war at home became more intense. This particular journey had kept him from home for just over a year. When on his return he was confronted with an unexpected new child he flew into a rage and accused Petronella of consorting with all and sundry, from neighbours to goats and devils. The child had been born six months ago, she answered calmly. Then it must be retarded, he shouted: anyone could see the baby was a puny little thing no more than a few weeks old. There were no neighbours to call as witnesses, as Petronella had kept to herself during the term of his absence; and not a single labourer on the farm could be induced, whether by plying them with wine, subjecting them to extensive sermons, or by the infliction of corporal punishment, to shed any more light on the matter. Instead of raging back at her husband, as Petronella was wont to do, she met his wildest accusations with a serene smile and the simple response that if the child wasn't his (and whose else could it conceivably be, since he knew all too well how loathsome she found sexual congress) it could only have been the outcome of an immaculate conception. In fact, she told him, gaining quite visibly in confidence and enthusiasm as she spoke, that the miraculous nature of the event had been announced beforehand by none other than God Almighty himself during one of his nightly visitations. Furthermore, it had been corroborated subsequently by the encyclopedia. He was free to look it up for himself, she'd made a note of it, page 463.

And nothing could ever prise anything else from her.

On one of the occasions when he brought the matter up again – it became the best opening gambit to any argument for the next forty years – she quietly countered, 'What did *you* do during that year, Hermanus? Were you faithful to me?' It was the first time, amazing as it might sound in retrospect, she had retaliated in kind: previously, whatever else she might have hurled at him, verbally or physically, his sexual fidelity or lack of it had never entered their quarrels. Being part, presumably, of woman's fate, she had tended in the past, with the grace of God and a silent grim wish for eventual divine retribution, to grin and bear it. But no longer.

Hermanus Johannes gaped at her. 'What do you mean? How dare you!'

'I was just asking. There was a woman with three children here on the farm while you were gone. She said she'd brought them to meet you. I sent her away, of course. Told her to come back later when you were home again.'

'Who was it?' he stormed. 'Did she say her name?'

'She did, but I'm not going to tell you.'

'Was it Susanna?'

She shrugged.

'Petronella, you're *going* to tell me! Was it Lavinia?'

She shrugged.

'Was it Maryke? Breggie? Ulrika?'

'Go on,' she said. 'I'm listening.'

'Why don't you say anything? Petronella, I'll – '

'I'm thinking,' she said. 'If one day all those women start coming here with their families we may have to add more rooms to the house.' Was that one of the reasons the house had taken the shape it had? Certainly it was no idle thought. In due course, at least until the time of Rachel's incarceration, strange women did occasionally arrive on the farm accompanied by what they claimed were Hermanus Johannes Wepener's offspring. Clearly, like the good sower in the Bible, he had visited indiscriminately the wayside, and stony places, and thorns, and good ground, bringing forth fruit, some an hundredfold, some sixtyfold, some thirtyfold. These visitors were lodged, their silence presumably bought at an acceptable price in order to safeguard the family's standing in the community; until after shorter or longer sojourns they could be prevailed upon to depart for destinations as far away as possible.

At least Rachel could not claim to have grown up lonely. Her own sister and brothers were around, all of them of an age where communication and interaction were possible; and then there were all these other visitors from afar. In spite of this, Rachel preferred to withdraw into her own games. It was not that she had trouble communicating with the others, but that she preferred her own company. Above all, she liked to paint, and in this, as in everything else, Petronella indulged her.

She grew into an exceptionally beautiful child, all the more reason for Hermanus Johannes Wepener to regard her with suspicion and jealousy. His own children, far and wide, tended to be plain, some of them quite severely and extravagantly so. But Rachel was a beauty. Petronella saw it as a sign of heavenly grace, confirming the girl's divine origins; for Hermanus Johannes she spelt bad news. Was it smouldering resentment, a guilty conscience, or an even guiltier awareness of sinful desire in his own heart that caused him to be so excessively possessive of the girl? And was that also the reason why, from the moment she reached puberty, his philandering came to an abrupt end? He wouldn't even go to town any more. Petronella had to take over much of the running of the farm while he stayed in the house to keep an eye on Rachel.

Which makes it all the more amazing that the girl could have fallen pregnant without his knowledge. Unless in this, too, it was the hand, if hand it was, of God that showed? In this wide district where gossip has always run wild like ostriches there were many stories, even though they surfaced only years later. If it wasn't God, or Hermanus Johannes himself, some averred, then it could only have been the dominee, who had been trusted ex officio. Or the doctor who had been called in once or twice when she'd been ill. Or the teacher hired to teach the children on the farm; but when was he ever allowed to be alone with her? The most likely culprit arraigned, tried and found guilty by the district, was one of the labourers on the farm. But really, there was no plausible explanation. And of course neither Hermanus Johannes nor Petronella was any help, ever; the shame was too great, and the front they kept up too impenetrable. Only on the day Jethro entered the family scene so many years later, did they briefly lift the curtain; but even that wasn't much, only the barest details.

It is known, now, that as soon as Hermanus Johannes Wepener discovered his daughter's condition he wanted to have her committed to an institution in Cape Town. After all, he reasoned, for a white girl to have relations with a coloured labourer (if that was indeed what had happened), she must have taken leave of her senses; and an asylum was the only safe place for such a one. But Petronella prevailed and had the girl locked up in the cellar, an act of mercy perhaps, however hard it may be today to interpret it as such. Certainly, that was how she tried to present it in her final illness. But there is so much we shall never discover.

All that is known for certain is the fact of her pregnancy and of her incarceration, the silent evidence of her paintings that no one could ever expunge from the basement walls – reappearing after every attempt like stigmata – and her unrecorded death. To this day, as far as I know, it has never been officially registered. There is that single unmarked grave outside the family cemetery, but we have only her mother's word that it is Rachel who lies there. All that the family has ever offered in explanation, was that she'd 'gone away'. Did she simply waste away, refusing perhaps to eat, until she drifted off into death? Was someone hired to kill her, either in retribution or out of mercy? Did she hang or stab herself, or take poison on one of the rare nightly excursions when she was let out to collect plants and soils to mix her paint?

On her death bed, long afterwards, Petronella divulged, not without a perverse sense of pride, that when she'd questioned Rachel about the pregnancy, the girl had smiled – much the same smile I imagine Petronella herself had once given in response to Hermanus Johannes Wepener's inquisition – and said, 'I slept with the King of Africa.'

And that is all we know. Once upon a time there was a girl called Rachel; and then one day she wasn't any more.

# 12

'I am her only flesh,' says Ouma Kristina, looking up at me again from another deep inhalation of oxygen. 'And it was only when I confronted Petronella and Hermanus Johannes with my decision to go away with Jethro that I came to know about her. I still do not know much more, although over the years I've worked through this whole house, every nook and cranny, in search of clues and signs. But there's nothing. Except the paintings. And I, her child. As I discovered on that momentous day.'

'And then you ran away with Jethro?'

'What else could I do? Hermanus Johannes would have shot me, both of us, if we'd stayed. Petronella was not so bad. She even told me, afterwards, that she secretly approved. At last, she said, one of her offspring would join the Jews, and return to the sea.'

'And did you? Return to the sea, I mean.'

'Not really. We did go to Cape Town, but only to catch a boat. Old

Moishe had arranged it through family and friends, and from there we went abroad.'

'Where?'

'We went to Persia,' she says without batting an eyelid. 'To Baghdad.'

'On a magic carpet, I suppose?' I ask tartly.

She stares quietly at me, quite unperturbed. 'I'm not asking you to believe me, Kristien. I'm only asking you to listen to me.'

I decide, not without a touch of irritation, to humour her. 'What was it like?'

'From the air it looked incredible. All those minarets and domes and spires covered in gold. Like the New Jerusalem, I suppose, all jasper and rubies and whatever. And in a way it was like a homecoming, I felt I knew the city so well from my readings in Revelations when I was a child, and the books old Moishe had brought me. My favourite used to be the *Arabian Nights*. And now we were there. It was almost too much to believe.'

'Didn't Jethro have problems?' I ask with a straight face. 'Being a Jew, I mean.'

Her eyes flicker, but whether it is in amusement or disdain I cannot quite make out. 'You're very perceptive,' she says. 'But that only came later. In the beginning – I mean, how were they to know? I was the only one who'd seen him naked. Very beautiful he was too, I may add.'

'Ouma, other men in the Middle East are also circumcised.'

'Are you telling this story or am I?' A petulant little shake of her head on its thin stalk. 'Anyway, I'm not talking about the Middle East. I'm talking about Persia.'

'And how did you find a place to stay?'

'I told you old Moishe had connections everywhere, being in commerce. And Baghdad was full of merchants, travelling across the seven seas and back. As a matter of fact, the man who first put us up was called Sindbad. Not *the* Sindbad of course, but a descendant. He lavished all kinds of splendid gifts on us and showed us all the sights. The days were very hot, but the evenings were divine. We used to stroll to the outskirts of the city to watch the sunset, when all the camels would climb into the palm trees and sing hymns in Latin. Every night there was a party, either at Sindbad's palace or at one of his friends'. With – what do they call those girls? – obelisks, and eunuchs, and veiled dancers, and storytellers, and the most exquisite food and drink, and opium pipes, and perfumes wafting about. During the daytime we were on our own. Jethro wrote poetry, or sang, he had an enchanting voice, and I painted. I'd always been fond of drawing and painting, and once the Wepeners had been persuaded that my interests ran to sweet little still-lifes and landscapes, nothing like Rachel's lurid imaginings, they'd let me have my way. But there in Baghdad I became more daring. My talent exploded. I must have made hundreds of paintings of Jethro.'

'All of them showing his Jewish streak?'

'Some more, some less.'

'Then why didn't you just live there happily ever after?'

'Because there's a snake in every paradise, even if it is Valhalla, or Nirvana, or whatever it was they called it in Persia. And this particular snake was a man called Achim Sidi Achim. One of the most powerful men in Baghdad, a personal friend of the Grand Vizier. He was quite young still, not yet forty, and he was very handsome, in a Persian sort of way I mean. Well, to cut a very complicated story short, he fell in love with me. And he wanted to marry me. He could see no obstacle, as Jethro and I were not legally married in terms of Persian law, or any other law for that matter; and Achim Sidi Achim had only three hundred wives of his own, so he had space and appetite for lots more. Those Persian men, I can tell you –

'Achim Sidi Achim took to visiting me late every afternoon, when Jethro was out with his friends. I tried my best to discourage the man, but he wouldn't listen to reason. He could easily have had Jethro removed, they have very refined ways of doing that, but because of his feelings for me he announced he would do the honourable thing and challenge Jethro to a duel. Which would have been all right, because among the skills Jethro had picked up in Baghdad was swordfighting and very few could match him. But the problem was that according to their custom such duels must be fought naked. It is part of the code of honour of those swordsmen – what do they call them again?'

'Samurai,' I suggest with a poker-face.

'Precisely. And so, with all the noblemen of Baghdad and their courtiers assembled in the main square, poor Jethro was unmasked, in a manner of speaking. And a great cry went up, "Infidel! Infidel!"

'Now I've already told you that Jethro was a consummate swordsman. And what he did, with a single almost unnoticeable flick of his wrist, was to strike at Achim Sidi Achim's manhood, deftly slicing off the foreskin, no more, no less.

'"Now we're equals," he said. "Let us fight till death."

'But he didn't stand a chance against that whole rabid multitude. I would have been willing to hurl my body on his to protect him against the crowd, but that would have been the totally senseless kind of bravery one finds only in stories, and the will to survive was uppermost in my mind. I ran home. There was no time to pack. All I could do was to throw over one of Jethro's burnooses or whatever you call them, and I grabbed and concealed under its folds the one small painting of Jethro. Then I fled.'

'But how did you get back here, all the way from Baghdad?'

'I won't bother you with that,' says Ouma Kristina.

'An elephant came and blew the story away?'

'It was not as simple as that,' she chides me. 'I had to walk for hundreds of miles through the Gobi desert. Thousands. At last I joined a caravan. And so I made my way back to England, where I boarded a steamer. By that time, of course, I'd already discovered I was pregnant. Only then did I begin to wonder whether I shouldn't have chosen to stay behind and die on the body of my lover. But it was too late for regrets. I had to face the future again. For the sake of the perfect love I'd known. And all I had to face it with was the baby in my womb and the one small painting, which is now lost. Like everything else.'

# 13

She is so weak now that I am beginning to fear she may not survive the night. But the indomitable will that helped her escape from the raging crowd in Baghdad and subsequently survive the ordeals of the desert, sees her through. That, and several slow deep breaths from the oxygen supply which I insist on placing on her tiny monkey face.

'Where was I?' she asks with a little gasp.

'We can continue tomorrow night,' I say. 'Please, you must sleep now.'

'Where was I?' she repeats, and I know there will be no respite.

'You came back from Baghdad,' I say with a sigh of resignation.

'That's right. That's right.' She is trying, as far as I can make out, to arrange her thoughts.

'Were you not rejected by your family when you came home?'

When she starts speaking again her mind appears less confused. The brief pause must indeed have composed her. 'Hermanus Johannes Wepener had died soon after I'd left, I think I told you, a stroke, the poor bastard had had it coming to him for a long time. But Petronella welcomed me back. She was overjoyed, in fact. She'd aged a lot while

I was away. It was almost pathetic to see how dependent she'd suddenly become on me. In those last months of her life – she was already over eighty when I came home and she didn't last much longer – we found a closeness that had never been possible before. As she approached death she even tried to talk to me about Rachel again. But she was very weak by then, and all those years of keeping quiet about it had made it almost impossible for her to discuss it. The night she died she tried, she really tried, but I think she'd lost the words for it by then.'

'So you were still in the dark?'

'More or less, yes. But there was one thing she said, quite inadvertently, I think, that suddenly opened a new window for me. Just before she died, it was a Sunday evening, Lizzie and I were with her. And she suddenly smiled, a strangely happy kind of smile, and said, "Yes. The two of you belong together. Like sisters." And died.'

'I don't understand.'

'Neither did I. Not right then. But it kept bothering me. And after the funeral I asked Lizzie whether she could shed any light on it. No, she said. But she'd been wondering about it too. And together we confronted her decrepit old grandfather Salie. He'd never spoken two words to me in his long life. Always treated me as if I were a contagious disease. But now his defences were down. His own wife, Nenna, had died while I was away, and I suppose Petronella's funeral at long last set him free to speak. Especially when I persuaded him that she'd already told us everything before her death.'

'But how could he possibly have known about it?'

'Because he might have been my father.'

I stare at her. 'No, please, Ouma – !'

'It was one of the strangest and most terrible things I've ever heard, Kristien. But I had no reason to disbelieve him. Even if it didn't prove anything, we all had to face the possibility. Because at long last he'd spoken what he'd never dared to utter before. He had nothing more to lose, you see.'

'But how – why – ?'

'Thirty-one years before, he told us, Hermanus Johannes Wepener had tried to seduce Salie's daughter Lida who was then a mere child of twelve or thirteen. Tried to bribe her with beads, with a gold sovereign, even a ring with bright stones. She refused. She was terrified. He paid no attention. He had the droit de seigneur. So he raped her.'

My face feels numb; at last I can see what is coming, even if it still impossible to believe.

'When Lida came home with blood on her dress, Salie took a spade and went in search of Hermanus Johannes Wepener. But the farmer must have been expecting something like that and he was waiting with his gun cocked. There was nothing Salie could do. Not directly. The only revenge he could think of taking was to do the same to Hermanus Johannes Wepener's daughter. That was Rachel.'

It takes a long time to compose my thoughts. 'Why didn't Hermanus Johannes Wepener kill Salie?' I ask at last. 'At the very least he could have driven him from the farm.'

'Until the day Salie spoke to Lizzie and me he'd never told a soul,' says Ouma. 'And Rachel, for reasons of her own, had kept it to herself as well. So neither Petronella nor Hermanus Johannes could ever be sure, whatever they might have feared or suspected. And he might well have had good reason to hide a guilty conscience of his own. In the end the two of them had each other by the balls. Which is the way men prefer to do battle, isn't it?'

'But how can you be sure that was what Petronella meant when she spoke to you and Lizzie?'

'I can't, and that's the point. No one will ever know for sure. Perhaps in her own mind it was no more than a befuddled wish or a lingering suspicion. Perhaps she'd even looked up something in her encyclopedia. The means and coincidences are not important. Only the story. And that goes on.'

# 14

A nightjar calls outside. In the corner the yellow-eyed owls are fidgeting. One takes off through the open window. I can hear Trui moaning in her sleep near by.

'What about you?' I ask Ouma Kristina. 'When you came home from Europe, pregnant and all: how on earth did you persuade Oupa – Cornelis Basson – to take you back?'

'He needed no persuasion. The moment he heard I was home he hurried over to visit me. Said he'd been waiting for me. And insisted we get married as soon as possible, which suited me. His parents disinherited him, of course, which made things easier for all the other brothers. Anyway, what I stood to inherit was certainly enough for both of us.'

'You moved in here after Petronella died?'

'Even before she died. We couldn't wait, you see. My pregnancy was beginning to show. And this house is big enough to hide a multitude of sins.'

I pause, and shake my hand to ease the circulation. Then dare to ask, 'How come Cornelis didn't mind? What did he say? Or didn't you tell him?'

'Naturally I told him. He went a little pale, but in his eyes I could do no wrong. Greater love hath no one. I'm sorry. I don't mean to sound callous. But it was a purely practical arrangement, and he knew it.'

'And then you lived happily ever after?'

'I never slept with him, of course.'

I find myself staring at her, but she keeps her eyes closed, imperturbable. It's like the game we played as children to end an argument: you would pull the most hideous face imaginable, then avert your eyes and make sure that for the rest of the day you didn't look at the other again, and so deprive your adversary of the satisfaction of responding.

'You never slept with Oupa?' I repeat, inanely. 'Yet you had six children.'

'Nine. Three died.'

'So the Holy Ghost got going on you too?' I say sarcastically.

'Like Zeus, the Holy Ghost has been known to assume many shapes.'

'I thought you were going to tell me the truth.'

'No. I asked you to come so I could tell you stories.'

'I'm no longer a child, Ouma,' I say, more sharply than I meant to.

'That would be a great pity.' Now she opens her blue-veined paper-thin eyelids again.

'Ouma Kristina – ' I make an effort to compose myself, reminding myself that she is dying; she has the freedom of imminent death, which I know nothing about. 'If you felt so strongly about not sleeping with Oupa, why didn't you just bring up Jethro's child and leave it at that?'

'That is exactly what I told myself afterwards. Hindsight is always easier, isn't it? But right then, suddenly finding myself pregnant – I had to give the child a chance in life. I allowed myself, for once, to be bullied by what others would think. But that was the last time, I assure you.'

'But then to have all those other children – ?'

The hint of a shrug. 'Most women embrace devoutness and dedication as destiny. I suppose I decided I'd rather be judged for my sinfulness. At least it would be less boring.' A tired but mischievous smile. 'Also, I discovered I loved being pregnant,' she says contentedly.

'Not the bringing up of the children afterwards. And certainly not having the fathers around. So I'm afraid Lizzie saw to most of that. But being pregnant – that feeling of wholeness, of being totally self-sufficient, of folding myself around my own centre. To feel my body growing heavy and to ripen like a big fruit, the fruit of myself, to feel my breasts swelling and filling with milk – I loved lying on my back and seeing the milk trickle from my nipples across my body and under my arms, and when I pushed myself up on my elbows, over my belly and round my popped-up navel, and into my pubic hair, and down the sides – to imagine it flowing from me, over the floor and out of the doors and across the veld, and to see the ants following the trails and crawling all over me – That was a fulfilment I could never have in any other way. Call it madness again, I don't mind. We all need our particular forms of madness, otherwise we'd just wither and die.'

'I still find it hard to believe that you really felt you should marry Oupa.'

'I married him for the same reason Petronella married Hermanus Johannes Wepener. For the same reason, I suspect, most of us marry.'

'Which is?'

'Because we're not permitted to lead a worthwhile life on our own. So we put up a front. As long as we can derive our worth, our authority from someone else, from a man, we are accepted. Mrs Cornelis Basson. How I fought and fought against that name. It was like cancelling myself. But what choice did I have, in 1921? With that name I could face the world. It would do for a safeguard and a passport, even for a widow, later, or at a push, for a divorced woman. But one is not free to go it alone. No, no. You see, when we try to do it on our own we can shout our heads off but no one pays attention. Not because we don't speak, but because no one will listen. So we try to survive, by hook or by crook. The first step is the worst. The rest is subterfuge.'

I gaze at her, uncertain about my own feelings.

'Don't look at me in that tone of voice,' she says. 'Why don't you say something?'

'What about love?' I ask, thinking, How corny can one get?!

She takes me seriously. 'I loved Jethro. I think. And I once thought I loved Francois Basson. But love is not so absolute that it cannot be imagined with other bodies.'

This time it takes a long while before I resume the conversation; she lies waiting patiently, with the faintest expression of amusement on her sunken face. (We *must* stop soon, I think; she cannot go on for much longer, she needs to rest now, she must be exhausted. But, like her, I suspect, I don't know how much time we have left.)

'Did you ever tell Mother – about Jethro? – about Oupa not being her father?'

'That was my only real indiscretion, I suppose. Some things are better left unsaid. I used to think the truth was always better. But some people cannot face it, not readily. And Louisa was one of them.'

'When did you tell her?'

'When she was twelve or thirteen. The worst possible moment, I realised afterwards. But I paid for it. She never trusted me again.'

'She never told me. She never told me anything.' I hesitate. 'Did you tell her about the other children too?'

'No. When I saw how she took the first bit I kept silent about the rest. One learns, even if it comes too late.'

For the first time in my life I become curious about my mother, that cold, aloof and secret woman I'd feared and resented so much; and Ouma Kristina is prepared to tell me; the little she knows, at least.

# 15

From the very beginning it was obvious that Louisa was musical. Before she was two years old she had the habit of waking up at the crack of dawn and singing in her cot until well after sunrise before she would call for food. She would sing throughout mealtimes; when there were guests they sometimes had difficulty making themselves heard through the performance. She preferred singing to talking. For Cornelis she was nothing short of a miracle; he couldn't have loved her more had she been his own child. What he enjoyed above all else was to go on his rounds to fields, bird enclosures, dams and sheep carrying the singing child on his shoulders. He pined when she went to school. It was hard for her too, but the opportunity of taking music lessons amply made up for it. Piano, recorder, singing, whatever was on offer. At home Kristina started a collection of records – all seventy-eights, of course, played on an old-fashioned His Master's Voice gramophone that had to be wound up by hand – which was worthy of the feather palace. Like the white dog on the label Louisa could spend hours beside the trumpet loudspeaker, singing to the accompaniment of the music.

'This child has too much talent for a small town like this,' the music teacher, who was also the church organist, warned Kristina. This was not an expression of unqualified admiration: it also carried the subtle warning that Louisa was getting too big for her lacquered shoes. Other teachers, and most of the school children, shared the feeling. But Louisa paid no attention. And Kristina took a well-considered decision to construct the child's whole future round her voice. As soon as she'd finished school she would go abroad to study with the best music teachers in Vienna. If necessary, Kristina would go with her. During the cavale with Jethro she'd seen something of Europe, and since then she'd collected enough books to have a fair idea of what to expect and what to do, and where. Her child wouldn't grow up in such restricted circumstances as she had had to do. All the opportunities of the new age, after the Great War, would be grasped.

Even the exorbitant expansion of the family – eight more children during the following seven years (five of which survived) – could not dampen the enthusiasm with which Kristina brought up her first-born. The only disruption of their relationship – unfortunately of a rather serious nature – followed her disclosure, with the very best of intentions, that Cornelis was not Louisa's natural father. Kristina seemed to believe that the discovery of her exotic origins abroad, far removed from this unimaginative and narrow-minded little place on the bare plains of the interior, would act as an added incentive to the child. But for Louisa it was a shock from which she found it hard to recover. One might say it was the only time in her cushioned youth when the outside world penetrated her active consciousness: previously she had been so lovingly protected by her family, her talent cherished with such dedication, that she appeared oblivious of anything else. That might also explain why the envy and viciousness of school friends and teachers left her so unruffled. Their world had nothing to do with hers. But Cornelis had always been a condition of her accomplishment, and the discovery that he was not her father affected her like a blight. Which explains why Kristina never repeated that sad mistake with any of her other offspring. Unless, of course, the whole account of the fatal revelation was fictitious, a cover-up, who knows, for something else that had gone wrong between mother and daughter, for which Kristina preferred not to take the blame?

Whatever the real reason, something happened in those vulnerable teenage years that shook Louisa from her insulated equanimity. Not that outsiders would readily discover it: the full extent of her anxiety remained concealed. The only sign was an even more passionate devotion to her music, the one enterprise that was sure not to fail her.

Previously her dedication had been spontaneous, like breathing or eating or drinking water; now she was driven by it as by an obsession; it seemed no longer healthy.

The same tendency towards exaggeration became evident in other forms. During her puberty she tried to deny all evidence of physical development by tearing her vests into strips and tying up her breasts so tightly that they couldn't be noticed; just before PT classes she regularly fell ill to avoid undressing in front of others. In later adolescence it became a form of self-denial, as she went about with knotted ropes tied very tightly around her body, practically cutting into the flesh, as if to punish it for being there. All her energies, her whole life, had to be dedicated to her music, and drastic measures were necessary to exclude all else. Her mother found out about it only when Louisa fainted one day and they tried to put on her pyjamas; by that time the gulf between mother and daughter had grown so deep that the girl refused to offer any explanation. When Cornelis, with the best of intentions, tried to coax something from her, she became hysterical and screamed at him that he was a dirty old man.

Towards the end of her school career, as her studies in Europe drew close, her life took on a calmer aspect. But another catastrophe was ready to break: Hitler's Anschluss just when Louisa was due to leave for Vienna. She trusted no one, confided in no one; so it was impossible for anyone ever to know just how profoundly this affected her. The only remaining option was the Conservatory in Stellenbosch. Not quite Vienna; but better than nothing. Had it not been for the diaries Ouma Kristina discovered many years later we would have had no indication at all of what she went through during those years.

She did well at the Conservatory. Exceptionally well, though one wouldn't have guessed that from her non-committal letters home. She could have become popular too: she was beautiful, there was no lack of admiring young men. But her response left them in no doubt: she either ignored them or bitched at them. That is, until the law student Ludwig Müller made his appearance. How can one ever explain that mysterious chemistry? Much later, in Louisa's diaries, Ouma Kristina would discover all about it: how he'd shared her passion for music, how they'd gone to concerts together, how he'd even sung with her; how he'd accompanied her on the piano, once or twice at concerts with the Cape Town City Orchestra. No one except Louisa ever knew that Ludwig Müller could sing a note, let alone play the piano; and whoever might try to page through old newspapers or the archives of the Cape Town City Hall in search of a review or an advertisement of a concert in which the two of them appeared, either jointly or severally, would end up empty-handed, Ouma Kristina assured me; she'd tried. The diaries were, in every respect, another story.

But whatever the nature or the source of the attraction, it existed. And in a way it must have done Louisa some good, drawing her out of her hermetic world of music to expose her to a kind of existence she knew nothing about. Ludwig Müller was a scion of an impoverished but furiously patriotic Afrikaner family (his father was a tenant farmer in the Free State) whose rhythms had been marked by the great events of the rebellion of Slagtersnek, the Great Trek, the two Anglo-Boer Wars, up to and including the reactionary movement of the Ossewa-brandwag that tried to sabotage the Smuts government during the Second World War. In fact, soon after Ludwig had begun to court Louisa, his father was arrested and interned in a concentration camp, allegedly after he'd been involved in an attempt to blow up a post office. The details of the exploit never fully came to light and one can only hope that some of the unsavoury accounts of it were exaggerated. At any rate, he remained in the camp until the end of the war in 1945. The event had radically influenced Ludwig's life. He was the oldest son, and when his father was interned he had to give up his law studies to support his mother and a number of younger brothers. As a result of his father's political involvement he was refused a career in the civil service, which left him with a lifelong chip on the shoulder.

After a series of humiliating disappointments, he was finally offered a job on a farm near Stellenbosch. Not very well paid, but at least a refuge from disgrace; and the farmer's family both understood and shared his nationalistic sentiments. The obstacles that faced him had strengthened the bond with Louisa; it is likely that the emotions bottled up in her during her isolation from her own family found some release in this relationship. There are indications (those diaries again) that they soon became intimate; if her account is to be trusted, it was ecstatic. There has always been this thirst for excess in the family.

Together they planned the future. As soon as the war was over they'd go overseas. He would complete his studies in Germany, following in the footsteps of a whole regiment of national heroes who had gone there in the Thirties; she would go to Vienna. The world would be at their feet. All that was required was for Germany to win the war.

Well!

At the end of 1945 Louisa completed her M.Mus. and took up a post at the Conservatory, teaching piano. Ludwig found work in a bottle store; he'd begun to study by correspondence. According to the diaries they attended concerts several times a week, meeting many international opera stars – among them, most notably, Amelita Galli-curci and Elisabeth Schwarzkopf, both of whom were so impressed by Louisa's voice that they offered her free lessons in the series of Master Classes they conducted. Unfortunately Ouma Kristina's subsequent enquiries failed to reveal any sign of visits to South Africa by Gallicurci and Schwarzkopf in those years; in fact, she found that Gallicurci had already stopped singing before the war. In the diaries the couple appeared to have led a life of success and fulfilment; the regrettably insufficient facts at the family's disposal tell a depressingly different story.

After the victory of the National Party at the polls in 1948, Ludwig was at last admitted to the civil service, in the Department of Justice. One would hate to sound disparaging, but it isn't unlikely that his father's war-time exploits at long last stood him in good stead, as his rise was meteoric. A year after the elections they were married. Soon afterwards Ludwig was transferred to a whole string of small villages in the deep interior, first to Calvinia, then to Carnarvon, later to Winburg, to Schweizer Reneke, to Lydenburg. In the diaries, according to Ouma, one could continue to read accounts of Louisa's enthusiastic correspondence with Gigli, with Richard Tauber, with Renata Tebaldi; there were entries on amazing offers – first of bursaries and openings for further study, then of recitals. Unseen, unheard, acting purely on the recommendation of divas like Schumann or Tebaldi, the managements of the great opera houses in Linz and Graz, Covent Garden, invited Louisa; there were even letters from the Vienna State Opera, later from La Scala, then the Met. All of which, of course, had to be graciously declined. Still, without singing another note, the name of Louisa Müller became, said the diaries, a household word all over the civilised world.

In 1951, coinciding with the transfer to Carnarvon, Ludwig was promoted to his first magisterial post. In the same year Louisa miscarried, as a consequence of which she remained ailing for a long time (which resulted in the cancellation of bursaries from Salzburg and Milan); and in 1952 their first child, Anna, was born. Her illness persisted, necessitating the refusal of passionate entreaties from Stockholm, New York and Paris.

By that time Louisa no longer gave music lessons. While it had been a useful help in paying for Ludwig's studies or complementing his initial meagre earnings, her contribution had been enthusiastically welcomed; but as he began to climb the social ladder he felt it no longer suited his status to have a wife who taught uninterested and uninteresting children to bang away at the piano. The diaries gave no indication of whether she resisted or quietly resigned herself to his wish; but there were persistent accounts of clandestine visits by Irmgard Seefried, Julius Patzak, Erna Berger and others, who were all so fired up by what they'd heard about her that they deemed it an honour and a privilege to offer her lessons. Some of them stayed over, Birgit Nilsson for three weeks. (An invitation to Marion Anderson had to be withdrawn at the last minute when Louisa discovered the singer was black.)

Fortunately Ludwig had no objection to his wife's eagerness to continue singing. In the church choir, for instance; or solos at weddings, christenings or funerals; or on special request at meetings of the church's women's group, the Women's Agricultural Association, or the Party.

As time went on Louisa began to accept the inevitable, although the diaries made it more than obvious that she deserved better than the small-town milieu to which her husband's career had doomed her. Conflict, one presumes, was unavoidable – between an increasing urge to withdraw into her own world, and the need to fulfil her role as one of the first ladies in whatever village they happened to live in. One gets the impression, according to Ouma Kristina, that her spirit began to wilt; in 1959 she spent three months at a mental institution in Cape Town to improve a 'nervous condition'.

It was soon after her discharge from the institution, while she and Ludwig were spending a week's holiday in Cape Town (having left little Anna at Sinai with her grandmother) that Louisa one morning found herself walking along the misty streets on her own. The mountain was invisible under its blanket, the air cool and damp, her breath puffed out in small white clouds. She was acutely depressed. In one of her rare confidences to her mother in those years she admitted that she'd begun to contemplate suicide. And then, quite suddenly, a young stranger turned up at her side. He didn't introduce himself, he made no attempt to chat her up; he barely looked at her. He merely walked along with her, took her arm, and burst into song: Mozart, Papageno's '*Vogelfänger*', then '*Dove sono*', then '*La cì darem la mano*', gliding effortlessly from one aria to the next, improvising his own words when he forgot the original. A pleasant, joyful tenor, nothing remarkable, not exceptional at all; but contagious. Soon she was singing with him. Until, a few hundred yards further, at a corner, she wasn't even sure of where they were, he let go of her arm, called *'Ciao!'* and went off on his own, disappearing into the misty day. It had all happened so unexpectedly that she couldn't even tell for sure whether it had been real.

The consequences were real enough. Louisa returned to the small German Gasthaus where she and Ludwig were lodging (he'd wanted to stay with relatives, but she'd refused), and confronted him with her decision: she was going on a trip to Europe. Life was passing her by; if she went on like this much longer she'd go mad. She would not deprive herself any longer of everything she'd given up for his sake. (Ludwig reported the whole episode, with righteous indignation, to Ouma Kristina, when he went there to arrange for Anna to stay on longer; surely it could not be expected of him to look after the child, his career was too important: and for once there is something more definite to rely on than the diaries.)

Louisa stayed away for three months, to sound out the possibilities; attending performances in London, Glyndebourne, Paris, Vienna, Bayreuth, Milan, recording each in great detail in her diary. Interestingly enough, says Ouma Kristina, there is no mention, during this period, of personal visits to any of the famous names who had become her intimate friends over the previous years. One gets the impression that she was relaxed, and happy; maybe it was no longer necessary to prove anything, not even to herself.

Upon her return she told Ludwig that she would stay at home until Anna was ten; then the child could be sent to boarding school, or to her grandmother (she refused to entrust her to Ludwig's relatives): and Louisa would go to Europe to resume the music studies she'd been waiting for all her life. She was not getting any younger, but hopefully it was not yet too late. There was a possibility of getting a small bursary to Vienna – nothing like the lucrative offers the diaries had recorded earlier, but not to be sneezed at either.

'On my salary – ?' Ludwig objected.

'Your salary, and the shares you've been buying through your relatives and your friends and your contacts, have been quite enough to see us through so far.'

'What do you know about my financial affairs?'

'More than you think. I've worked it all out. With my bursary, and a small monthly contribution from you, and a loan from my mother – I'll pay back every penny, don't worry – I can manage. And this time nothing will stop me.'

Three months later she was pregnant.

Ludwig was ecstatic about the prospect, at long last, of a male heir. He couldn't stop enthusing. He even had the name ready; he had no doub^ at all that it would be a son.

On several occasions Louisa came close to losing the child. You may think what you like, says Ouma Kristina; but no one can prove anything. And in the end a healthy daughter was born, and named Kristien after her grandmother.

From that day, according to Ouma Kristina, the diaries once again began to expound at length on illustrious operatic visitors from abroad; throughout the apartheid years most of the greatest names – Victoria de los Angeles, Joan Sutherland, Janet Baker, Kiri Te Kanawa, even, once, Maria Callas – paid clandestine visits to the villages where Ludwig Müller was magistrate, lodging with the family and getting to know that disgracefully undervalued talent. In due course even journeys abroad were recorded, mainly to Vienna, which Louisa appeared to know intimately, but also to New York or Milan: mostly courtesy visits to friends and admirers, but occasionally, on the insistence of Von Karajan, or Solti, or Davies, for closed recitals to invited audiences.

If this were Ludwig Müller's biography, those would have been eventful years; it would have been revealing to trace the interlinking of his personal career with the larger history of the country. First, in the Fifties, the gradual unfolding of a new system of legislation and the manifestation of a growing passive resistance: through trials involving passes or protesting women disturbing the public peace Ludwig acquired quite a reputation. There must have been the heady discovery that he was making a personal contribution by handing down verdicts in terms of an elaborate system based on nuances of skin colour or the texture of a human hair or the crescent on a thumb nail. Then the watershed of Sharpeville in 1960, the year before my birth: the increasing polarisation, the banning of the ANC and other liberation movements, the first signs of armed underground resistance – coinciding with Ludwig's first political trials, sabotage trials, his growing popularity with the police for his 'firmness', for verdicts that left no doubt about the need for law and order. The Seventies: the rise of Black Power, the school boycotts and the eruption of Soweto, the murder of Biko, war on the borders, the escalation of resistance, stirrings of industrial unrest – while Ludwig issued fuel permits, sat as an assessor at terror trials, composed confidential reports to Pretoria on subversive action in the platteland. The successive states of emergency during the Eighties, increasing corruption, the arrogance of unchecked power: while Ludwig sentenced conscientious objectors to prison, acquired ever more shares and properties, following the informed hints of insiders and fellow campaigners within the grand system. Brother among brethren, rising to the position of chairman of his branch in the organisation of *éminences grises* that controlled the power, onward Christian soldiers. Clandestine meetings once a month, the hectic circulation of confidential documents to expose traitors and promote the cause of the volk . . . The fascination of power that can be shaped and fashioned in one's hands the way one shaped clay oxen as a child (somewhere, somewhere hidden in the mind must lurk the barefoot boy jeered at by the superior English, by city-dwellers, humiliated for being a little Boer and a bywoner). The appointment of teachers, the calling of pastors, the manipulation of posts on city and school and church councils; the ingenious organisation of fêtes and bazaars and cultural actions and meetings on moral standards. The triumph of the man who as a student was forced to leave university for lack of money: now a key figure in chambers of commerce and among brokers and the organisers of Days of the Covenant and Heroes' Days. The private grudge which coincides with memories of the suffering and humiliation of a people, the assiduous exploitation of the agony of mothers and children in British concentration camps, of barefoot women crossing the Drakensberg – all of this dutifully harnessed to the cause of the establishment.

Of all this there is no sign in Louisa's story; it is as if she's never been there, never looked over his shoulder. All she could leave behind was the diaries, and those were too private for the eyes of others, flights of the imagination described on the tablets of her secret resistance and suffering, worthless to outsiders. Only Ouma has read them, understanding (perhaps) more than Louisa could ever have expected.

Late in 1989 Ludwig died of a coronary, at the respectable age of sixty-nine, after devoting the last years of his life to full-time political campaigning. The grateful community (the Party, to be exact) arranged a memorial service, attended by officials from as far afield as Pretoria; afterwards his remains where laid to rest, for some inexplicable reason, in the family graveyard at Sinai; even ex-president Botha attended, trembling, in a collar much too large for him.

Louisa moved into the feather palace with Ouma. A strange decision, to say the least. Was it another demonstration of her urge for self-flagellation? Did she think it would heap fiery coals on her mother's stubborn head? Or did blood in the end prove to be thicker than water anyway? There was another, more banal, possibility: the discovery that Ludwig's political campaigns had financially ruined him to such an extent that he left her nothing but accumulated debts. So the only way to salvage her pride was to move to the farm. She became a recluse; people seldom saw her in town. Like two shadows she and Ouma Kristina continued to live alongside each other. She was a stickler for order and ceremony: one had to 'dress for dinner', taking turns with her two full-length evening gowns, even when she found herself alone at the head of the long mahogany table in the dining-room, with only a boiled egg for dinner, served by Jeremiah in livery. That, she explained when Ouma once dared to enquire, was how it was done in Europe. When she was at the State Opera, or Callas's guest on the yacht of Ari Onassis, or with Rainier and Grace in the pink palace. One has one's pride.

After Louisa's death in a car accident – on that straight stretch of road in to town, says Ouma Kristina, with no tree in sight; no sign of a burst tyre or mechanical failure either – Ouma wound up the estate. That was when she first discovered the diaries. She thought of burning or burying them, out of consideration for her daughter's memory; but then decided to keep them for me, confident that one day I would come home.

Now, regrettably, they have all been destroyed in the fire, together with everything else she had in her room.

# 16

Already the early birds are causing a racket in the trees around the house. Trui comes in from the passage, shuffling on bare feet, yawning, her head a bargain basement of green and pink curlers.

'Why you didn't call me, Miss Kristien?' she scolds me in a guilty tone of voice. 'Here the night is almost over. You must be dead.'

'I'm sorry, Trui. I meant to. But we've been working – '

'Working?' She looks, openly incredulous, at Ouma Kristina who seems to have sunk right into the bed, in a deep sleep. For the first time I discover how exhausted I am. I sleepwalk round the bed to help Trui change the drip and pat down the bedclothes. On automatic pilot I head for the chair again, but Trui resolutely pushes me towards the door. 'You go to catch some sleep now. The nurse will soon be here.'

From the door I look back in a sense of amazement that seems remote to myself. How fitting, after all, I think, that Lizzie's child should be taking over from me. All in the family. But I'm too flaked to control my thoughts. Sleep; I need sleep.

Yet when I do collapse on my high single bed in the adjacent room, too tired even to undress, sleep eludes me. There is simply too much on my mind. The stories Ouma Kristina has told me: old ones, new versions of old ones, new ones; but what used to be stories has suddenly begun to coalesce into a history, hers, ours, mine. Ouma and her Jethro on their magic carpet; Ouma and Oupa, a lifetime beside one another, yet never together; the Girl who has now been named, Rachel, the paintings on the crumbling walls, down below where a stranger hovers, dangerous perhaps, or merely in fear; the mystic Petronella, fraud or fanatic?; her daughter who swallowed glass and left the date of her death embroidered on a square of cloth; my mother and a stranger, Papageno, on a misty morning, a pile of diaries, now burnt, the truth masquerading as so many sad lies; immaculate conceptions and revenge rapes; the fantasies of a frontier world, all larger than life, the exaggerations of a mind on the threshold of death, or a vision of some deeper darker truth? Does it matter, does it make any difference? I have listened to her, I have written it all down, I've appropriated it, claimed it as my own.

And the stories, history, mingle with the stream of events that has carried me through the past day, from the nocturnal discovery of Jacob Bonthuys on the stairs, past Casper's dawn visit, his proprietary eyes on my breasts; breakfast in the kitchen with Trui and her family, Jonnie's smouldering aggression; Jeremiah's stung pride, his anger at having to drive me to town in the hearse; the rediscovery of all those places from summers I've come to think of as lost and possibly invented, butcher's and baker's, chemist, the church with its memories of mice devouring the sacred body of Christ, green figs in the Home Industries and the news of the new atrocity in the township, Casper's desperate rage. What has really happened here, is still happening around us, or waiting to break on us tomorrow, today, any moment? A whole country in the grip of madness, drifting like flotsam on a churning flood towards that event, mere days away, which may seal our collective fate. And what am *I* doing here, in the midst of it all, drawn into the vortex of a history I'd prefer to deny? This is no place for me; no place for anyone who wants to preserve some sanity. I must get out while it is still possible. Yet I cannot move before Ouma Kristina, a whole virulent past made flesh, releases me.

To sleep, to sleep, perchance to dream. Jesus, Michael.

# THREE

## *Among Strangers*

# I

I wake up to find Anna beside the bed, in a crisp white embroidered blouse and navy skirt; she has done something to her hair and looks groomed. I cannot believe my sleep-heavy eyes.

'I'm sorry,' she says in her apologetic way. 'I didn't mean to wake you up.' She evidently finds it necessary to explain herself: 'But it *is* past ten o'clock, you know.'

'Is Ouma all right?'

'She's sleeping. The nurse is with her. She says the doctor's already been.'

'What did he say?' I ask, reproaching myself.

'She's still serious. But he thinks she's doing okay, in the circumstances.'

I relax. For a moment I study her, not quite sure how to react. 'What have you done to yourself?'

She blushes like a teenager. 'Is it all wrong? I just felt like putting on some make-up. Haven't really had time for it lately. And I had my hair done.'

'You look ten years younger. You should do it more often.'

'Ag, well – ' She brushes imaginary dust from her shoulders. 'You sure it doesn't look too mutton-dressed-like-vixen?'

'I rather fancy the vixen look.' I push myself up against the head of the bed, yawn, stretch. 'You really look good, Anna. I'm afraid I must be a sight.'

'Did you have a bad night?'

'Late. But not bad. In fact, it was wonderful. Ouma started telling me the family history.'

She pulls a face. 'Haven't you heard it all before, over and over?'

'Not like this. Not all these skeletons in our cupboard. And even the parts I'd heard before now sound different.'

'Like how?'

'Well, for one thing, what I used to take for stories she'd made up now turns out to be – ' I hesitate. I meant to say 'real', but that is not true. The mere memory of the trip to Baghdad makes me smile. Yet even as I smile I feel caught out: Ouma was trying to tell me something and if I failed to understand the fault was not hers, but mine. Anna's gaze exacerbates my dilemma. How can I defend Ouma's stories against this level-headed woman who is my sister and who comes from a world where blood and violence and fear are everyday realities, not fantasies or nightmares? Is this what it is about? – that the very fabric of our fictions betrays the predicament of a culture? 'She held me spellbound,' I protest, not very convincingly.

'But her mind is wandering. How do you know she's to be trusted?'

'I *have* to trust her, Anna. This is the last chance.'

'Even if it's true, what's the point? A lot of useless baggage.' A touch of mischief: 'And I thought you always travelled light.'

'Perhaps I've been travelling too light.'

'Don't tell me you're developing a conscience.' Her face immediately betrays consternation. 'That's not what I meant. I – I'm sorry, Kristien. I was just being flippant.'

'Many a true word . . .' There is an awkward silence between us. I feel inexplicably naked. 'It wasn't easy to come back, Anna. I'd thought – hoped – I'd freed myself from everything I left behind here. But it's not that easy.'

Almost in spite of herself, it seems, she approaches and sits down at the foot of the bed. 'What did she talk about?'

'Herself, her parents, grandparents. Mother.'

'And me? Did she turn me into a story too?' Before I can answer she says, more vehemently than I would have expected, 'But of course I'm not interesting enough, I have no story. I was born, and did my best to please everyone, and experimented a bit at varsity, and then met and married Casper.'

'And then he took over?' I say pointedly.

She draws her breath in sharply and presses her hands to her face.

It is my turn to say, 'I didn't mean to hurt you.' I feel genuinely contrite. 'But for Christ's sake, Anna, why are you always so hard on yourself? You have a life of your own. You're not just part of Casper's.'

'Have you sorted out your own life?'

'At least I'm trying.'

'I know so little about you.'

I find her frank eyes unnerving. Trapped in bed like this, dishevelled and befuddled, aware of my own stale smell, I feel at a disadvantage. Resolutely I get up, shaking back my tangled hair. 'I must have a bath and get dressed first. I won't be long.'

'I'll come with you,' she says. Pressing her advantage? – the right of the older sister again, denying me a right to privacy. But I try to put up a bland front as I rummage self-consciously through the drawer in which, on moving in, I dumped the contents of my suitcase. I've been meaning to tidy it up, but somehow I haven't got round to it yet. Story of my life.

Through the window, on my way past, I check the weather; a habit I must have picked up in London. The sky is sunny and flat, without depth, a day not so much tranquil as placid.

Anna follows me to the bathroom.

'Any new developments?' I ask as the water begins to run – but it is cold, fuck it. So I resign myself to a shower.

'Actually, yes. They've arrested the arsonists.'

'What? Why haven't you told me before?'

'It was on the early news. Casper has gone off to find out more.'

'Who are they? How many? Where did they find them?'

I strip off my clothes and draw the skimpy plastic curtain, stained with ancient mould, in front of the bath.

'"The police are still continuing with their investigations." That was all they said. But at least it's something.'

'So the brave farmers of the district will start calming down now?'

'I don't know.' She sounds defensive. 'There's still all the unrest in the township after yesterday's attack. And now the ANC are sending down some of their top people. To defuse the situation, they say. Whatever that may mean. There's a whole new language developed in the country these last few years.'

I shampoo and rinse my hair; I soap my body, sponge it off, more vigorously perhaps than necessary. It isn't only to resist the shock of the cold water, but to try and work up some indignation about Anna's news. Why does it all continue to sound so remote, as if nothing really concerns me? I'm not involved; whatever I discover is communicated to me by others; by Anna, in that restrained voice. Yet how can I feel so untouched by it? Here I am only a few metres away from Ouma's room: an old woman in the process of dying, slowly and painfully, from the wounds she sustained in an attack; I'm in the remains of a house that was practically burnt down. So why am I not outraged, why do I feel no urgency, not even anger, or anguish, or fear – as if I'm still ten thousand kilometres away? Can one really lose touch so totally? Or is there an entrance fee to be paid, in kind, in pain of one form or another, in suffering, before admission, readmission, is permitted? But surely this is the kind of reasoning Anna might indulge in, not I. Am I so out of touch that I'm not even sure about my own reactions any more?

When I step out of the bath, dripping, shivering, my skin glowing, I avoid Anna's eyes as I briskly go about the business of drying myself and getting dressed. Only much later, dressed in my shirt and jeans, my hair dried, the tea made (Trui is bustling about somewhere else on a spring-cleaning spree clearly designed to extend, in due course, to the whole house), I face Anna across the breakfast table in the kitchen.

As I spread my bread with Ouma's home-made apricot jam salvaged from the pantry, her eyes caress Michael's watch on my wrist – I have a weakness for men's watches, as I have for large-buckled belts – and follow the motion of my hands.

'You have nice hands,' she says.

'Practical.' I briefly spread them out: the fingers longish but square-tipped, short nails. No-nonsense, I suppose. 'Not like those exquisite tapering fingers Mother had. Remember?'

She gets up to pour the tea. 'What was it Ouma told you about her?' she asks, nonchalant, but I notice the underlying tenseness.

'Did you know about Mother's diaries?'

'What are you talking about? Mother was not the type to keep a diary, and you know it.'

'What do we really know about her?'

'If she kept them, where are they now?'

'Destroyed in the fire.'

'Of course.'

'Anna, I'm sure Ouma told the truth.'

'Scandal. She's always thrived on scandal.'

'Why should you try to protect Mother? She's dead now. And it's not as if you were close. She never allowed anyone close to her.'

She makes an effort. 'All right. Tell me.'

I offer her a brief account of Ouma's story: the diaries; the inexplicable accident.

'So what does it all come down to?' she asks. 'That she sacrificed all her ambitions for our sake? To fulfil her duty towards her family? But hell, she certainly made us pay for it.'

'Sure. That's what I've always reproached her for. But last night – Ouma suddenly made me realise that there was another side to it. She had a whole secret life of her own which we knew nothing about.'

'So? Who doesn't?'

I take the bait: 'You too?'

She takes her time over a sip of tea, then puts down the cup. 'Did you know,' she asks in a wry, self-mocking voice, 'that I once wanted to become a doctor?'

'Why didn't you?'

'Father asked the dominee to come and talk to me. He explained that if I really was interested to help the sick and suffering I should become a nurse. That was more suitable for a girl.'

'And was that why you wanted to do medicine? To help the suffering?'

She sniffs. 'Not really. I suppose I just wanted to do something that would get me away from home. To learn more about the world, to dissect, to speak with some kind of authority.'

'And after the dominee's visit you resigned yourself?'

'Of course. I always did, didn't I? I did the next best thing, became a teacher. It was good to be liked. By Mother, above all. As a child I thought she was perfect. All I wanted was to be like her. So I became her devoted slave. I'd do everything and anything as long as she approved. It's odd to think, now, that she probably needed my adulation as much as I needed her approval.' She is silent for a while. Then she looks at me with a crooked smile. 'Even that wasn't enough. I wanted to be liked by everybody – by Father, by the teachers at school, by friends.'

'By boys,' I remind her with a smile. 'Because you had the boobs.'

'Sure.' Her frankness surprises me. 'It was the most remarkable discovery of my life. I was the first in our class to have them. In the beginning it was painfully embarrassing. Until I discovered there was another side to it. Suddenly boys began to notice me. Even bigger boys. It was not like the teachers who liked me because of my good marks or my exemplary manners or the neatness of my homework or whatever. For the first time in my life people seemed to be looking at *me*, however dubious their reasons might have been. I began to think I mattered. It was extraordinary to discover what boys were willing to do in exchange for the smallest favours.'

'What kind of favours?' I push her.

For an instant she is flustered. But with a touch of bravado she looks at me again. 'What do you think?'

'Anna, *you*?!'

'I wasn't always the goody-goody you thought.' She busies herself with her tea cup, spilling on the table. 'But don't get me wrong. I might offer one of them a glimpse. Or perhaps a feel. It never went beyond that. I was much too straight-laced. The fear of God kept me on the straight and narrow. And every time I did grant a favour I prayed for days afterwards, dreaming of fire and brimstone. At the same time it was such an exquisite feeling to know I was liked, I wasn't worthless, I could turn the boys round my finger. It certainly made up for a lot.' A nervous smile flickers across her lips. 'In a sense it made me believe I was actually real.' She puts down her cup. 'While the only things that were real about me were my boobs.'

'They must have been an asset at university too,' I say lightly.

She gets up, goes to the washup, picks up a cloth, looks round aimlessly, puts it down again and comes back to the table.

'That made it all the more humiliating in the end,' she says. 'To admit that whatever I achieved was due only to the shape of my boobs. Not because I was a woman, but because I was made to feel like a kind of female impersonator.'

'What happened?'

'Nothing special. It was the whole experience of being away from home, suddenly feeling free, exposed to so many new things, that made my head turn. I thought I was queen of the castle. Almost literally: when I was crowned Jacaranda Queen . . .' A disparaging little laugh. 'Can you imagine anyone whose highest achievement in life is becoming Jacaranda Queen? What a future I have behind me. That was also when I met Casper.'

'I've always wondered how he came into the picture.'

'At the coronation ball. He took me home. Except we only got there the following morning. It was the first time I'd ever gone all the way with a man. Although I must admit that by that time I'd come pretty close. But you know how it is: you come to persuade yourself that as long as that little membrane is more or less intact it's still okay. Anyway, that was that. And so naturally I had to marry him.'

'Shotgun?'

'No, not at all. Nothing as melodramatic as that. We only got married two years later. But that's beside the point. It was just that I believed I had no other choice. You sleep with a man, you marry him. Otherwise it's straight to hell.'

'Not that you escaped it altogether.'

She fastidiously lines up her teaspoon with the angle of the handle on her cup. 'No,' she says at last, almost inaudibly. 'But then that's where responsibility comes in, isn't it? You transgress, and then you pay. You can't expect to go scot free.'

'That's shit.'

'Shit is very real.'

'Anna, you've got to get out of this rut.'

'It's easy for you to talk.'

'You really think so?'

'You always did things your own way.' She chuckles, in spite of herself. 'Remember when you were small, one summer when we were here with Ouma, and you were climbing trees? Then Mother told you to stop it. You wanted to know why – you always did. She said you shouldn't let the boys see your panties. So you promptly took off your pants, and hid them where the boys wouldn't see them, and went up the tree again.'

I smile at the memory.

'And in your very first year at school – was it? – the music teacher came to see Mother about you. She complained that you refused to utter a sound in singing class.'

'What else did you expect? We had music shoved down our throats at home all day.'

'And then the teacher decided to punish you. She ordered you to stand, and said you'd remain standing there all day until you agreed to sing.'

'And then I told her, I was still lisping, "Will thow you. Will thtand. Won't thing." And stood there until the last bell went.'

'Can you imagine how it stung Mother? Because she knew, we all knew, you had talent. I once overheard a man saying you had a voice that caressed not only the cochlea but the coccyx. But you always refused to sing. The stroppiest person I've ever known. While I never had much talent, but I practised till I was blue in the face, to please Mother.'

'They tried so hard to break our spirits. All for our own benefit, they said, in the name of love and of God, Father, Son and Holy Ghost. Whereas the dirty little secret was quite simply that it made it so much easier for them to control us. You let them, I didn't.'

'It's damn unfair,' she says. 'I tried so hard, and what can I show for it all? While you – '

'Don't overestimate what I've got, Anna.'

'At least you're independent. You make your own decisions. You follow your own mind.'

'So can you.'

'No. *That's* the difference. I'm married.'

135

'How nice to have a ready-made excuse you can blame for everything,' I say, rather more sharply than I meant to.

On any other occasion this would have triggered a no-holds-barred fight; our whole relationship over the years, until I left, was marked by such quarrels. But it is different today: have we simply become battle-weary? or more circumspect? or is there a more profound, submarine, change taking place?

'I wasn't looking for excuses,' says Anna. 'If it is one, then how do you explain your decision to leave – what was it? – eleven years ago? Was that rebellion, taking a stand, making a statement – or running away?'

'I wish I knew,' I say, and mean it.

'Can you bear to tell me about it?'

I hesitate. I pour another cup. I look at her. 'I can try. I've never really discussed it with anyone. The only time I wanted to, quite desperately, was after I lost the child. After the abortion, I mean. I wrote to you, remember? For once I needed a big sister.'

'I didn't write back,' she says quietly. She cradles the cup in both her hands and looks into it. 'I failed you, didn't I?'

'I thought so then. Now I'm not quite so sure any more.'

'Your letter came just after I first found out that Casper was cheating on me. I remember every moment of it. I'd just come home from hospital with my third child. There was a party to welcome me back. I had to go to the bedroom to feed the baby. I was rereading your letter with the child at my breast. It was so upsetting – I was so furious with you – that before joining the others in the sitting-room again I went outside to compose myself. And found them on the side stoep.'

I stare at her, unable to comment.

'Do you know what my first reaction was? I wanted to go back to the bedroom and smother the child with a pillow. I wanted to kill him. And after that I was feeling so guilty I couldn't write to you.'

'There is so much we still need to sort out.'

## 2

There was no Damascus experience for me, no great leap for mankind (or womankind for that matter), only a series of small shifts, each insignificant in its own right, but each making possible the next. A rebellion that sometimes assumed weird and rather distorted forms.

Fighting against the idea of being the dutiful daughter, but going about it so skilfully – although there was always a risk – that I wouldn't get caught: stealing little objects from class-mates, things they prized, and then throwing them away because I didn't want them anyway. Once, I remember, I stole a tiny ceramic figurine of a rooster, quite exquisitely painted – and then had no idea of what to do with it. In the end I spent a whole afternoon making a little matchbox dresser, covered in brightly coloured paper, with a silver-paper mirror; and then I placed the rooster on it and offered it for sale at the church bazaar, which somehow cancelled the guilt. That kind of thing.

When I was already in London I remember once walking past a large sign on someone's garage door that said:

DON'T EVEN THINK OF PARKING HERE.

And all of a sudden parking there was all I could think of, although I didn't even own a car. In fact, I spent days, if not weeks, trying to figure out how I could get hold of a car just for the sake of parking it there. See what I mean?

As a child, in the games we played, I always wanted to be the robber, not the cop; or the knight, not the sweet little lady waiting to be rescued; the one who fought the monsters and sometimes won and sometimes lost, not the one who had to be saved. Even at high school I was beginning to have doubts about my female fate: not only the idea of getting married, but that having a husband and children should be the be-all and end-all of my life. I suppose Mother had a lot to do with this. Because of what she did to us; but also because of what she allowed Father to do to her. Most of my friends revelled in the prospect of being let loose to flirt and experiment with the passions and try their wings, safe in the knowledge that afterwards they would settle down peacefully for ever and ever, amen. As though the fascination of seeing male desires focused on yourself could blind you to what was in it for *you*. To me the idea was repulsive.

We once had dinner with a friend of Father's. It was a Sunday, after church, we were all straitjacketed in our finery. We'd been warned beforehand that this was a very important man, we had to behave ourselves and be as quiet as mice. Which we were. But the man's own two kids were quite small, three or four years old or thereabouts, and *they* were pretty rowdy; and halfway through dinner the man looked at his wife and made a motion with his head, and she took them outside to play in the garden so as not to disturb her husband and the guests, and she had her meal by herself, afterwards, while the others were taking coffee in the lounge. I remember that I, too, ran out to play in the garden with them, although I was already about eight or ten and should have known better, but it seemed so much more fun outside. Except it was so awful seeing the woman sitting there on the swing crying but pretending not to. I went over to her and pressed myself against her where she sat, and decided to tell her my 'secret' to make her feel better – which was that when I grew up I'd never have children – but that made her cry even more.

In one sense university improved my life, but in another it made it worse. It was an improvement, because for the first time I was tasting a kind of freedom. But it was worse, because I knew a moment of decision was approaching. Holidays were terrible, except in summer when we came here to Sinai. There were always arguments with Father – about not working hard enough, or taking 'useless' subjects, or reading the wrong books, or turning my back on 'my people', or wearing the wrong clothes. Jesus, there was one argument that went on for days, simply because I'd put on what Father regarded as a see-through blouse that showed my nipples, which was about all I had up there. A girl who flaunts her nipples, he maintained, is making herself cheap by blatantly announcing her general availability. For once, Mother took my side, although her argument was somewhat back-handed: I had nothing to flaunt anyway, she said, so what was the fuss about? I tried to be aloof, then became sneering, then shouted at him, then made a fool of myself by bursting into tears of rage, and in the end only felt sick (although I refused to change my blouse). What really scorched into my mind was his ultimate warning, 'Well, don't come to me for sympathy if you get raped.' To which I could not help but shout in reply, 'And don't expect sympathy from *me* if you get kicked in the balls.' That cost me the final humiliation of a thrashing, even though I was supposed by then to be too old for that.

Towards the end of my university career – I went to Stellenbosch, not Pretoria where Anna had gone; my only reason being to put as great a distance between me and my parents as possible, but it was not without irony, because as Stellenbosch was their own alma mater they enthusiastically supported the move – we made a family trip to distant relatives in Namibia (which was then still 'South-West Africa'): he'd always been very conscious of family ties. The only worthwhile moments on that whole wretched journey were the visits to the Namib, the shifting dunes outside Walvis Bay, where every time one returned one would discover them in new configurations – and yet they seemed eternal and immutable. I could have stayed there, I think. I fell in love with the desert; it was the first time I formed an image to match the name of Africa, and until today it is the most vivid in my mind. The rest of the holiday was miserable. Mainly because the whole trip was organised around a hunting expedition, which sounded exciting beforehand, but turned out to be less than inspiring.

We spent most of the time on this vast farm, north of Okahandja, stretching to beyond the horizon. A whole army of relatives and friends had descended on the place, most of us camping outside because the low, grey, depressing farmhouse was much too small to lodge us all. That in itself was no problem, except that the tents pitched in a sandy dried-up river bed under tall camel-thorn trees were soon infested by bird-lice of a particularly venomous kind; and Mother complained endlessly about the lack of amenities. Also, she was scared by every night sound. Once, when a donkey brayed in the vicinity, she was convinced it was a lion and sent Father scuttling outside on all fours, presumably to kill the predator with his bare hands.

Before sunrise every day the men drove off with their guns in their bakkies while the womenfolk stayed behind to work. And work they did, from long before dawn until the men came home at sunset, because only through slaving away could they justify their existence. In the very biltong they cut, in the marinades they made and the miles of sausage they stuffed, I could see the system itself going about its inexorable business.

After a few days I couldn't stand it any more. So I fled – accompanying the men on the back of a bakkie, where the previous day's blood had coagulated in a dark jelly on the metal floor, covered in red dust. I took an orange with me, and a can of beer, a length of stringy biltong, and a book. I spent most of the day nearly passing out in the sweltering heat, trying to read Jung's *Memories, Dreams, Reflections*. Third-year Psychology. Until in the hazy afternoon the men returned, an almost totemic sight, carrying on their shoulders the bleeding carcasses of the game they'd shot.

After that I stayed behind again; but leaving the women to their energetic duties, and ignoring Mother's dire warnings about lions and leopards and the more nameless terrors of Africa, I strode into the veld resolutely carrying a pair of binoculars, a knapsack of provisions and Roberts's *Birds of South Africa* to do some bird-watching (though any other pretext would have done as well); and of course I got lost, and soon consumed my sandwiches and dried wors and tepid cooldrink and was beginning to believe I'd die of thirst when I was found, humiliatingly, by a search-party of men, led by Father and our host, well after sunset.

It is hard to tell whether I was more furious with him for finding me or for having caused me to wander off on my own in the first instance. Perhaps an awareness was already beginning to dawn that a time would come when I wouldn't take it any more. There was no future for me in this fucked land. Even then it wasn't easy to take a decision that meant a total uprooting. At university I'd become involved in mildly leftist politics (there were no more radical options available on that campus). At least part of my motivation must have been the knowledge of just how much it would irk Father. He was so smug in his dedication to the great causes of Afrikaner politics (which as far as I could make out in practical terms meant only his own advancement) that it was almost obligatory for me to find ever new ways of mortifying him.

But it wasn't all self-interest. Inasmuch as such decisions can ever be pinpointed in time and space I recall a party, towards the end of my second year, at the house of friends in the exemplary suburb of Dalsig – all pseudo-Spanish architecture, landscaped gardens with indigenous shrubs and trees and triumphant middle-class values. Somebody's birthday, I think. The weather was perfect and we were lounging around the illuminated pool in the afterglow of too much to eat and even more to drink; it must have been near midnight. The conversation, prompted by God knows what, was, as befitted a group of students carried away by a reckless overestimation of their own intellectual faculties, the human condition, nothing less. All of it solidly embedded in European tradition, all Hegel and Heidegger, Sartre and Camus, a dash of Foucault, and of course a thoroughly disinfected and sterilised Marx. In the midst of all this half-baked erudition there was a sudden irruption into our cosily sequestered world as a man, a black man in ragged overalls, came bursting through the privet hedge, scuttling across the lawn, colliding with chairs and upsetting trays and tables, dashing past the edge of the pool, and crashing through the opposite hedge into the neighbours' garden. Before we had recovered from the shock two more men came tumbling through the privet in his wake, two constables in blue this time, guns in hand. Bang-bang, you're dead. Quite oblivious of our presence, intent only on their furious pursuit, past the pool, through the shrubs, and off into the next-door garden. It was all over as abruptly as it had begun. The whole thing had been so surreal that it was hard to believe it had ever happened. It was as if a sudden squall had struck the place, leaving havoc in its wake, then disappeared.

A few of us went over to the neighbours to enquire, but they were blissfully unaware of anything. (We also checked the papers the following day, but there was no mention of anything untoward.) A few intrepid souls tried to resume the conversation, but there was no spark left and soon it petered out and everybody went home. I have no idea of whether any of the others ever gave the incident another thought; none, as far as I can remember, brought it up again. But to me it was another shift, as if the whole submerged other half – four-fifths – of life in South Africa had suddenly, forcibly, broken into the comfortable little enclave in which I'd been brought up. It was as if that other man, the one who'd once come to Father for help, with blood on his head, had been resurrected to come and haunt me. Perhaps my reaction was ineffectual, and sentimental, and certainly embarrassingly 'white'. But having been brought, for one shocking instant, face to face with that secret dark segment of life in this country on which everything else is predicated, I couldn't just blithely return to the bliss of my habitual ignorance.

Had I been religiously inclined I might have been inspired, like most of my fellow students with bad consciences, to join some missionary action of the church. As it was, I had pretty little choice. But I did become active in whatever leftish political activity was permitted on our campus, where even the suggestion of questioning 'traditional values' was regarded as a potential act of terrorism, Communist-inspired.

So it was all very safe, really. But it did provide me with some sense of becoming a part of larger issues, of a movement gathering momentum and running diametrically against what Father had always so passionately described as 'our people's struggle for recognition'. And it helped me through the next few years. The most remarkable – and gratifying – discovery was that, however cautious and tentative our position was in real terms, within the context of campus life it was regarded as very dangerous indeed.

What was particularly frowned upon was my relationship, in my Honours year, with Eric Olivier, who was regarded as something of an oddball at Stellenbosch: artistic, unconventional, with an angry satirical streak that did not go down well among the rugger-bugger crowd which dominated student life. What brought Eric to prominence was his involvement in anti-military campaigns, burning his call-up papers, advancing in the ranks of the End Conscription Campaign. It was amazing to see that shy, stuttering boy suddenly fired by a conviction I found almost frightening at times. I was fascinated by Eric. But the relationship didn't last long. One day as he came from an art class he was whisked away in a car; and I never saw him again. We – some of us, at least – staged demos, wrote to the newspapers, plastered the admin buildings with posters demanding that the university step in to have him released from detention, but no go.

And then it was my turn.

I was called in by the primaria of my residence, ticked off by the house committee, eventually summoned and officially reprimanded by the rector. My behaviour was termed unacceptable for an Afrikaner, particularly reprehensible in a young woman. I was asked to resign from the SRC and sacked from the editorial board of the student newspaper. People were warned against associating with me. It was great.

The rest of my student life followed what must be the standard Afrikaans-student-having-seen-the-light pattern: I lost a few friends, I also made new ones, particularly coloured ones, comrades from the United Democratic Front. Among them, Jason. He was a coloured teacher, twelve years older than I, an organiser for the UDF, who'd already been detained twice. Had the circumstances been different I could easily have fallen in love with him, but our relationship was strictly platonic. I knew his work in the UDF was too important to be jeopardised by complications of a different kind.

There were others who could fulfil my physical needs as and when these obtruded. I rather liked men, and going to bed with them when the mood was right, but I saw no need for involvement except on my own terms. One or two episodes had turned out badly and made me more wary; but I acknowledged the needs and desires of my body and I prided myself on being able to make, by and large, I hope, sensible judgements. If the great consuming passion in which I confess I still secretly believed had not yet come my way, I felt sure it was just a matter of time.

The dénouement was quite unexpected. At the beginning of my MA year I was visited in the residence lounge by two stereotypes in sports jackets and Terylene trousers; and after some heavy-handed banter they came to the point. I was invited to keep tabs on certain fellow students and report regularly to the two nice gentlemen. It was all so crude that I could scarcely believe it. Rightly or wrongly, I saw Father's hand in it. I'm afraid I laughed outright at their proposal. They dropped the bonhomie. 'Think it over first,' said the older of the two. 'We don't want an answer today. It's entirely up to you.' The briefest of pauses, before he added, 'Of course others may be affected by your decision. Man called Jason Smith? Now I'm sure you wouldn't like to cause your parents the disgrace of an immorality trial.'

I refused to accord them the satisfaction of seeing me shaken.

The visit had been like a tremor, a detonation, under water, that caused all kinds of long-discarded debris, and dead fish, to drift up to the surface. My first urge was to drive to Jason's small square house in Belhar and warn him; but of course it would be foolish to expose him to any further risk. And it was as much for his sake as for mine that I took the decision – it did not even have to be taken, by that time it seemed ready-made within me – to leave the country.

# 3

I get up and take my breakfast things and Anna's cup to the sink. The sun falling through the window draws a sharp line across the quarry-tiled floor. Ouma Kristina's clock. She's never worn a watch in her life; there used to be any number of clocks in the house, but although she would occasionally wind them up she never bothered to correct the hands, with the result that they – all fifteen or twenty or more of them – showed, and chimed, different hours. The only reliable timepiece was the sun sliding across the kitchen floor; and she could tell, within a margin of ten minutes or so, the exact hour by just glancing at the joint it had reached (allowing, of course, for the time of the year, which made it quite a complicated calculation). On the rare overcast days she was stranded, but that was neither here nor there; mere mathematics has never concerned her much.

'Would you like to go to town?' Anna asks.

'Do you have time?'

'Oh yes. It's Saturday. I thought it would make a good excuse to get away from the children for a morning.'

'Good,' I say approvingly.

But before we can proceed there is a hectic invasion of the yard outside, accompanied by a cacophony of bird sounds. We reach the kitchen door in time to see a yellow police van pulling up, followed by five or six other cars in a swirl of red dust. The open windows all bristle with guns so that the procession resembles a cohort of outsized mobile porcupines. As soon as the escorting vehicles come to a standstill the doors swing open and amid a racket of shouting male voices at least twenty armed men in blue fatigues come tumbling out to form an irregular circle around the van. From the front of the van two policemen in uniform emerge, run round to the back, pistols drawn, unlock and unlatch the doors and jump back in anticipation, like the trainers of dangerous predators in some circus act.

There is a chorus of orders shouted at full blast – 'Move it! Move it! Move it!' – while some of the escort drum on the sides of the van with the butts of their rifles or the reinforced toes of their huge boots. Expecting at least a pride of lions or tigers, if not an elephant, to come charging from the open door, I approach a few curious steps. Becoming aware of a female presence the display of male power rises to a near-hysterical pitch. Then, from the back of the van, four dishevelled figures dribble to the ground. Around them the dust begins to settle. A hush falls upon the military assembly. In the background the prostestations of the birds subside.

One of the two uniformed men, presumably the commanding officer, judging from his corsage of pips, clicks his heels together and makes a movement with his right hand (still clutching the pistol) as if to announce, '*Voilà!*'

Their quarry, their insignificant bodies huddled together in fear, turn out to be a bunch of teenagers, the youngest looking barely twelve, a boy with bony knees and elbows. The handcuffs holding his too-big hands together appear exaggerated on those thin wrists. He has peed in his short khaki pants; his face is covered in tears and snot, streaked with dust, and from time to time his rib-cage is convulsed with a sob. All around the kids the men still stand, their guns pointing inward.

It takes a while for me to tease some sense out of the scene. They are all, clearly, awaiting my reaction, like boys anticipating parental approval of some quite extraordinary feat.

'What the fuck is going on here?' I manage to ask at last.

The officer, taken aback, opens his mouth; but all he can do in the end is just to point. Behind me, Anna is uttering a barely audible, warning sound, but I pay no attention.

'Well?' I ask. 'Corporal, or General, or whatever you are – what in God's name is all this?'

'Miss,' he says, 'we've caught them.'

'Who are they?'

He stares at me as if I'm soft in the head. 'It's them,' he says. 'They're the ones who set fire to this place, man.'

It is my turn to stare.

'But I thought – people said – they were supposed to be disaffected MK soldiers or something?'

'Let me tell you, they're never too young to join, Miss,' he says. 'I mean, at the end of the day it's the young ones what's the worst.' Without warning, even without turning his head, he lashes out with his left hand to give the nearest prisoner, the stick-like boy, a cuff to the side of the head that sends him sprawling, with a shrill cry like a girl.

'Get up!' orders the officer and I see him positioning himself for a kick at goal. (One of my first boyfriends at Stellenbosch played flyhalf.)

'Stop that!' I shout, using all the lung capacity I've inherited from my operatic mother.

He gapes at me in disbelief. Even the boy has stopped moaning in mid-sniff.

'But these are they!' reiterates the officer, gesturing helplessly. 'Don't you understand?'

'They're just a bunch of kids.'

There is a muted rumbling among the assembled men.

'But I told you – !' A tone of triumph creeps into the officer's voice. 'They already confessed.' He turns to the tallest boy and bellows at him, 'Hey, Georgie boy?'

The youngster mumbles something incoherent. His mouth, I discover, is swollen so badly that he has difficulty speaking.

'You hear?' asks the officer. 'They sang like canaries, I tell you.'

'But why would they have set fire to this place?'

'For the hell of it. Because they felt like it. Because they had nothing else to do.' He looks at me, exultant. Then turns towards his men. 'Okay, boys, take them round to the front.' And looking over his shoulder he says laconically, as if I'm a child to whom everything has to be explained, 'We just brought them round for a final check.' And in a louder voice again, to his cohorts, 'Move it!'

I turn to Anna. 'You coming?' I ask.

She shakes her head, supporting herself against the door frame. Behind her I see Trui's bright red doek appearing, and further back, in shadow, Jonnie.

The officer appears surprised, even discomfited, when I fall in beside him. We go round the house to the devastated stoep on which the gutted window frames still stare like gouged-out eyes.

'It's really not necessary, Miss,' he says officiously.

'What has happened is bad enough,' I tell him curtly. 'I want to make sure that nothing untoward goes on.'

'The old lady was nearly killed,' he says, a touch of annoyance now creeping into his voice.

'She's my grandmother,' I say.

'Well.' He smiles conspiratorially. 'Then you'll understand.'

'I don't understand how these boys come to look the way they do.'

'When it's life or death one can't always wear gloves, Miss. I'm sorry. It's not that we like it or anything. But we've got a job to do.' Adding pointedly, 'So you can sleep safe in your bed at night.'

'I'll sleep a lot better if I know *they*'re safe.'

'Look,' he says suddenly, 'what's your case? Are you now blaming us for catching a band of terrorists?'

'A band of terrorists?' I feel a very rigid smile on my lips as I motion with my head towards the four boys surrounded by the squad.

'You obviously don't know these types. Let me tell you – '

'No,' I stop him short. 'Let me tell *you*: I'm going to arrange for a check on these kids. And if anything more happens to them – you understand me? – if anything more happens to them, you're going to end up where they are now.'

'Excuse me?' There is a hint of real amusement in his eyes. (Perhaps, it occurs to me, he is really a very nice man. Probably an excellent father. All fun and games.) '*You* are going to arrange – ?'

I feel my throat contract. But I say, 'Yes. Because a week from now there's going to be a new government in this country. You won't be calling the shots any more. And I happen to have contacts.'

His blue eyes narrow as he gazes at me, hoping, I'm sure, he can call my bluff.

'I'm in the ANC,' I say in a straight voice. 'I'll be speaking to their representatives within the next few days.'

Now he seems totally at a loss. 'But aren't you an Afrikaner?' he asks.

'Of course I am.'

'Then I don't understand.'

'There's a lot of understanding you'll have to do in the next week,' I tell him. 'And you'd better start right away.'

It is fascinating to see his features change. So far, he has been at times condescending, or annoyed, or irritated, having to deal with a woman's inability to understand; but we were, he must have thought, on the same side. The look on his face changes from puzzlement, to suspicion, confusion. Now it becomes simple and precise, in a hatred as intense as a laser, almost exhilarating to watch, the kind of pure and focused emotion that can free a man to commit the worst excess.

'They burnt this house,' he says softly.

I walk into the circle of men. My legs are unsteady, but if there's one thing I can do it is to keep up a front; we learn that from childhood.

'Listen to me,' I address the four boys. 'If anyone here' – I make a slow sweeping gesture – '*anyone*, no matter who, if anyone hurts you, I'll be around to check up.' I look past the men at the officer. 'And there will be hell to pay.'

The laser beams back at me.

I try to round it off with an exit, stage centre, worthy of my mother; but discover too late that, of course, the charred front door has been boarded up. No way out in this direction. So I pretend that this has been my intention all along, and I turn back to face them, from my elevated position on the stoep, crossing my arms on my chest to control their trembling; and, legs astride, Wonder Woman, I stand there in silence until the squad turns away and trundles round the side of the ruined house. Moments later there is a battery of car doors slamming, followed by engines revving and, as they say, roaring into action. Soon the cortège comes driving past again, following the contour of the front lawn, past the rose garden and the trees, and off along the farm road to the ostentatious palace gates. The dust takes a long time to settle.

# 4

Anna and I follow the same road, half an hour later.

'They *were* trying to do their job,' she said over the cup of tea we felt obliged to drink after the commotion had subsided.

'Their job isn't beating the shit out of kids.'

'Their job is to catch the people who killed Ouma.'

'She's not dead.'

'Not yet. But they killed her. Whether they're twelve years old, or twenty, or fifty.'

'Who are you trying to convince?'

'You don't know these people, Kristien. They may be kids in terms of years. But they grew up in the streets. They're the generation that shouted *First liberation, then education*. Violence is their only language. They don't understand any other. Just look at this place, look at what they've done.' She took another sip. 'You've been away for too long. I've told you before: you don't have the faintest idea of what's going on here. It's no use trying to be a goody-goody-gumdrops bleeding-heart liberal. This is for real, Sis.'

'I'm for real too,' I said, feeling sick.

She smiled, commiserating, condescending; and put down her cup. 'Well, shall we go?'

'Where?'

'I thought we were going to town?'

'Oh. Yes, of course.' I took a deep breath. 'I have to get my bag and some stuff I need for the bank. Will you wait for me in the car? I won't be a minute.'

I wasn't. I had to go and wash my face in cold water. I dropped in on Ouma, but she was still asleep. Beside the bed sat the gawky nurse like a many-limbed insect, preying on her magazine. I gathered my things, fobbing off Trui who was clearly preparing for a discussion. ('We'll talk later, I promise, okay?') From the kitchen window I made sure that Anna was in her bakkie under the pepper tree. In the distance I could make out Jonnie, still hovering. I turned back into the darker recesses of the tumbling palace and hurried down the stairs to the basement.

Jacob Bonthuys was still sitting where I'd last seen him, yesterday, staring at me in a daze, unsurprised, resigned. He looked older than before. I stood with my back against the door.

'What happened?' he asked. 'Who was here?'

'The police.'

He stood up, backing away.

'They were not looking for you, Mr Bonthuys. They said they'd caught the people who bombed the house. That means you're safe now.'

He looked at me warily. 'Miss isn't just saying so?'

'No. I'm sure. You can stay here for as long as you wish.'

'Thank you, Miss,' he said. 'The Lord will bless Miss.'

'Leave the Lord out of it,' I said in a huff, then checked myself. 'Is there anything you need?'

'No, Miss. Trui already brought me breakfast, early, early.'

'Wouldn't you like something to read?'

He looked down, embarrassed. It suddenly occurred to me that he might not be able to read. If so, it was too late to backtrack now. For a moment I reproached myself. When would I learn to think before I plunged in? But then he said, 'If Miss could bring me something by Langenhoven? There's a book called *Loeloeraai*.'

I mumbled a response. What on earth could interest him in the writing of a staunch old Afrikaner patriot? Ask no questions, I decided; and left.

'Where were you so long?' asked Anna when I finally moved in beside her; she sounded more resigned than annoyed.

'Just did a check on Ouma.' I was still trying to organise my thoughts. 'Incidentally, is there a bookshop in town?'

'There's CNA.'

'Would they have Langenhoven?'

She glanced at me and shrugged. We drove through the gates; Anna waved at the guard on duty, I stared straight ahead.

We are driving along the farm road. There is no wind, and some dust churned up by the police cortège still hovers in the air, prickling the mucous membranes.

I remember the last time I visited the farm before I went abroad. I tell Anna about it. I couldn't leave without talking to Ouma first.

She just smiled. 'Did you come to ask me, or to tell me?'

'I think – to tell you.'

'Then you must do it.'

'But suppose it turns out badly?'

'Anything can turn out badly. It's the plunge that's important.' Ouma had a way of infusing clichés with conviction, every word weighted with her own experience.

On the last afternoon I walked along this road, for hours, blindly. Ouma's territory. Mine, by adoption, appropriation. At some stage I reached a fence. I hesitated, but not for long; then climbed through – a small bright blue patch from my dress got caught on a barb and remained behind to signal the transgression – and stalked on. There was something unexpectedly profound about the experience: reaching the limit of the farm, the edge of the familiar, of the permissible – the neighbour was reputed to be an irascible old bastard who shot on sight – and to discover it was not the end of the world. The limit of one space was simply the beginning of another; it was possible to go beyond. I knew then, yes, that I should go. I would leave the margin and move into another territory. Its name was history. The sweet presumptions of youth, if no longer of innocence.

# 5

For the first few months in London I was on a high. I was driven by the compulsion to 'make it work', to 'show them', to get involved – as I had so recklessly presumed – in history, above all to prove to myself that I could succeed. I was eager to burn as many bridges as possible. While they existed turning back, the past itself, remained an option; and that I did not want. I first landed in Earls Court, but the vibe was bad: too many South Africans, the wrong kind. Following some recommendations and introductions I'd brought with me, I drifted down to Stockwell, then picked up, or was picked up by, a compatriot in exile, a louche attorney who later turned out to be no more than a second-hand confidence trickster, and moved to North London. I'd had no compunction, before I left, about selling the small car Father had given me for my twenty-first and which I'd accepted with bad grace; so I had some money to see me through the first months. But I needed to find a job, both for the money and the independence; and because hanging around and doing nothing would kill me.

Through some of my UDF contacts I met ANC exiles, and people from Anti-apartheid and Amnesty International. That meant odd, and mostly illegal, jobs here and there, making posters, organising gatherings, writing pieces for various small papers, even acting as editing assistant for a couple of low-budget Third World documentaries. But there was little security in these ventures and in spite of a measure of protection offered by Anti-apartheid, and some sympathy from the GLC, one knew all the time that the Thatcher government, in cahoots as it was with the regime in South Africa, did not take a kind view of aliens in my situation. I had to place my presence on a more secure base. To start with, I needed better – more acceptable – qualifications for a career. And once I became more reassured about the very basic and physical aspects of survival I registered for an education diploma. Not exactly an inspiring or enriching experience, but I attended lectures with commendable dedication.

Now the marriage. I'm afraid there was neither glamour nor romance involved. It was an eminently practical solution to several irritating problems. First, after the rather sleazy beginning with the fake attorney, I withdrew, for quite some time, into the safety of celibacy; but natural inclination, and an exceptionally cold winter, prompted reconsideration. There was a fair amount of fucking going on in the circles into which I'd moved, and as the temperature dropped and nocturnal loneliness became acute, I availed myself of some of the opportunities on offer. Not bad; not particularly good either, and certainly not earth-moving. For a while it served its purpose in making friends and influencing people; but in due course – in the 'medium term' as the bright and eager political analysts around me would say – it also created enemies, and there was a hint of the vicious circle about the whole exercise. While I've always tended to agree with Ouma Kristina that only a person who dares to make enemies deserves friends, there was little sense in gratuitously accumulating resentments. Also, quite frankly, I discovered, to my bemused reassurance, if not entirely without alarm, that I am at heart more monogamous than I'd thought. And as I happened to find myself, at that time, in a reasonably pleasing relationship with one of the AAM leadership, I proposed marriage and was accepted. Jean-Claude Thompson was his name, JC in the inner circles, a name stuck on him by a doting French mother. This connection might have contributed something to his prowess as a lover, notably in the oral department; I shall not deny that it pulled some weight in my decision, which really was not taken quite as lightly as it may sound, but the primary consideration was that matrimony provided the readiest access to a work permit.

If this sounds callous, I should argue that there was no deceit between us, both knew exactly what was involved; above all, it was a strategy for survival, and at that time this was what being in London was about. I obtained my qualification; I plunged into teaching, first in a maddening comprehensive in Hackney where all-out war character-ised the milder days, later in a somewhat more manageable school in Camden Town, and finally in one near Paddington (which made the flat in Sussex Gardens particularly useful); and I tried to do my bit for the Struggle. It hardly amounted to much more than taking part in demos and drives, getting involved in fund-raising, doing some public liaising (JC proclaimed that my backside could make the difference between a two-hundred- and a five-hundred-pound donation; and this was why I eventually gave it up), acting on committees dealing with women's issues. Enough, certainly, to keep me occupied for forty-eight hours a day. Its real reward lay in the knowledge that with every action I was striking my little blow against everything my father represented.

Life changed when I fell pregnant. Both JC and I were caught, in every sense, unprepared; the urge had overtaken us one summer weekend in a field of grass near Stowe-on-Wye, JC had done his reputation proud, and there it was. I must try to be as matter-of-fact as possible. Am I – still – scared I may not be able to handle the emotion? Perhaps it is just a natural aversion of melodrama, in a family that has seen more than enough of it over the years. I made no scene then, at least not publicly; I shouldn't now.

But why did it leave me with such a feeling of devastation? Perhaps it began on the day, a week over my time, when I took the test. It was like having been caught out in some minor misdemeanour, no more; but when, affecting nonchalance, I communicated the result to JC that evening, his only reaction, without even looking up from his paper, was, 'So when are you going?'

There was no reason at all to turn it into an argument; but his total lack of concern – his automatic assumption that there would be no discussion – provoked me.

'Going where?' I asked.

'To have it done.'

'To have what done?'

'Are you daft or something? The abortion.'

We'd agreed, long before, that we never wanted children; that was not the issue. It was the way he took for granted that it would be done, as if I had no choice at all, as if it should concern me no more than an in-growing toenail or a bunion.

'Why are you looking at me like that?' he asked with a touch of irritation. 'Don't tell me – '

'I'll make an appointment for some time next week,' I said, and left the room.

That week, and the weeks after the brief impersonal visit to the clinic, were the only time I felt a pang of missing my family. No, not my family. My sister. And of course Ouma Kristina. For some reason it was Anna I chose to write to. Ouma, I knew, I could talk to on one of her nocturnal visits. To my parents, in due course, I would only mention that 'I'd lost the baby'. But what I was in need of now was sisterly closeness. In a way it served me well, if not right, when no reply came. It finally made me accept, as if there'd ever been any doubt, that I would – could – never go back. Nothing, not even the deliberate burning of my bridges through my involvement with the anti-apartheid cause, had been so emphatic in driving home to me just how irrevocable my decision had been.

All that I could absorb. What was more difficult to deal with was the loneliness of my nights, JC sleeping peacefully beside me; or feeling my stomach contract whenever, in bus or tube, or walking past a block of flats or a green enclosed garden in an oval square, I would hear a baby cry. The kind of sentimentality I'd never have given myself credit for. I actually became weepy, for several months. I had bad dreams. I even went for therapy for a while. In the end, an end that was not very long in coming, it caused JC and me to split up. I accept my share of responsibility. But what got me in the guts was the way he became distrustful of me, as if the experience had revealed a lack of substance and dependability, even of credibility, in *me*; a kind of female instability that somehow threatened his male certainties, even the range of future choices available to him. So I told him, in as businesslike a manner as I'd once asked him to marry me, to fuck off; and we went through the necessary legal rigmaroles, and one particularly pleasant late September day we were divorced.

JC was considerate enough to move to the Paris office, or perhaps it was simply a better offer. What mattered was that his move made it possible for me to continue with my political activities, even though 'dabbling' might be a better word. There was some necessity for it, a need to persuade myself, perhaps, that there was a larger destiny involved; most importantly, I needed the sense of involvement, of solidarity, of a ready-made circle of friends to stave off loneliness; in due course I could come to terms with what had happened, life does have a way of going on; but I doubt that I could have faced the humiliation of admitting, to my family, that the move abroad had been a failure. There remained an urgency to prove that I could make it.

Contact with the family in South Africa (I could no longer bring myself to think of it as 'back home') tailed off to the perfunctory card at Christmas, the brief scribble for birthdays. Only with Ouma did I carry on a more regular, if by no means substantial, correspondence – a letter of two or three pages, perhaps four, a couple of times a year. She made it clear that she missed me, but she never exhorted me to come back; if that had to happen, as she believed it should, it would. She knew me too well, and herself too well, to insist. And in her wise, unflappable way, in a handwriting that grew steadily larger and more erratic over the years, crawling across the page like the irregular footprints of some unclassified insect, she sustained me in whatever I undertook, without ever presuming to enquire precisely what it was.

More important than her letters were her visits. Shifting sands, these, I know; but among all the quirks of our family this one, perhaps, is not so outlandish. Others would call it dreams; *I* knew they were nocturnal visits, in the course of which she would allow me to unburden myself and then offer the simple but profound reassurance of her solidarity. She might not always approve, but she was always there. 'If that is what you really want to do, then by all means do it.' And if it appeared mad or irresponsible to others, she couldn't care less. '*You*'re the only judge, Kristien. Go for it.' That, more than anything else, kept me going for eleven years.

There is not much more to tell. The odd affair, some quite fulfilling in their way, others considerably less so; the unavoidable occasional one-night stand, ranging from the hilarious to the briefly ecstatic to the unsavoury. Then settling down, if such a phrase dare be used, with Michael, whose worst demonstration of eccentricity, during the three years of our shared life, was waking up with a muffled scream one night, explaining that he'd seen a footnote crouching at the end of the bed.

The only exception to it all was Sandile Hlati. For once in my life – so far the only time, although I reserve the right to be surprised again – I was in love. Unquestioningly, unconditionally, un-whatever-elsely, proverbial head over real heels. If we didn't have to leave so early on the first morning after the first night, I'd have hung out the sheets. Sandile was in the ANC office, he'd just recently been posted there, after a spell in Prague. A beautiful man; but let me not wax lyrical. He was considerate, he discussed everything with me, he cared for my opinion, his laughter was infectious, his enjoyment of life brought a glow of embers to the stomach; thank God he was also human, which means that he could be, at times, headstrong, infuriating, overreacting, pedantic or suddenly morose; we could talk for eleven hours without stopping for a break, and then make love for – I never counted. I just know how surprised I was, without fail, when it was over, at how incredibly late, or early, it had become. Sandile was a source of constant wonder. He could be endlessly attentive; yet when there was work to do nothing, not even my most provocative attempts at distraction, could succeed. He was dedicated. He was passionate. He loved my feet. He was left-handed, like me. He was, secretly, a poet. He was brilliant. He was, above all, married.

I'm not particularly proud of any of my relationships with men. But I had always, out of an old-fashioned, perhaps atavistic, sense of propriety, meticulously steered clear of married men; and I had an unfailing instinct to detect matrimony. In another life I might have been a customs officer's drug-sniffing dog.

When I first met Sandile, at a drab office function on a drab day that suddenly lit up, all the signs were there; and he made no attempt to dissimulate. Even when, as Ouma Kristina might phrase it, the wetness came, I was resolved to steer clear. We very quickly became good friends. It would be, I resolved, as it had been with Jason, if for quite different reasons. But even Jason would have been no match for Sandile. I'm not going to blame the stars, or destiny, or poor old God. It was us. After a certain cape had been rounded we refused to resist any more. And we didn't try to find excuses or explanations either – the pressures of work, the reality of the threats under which we lived (even in London there were agents and killers about; recently, in Lusaka, a whole ANC safe house had been blown up), the misery, real or imagined, of exile, the shortness of life, or whatever other pretext that had served its purpose in the course of human events – but, when the time came, acknowledged our love, for love I maintain it was, and plunged into it as one would dive, naked, into the cliché of a fathomless pool.

Even so we were extremely discreet about it: it was the very condition of our love, and I don't think anyone ever had the slightest whiff of suspicion.

It lasted for five months, seventeen days, and thirteen hours.

Then I met his wife. Nozipho. She had just returned from an extended visit to her family who'd travelled to Botswana to be with her since she was, obviously, barred from South Africa. He had spoken to me about her; I had asked. We had never pretended that she didn't exist. But meeting her, with two bright-eyed small children in tow, six and four years old respectively, was different. Nozipho was slight and very well dressed, not particularly beautiful, but with a wide and wholly trusting smile, and eyes that showed a deep contentedness with the world, however horrible it was. She had a relaxed manner with the children; an even easier way with Sandile, the easiness of a body that has no secrets for another, yet has retained its core of mystery. If that doesn't sound too corny.

We spent only an hour or two together; there were several of the other ANC people with us. It was a very curious experience. For the first time – and that includes the bad cramps I'd suffered after the abortion – I discovered what it really means when one's womb contracts, a pain more acute than anything merely physical. Yet at the same time I felt incredibly aloof, distant, detached, knowing with unflinching clarity what I should do. And when he kissed me good-night as I left the party, I pressed his hand; and he acknowledged it.

The real hurt, the tears, his and mine, came afterwards. But the worst was already over. And we were both strong enough to see it through. To say that it was for the sake of his family makes it sound sanctimonious, or trivial, if not both. There was no feeling of doing a noble or a lofty thing; only the inevitable thing. What they had, in that family, should not be jeopardised by anything as selfish and private as passion. He made it easier, after a few months, the blackest and most desperate few months of my life, by asking to be posted elsewhere. The executive was reluctant; they needed his skills in London. Also, since he couldn't divulge the real reason for his request, it wasn't easy to persuade them. But Sandile went to see the president himself, and I presume that speaking man to man he was able to confide the full situation to him, for his request was granted and he was sent to Washington. We've been in touch since then, not all that regularly, our letters marked by the restraint our memories necessarily imposed on us. And eventually, as it does tend to happen, alas, the fierceness of the passion subsided into a dull ache, until even that seemed resolved – except, rarely but preciously, in an unguarded moment.

I continued to work for the ANC, over weekends mainly, but gradually the early enthusiasm wore thin. Without my wishing to admit it, the time for stocktaking and soul-searching had come. There was nothing wrong with the Struggle; on the contrary. Its issues were real, urgent, clear-cut. But that was part of my problem. I suppose the context of British politics, so prosaic and predictable (at least on the surface), drained some of my enthusiasm, made me dubious about any issue where manichean choices appeared possible. More importantly, there was the growing feeling, right or wrong, that I was nowhere near anything like the eye of a storm, but floundering somewhere on the sidelines, part of a support system, not the real thing, doing manageable womanly things, expected to toil selflessly in the shadow of the men. In the distance, in the far south, under the fulminations and shaking finger of a demented president, the convulsions of a white regime in its final, dangerous agony sent dark and desperate waves across the world: massacres, assassinations, disappearances, torture, detentions, corruption, necklacings. To all of that we had to find answers, drawing up plans and programmes, devising counter-attacks and infiltrations, arranging conferences and clandestine meetings. I felt myself more and more of a futile appendix, no vital organ. If there was a rainbow of hope, ever, I belonged to that other, mistier, hazier shadow-image of the true rainbow in its full spectrum of glory. Blame me; not the ANC. There *were* women in the forefront. But I was never one of them, and gradually my enthusiasm waned. History had passed me by; at best, I'd been relegated to a kind of easy alternative. After the news of Father's death I stopped altogether. There was nothing dramatic about it; I just couldn't see much sense in it any more, it had gone on for too long. I couldn't see it ever ending – those terrible states of emergency, one succeeding the other, murders, raids on neighbouring countries, the whole subcontinent appearing to be spiralling down a drain of mindless violence. Had I become a traitor to the cause? Hardly. I just didn't have enough energy left to go on hoping, believing; unlike those who'd dedicated their whole life to the Struggle, I was gently spilled on a sandbank and left behind, a bit weary, a bit cynical, a bit guilty, nothing really profound.

The last time Sandile wrote to me, already well over a year ago, was to say that they were going back, going home. There was no need to stay away; the exiles were returning, amnesty had been accorded, he was to be part of the transitional processes leading to these elections, next week, everybody is expecting with so much uncertainty, spoken or unspoken. Not a word since then, although his name has often cropped up in the newspapers, sometimes his photograph. Sandile, my love. Part of the entire unresolved past. No, Anna, I do not travel lightly.

# 6

We are sitting in a tea room in the main street, our business accomplished. I look around, invaded by memories of coming here on Saturday mornings, with the family or with Ouma, on summer visits to the farm; of arguments between Anna and me over ice-creams and milk shakes, while Father and Mother sat staring past each other, having run out of conversation years before; or of animated discussion and uproarious laughter with Ouma when the two of us were alone. (This was where we celebrated the acquisition of the bra at Shapiro's emporium: I was already wearing it – feeling unspeakably dignified and mature – under my T-shirt, where it must have shown up at best as an untidy bandage.) The place has undergone the predictable renovation: knotty pine, Formica, red curtains draped on brass rails in home-made swags and tails, huge laminated – and already fly-stained – menus.

Just after the tea and scones have been flung down before us by an inept but well-meaning waitress in a stained pink uniform with a frilly cap, I catch sight of Anna's face as it pinches up into a fixed gaze; looking in the direction of her stare I see a stranger approaching from the door. Tall and lean, almost gaunt, sun-tanned, in rolled-up shirt-sleeves and jeans, he appears to hesitate when he notices her expression; but he is already committed to the approach.

'Yes, Anna.' A wiry arm reaches past my shoulder. There is an uneasy pause before she accepts his hand. 'Am I interrupting something?'

'My sister, Kristien,' she says in a flat voice. 'Just arrived from London.'

'I can see that.' He turns two keen blue eyes to me. His dark hair, cropped short, is turning grizzly. He offers me a hard hand. 'You need sun. You look like something that's been living under a wheelbarrow.' A nod, a bright grin. 'Abel Joubert.'

For a moment I search my memory, then find the name, superimposed on Casper's disapproving face. 'It's on your farm that the shooting took place.'

'Ja.' He pulls out a chair. 'Mind if I sit down for a moment?'

I can see Anna urgently trying to mouth something at me, but he is already seated, sideways, at the narrow end of the table.

'Would you like to order something?' I ask.

'No thanks. I'm supposed to meet my wife. She should be here any minute.' He looks quizzically at me with those frank blue eyes. 'Come for the elections?'

'No. My grandmother – '

'Of course.' He shakes his head. 'I'm so sorry. We were all shocked. What an awful thing to have happened. How is she?'

'I didn't think you would care,' says Anna crisply without looking up from her scone.

'Why shouldn't I?'

'Because she's white.'

He looks at her in genuine surprise. 'Why should that make a difference?'

'Because you always blame us for everything, don't you? So when something like this happens you say that's what we deserve, we've been asking for it. While no one with a black skin can do anything wrong.'

'Now wait a minute.' He smiles, but I notice a tightness round his jaws. 'I don't think it's quite so simple. What we need is to start seeing more than just black and white.'

'This *is* South Africa,' she reminds him.

'All the more reason for breaking the stereotypes. The country is no longer what it used to be.'

'A change for the worse.'

'No, I don't agree. We've been going through a very bad patch, I know. So much violence. Everybody has been jittery. But don't let that fool you. The moment the elections are behind us – '

'I'm afraid I have to go.' She pushes back her chair very suddenly and gets up, casting me a meaningful look. 'You coming?'

But I won't be manipulated like this. 'I haven't finished yet,' I say, pointing at my tea. 'You go and finish what you have to do. I'll be here.'

'Well, suit yourself.' She strides out, head high.

'I'm frightfully sorry,' says Abel, half-rising. 'If you want to go – '

'I want to finish my tea.' I fill up the cup. 'Don't mind Anna. She's on edge.' I try my best to be fair. 'Not entirely without reason.'

'It can't be easy to be married to Casper.'

I shrug, non-committal, family loyalty briefly balanced against frankness. Then, true to form, I barge in, what the hell. 'It's people like him who're threatening to derail the whole process.'

'Don't overestimate them.'

'What do you mean? Haven't you seen them swaggering about with their guns and holsters and walkie-talkies?'

'I know. I've had my own problems with them.'

'Of course.' I feel a fool. 'That shoot-out . . . It wouldn't have taken much for them to have killed you too. And after next week, if they really get trigger-happy?'

'Sound and fury.'

'Don't kid yourself.'

'I'm an Afrikaner too, remember. I can understand the despair they're feeling, faced as they are with something they've never thought possible, not in their worst nightmares. But once they discover it's not the end of the world and they can go on living, living and partly living, they'll settle down and become good solid citizens again.'

'You're very sure of yourself.'

'I'm just trying to read what's happening. Why do you think people like Casper are in such a frenzy? It's fear. They're scared of losing what they've got. And what is that? Not just their possessions, their comforts, their privileges. Deep down it's this place. It's Africa. There's nowhere else they can go to. This is where they most urgently want to be. And as soon as they discover that the only way that can happen is to accept majority rule they'll be ready to shake hands. Especially if they realise that what they regard as "the other side", the blacks, have exactly the same feelings about the same country. We all love it. So let's start sharing instead of fighting.'

'You're an optimist. That may be dangerous in the present circumstances.'

'I'd rather be an optimist in the wrong than a pessimist in the right.'

'Where do you get that from?'

'I've done my bit of travelling. Even thought at one stage I should settle in Canada.' His smile reveals very white teeth against his tanned skin, stubbly with new beard. 'But this is home-grown. For better or for worse.'

'What were you doing in Canada?'

'Travelling. Studying. Even got myself a job in Toronto. Then found out the obvious: that one never gets away. Same problems there. And I decided in that case I'd rather deal with them here. Also, I couldn't stand the climate. We need the sun.'

'We?'

'You too. Or am I presuming too much?'

'You are. I've just come to – to see Ouma through this. Then I'm going back.'

'The good life?'

'No!' I am surprised by my own vehemence. 'But – ' I push back my cup. 'I have my reasons.'

'I'm sure you do.'

I decide to change the subject. 'That shoot-out on your farm. Those people had nothing to do with the attack on my grandmother's place.'

'I know that.'

'How could you be sure?'

'I've known most of them for years.'

'Jacob Bonthuys?'

'What about him?'

'He was wounded.'

'How do you know about him?'

For a moment I feel trapped, but I keep my pose. 'People talk.'

'We're all very concerned about him,' he says. 'After that night he just disappeared.'

I weigh the evidence; but I cannot tell him the truth, not yet. It would betray a trust.

'The police have made some arrests,' I say, playing with my teaspoon.

'I know. It was on the news.'

'They brought them to the farm this morning.' I look him in the eyes. 'Four youngsters. Probably in their teens. The youngest cannot be more than twelve or so.'

He looks at me in silence.

'They were beaten up.'

A muscle flickers in his left jaw.

'We've got to do something about it,' I insist.

'There's a good lawyer in town.' He reflects. 'He's black. Sam Ndzuta. He's also the local ANC chairman. Some people have tried to boycott him because of that, but he's tough. Running battle with everybody in authority. But he's good.'

'I told them I'm in the ANC and I'd make sure someone would keep an eye. So now I've got to do something.'

'Are you in the ANC?'

'I suppose so.' I offer him an apologetic smile. 'I was. For years. In London. Then I – sort of lapsed. Like Christians do.'

'You're not a Christian?'

'No.'

'Pity.'

'Are you?'

'Yes, I am. But right now that's beside the point. You were talking about the ANC. They're sending a delegation here on Monday.'

'So I've heard.'

'I know Mongane Yaya who's leading the group. I've been involved in some negotiations with him over the last year or so. Land matters, resettlement programmes, things like that. If you want to I can arrange for you to see the delegation.'

'I'd appreciate that.'

'In the meantime, that lawyer.' He looks at his Seiko. 'I could take you there if you want. He works on Saturdays. It's just round the corner.'

'You were waiting for your wife.'

'I'll tell the people at the counter.'

Ten minutes later a sharp-faced white secretary waves us past a crowd of waiting people, all black, in a sparsely furnished waiting room into Sam Ndzuta's office. I feel briefly offended by the blatant privilege accorded our whiteness; but it is soon evident that the priority treatment is based on friendship, not colour. Sam Ndzuta is a large avuncular man; his spectacular tie has been loosened around his bull-neck. There is much embracing and backslapping between him and Abel before he turns a benign if somewhat bloodshot eye in my direction; the African double handshake I offer him appears to amuse him hugely, which briefly gets my female hackles up. But there is so much irrepressible humour in the man that he is soon forgiven.

'So what's the trouble this time?' he asks, waving us towards two rather worn easy chairs.

I explain briefly. My account of the encounter with the police, which does not sound particularly amusing to me, causes him to double forward in mirth, practically wiping his face on his variously stained green blotter.

'What are the chances of intimidating the police?' I ask.

'Normally zero.' He is racked by another fit of laughter. 'But right now they're jittery. And the one thing they're as scared as hell of is Monday's visit. So I think you did exactly the right thing.' His eyes narrow. 'Only, don't get too carried away, hey? Those kids *did* try to blow up the house. They're capable of committing murder. It's a desperate generation. But don't worry, I'll keep the pressure on.' He leans forward. 'So how come you have ANC connections?'

I give him a very brief survey of my time in London.

'Who did you work with?'

'Is this an interrogation?'

He finds this excessively funny and it takes a while before he answers, 'No, my dear. I just thought we might have some friends in common.'

'You also spent time there?'

'On and off. Mostly clandestinely, for the UDF.' He flashes his smile at me. 'Did you know Johnny Mphahlele?' This is only the beginning. Did you know – did you know – have you met – do you remember – ? There is no one, it seems, he does not know one way or another.

And then – prompted by what perversity? – I lean forward and ask, trying to keep my cool, 'And Sandile Hlati?'

'My God, Sandile! Saw him in Joh'burg last week.'

'Last week?' I repeat idiotically.

'Sure. Had to go up for a case.'

'Is he – well?'

'He's very well. Working like a madman. You know he's been a big shot in the transitional council. Anyone else would have been exhausted, but he seems to thrive on deadlines. I love the man.'

'So do I.'

Has he caught something? Below the rollicking exterior I am becoming aware of a shrewdness which nothing escapes. 'You knew him well?' he asks.

It takes a moment to compose myself and meet his eye. 'I worked with him. Before he went to Washington.'

'Of course. We must all get together.'

'What' – there is a dryness in my throat which I have to clear before I can continue – 'what do you mean?'

'I'm hoping he may come down with the delegation on Monday.'

I look at him in consternation.

'What's the matter?' he asks.

'Nothing.' I shake my head but dare not face his disconcerting gaze. 'Nothing at all. It would – it would be good to see him again.'

'I may be phoning him tonight, in fact. Shall I tell him you're here?'

'No!' I exclaim. Then recover, though it takes some effort. 'Please don't say a word.' Realising that this might sound too intriguing I hastily add, 'I'd prefer it to be a surprise. Okay?'

'Okay.' He gets up, a huge beaming presence behind the scuffed desk. 'Well! We'll be in touch then.'

On the way back to the café Abel Joubert says, 'This Sandile Hlati sounds like a special person.'

I glance at him, but his face is neutral. 'He is,' I say demurely. 'Or was. I haven't seen him for the last five years.'

Then how is it possible, I wonder, to feel so dizzy? It has all been over for a very long time. There is Michael. There is – well, everything. And being here, now, makes a difference. My life here has no link with that alternative existence over there. It is not only better that the twain should never meet, but unthinkable that they might.

## 7

On the way back, Anna is silent at first – a deep, crushing, offended silence, such as only she can muster, gathering it round her like an impenetrable kaross – but after a few minutes she asks, without turning her head, 'I suppose you blame me for walking out on Abel?'

This in itself is new; before, she would have withdrawn into a sulk that could last for days.

I look at her through the large bunch of flowers I have bought in town. 'Would you like to be blamed?' I ask mischievously.

'Of course not.' In spite of herself, she laughs, a yellowish laugh. 'But you didn't approve, did you?'

'To tell you the truth, we had such a good conversation that I didn't think of blame or approval at all. I never expected to find a man like Abel in a place like this.'

'Who *do* you expect in a place like this?' A brief but heavy pause. 'People like me and Casper?'

I refuse to take the bait. 'He doesn't live in fear. He's an optimist. At the same time he isn't unrealistic. He has no chips on either shoulder.'

'He's just sucking up to the new rulers.'

'Is that what you think? Or is it what Casper says?'

'You really regard me as a very low form of life, don't you?' She says it lightly, but there is a catch in her voice.

'Only when you're playing the doormat,' I retort. 'Is that why you

163

walked out? Was it really because you couldn't handle what Abel said? Or because you were scared in advance of what Casper would say if he found out you consorted with the enemy?'

'You don't know what he is capable of.'

'At the risk of sounding like an Agony Aunt: he may actually learn to respect you if he discovers you have opinions of your own.'

'One falls into a habit.'

'You've already shown that you can make your own decisions.'

'Like what?'

I smile. 'When you came to visit me this morning. I bet he didn't approve.'

'You are my sister after all.'

'Do you regret it?'

She slows down to take the turn-off to Sinai. 'You know, I don't think we've ever spoken as frankly as we have today.' After changing gears she briefly puts a hand on my knee. 'You've trusted me with a lot. I never thought you would.'

'What a secretive household we've always been.' I cannot repress a sigh. 'Father and Mother too. I've never known a more ill-suited couple. 'She with her music. He with his *volk*-and-fatherland stuff – he should have lived in the Boer War or the Great Trek when there were enemies to kill and lands to conquer. When it all turned inward he just couldn't cope any more.'

'Do you know about his political aspirations?'

'What were they?'

'After he retired he actually stood for parliament in the last elections.'

'And lost?'

'How do you know?'

'A guess. Wishful thinking perhaps.'

'He didn't just lose. It was a landslide, in what used to be regarded as a safe seat. He blamed it on everybody except himself, of course. It put paid to all his ambitions, and less than two months after the election he had a coronary. But the really ticklish thing about it all was that Mother voted against him.'

'I don't believe it!'

'She did. Never told him, you can bet on that. But after his death she told me. Her only chagrin was that he'd lost by so much. She'd cherished the hope of seeing him defeated by a single vote: hers. So her only act of revolt came to nothing after all. Poor man. Poor woman.'

'I'm sure we can do better.'

We are escorted, over the last few hundred metres, from the gothic gate, by a cloud of birds. In the yard I shield the flowers against the shock of Anna's abrupt stop.

She keeps the engine idling. 'I'd better go now. There are hungry hordes at home to prepare for.'

'They can forage for themselves, for once.'

'But – '

'What you really mean is: What if Casper comes home for lunch?'

She doesn't answer.

'If I remember correctly there are about eight hundred servants at his beck and call. Why must you also be there?'

'But what will he do?'

'Wouldn't it be wonderful to find out? A whole new world may open in front of him.'

She turns off the engine.

# 8

Ouma is beginning to surface when I come into the bedroom, but her mind is still befuddled. I leave her to the care of the nurse while Anna and I make a salad for lunch. Afterwards she helps me to arrange a small vase of flowers for Ouma's room. The rest, a huge armload, we carry to the graveyard where we divide them up among the graves. I save the last few for the unmarked rectangle outside the walls. Anna looks at me quizzically, but makes no comment. Neither do I. For the moment this is between me and them. Years ago I turned down Ouma's invitation to join her here in her nightly conversations with the dead. Now I am obliged to meet them only in the imagined selves of her stories. They can no longer be avoided. This is some kind of contrition, perhaps.

As a result, who knows, we find Ouma awake upon our return. She knows without being told that we have been to the graves.

'Is mine ready?' she asks tranquilly.

'Now Ouma – ' Anna admonishes, but I shake my head at her. Flustered, she stops.

'I want you to bring the coffin down from the attic,' says Ouma. 'It's not the sort of thing one should keep for the last moment. There's a long sleep ahead and I want to be sure I'll be comfortable.' She grasps my hand. 'Or was it also destroyed in the fire?'

'Most of the attic escaped,' I assure her. 'There is still one coffin up there. I had a look.'

'There used to be enough for the whole family. But so many people have died.'

'You'll be all right, I promise.'

'I want more than a promise, Kristien. I want to try it out for myself. Will you do that?'

Anna is looking on in revulsion. But what can I do? I nod and press her hand. 'We'll see to it, Ouma.'

'I have to go,' says Anna. Now she's in a hurry. Perhaps she has begun to regret her decision to stay for lunch. But I give her a special hug when we say goodbye. She is, unexpectedly, tearful.

I remain standing in the yard until long after she has gone. Then turn back to return to Ouma.

But only a few minutes after I have relieved the nurse there is another interruption. The dominee, Trui announces, has come to visit.

'This is not the time, Trui,' I tell her, sternly; but he is already entering the room unbidden.

'It is always time for the work of the Lord,' he says cheerfully, having evidently overheard us.

He appears fortyish, pink and plump, with small, soft, damp hands, his hairline receding quite drastically along his globular head (a gibbous moon is the image that comes to mind); a few long thin strands of pale hair have been draped across the pate, in a style Ouma used to call 'seaweed on the rocks'. He is beaming goodwill and salvation. Under one elbow, close to his plump body, he clutches, like a life-jacket, a Bible.

'You must be Katrien,' he says, smiling as if he has received the tidings straight from God.

'Kristien,' I tell him.

'Same thing,' he says. 'Welcome, welcome. What a lovely thing to do, coming all this way.'

'From distant heathen lands,' I say, wincing as I accept the limp, moist hand.

'And how's our girl today?' he beams at Ouma.

'Dying,' she replies calmly.

'Now, now, Granny,' he remonstrates with a beatific smile which fades very slowly under her ferocious stare.

'Dominee,' I say firmly, 'I really don't think – '

But having put on the full armour of God, he brushes me aside. The pink expanse of his head shines dully in the light that falls from the window.

'I have come to give you some courage for the road ahead,' he says, taking the nurse's chair beside the bed.

'I'm doing all right,' Ouma says. He clearly doesn't catch the warning in her voice.

'Dominee, please!' I try to intervene as tactfully as possible.

'Now don't you interfere with the work of God, my girl,' he admonishes in a surprisingly stern voice.

'What do you know about God?' Ouma asks unexpectedly.

'But Granny – '

'If I were you I'd stay out of this,' she says, staring serenely at the ceiling. 'God can be a very cantankerous old woman.'

The argument, in the circumstances, might well have turned unpleasant. I'm not sure how the twist comes about: my impression is that Ouma utters a high, shrill, wheezing sound, which may or may not be a mere sign of discomfort. The next moment the birds are there. Not all of them, only a few, but clearly well chosen for the occasion: buzzards at the top and bottom of the bed, a line of cranes at the sides, and a single pure white egret that turns overhead and deposits a splotch of shit on the holy man's exposed pate before it dives out again.

The delicate pink of his face changes to cerise, then deep crimson. Patting the top of his head with a large damp handkerchief, which only serves to spread the blob evenly across the globe, the dominee gives up and retreats into the passage.

'Kristien, will you please see the silly man out?' asks Ouma innocently, making sure he can hear.

'I'll try again some other time,' he mumbles as we reach the ground floor.

'It might be a good idea to telephone first,' I say. 'Ouma is not always in a fit state to see visitors.'

He looks annoyed. 'Look, I'm sorry to say this,' he blurts out, 'but however terrible a thing it may be that's happened to her, we must see the hand of God in it.'

'I'm not sure what you mean, Dominee.'

'God doesn't sleep.' His voice climbs a few notes. 'I'm afraid your grandmother has defied Him in many ways over the years. I had hoped, I had prayed, that there would be a sign of repentance as the end draws nigh. But what has happened here today – ' He lowers his voice again. 'It is a fearful thing to fall in the hands of the living God, Katrien.'

Outside, undoubtedly reassured by the light of day (although he continues to cast apprehensive glances at the sky), he makes an attempt at damage control, even though I still detect an undertone of reproach. 'From what I've heard, here and there, you must have a very interesting life abroad.'

'I don't know what you've heard.'

'Oh, news travels, you know.' He beams. 'We're so glad to see you back. You know, God cherishes the one lost sheep much more than the ninety-nine that stay in the fold.'

'I'm not sure I was lost, Dominee. Neither am I exactly back in the fold.'

He doesn't hear, or pretends not to. 'And at a time like this,' he says. 'At last we can all breathe freely. After all the terrible years of apartheid, the indignities, the injustice – '

'You actually fought against apartheid?'

'Well.' Various gradations of colour once again move across the smooth surface of his face, like a boiled sweet that changes hue, layer upon layer, after every suck. 'I've always been in the forefront to condemn the wrongs of the world, you know.'

'Were blacks allowed in your church?'

'Good heavens! I don't think you realise what times we've been living through – '

'I'm sure you've set an example for many, Dominee,' I say.

Now he seems in a hurry to leave. And a flock of birds escort him overhead, presumably to monitor his progress and wish him God-speed. I hope they will not spare his bonnet.

# 9

On my way back I am so deeply lost in thought that I only notice Trui when it is already too late to avoid her. She has taken up position opposite the kitchen door, cutting me off squarely. 'I want to know what's going on in this place, Miss Kristien,' she says, drying a plate.

'Why don't you leave the dishes to me?' I ask. 'You need some rest.'

'I'll rest when I have to rest,' she says. 'The dishes are almost done anyway. I want to know about this morning. People are coming and going all the time but nobody tells me nothing. First there was the man down there in the cellar, then the pollies, now the dominee.'

'The dominee came to see Ouma.'

'But I heard you arguing and one doesn't argue with a man of God.'

'He was nagging Ouma, he has no respect for old age, so she told him where to get off.'

'That old Missus is going straight to hell.' She puts the plate on the dresser and starts stacking away the dishes; I give her a hand. 'And that man down there?'

'It's all been cleared up, Trui. The children who came with the police this morning were the ones who set fire to the place.'

She stares at me in disbelief. 'Is that genuine, Miss Kristien?'

'It's genuine, Trui.'

'So it was because of those snot-nosed kids the pollies gave us such a hard time?'

'I spoke to them. They won't dare to do it again. With nobody, and that includes the kids.'

'That was a terrible thing they did, Miss Kristien.'

'We don't know what made the kids do it, Trui.'

'This whole country is up to maggots.'

'The important thing is that from now on you – all of us – can sleep more easily at night. The man in the basement is innocent. I told you from the beginning, didn't I?'

'He's not a bad one,' she admits with some reluctance, then shakes her head. 'But where is it all going to end? Next week we're getting a black government, then we'll all be killed in our beds.'

'That's nonsense, Trui. You should be ashamed of yourself.'

'The blacks have never cared one bit about us coloureds, Miss Kristien. First the whites gave us hell, now it's the blacks. For us in-between people nothing will ever change.'

'I promise you, Trui – ' For a moment I consider giving her a more cautious reply; then I rush in headlong. 'There's good and bad on both sides. And I came to know many of the good ones when I was overseas. I almost got married to one of them, you know.'

'Good Lord, Miss Kristien, what are you telling me?'

'I may be seeing him again. He's coming here on Monday.' I take her hand in both of mine. 'You're the only one I can tell this to.'

'Why would that be?' she asks with healthy suspicion.

'You've always understood.'

'Shame.' She sighs. 'One shouldn't speak bad about the dead, but your mother never cared much about you, did she?' Just in case I think she is giving way, she adds more sternly, 'But you were always looking for trouble too, ever since you were this big.' She gestures with her hand close to the floor. 'Naughty little bugger you were, no matter how often they gave you the strap.' A chuckle. 'But then one couldn't help loving you.'

This unexpected motherliness, taking me back so many years, makes me feel sorry for myself; for a moment I press her against me.

But she breaks loose very soon. 'Now what's this nonsense?'

'You should have been my mother.'

'Miss Kristien is just being contrary again.'

'I'm serious, Trui.' Why shouldn't I say it? 'Ouma was telling me stories last night, about the old days: about her mother and grandmother, long ago.'

'The old Missus is always telling stories, you can't believe them all.'

'Do you know about your ancestors and mine?'

'What is there to know? I don't have time for nonsense.'

'I'm talking about Ouma and your mother.'

She goes down on her haunches in front of the dresser and starts rearranging the crockery at a furious pace, her back to me.

'So you know?' I say.

'I know nothing about nothing. Leave the dead alone.'

'But *we* are still alive, Trui.'

'Miss Kristien must stop this now. I have my people, you have yours. That's the way it's always been in this country.'

'But now things are changing.'

'Nothing changes for me.' She gets up suddenly and turns to face me. 'You understand, Miss Kristien? The Lord made us the way we are, and that's that.'

'The Lord made us near family. My great-grandfather and your grandfather both grazed on the other side of the fence.'

'It's not for me to say, Miss Kristien. It's too far back.'

'That's how I used to think, Trui. But last night Ouma made me see things differently.'

'And suppose it's true?' she asks, helpless, but resentful too. 'What's the use? What can we do about it?'

'We can learn to live like family.'

'Who knows for sure that was what happened?' she persists. 'We've always got along just fine the way we were.'

'With your family living in the little box of a house back there and Ouma's family in this palace? You call that getting along fine?'

'One doesn't interfere with the will of God.'

I'm on the point of snapping, Fuck the will of God. But for her sake I say, 'No, Trui. Some things may be his will. But others are up to us to put right.'

She starts taking off her apron. With great precision she folds it up and puts it away in a bottom drawer.

'We're Christian people, Miss Kristien. We do what the Bible says. It's not for us to complain.' In a flush of anger she slams the drawer shut. 'There's only one thing the Lord will hear me complain about and that's a black government.'

'It's precisely because we're getting a new government that we can start burying yesterday's wrongs, Trui.' I take her by the arm. 'Please help me!'

She disengages herself, but gently. 'I need more time, Miss Kristien. This is too much for one day.' She goes to the back door. There she turns round. 'There's one thing you must promise me,' she says. 'Don't talk to Jonnie about this. He'll go right over the top.'

'It will remain between you and me,' I promise. 'But on one condition. You must never ever call me "Miss" again.'

'I'll do what I think best,' she says, but she cannot suppress a smile.

'Think about it, Trui. We'll talk again.'

'I suppose so,' she says. 'Kristien.'

## 10

Ouma Kristina has again drifted off by the time I return to her room, sleeping with an expression of satisfaction on the wasteland of her sunken face. I warn the nurse not to overdo the sedatives. Ouma will want to be awake tonight. Then, with a mixture of curiosity and guilt, I collect the fat tome of Langenhoven, volume one of the *Collected Works*, from the kitchen table where I left it when we came in for lunch, and take it down to the cellar. I couldn't find *Loeloeraai* in the bookshop ('Lulu who?' the assistant had asked. 'No, sorry, Miss, but we do have a nice book on leopards') so we had to make a stop at the library where, fortunately, Anna is a member.

Jacob Bonthuys is lying on the rickety iron bed when I enter, sitting up very quickly, rubbing his eyes.

'I'm sorry, I didn't mean to wake you,' I apologise.

'It's all right, Miss.'

'I found *Loeloeraai* in the library for you.'

His reddish eyes light up. 'Ai, Miss.' Almost reverently he takes the book from me, open it, pages through it. It looks rather dusty; it must have been sitting on its shelf untouched by human hand for years. But he seems to be greeting an old friend.

'Mr Bonthuys.' I'm not sure how to go about satisfying my curiosity. 'How did you get interested in Langenhoven? He's such an old fogey.' Nobody reads him any more.

'Ai, Miss,' he says again. 'The two of us come a long way.' He caresses the spine of the book; it is a gesture almost too intimate for prying eyes. 'I was just a young boytjie when I discovered this man. 'The teacher read us one of his stories in class. About those two ugly cannibals, Miss knows, Brolloks and Bittergal. But after a few periods she had to stop because the principal said we had to learn for the exams, he didn't like us wasting time on stuff that wasn't in the syllabus. A very hard man he was, we were all scared of him, the teacher too. I asked her to lend me the book, but she said if the principal found out he would give her hell. And besides, the book was already back in the library. It was too bad, Miss. I just had to find out what was happening in the rest of the story. You see, we only got to the place where the beautiful girl that was living with the monster tried to save the lives of the two little children he wanted to catch. He got suspicious about it and then he trapped her with the children. And just there the teacher stopped reading. So Miss can understand, I *had* to get the book. But it wasn't easy.'

'Couldn't you get it from the library?'

'I was scared of just going there and asking for it. Our people weren't allowed there, it was mos just for whites. Besides, we only got to town once a week, on Saturdays, when Abel Joubert's father took us in on the lorry for shopping. So for three, four weeks I just walked round and round the building, not daring to go in. But that story was killing me. I was having nightmares about old Brolloks and that girl. I knew I wouldn't have peace in my mind again before I knew what happened. In the end, one Saturday, I took my heart in my hand and I went inside and asked for the book. But the madam at the desk didn't even look up, she just chased me out. Yissus, Miss, she was a kind of Brolloks herself, with glasses on her nose and her hair in a bun, so tight it looked like the cud of a cow. Three times I came back, and three times she threw me out. The last time she said she was now going to call the police.'

'What did you do then?'

'Then I asked the Madam on the farm where my ma worked. That's now Abel Joubert's mother. I knew she went to the library on Fridays when she fetched the children from school. And she was a good woman, she really was. Just like Abel Joubert today. He got it all from her. From his father too, I must say, but mostly from her. Also his love of books, if Miss asks me.' Now that he has begun, there is an uncontrollable flood of words washing over me; and no way out. So much dammed-up urgency to talk that I have no choice but to resign myself to it.

'And so she brought you *Brolloks en Bittergal*?'

'Yes, Miss,' he says, smiling broadly, revealing the gap where his upper front teeth are missing. 'And at last I could finish the story of Brolloks and the girl and the children. And then the story of old Bittergal. But you see, there were other stories in the book also, about the Christmas children and them, and I read the lot of them. I almost didn't sleep that whole week. My ma said if it didn't stop she'd strip the skin from my backside.'

'But you carried on?'

'How could I stop, Miss? The next week I asked the Madam to bring me another book by this Langenhoven. This time it was ghost stories, the most terrible things you ever heard of. I mean, you look at the world and you have no idea of what is hiding behind it all. I was almost too scared to go on, but I couldn't stop either. And by that time I was hooked. After that the Madam brought me all the other books, one by one, I think there were fourteen altogether. Some of them I couldn't understand head or tail of. They were just too damn difficult, no matter how hard I tried. I even copied whole pages of it out in an exercise book I bought with some money I got from selling a few of old Mr Joubert's ostrich eggs. That was a sinful thing to do, but the reading was more important. But on some of those books I had to give up. And there were others that was boring. I suppose I was just stupid, but I couldn't help it. So I went back to the stories. And the one I got to like best of all, in the end, was this *Loeloeraai*. Does Miss know it?'

'It's about this spaceman who comes down to earth and then takes Langenhoven and his family to the moon?'

'That's right. Can Miss imagine that? – he comes all the way from the planet Venus and he lands in the garden of an ordinary house in Oudtshoorn, right here in the Little Karoo. What makes it so special is that of all people he found Mr Langenhoven, who could write it all up so he could tell the whole world about it. I can't wait to read it again.'

It takes him another fifteen minutes to wind up, all the while caressing the book like a cat on his lap. By this time the accumulated fatigue sits heavily on my eyes; and leaving him to his Langenhoven I drag myself up the stairs to my room. If Ouma has another tale to tell tonight I'd better catch some sleep.

# 11

'This time we must go further back,' says Ouma Kristina.

'Why don't we start at the very beginning?'

'And what do you think is the very beginning?'

'The arrival of the first Müller at the Cape?' I suggest, 'Or the first Basson? Or the first Wepener?' I'm aware of the provocation in my answer; my only aim is to get her going.

'What have the Müllers got to do with it?' she asks, irritated. 'Let's keep the men out of this. They came with verse and chapter. Our story is different, it doesn't run in a straight line, as you should know by now. You and Anna come from Louisa, your mother; she from me. And I've already told you something about the ones who came before me.'

'Rachel. Petronella Wepener. Wilhelmina – what was her surname?'

'The surnames are of no importance. Those have all been added on, you can't rely on them. Every time a man becomes a father he's all too eager to get his surname into the picture. But how can he be sure that what he put in is the same as what comes out? We're the only ones who can tell for certain, and sometimes we prefer to keep it secret. It's us I'm talking about. The womenfolk. I told you it's my testament. And now that I'm getting close to death this is all that really matters.'

'How far back do you know the story?'

'Far enough. In our family we've been fortunate in always having storytellers around. You have me, I had Petronella, she had Wilhelmina, and so on, far back, all the way to the one who had two names, Kamma and Maria. That makes nine of us all told, if I remember well.'

'So Maria-Kamma was the first?'

'Of course not. Aren't you listening? No one knows where we began. We go back to the shadows. I think we've always been around. There are some old stories about a woman deep in the heart of Africa who came from a lake with a child on her back, driving a black cow before her. Or from a river, the snake-woman with the jewel on her forehead. Or from the sea. One day a small wave broke on the beach and left behind its foam and in the sun it turned into a woman. But that we don't know for sure and I prefer to talk only about the things I know.'

'This Maria you spoke about?'

'It's a useful beginning.'

'Was she the same Maria you told me about years ago?'

'The same.'

'But in those days you never told me she was family! I thought it was just a story.'

'You should have known better. Nothing is just a story.'

I need time to grasp what she has said; I'm beginning to catch a glimmer of why she felt this urge to bring me back to her. To foretell the past, the way prophets foretell the future.

'That's why you had to come home,' she says as if she's read my thoughts. 'To know where you come from. To have something you can take with you. Perhaps to help you understand.' Her crooked hand contracts into a small fist, then relaxes again.

'How long ago did this Maria live, Ouma?'

'How must I know? Does it matter? My memory doesn't depend on dates and places. If you really must know, I'd say it was somewhere up along the West coast, but far away, where it reaches the desert, where earth and sky meet. And long ago. In the time the first colonists began to travel up that way to barter and hunt and kill and lay waste, measuring out their farms further and further away from the Cape, you know what it was like, riding on horseback from sunrise to sunset, in a wide circle, returning to where they started from.'

Slowly she moves into the telling of her story. And I write as she speaks. This afternoon, after I'd been to see Jacob Bonthuys, I slept for an hour; I'm ready now.

Maria was a name the whites gave her, much later. In the beginning she was Kamma – the word the Khoikhoi, the People-of-People, had for water. That's why I believe that one way or another she must have been born from water, but we can't say for certain; it might have been one of her foremothers. The first that was known of her was when a group of trekking farmers reached her people's settlement. They'd come all the way from Cape Town, with wagons loaded to the canvas tops with beads and copper wire and brandy and tobacco and other stuff they used to barter for ostrich feathers and eggs, ivory, musk, tortoise shells, cured hides, honey, and of course for as many wide-horned cattle and fat-tailed sheep as possible. They were also eager for information about good grazing beyond the colony's frontiers, and rivers with a steady water supply.

On this trek trouble broke out between the Khoikhoi and the farmers – a heathen lot, if you ask me, with long beards and short tempers, always ready to pick a quarrel and use their fists or grab for their guns. You see, there were different tribes among the Khoikhoi, some of them well-disposed and rather spoiled by years of lucrative bartering with the people at the Cape; but the further you moved away from Cape Town, the more difficult it was to get along with them. And during the last month or so of the trek things had been going from bad to worse, because the tame Hottentots the boers had brought with them had begun to get fed up and were absconding at every opportunity; and the cattle were dying of thirst. That was more or less the stage they'd reached when they met a tribe that had never had any contact with whites before. Language served almost no purpose. Misunderstanding was rife.

As I have it, those Khoikhoi wanted the trekkers to remove themselves as soon as possible, which the boers refused to do before they'd acquired a large herd of cattle; and this the Khoikhoi were not interested in. To complicate things further several of the men, weary and frustrated with months of travelling, were getting randy, and the Khoikhoi were possessive of their womenfolk. With good reason too, as that tribe was reputed to have the most beautiful of all indigenous women.

And the most ravishing of these was the daughter of the headman. The very Kamma we spoke about. She was also known, for good reason, as The Little One Who Sings, but I have now forgotten the indigenous name for that. Kamma was a girl to whom praise songs had been composed, comparing her to *t'kamkhab* the new moon, or *khanoes* the morning star; a girl with the grace of a gazelle, lithe as a reed, all those poetic phrases, you name it. One can understand that the boers were hot for her, and day after day they pestered her father with ever more generous offers, but she was not for sale. Not only because the father was obstreperous, but because Kamma herself was too proud. The man who won her would have to be a prime specimen, not one of those unsavoury ruffians.

That charged the men up even more, and you can imagine the kind of dreams that were dreamed around the camp fire at night; it was said that for years afterwards nothing would grow on the spot. But in a dry land in summer, sooner or later, desire tends to burst into flame, and that was how the trouble started.

One evening a few of the boers abducted a woman from a hut which was set somewhat apart from the others. It also looked different. Whereas most consisted merely of a framework of branches covered with reed mats, this one was covered in skins. What the boers didn't know was that it was the taboo hut, the *t'nau* hut as it was called, that is the hut in which women were segregated for their monthly bleeding. That, of course, made matters even worse.

A short distance away from the huts was a small water course with dense vegetation along the banks. This water was one of the reasons why the boers had decided to make a halt there, and one of the reasons why the Khoikhoi didn't want them there. That was where the abductors had their rough way with the woman, after which they simply abandoned her.

During the night, crawling painfully up the slope, the woman found her way back to her people and told them what had happened. Some of the men wanted to attack the boers on the spot and massacre the lot of them, with their cattle and all. You must understand that it was a deadly sin to have intercourse with a woman who was *t'nau*. But others were more refined. They overpowered a boer who was sleeping a few yards away from the rest, dragged him to the very spot where the woman had been raped, and there deprived him of his manhood.

Now it was his turn to crawl back to the wagons, and at daybreak war was ready to break out. It began with angry posturing on both sides, until one of the boers got so carried away that he grabbed his gun and shot one of the Khoikhoi. Some of the others followed his example; but their comrades managed to subdue them. An armistice was observed, at least until nightfall. But in the dark – it was new moon and light was scant – the Khoikhoi crept to the wagons and set them alight. Two were destroyed totally, with three men inside.

The next day the furious negotiations began anew, difficult as it was with only signs to go on. The boers demanded compensation. But the Khoikhoi stood their ground: if compensation had to be paid, they should start with the woman who'd been raped. That could not readily be calculated in economic terms, but what about ten cattle and thirty sheep for a start? Then what about the castrated man, countered the boers? Twenty cattle and fifty sheep. The inevitable result was a new outbreak of violence, another five or six Khoikhoi killed. That night the boers stayed awake to avoid being surprised again. What they didn't know was that the Khoikhoi quietly poisoned the waterhole where the boers' cattle used to drink; the outcome was devastating. Moreover, the boer who'd had his candle snuffed blew out his brains with a pistol – not so much for the pain, it was said, as for the shame. Which immediately fired up the rest again.

If ever war was close, this was the day. *Kharab* they called it: blood-vengeance. And it was more than likely that the whole lot, boers and

177

Khoikhoi alike, would have been massacred right there had a woman not intervened. A very young woman, practically a child still, one might have thought at first sight as the Khoikhoi are so slight of build. This was none other than Kamma, the headman's daughter.

Don't expect me to repeat the whole argument, I wasn't there; but the point she made, as it was later handed down to her offspring, was that the men should stop before everybody, white and brown, man, woman and child, was killed. If it would prevent bloodshed, she was prepared to offer herself: the boers could choose anyone from their midst to *kwêkwa* with her, that's what the Khoikhoi called it; afterwards each group was to pack up and move as far away as possible from this place, the Khoikhoi to the north of the setting sun, the smooth-haired men, the *honkhoikwa*, to the south of the spot where it rose.

Consternation among the Khoikhoi. This was unheard of. Kamma was the pride of the land; her motion in the dark was like a string of glowing embers, a line of fireflies, like *tsaob*, which was what they called the Milky Way. To lose her would be worse than abandoning themselves to the fury of Gaunab, the evil god of the black heavens. But Kamma was adamant. Surely the life of the whole tribe was worth more than a single girl's maidenhead. The old women warned her to be careful: one doesn't speak of such things lightly; intercourse with a girl might lure the Dusky-feet, the *hei noen*, to the tribe. Look, there in the distance a *sarês* was churning up dust, a whirlwind, harbinger of death; and high overhead the death-bird was wheeling. After the women the old men took over. Then the young ones. But no one could persuade Kamma to change her mind. And already the boers were getting restless: further procrastination might lead to disaster.

Another commotion followed when the boers elected their man. He was Adam Oosthuizen, the tallest of them all, a man like a tree on the plains, with a shock of unkempt blond hair and a red beard, a giant who'd once strangled a leopard with his bare hands. No, no, said Kamma's father: this was murder. His daughter wouldn't survive the ordeal.

If Kamma could turn pale, she would have rivalled the moon in its last quarter. But she persisted. 'My word is my word,' she said, 'and if I can help to avert war, so be it.'

About the rest of that night Ouma Kristina is reticent. This is not the way I've come to know her. I remember a previous occasion when she told the story – admittedly it was after several glasses of jerepigo – and turned it into a spectacular account of the Khoikhoi and the boers forming a wide circle around the two, and the epic night that followed.

178

How the girl, for the sake of what Hollywood would call special effects, had caught a skin bag full of fireflies which she set free in little spurts, one or two at a time, as the night went by, greeted with enthusiastic applause by the spectators who took them for sparks. And how, at the final climax, she released the whole remaining bunch: it was pitch dark by then, and all one could see was this rain of sparks like when a great trunk erupts into flames – and how the assembled people broke into prolonged cheering for a performance the likes of which they had never seen.

Ouma has often gone right over the top with her stories. But tonight she is subdued. What she tells me this time is that when the huge boer took hold of Kamma she started singing to him, the songs she'd picked up from the tribe since childhood, the way other children collect coloured pebbles or birds' eggs or feathers. Songs about the Moon and the Dawn, about the Chameleon and the Hare and Death, about the Water Maidens and the Dusky-feet that walk in the dark, about the girl who made the Milky Way by emitting sparks from her sex when she made love with the great hunter-god Heitsi-Eibib, about Tsui-Goab the god of the red dawn. Adam Oosthuizen was so enchanted by the cadences of her voice that he fell asleep; and nothing further happened. But by then it was so dark that no one could see, and the only sound in the night was that of the Khoikhoi singing their saddest songs to Tsui-Goab to spare their child.

The following morning the girl returned to her people. But this was really the worst: they refused to take her back. Whatever had happened had not been her fault, they admitted; but having consorted with a stranger she was now, according to the customs of the tribe, *t'nau* for seven winters.

## 12

Was it with a kind of crude compassion, or from spite, or in a flush of triumph that the boers took Kamma back with them? One will never know. All she took with her was a couple of mahems, you know, those long-legged birds with the beautiful golden crowns. Sometimes they followed Adam Oosthuizen's wagon; otherwise they sat perched on either side of the girl, standing guard over her. She was seriously ill. The cause would depend on the version of her story one chooses: if Adam Oosthuizen had indeed had his way with her on that night of the flying sparks, she might have been suffering from the inevitable consequences; but her sickness might just as well have been one of the mind, following her rejection by the tribe. Whatever the cause, she was close to death, and the two mahems kept watch.

The trek made slow progress. The cattle that remained after the poisoning of the water had to keep up with the wagons, and the oxen were worn out. After a number of weeks the boers began to disperse. Those who'd come all the way from Cape Town continued on their journey. The rest, who had already measured out their farms along the coast, returned to their desolate abodes. Among those was Adam Oosthuizen; and he took Kamma with him.

If he'd had any inclination during the journey to use her again, her condition would have made it impossible. Once or twice in fact she was so bad that they had her taken from the wagon to leave her body behind on the veld; and high up in the sky, drained of colour and curdled like sour milk, the vultures were making their clairvoyant loops.

But if they were, then this time they were mistaken. With her thin arms Kamma kept hold of the legs of the man who tried to get rid of her; it was impossible to shake her off. Like dung to a veldskoen she clung. And the mahems would turn on him too; and out of the clear sky other birds would make their appearance – hawks, sparrowhawks, falcons, peregrines, even eagles of various kinds, and secretary birds – diving down to the wagons and causing such havoc that Adam was forced to give up and take her all the way back to the farm with him. That might have been on the banks of the Olifants River, but don't take my word for it.

It was a complicated family Adam Oosthuizen took the girl back to. He had a wife and something like thirteen children, but there were no strict demarcations between the generations. He couldn't read, which made it easier to get along with the Word of God. While the old State Bible, inherited from his ancestors or his wife's, lay holier than thou on a rough chest in the voorhuis, the brass clasps neatly closed on the dark brown leather binding, Adam visited his daughters as regularly and as enthusiastically as he did his wife. Which wasn't all that unusual in those days: according to one tradition Adam himself was his oldest sister's son. Everybody had something going with everybody else, all in the family; no wonder that some of his children were beginning to show the consequences. One more generation like that and they might start walking on all fours again. So what? Those were times when a man's only wealth was land and cattle, perhaps a field of wheat along a river; this required hands, and it was cheaper and more reliable to produce these from one's loins than to buy or hire them.

Kamma was first lodged in a reed hut with the labourers, where the women tended her. No one really expected her to survive. But thanks to the stomach contents of a steenbok and still-warm musk-cat skins, to seven ticks in sheep's fat, to bitter roots and bulbs, to a pinch of ground rhino horn and the sun-dried eyes of a jacopever bird, the chopped hind leg of a red-winged male grasshopper and three drops of blood from the comb of a black rooster, to a newly born striped fieldmouse swallowed whole, to the urine of rock-rabbits and the uterus of a pregnant porcupine, they saved her life.

As soon as she was back on her feet and more or less in shape she was given work on the farm, herding the sheep. In the beginning she was sent out with Adam's oldest son, then with the others, but that was asking for trouble; because the brothers all had their father's disposition, and Kamma was a winsome girl, all the more irresistible to the men for going about as naked as my finger, except for a minuscule apron. In a way she was even more beautiful than before and her habit of singing her songs all day long was enough to turn a man's head. But all to no avail, as far as the sons were concerned. Not because of anything she did to prevent them: she never acted in a way which could bring her trouble. Every time it was pure coincidence. That, at least, was what it looked like. Until one started adding it all up.

The oldest son was the first to try. Right there in the veld where he was overcome by his desire. But she played the fool with him, luring him this way and that, dancing across the plain, singing all the time, until she reached a large flat-topped anthill where she lay down. There the large black ants known with good reason as ball-biters set to work on him and sent him home hobbling, with legs wide apart; while not a single ant attacked her. The second time, with the same pigheaded man, it was a billygoat that charged him from behind just as he was on his knees, preparing to enter her. He was sent tumbling through the air, landing three yards beyond Kamma, in a porcupine hole where the animal attacked him so viciously that for a month he didn't know whether he was coming or going. The third time it was a ringneck adder that bit him on the backside just as he was aiming to take the plunge. And that was the end of the poor bastard.

The second brother was given an early warning when soon after the funeral of the first, as he was crouching on his knees in front of the prostrate singing girl, a lammergeyer passing high overhead dropped a tortoise on his head. The second time, barely a month later, a rabid meerkat sank its teeth into the youngsters member at the crucial moment and refused to let go. With the meerkat still dangling in front of him, and followed by the girl who was singing a song she'd made up the previous day about a man and a meerkat, he stumbled home. Three days later, by way of precaution, a new grave was dug in the backyard, but in the nick of time he was saved by a concoction Kamma had brewed. The youngster never went out with the sheep again, and just as well.

The third brother was still quite young and less impetuous than the others, but the girl's songs drove him mad with lust. A long white thorn lodged inexplicably in his left testicle soon put an end to that.

The fourth – but by this time the picture should be clear. Henceforth Kamma herded the sheep on her own. But for someone like her, who loved to have an audience for the stories she sang, it wasn't much of a life. And tending a flock of sheep hardly presented a challenge. So she soon took to leaving the sheep to the care of her mahems and a couple of secretary birds that sometimes came to keep her company, or to a lynx she had befriended. Once she invited a leopard, but that didn't work out all that well and it earned her a thrashing when she came home missing three of her flock. Adam Oosthuizen had a hard hand with the sjambok he'd made himself, so he bragged, from the penis of a buffalo. After that, to save her skin, she changed the sheep into stones when she felt like wandering about on her own.

There wasn't an animal or a bird on those plains she did not speak to. In her stories she could mimic the songs of birds so perfectly that one couldn't tell the difference: the cry of a kiewiet or a kelkiewyn, the calls of finches and starlings and bokmakieries, the shrieks of hawks or mountain eagles, the twitterings of guinea-fowl or partridges, the maniacal laughter of the katlagter. She could spend whole days amusing herself in this way, and large swarms of birds would turn and tumble in the sky about her. But she spoke to the animals too and engaged in endless conversation with jackals and meerkats and lynxes and wild cats. She certainly had a way with languages; and in the end it was her downfall.

# 13

After some time – a month or months, or years, what's the difference? – Adam Oosthuizen had her brought back to the farmyard, and into his home. That must have been his design all along. Because somewhere in his thick Cro-Magnon skull the memory of a distant night of fireflies and stars had lodged; he was to remember it to the day of his death, and maybe afterwards as well.

Many times Adam went out to the veld to spy on her from a distance, her long-legged gait, the enticing rhythm of the small apron that danced at the meeting of her thighs, everything that tends to catch a man's eye and mind. She must have been aware of his presence, but she never betrayed that knowledge by any sign; and he was hesitant to go closer, no doubt expecting her to dart off to the horizon like a duiker the moment she saw him coming. So he waited for her, until at last he felt she was tame enought to be brought inside to the hearth of the house that had begun as a wretched little one-room shack of wattle and daub, gradually expanding in all directions like a sociable weaver's nest to accommodate the increasing number of offspring. Once inside, Kamma had to exchange her skin apron for a dress. This took a considerable amount of coaxing and several thrashings, but gradually she not only became used to it but learned to wear it with a certain grace. But no fire or brimstone could persuade her to wear shoes.

Whether Adam's wife Johanna had become too worn out to object, or whether she really had no inkling, is impossible to tell; but not only did she accept Kamma's presence, she actually became fond of the girl; and between her and her daughters they began to teach her the skills a young woman ought to know. Sewing and darning, making moleskin clothes, rudimentary cooking. Even a smattering of reading from the State Bible. Adam and his sons didn't care about learning; on the rare occasions when they had to sign a document at the Cape to confirm a birth or death, a spidery cross sufficed. But the daughters were expected to read; and sometimes of an evening they would sing a hymn, so they enjoyed drawing Kamma into that. (Her own click songs were much too intricate for them.) In due course she became so fluent that on one of the family's annual trips to Cape Town she was taken along and baptised in the church. From then on she was Maria, no longer Kamma.

It was a whole new way of life she had to adapt to. Even the food was different: instead of the veld food she'd grown up with – tsamma melons and kambro roots, flying ants and partridge or ostrich eggs, locusts, sour milk, honey, things like that – she now shared the Oosthuizens' meals of sour bread baked in an anthill and soaked in milk, pumpkin, sweet potatoes, crushed wheat. The only item that appeared on both menus, only much more copiously on that of the Oosthuizens, was meat, whether of goat or sheep or cattle, or venison, guinea-fowl, pheasant, partridge. Most difficult of all to get used to was the routine of regular meals, morning, noon and night. But Maria proved to be an astute learner, and within a few months one would have thought that she'd grown up in a house.

Only one object in the house never ceased to mystify her, and that was the single mirror in the voorhuis. Johanna had inherited it from her mother, who'd brought it from Holland; and she'd refused to part with it, even on the interminable honeymoon voyage from Cape Town all the way up the West coast. Now it was hanging on the crudely whitewashed wall, the only ornamental object in the house. The first time Maria walked past it she stopped in her tracks, cautiously retraced her steps, and took another look; she turned her head sideways and saw the person on the wall imitate her; then put out her tongue, to find that gesture, too, repeated; she called upon the great hunter-god Heitsi-Eibib and ran for her life. It was dark when they finally brought her back from the veld, and then she refused to cross the threshold into the house.

It was days before she could be coaxed inside again. This time she crept up to the mirror very cautiously, sidling along the wall with her back pressed against it; standing next to it she took the precaution of first pulling the heavy mirror a few inches away from the wall to peep behind it. But there was nothing, only the roughcast whitewashed mud surface. That reassured her. Her body still pressed against the wall for security, she slowly moved her head to the edge of the frame and then very quickly peered round it. And once again called on Heitsi-Eibib as she took to her heels. At the front door she collided heavily with Adam Oosthuizen who just happened to be on his way inside.

He gave her a backhanded cuff that sent her sprawling against the opposite wall. For several minutes Maria remained there, huddled in a small bundle, clutching her knees and uttering small whimpering sounds which brought back tempestuous memories to Adam's mind.

'What the hell is up with you?' he asked, not too angrily.

She buried her head more deeply in her arms.

'Maria, I'm talking to you!'

This time she made a half-hearted gesture with one hand, still without daring to look up.

It took Adam Oosthuizen a while to catch on. Then, guffawing from his guts, he picked her up in one hand and carried her across the dung floor to the mirror, forcing her forehead against its cool smooth surface.

184

With an anguished cry she tried to disengage herself, but she was helpless in Adam's mighty grip. She opened her eyes, and stared in disbelief.

'*Ammase!*' she gasped. Which, translated, was a crude variant of 'Good heavens!'

What she saw in front of her was not only the strange young ghost-woman she'd seen before, but also Adam Oosthuizen's familiar broad face framed in blond hair and red beard. You must remember that she'd never seen herself before; but she was quick-witted enough to grasp that the face beside Adam Oosthuizen's heathen head could only be hers. Still disembodied, only head and shoulders; but during the next few days she discovered that the rest could be discerned as well, provided one came close enough and then looked down. From time to time she still checked behind it, just to make sure; and she never disgraced herself again in front of others. But she never became entirely at ease with the mirror.

At the same time she was too fascinated to stay away. She could be so absorbed in the mirror that she'd forget all about her duties, which would inevitably result in punishment. She also brought her birds into the house to show them the miracle – at first it was only the mahems, but soon all the others came too, which necessitated quite drastic cleaning up afterwards.

One day the mirror disappeared. Johanna was frantic; and there was only one suspect. It took another flogging, poor thing, before Maria took them to where she'd hidden it in a hollow anthill. Yet that very night, after the punishment, the mirror went missing again. This time it was found in one of the many added rooms – the one Adam Oosthuizen had set aside for his own use to fulfil his patriarchal obligations towards wife and daughters. Curled up in front of the mirror, her body still racked by sobs from time to time, was Maria; and this time Adam let her be and instructed the rest of the family to keep away too. Later that night he went to the room to comfort Maria in his own manner. It was the first time since Maria had been brought into the house that he'd done it openly. Soon it became a habit. And the family dutifully acquiesced in the inevitable. For some of the daughters, of whom five happened to be pregnant at the same time, it might even have come as a relief.

# 14

One day a large group of farmers from the Stellenbosch region visited the farm with their fleet of wagons on a bartering trip inland. They knew that Adam had travelled that way before and invited him to accompany them as their guide. Annoyed by a houseful of babies and with ants in his arse from having been confined in one place for too long, Adam was more than willing. And with shrewd foresight he took Maria along too. She, in turn, refused to budge without her mirror. This sent poor Johanna into such a rage that she had a stroke which paralysed one side of her body. She could never close her left eye again. In an unsettling stare it remained open night and day, missing nothing. During the day it was blood-red, and at night, people said, it glowed in the dark as if it was lit up from inside. No wonder that Adam Oosthuizen was relieved to leave his wife to the care of his many daughters while he took his sons along with him.

Hunting and bartering as they went, the group of trekkers moved ever deeper inland. Maria behaved herself very well. But once they'd crossed the Gariep, she unceremoniously stripped off her demure dress and reverted to wearing only the minuscule apron of long ago. Adam remonstrated with her, not because it displeased him, but because of the way the other men looked at her. However, no one ever dared to go beyond looking, they were all too scared of the giant.

In due course they reached frontline settlements of the Khoikhoi. Strange, distant tribes who had never encountered whites before and spoke no comprehensible tongue. That was where Adam's design in bringing the young woman along became clear. Even the boers who had resented her presence (for whatever obscure and troubling reasons) discovered that she was worth more than coral or rubies or whatever it was the wise Solomon had once spoken about. Khoikhoi who at first sight appeared sullen or suspicious changed their manner the moment Kamma – who had shed her white name together with her European dress – addressed them in their own tongue. Whether they all spoke the language with which she'd been brought up no one could tell; but she seemed at ease with any sound a tongue could produce. And it turned into the most lucrative bartering trip ever.

Kamma even went further than was strictly expected of her. If they reached a settlement where the cattle looked scrawny and not worth a second look, she would surreptitiously warn Adam, 'These sickly oxen and sheep were brought here to deceive you. The good cattle are all kept behind those hills until you're out of the way.'

Then Adam would send his men round the hills to drive out the good cattle. There were times when the discovery of their ruse so angered the Khoikhoi that they threatened to make war, only to be shot to pieces with the boers' guns. This ability to kill from a distance was enough to persuade the Khoikhoi that they were dealing with sorcerers; and in this way the boers got away with murder.

'How come you don't mind betraying your own people?' Adam once confronted Kamma.

'These are not my people.'

'They may not be your tribe, but they're Khoikhoi.'

She only shrugged. But when Adam persisted she explained, 'My people disowned me. After I'd *kwêkwa*'d with you they didn't want me back.' One would never have expected such a meagre body to harbour so great a grudge.

Adam never pressed her for more.

## 15

Upon their return there was a new grave behind the farmhouse. Johanna had passed away. At night the red eye still smouldered on the pillow of the bed she'd slept on; the rest of her was underground. Adam solved the problem by avoiding the room and moving in permanently with Maria. If his conscience felt uneasy it was amply outweighed by his elation at discovering that Maria was pregnant. The baby was due in midwinter, the seventh winter of her stay on the farm.

But in the late autumn, about two months before the baby was due, Maria disappeared. When they woke up one morning her chintz dress lay neatly folded in the kist in the voorhuis; and the mirror was missing from its peg.

Adam called up his host of sons and set out on horseback in search of her, each galloping off in a different direction. They searched all day, to the horizon and beyond, but there was no sign at all of her. She might just as well have changed into an anthill or a rock or a tree or a bird; and perhaps she had. Adam Oosthuizen was convinced that he'd lost her for good, and his mourning was fearsome to behold.

Yet six months later she was back, blithely wearing the small apron and carrying the mirror in her arms. Without saying a word to anyone she came past them all, went into the house, took her dress from the kist and put it on. The mirror was hung in its old place. Then, as if nothing had happened, she asked whether anybody wanted coffee.

Even Adam was so overwhelmed that it took days before he ventured to enquire about the child. Maria shrugged. And that was the only reply she ever gave.

From then on she made a habit of going away towards the end of every summer, sometimes pregnant, sometimes not; returning six months later all alone and as bare as my finger. Then she'd put on the dress that had been stowed in the kist, and resume her life among the Oosthuizens as if there had been no interruption at all.

And the mirror? As far as Adam could make out, after many interrogations, she'd taken it with her so that the Khoikhoi she encountered could be shown in it the reflection of the Oosthuizens who had adopted her. But whether it really worked that way remained a mystery. Certainly, when she tried to show Adam the reflections she'd brought back from the people she had been visiting there was nothing but his own face in the mirror.

The third or fourth time she returned – by then Adam Oosthuizen and his brood knew better than to ask any questions about her whereabouts – she brought a small band of Khoikhoi with her, loaded with elephant tusks, ostrich feathers, gazelle skins, tortoise shells and other wares. What was the meaning of this, asked Adam. This was a different tribe from any of those the boers had had dealings with before, Kamma explained. They had come for help. There had been war in the interior and all the tribe's cattle had been driven away by other people from far away. They wanted Adam to reclaim their property.

Adam Oosthuizen felt no inclination to get drawn into other people's quarrels. But Maria, still pale with the dust of her long walk, took him aside for a long and serious discussion. These were important people, she explained. If he could win them over to his side the whole interior would open up to him. He and his sons could accompany the tribe on a campaign against the malefactors, and this would make him the most important cattle farmer of the hinterland.

The next morning the Oosthuizen men set out with the Khoikhoi, accompanied by Kamma – since without her it would be impossible to make themselves understood to each other. Many evenings she spent with the Khoikhoi at their camp fire, and from a distance the Oosthuizens would watch and listen to her talking and revelling with them till the small hours. It killed Adam. He could swear she was colluding with the strangers. But whenever he tried to confront her, she would avoid the direct questions and assure him that the men were strangers to her too. Adam should stay out of it, she warned him, because it was important to retain the goodwill of the tribe.

Here one can turn a long trek into a short story. The journey ended in a battle in the land of the enemy Khoikhoi who naturally proved helpless against the gunpowder and bullets of their attackers. Two of the Oosthuizens were killed and a couple more wounded; but among the Khoikhoi few escaped unscathed. With a vast herd of captured cattle the victors returned to their own settlement, seven days from there, in a narrow kloof between tall outcrops of rock. There they rested for several days. The honey-beer flowed like water; below the moon at night there were celebrations that lasted until daybreak; everything was covered in dust.

After prolonged discussion the cattle were divided into two herds, one for the Khoikhoi, the other for the boers. The negotiations took a whole day; at sunset everybody was satisfied, and the Oosthuizens announced that they would be leaving at first light the following morning.

That night Kamma once again spent in celebration with her people – inasmuch as they were her people; but blood is thicker than water – while the Oosthuizens retired to have a good rest before their long journey. They awoke at daybreak from the unnatural silence surrounding them.

Can you believe it? There was no sign of the settlement in the kloof. Men, women, children, all gone. Not a hair or a turd left of cattle and sheep. Worst of all, as far as Adam Oosthuizen was concerned, was that most of the cattle allotted to his family – including by far the best animals – had disappeared as well.

He was all set to go in pursuit and reclaim what was his. After all the trouble, after months of trekking, of war, after losing two of his sons! But there were no tracks they could follow. He swore that Kamma was to blame; he was ready to murder her. Lodged in the recesses of his mind a dark suspicion had taken root that she was not to be trusted, that all that talk about having been rejected by her people had simply been part of an elaborate ruse to avenge herself on him for that unforgettable and terrible night of years ago. At the same time he was besotted with the woman. Certainly, for the time being, there was nothing he could do. He had the unnerving hunch that raising a finger against her would mean that he and his sons would never reach home again.

# 16

Barely a month later the farm was attacked, out of the blue, by what must have been a whole locust swarm of Khoikhoi, arriving on a moonlit night without making a sound, and disappearing again with every hoof of cattle the Oosthuizens possessed. No doubt about the identity of the raiders: they could only have been the recent enemy, probably in league with a host of other tribes, bent on avenging their defeat in the deep interior. This was exactly what Adam Oosthuizen had feared, and the reason why he hadn't wanted to get involved in the first place. Now he was as poor as Job, without a cob to scratch his arse. But he had no choice: it was clearly the will of God that he should go back into the land to avenge his male honour. And Kamma had to go with them as guide and interpreter, knowing the country as she did like the pale palm of her narrow brown hand.

Initially she was reluctant, but Adam had his ways of persuading the obstreperous. He and his sons rode down the coast, at least as far as Saldanha, rounding up all the boers they could find – most of them required little persuasion – and soon the awe-inspiring commando rode off to the north-west across the uninscribed plains.

Three more of Adam Oosthuizen's sons were buried in the hard land on that journey, as well as ten or twelve of the other farmers. This was no ordinary war, man to man, the Khoikhoi were much too sly for that. A sudden attack, an ambush, a nocturnal raid, luring them deeper and deeper into the wasteland. Worst of all was a skirmish one rainy day among bare mountains: Kamma had been sent out the previous day, as usual, to reconnoitre; and she'd come back with a bedraggled collection of Khoikhoi eager to make peace. The discussions were protracted for hours. Then the rain came down. And without warning the delegation grabbed their bows and arrows and kieries and attacked the unsuspecting commando. The boers instinctively reached for their guns, but these were useless in the rain, as if the Khoikhoi had known it in advance.

A bitter campaign followed, that lasted many months and wore out the men. But in the end law and order triumphed, when God is with you no one can withstand you; and at last the commando turned back, encumbered with enough cattle and sheep and ivory and feathers and hides to ensure a lifetime of prosperity.

Except that, less than a year later, while Maria was gone on one of her solitary wanderings, everything was taken once again.

This time, when Adam Oosthuizen saw her approaching from afar, he went out to meet her at the farmyard gate. Delighted as he was to see that reed-like figure with the dancing apron, with a shadow of finches overhead, there was a heaviness in his heart as well. He'd had time enough to think, something which in the best of circumstances did not come easily to him. But slowly, trickling through the dull grey folds of his brain, a lump of thought had coagulated: why had the raid happened while she'd been away? why was she the one who'd brought the first group of clients to the farm? how had the Khoikhoi known so accurately that the boers' ammunition would be useless in damp weather? why this? why that?

He didn't beat her. He merely blocked her way with his massive body and told her to go; for good. He couldn't trust her any more. He never wanted to see her again.

She was crying when she left.

She didn't speak a word. She couldn't. Her tongue had been cut out.

# 17

No one will ever know for sure. Was it Adam who'd done it, to punish her for her betrayal and ensure that she would never carry gossip to the Khoikhoi again? Or was she already tongueless by the time she arrived at the gate – in which case the Khoikhoi would have been the perpetrators, to prevent her telling the whites their secrets and the location of their herds and watering places?

She herself couldn't tell. So we shall never have an answer: had she devoted her whole life to avenging herself on the Khoikhoi for rejecting her? Or on the boers for what Adam Oosthuizen had done to her?

Not that this was the end of the story yet.

Adam Oosthuizen stood looking after her until she'd disappeared in the distance; then, with hanging shoulders and heavy tread he went back home. As he came past the mirror in the voorhuis he stopped. What he saw there was, surely, impossible. Yet there it was: Maria's face. Kamma's. Not clear and sharp like his own, but a vague smudge, as if she was looking at him from very far away, like a face seen under water, but unmistakably hers.

With a groan he took the mirror from the wall and carried it to the outer room where he'd used to lie with her. More and more, as the months dragged by, he withdrew into that small room. Surly and glowering, Adam Oosthuizen isolated himself from his brood, dangerous as a lone elephant bull. He refused to speak to anyone.

At last loneliness got the better of him. He brought out the strongest ox from his kraal – by that time his sons had acquired a small new herd – and rode off into the wide land. In a large knapsack he'd made himself from well-cured wildebeest hide he carried the mirror. As time went by the image began to fade, but it was still visible. And when he stopped at night to rest, he'd take it out to stare at her face. He held long conversations with her. But of course she never spoke back.

Whenever he reached a Khoikhoi settlement he enquired about her, the thin young woman who moved like a shadow across the veld. And when the people couldn't understand he took the mirror from his knapsack to show them her image. Invariably it caused pandemonium. But curiosity tended to get the upper hand as the frightened people thronged for a closer look. In the end, however, they all shook their heads and indicated that they knew nothing about her at all.

He must have searched for years. Gradually he turned grey, but that might have been from suffering; and his body, once as proud and tall as a tree, became gnarled and shrunken like driftwood. On and on he travelled on the back of his ox, knapsack on his shoulder, enquiring as he went. But no one would help him.

Except, one day, a honey-bird. Exhausted with hunger, he'd been following the little creature for a day. It had come upon him when he'd been sitting in a spot of shade staring at the remains of that faded image in his mirror; he'd heard the excited twittering, looked up, saw the bird, then started following it. What he hadn't realised, of course, was that the bird had recognised the image. And so the journey brought Adam, not to a hoard of honey, but to a straggling group of Khoikhoi huts.

From a distance he recognised her. And when he saw the children with her – a motley group they were, but the oldest girl, who must have been thirteen or fourteen years old, was startlingly fair – he immediately realised that they were hers: the children of which she'd deprived him year after year.

According to the story he started crying into his unkempt beard; but all he could do to express his feelings was to raise high above his head his sjambok, that vicious buffalo penis with which he'd ruled his world, as he uttered a bellow like the sound of a wounded bull. How could anyone tell if it was an expression of rage or delight?

Surrounded by her children, Kamma jumped to her feet when she heard that roar. She recognised him and started to tremble. She couldn't call out to warn the people as she had, of course, no tongue. The only sound she uttered was an anxious moan.

And then, all of a sudden, she changed into a tree, a small thorn tree, with ample space for birds in her branches, and shadow below for her two mahems.

Adam raced towards her as fast as he could. Beside himself, and most likely without realising what he was doing, he started flagellating the tree with his sjambok. The tree began to cry, its tears running down the trunk like gum. Then all the birds in the wide-spread branches started flapping their wings, and in front of Adam's eyes they flew off with the tree, past the horizon, gone; the two mahems followed on the ground, racing with their spindly legs. And Adam, too, followed, on the back of his ox, but he didn't get very far.

His skeleton was found many years later, bleached on the plains. It was only through the mirror in his knapsack that he could be identified.

And then an elephant came and blew the story away.

# FOUR

## *The Coffin*

**I**

Adrift in the present. Thoughts on waking: how disconcerting to discover that there is nothing real about the present, that it can be grasped only after it has already slid into the past. From moment to moment it eludes me. I write: I get up, I look through the window, the shadows of clouds move across the landscape. But what I ought by rights to be writing is: I write that I get up, look through the window; I write that the shadows of clouds move across the landscape, and even as I write it is no more. Sooner or later I shall write: Ouma is dying – but she will already be dead. I write: Today we'll have to bring the coffin down. I really don't like the idea at all, but for once there may be some practical sense in Ouma's instruction, not mere whimsy. If there is anything to be done to make the coffin serviceable again after so many years, today is as good a time to start as any.

It is Sunday. There will be fewer demands from the outside world. (I prefer not to think about tomorrow yet, in case, as has happened so often, I'm disappointed. So I shall write down Sandile's name, but not dwell on it.) It is already a week since I arrived. So much has happened; nothing has happened. An existence in suspense, somehow, in which, curiously, Ouma's stories seem almost more real than the events surrounding me – even though I'm still not altogether sure why she has felt this urgency to tell all before she dies. At the same time I cannot ask; she will not answer, this has always been her way. The cryptic remark, the look askance, the indulgent little smile. *You'll get there; don't worry, you'll get there.* Before she retreats into her inner desert again, that place of moving dunes that shift position from one day to the next, ceaselessly rewriting their landscape and redefining their space.

Before I shower I go through yesterday's clothes, a quick check on each garment to decide which to fold and stow, which to discard (I must find time for doing some washing today). I presume I do it every day, unconsciously, second nature, a measure not so much of hygiene as of atavistic animality; but this morning I suddenly catch myself in the act of holding up panties, a bra, a shirt, a sock against the light, then sniffing it. What surprises me is not the recovery of a faded yesterday – lotion, eau de toilette, deodorant, body, me – but the *fact* of doing it, the need it suggests of having to check on myself like this, reassure myself, acknowledge my physicality, locating myself in time, in space. The discovery is disturbing (why?), and almost irritably I cut short the sorting.

After my shower I choose a dress for today. Even though I've brought only some very basic clothes along, it takes a while. The sense of colour, texture, smell, establishing relationships. Back home, in London, Michael invariably watched, from the bed or the bathroom door, as I went through these processes of selection in which I tended to lose myself – a ritual which, depending on his mood, would either amuse, or arouse, or exasperate him; yet it was not, or only rarely, a show put on for his benefit. Much more important was the need to find, to appropriate, a self for the day, going through elaborate motions to work my way through open possibilities until something gelled and the day became, if not predictable, at least more graspable. This day I find difficult to assess, to move towards. My period has begun, catching me, as usual, unawares (I must have a tampon or two, somewhere, but a remedy will have to be found before long). Also, it is Sunday, a day on which I always feel somewhat displaced, and today it is worse because I also have to please Anna who has invited me to lunch: I do not relish the prospect, especially not with Casper there, but I owe it to her.

Having laid out the dress on the bed I put on the gown Anna has insisted on lending me and first set out on a morning round, checking on Ouma (who is emerging, with an unnerving series of muffled moans and gasps, from sleep), discussing the prognosis with the nurse (who appears in a hurry to clear her preliminary duties out of the way so that she can return to her glossies), tracking down Trui to plot the broad outlines of the day, even descending to the cellar to make sure Jacob Bonthuys and Langenhoven have had a satisfactory night (Langenhoven seems in good form, but Jacob Bonthuys looks feverish and weak). At last I return to the bedroom, where I decide against the dress laid out in favour of a long skirt and blouse, which I put on briskly and with a feeling of efficiency.

There is considerable resistance to overcome, I find, when after breakfast (I'm beginning to feel bloated from Trui's elaborate farm breakfasts; I shall have to persuade her, without hurting her feelings, to reduce these to the single slice of bread and the fruit I've become used to) I muster the available forces to fetch the coffin upstairs. The nurse, justifiably, finds the exercise premature and in bad taste. Trui refuses point blank. 'That's a second-hand thing, Kristien. It's bad luck.' Even the reminder that it is Ouma's own wish will not sway her, and the way in which she sets about scrubbing the kitchen floor, which I saw her do half an hour ago, makes it clear that her mind is made up. This leaves Jeremiah and Jonnie; and perhaps the tone of voice in which I round them up – resolved to lug the bloody thing down the stairs myself if they refuse – does the trick. Having first emptied it of its mouldy contents, and with some cautious footwork down the narrow unsteady steps from the attic, we carry the heavy dust-covered coffin to Ouma's room where I spend an hour dusting, wiping and polishing it. The nurse has moved her chair to the window, ostensibly for more light on her lurid reading matter, but really, I'm convinced, to distance herself more visibly from my activity. Ouma, on the other hand, is watching contentedly, even avidly.

In spite of scuff marks and scratches and even burns (in our childhood we surmised the coffin had been retrieved from hell), in spite of dents and chips of indecipherable origin, the wood begins to show up beautifully, with the patina of great age. But the lining is a different story. The silk has decayed and turned yellow; it is torn and frayed in places, and irreparably stained, not just by the feathers and dried fruit and the bird and bat droppings it has housed for what must be more than a hundred years, but by mud and water and mould, and, who knows, blood, that have marked it like a dirtier version of the Turin Shroud.

'The others were in better condition,' I say. 'What's happened to them?'

'People have a habit of dying. I helped out when I could. Your mother got the last one.' At the window the nurse sniffs pointedly.

'When we were small you told us that this one was second-hand.'

'Yes.' A brief clutching motion of her hand. Then it relaxes again.

'Is it?' I prod her. The nurse is pretending not to listen, but I can practically see her pointed ears prick up.

'Does it matter?' asks Ouma. An almost inaudible chuckle. 'I used to enjoy getting news of everyone who died,' she goes on, clearly not concerned with whether the connection makes sense or not. 'It's one of the few remaining satisfactions when one gets old. Especially when the people who die are younger than yourself. But of course it catches up with one, sooner or later. That's why I kept this coffin out.'

I point at the inside. 'We'll have to rip all this out and make a new lining.'

Ouma Kristina shakes her head. 'The stains are all right, I don't mind. Just dust it properly, I don't want to start sneezing when I get to the Throne: I might miss some of the more interesting remarks.'

The nurse shakes her magazine in disapproval, flipping over a page so energetically that it tears. Briefly, as if it's all my fault, she glares at me over her shoulder.

'The main thing is that it is comfortable,' says Ouma. 'It's a long sleep.'

I move my hand over the stuffed bottom of the coffin. 'It's soft enough. A bit lumpy.'

'Try it,' she says quietly. There is no mistaking what she means.

The nurse raises her head.

'I don't think I can,' I protest weakly.

'Of course you can. You kids did it all the time when you were small.'

'That was different. Those were games.'

A click of her tongue; I can't make out whether it is meant to convey annoyance or commiseration. 'Come on, get in,' she says.

I kick off my shoes, take a deep breath, then stretch myself out in the coffin, the way we used to do, taking turns, in those summer holidays when death was still remote, unreal, the underbelly of our games and stories. It was the best of hiding places. We had nocturnal contests to see who could last longest with the lid closed. Once some of the older cousins forgot about me; I was already limp when I was retrieved the following day. That should have cured me, but it didn't. This, though, is different; a game that is suddenly no longer a game.

'Well?' asks Ouma.

'Not too bad. But it's a tight fit.'

'I don't need much space.'

This is how the doctor finds us. I become aware of him when he is already standing in the door, staring down at me in utter disgust. He is not, I have already discovered, the most humorous of men.

The nurse has risen, ready to deny guilt and apportion blame.

'Miss Müller!' A voice from my youth; all those voices: Father, teachers, the rector, men. 'What in the name of God are you doing there?'

'She's just trying it out for me,' says Ouma Kristina from the bed, her tone that of a cajoling girl, grotesquely unsuited to her wasted appearance. Even so, fleetingly, I realise how irresistible she must have been in her bloom.

Red-faced, and not very elegantly, but defiant, I disengage myself from the coffin.

He looks at me as if I'm a new and particularly virulent disease, then obviously decides to ignore me altogether as he advances towards the bed, stethoscope and briefcase in hand. 'And how are we this morning?'

'Preparing to meet our Maker,' says Ouma Kristina. 'But some of us still need more time from you.'

'Mrs Basson, really.' He looks at the nurse. 'Has she had a good night?'

She seems offended by his mistake. 'I'm a day nurse, doctor.'

'I gave her oxygen twice,' I say. 'She's comfortable. But I think the pain is still bad.'

He ignores me and bends over Ouma.

'I'd like to see the week out if I may,' says Ouma

'You really ought to go back to hospital, Mrs Basson.'

'You just do your best to see me through a few more days, doctor.'

He makes a sound of exasperation and motions to the nurse to give a hand. The bandaging has to be changed, which involves a painful sponging with Dettol, her blood pressure must be taken, her frightfully scorched body – a little flour-bag half-filled with brittle bones – swathed in new Betadine bandages. I approach to offer two more hands, but he studiously avoids me; in fact, he makes it clear that I am in the way. Annoyed, but not entirely without a sense of relief, I wait at the window, my back to them. I prefer not to see too much; what little dignity she has left deserves to be kept intact. But her small gasps and suppressed moans ache in my ears.

He gives her a morphine injection. Only when he picks up his bag again and prepares to leave does he address me again.

'Will you please see to it that this thing is removed as soon as possible?'

'This thing will stay exactly where it is,' says Ouma. 'It was brought here on my instructions. Kristien tried it out because I asked her to. And I want it there so I can look at it.'

'Mrs Basson, there will be a time for this.'

'No better time than right now, doctor. I'm not having old Piet Malan mucking around with my corpse.'

'He retired years ago, Mrs Basson,' he remonstrates in the long-suffering tone one uses only with the very young and the very old. 'His son has taken over the business. At any rate I fail to understand – '

'But he's still *there*,' she says calmly, 'waiting for me to go so he can bury me.'

'What earthly difference could that make to him?'

'More than you think, doctor. He does things to women's bodies.'

'Mrs Basson!' he exclaims, scandalised. 'Mr Malan is a highly respected member of the community.'

'Of course. That's why no one suspects him. But I won't have him near me when I die, so I'm taking precautions.'

'There are all kinds of arrangements we can make when the time comes.'

'I'll make my own arrangements while I still can.' She looks straight at him. 'And tomorrow, if I'm stronger, you can help Kristien to put me in the box. I want to get used to the feel of it.'

Poor man, he is now in the invidious position of having to appeal to me as an ally.

'Miss Müller, do you think you could persuade her to – ' He represses an expression of resentment as he takes me by the arm to continue the conversation outside. As we move towards the staircase he says, 'I may be mistaken, but I get the impression that you're aiding and abetting her in this outrageous business.'

'If it makes her happy, doctor, surely the best thing we can do is to play along.'

'But it's preposterous!'

'What if it is? She's dying. She needs every bit of indulgence we can offer her.'

'Well!' His mouth is set in a pout, like a prune.

'There is something else,' I say at the bottom of the stairs.

He looks warily at me.

'I have another patient for you. If you'll be so kind.'

## 2

In the early afternoon, after I've returned from the Sunday meal with Anna's family, I find Ouma awake and waiting for me.

The nurse, at the other side of the bed, makes a face. 'She doesn't want another injection, Miss. She says she wants to talk to you. I told her – '

'That's all right then. If you want to take a nap . . .'

I wouldn't have minded one myself. But Ouma is fidgety and anxious to talk. It's the coffin that has brought it on, I think. There are things she wants to clear up, she tells me.

'You've already cleared up so much,' I try to calm her down.

'I haven't even begun yet.' A weak but irritable gesture of her hand. 'So many things still to tell you, Kristien.'

'I'm ready for anything,' I say quietly.

'We never went to Baghdad, you know,' she says unexpectedly. 'I mean Jethro and I, when we ran away.'

'Really?' I pretend to be surprised. 'I thought every word was true.'

'We never got beyond Cape Town,' she says, as if she hasn't heard me. 'Stayed with old Moishe's relatives to start with, in Sea Point. But it was cramped, and they kept on nagging us about not being married. So we moved on. A small flat in Woodstock. Then a room in someone's backyard in Gardens. In the beginning it didn't matter, we were so in love. But soon it just wasn't fun any more. Our money ran out. Jethro found work in a bar for a while, I did some typing. But we weren't cut out for it. I could still take it if I had to, but he began to sulk. This was no life for an artist, he said. We started bickering and bitching. He was going out more and more, on his own, never telling me where he went, or when he'd be back. I began to suspect something. I could smell it on him when he came back. Then I discovered I was pregnant. He was out again, but I waited up to tell him. It was two or three o'clock before he came in. When I kissed him the smell was there again. I asked him what he'd been eating. He said crayfish. Where'd you find crayfish? I asked. And even while I was asking it I knew. And that was the end. The next day while he was out I took the last bit of money I'd saved from my job and walked all the way to the station and caught a train home.'

'And the little painting you brought back?'

'Bought it at the flea market on the Parade. I was never a painter.'

I bend over and press my lips against her burning forehead. I don't want her to discover that I'm crying. But I've never been able to hide anything from her; and from the way she gently pats my cheek I know she knows.

'For heaven's sake, sit down,' she says brusquely. 'I have no wish to be drowned at my age. And there is business to attend to.'

'Tell me,' I say, recovering my composure as best I can.

'This place,' she says. 'It's been built around so many wrongs. You must help me sort it out.'

'How, Ouma?'

'My testament.'

'But I thought that was all done long ago?'

'I want to make sure. I don't want Casper to take over the farm.'

'What about Anna?'

'Anna is well looked after.'

'Who then?'

'You, of course.'

'I can't inherit this place, Ouma.'

'I want you to.'

'That's not enough reason.'

'For me it is. You've come back and you must have it.'

'I only came back because – ' Now, of course, I cannot say it. I rearrange my thoughts. 'My life is in England, Ouma. I'm going back soon.'

'That's what you think.'

'Ouma, please. I won't be persuaded. It's useless even to try.'

'One doesn't contradict the dead and the dying, Kristien.'

'I won't be blackmailed either, Ouma.' Impetuously I rush past all hovering angels. 'Besides, there are others who deserve this much more than I do.'

'Like who?'

'Like Trui.' It is the first thought that comes into my head; but it makes sense. 'She's family, after all.'

She looks at me, her eyes inscrutable.

'That is, if what you told was the truth.'

In her infuriating but characteristic way she simply drops the subject. 'And you must see to it that the undertaker, old Piet Malan, the turd, doesn't come near me.'

'Why are you so set against him?'

'That man – !' For a moment I am worried that she is getting too upset; then she relaxes and gives a dry chuckle. 'You know, sixty years ago that little man was all over me. Wanted to get into my pants.'

'But Ouma – !'

'Mind you, he was quite good-looking then. Half my age, of course. But at forty I was in my prime, even if I say so myself. Now if he'd just come to me to try his luck like an honourable man I might have let him.' A pause. 'But you know what? He tried to blackmail me into sleeping with him.'

'But why – ? How – ?'

'He'd found out – about my children. Their fathers. You know? One

204

of them had told him. The bastard. You just can't trust men, can you? So young Piet Malan thought he could try his luck too. I kicked him out of here, tail between his legs. And you know what he said then? "Kristina, I'm going to possess that body of yours even if I have to wait a hundred years." I swear he became an undertaker just for that. And he has a dirty habit of visiting all his prospective customers on New Year's Eve, every year, regular as clockwork. Some people find it reassuring. Looked after, someone caring about them, you know. But I've never allowed him to set foot in here. Even so, for the last twenty years he's been turning up at the front door every year, thirty-first of December, you could count on it. Just looking at me – a kind of measuring look, as if to say, "Five foot four" – and then leaving again. So how can I trust myself to those clammy hands of his?'

'But Ouma, he must be almost ninety himself.' I dare not let her discover how appalled I am.

'So what? He can wait. And he will, I swear. That's why I want you to promise me he won't be allowed to set foot on this farm.'

'You can count on that,' I say grimly. 'But what I'd like to know – '

'That's all right then,' she interrupts. 'But there are other things too.'

'What kind of things, Ouma?'

'Things I don't want people to find here when I'm dead. I want you to destroy them.'

'Where are they? What are they?'

'Will you promise?'

'I have to know first.'

'Then I won't tell you.' Like an ancient wizened naughty child she stares at me.

I sigh. 'All right.'

'Put your hand between your legs and swear.'

'Ouma!'

'That's all we have to swear by, child.'

Feeling my face flush, more in anger than embarrassment, I do as she tells me.

'It's on the floor above. There's a room off the small passage that leads to the red bedroom where your parents used to sleep. The green door. There's a picture of the Broad and Narrow Ways beside it.'

'The one with God's eye on it? The door that was always locked?'

'So you know it.'

'I can't tell you how many hours I used to spend as a child, every single holiday, trying to get in. No key would fit it.' Once I even tried to reach it from the outside, lowering myself from the attic with two sheets tied together; but the shutters wouldn't budge. On one occasion I took a stepladder upstairs, and a torch, to peep through the fanlight above the door in the passage, but all I could make out was stacks and stacks of indefinable bulky objects, obscured by dust. And when I carried the ladder downstairs again I bumped against a huge Chinese vase in a niche off the landing, and the thrashing I got from Father was enough to dampen even my spirits.

'The key is behind the picture, the upper right-hand corner. There's a small sliding lid in the frame.'

'But what's in the room?'

'My life,' she says, not melodramatically at all, but quite casually, as one might say, 'A bunch of feathers.'

'Shall I go now?' I propose eagerly.

'No, later. I don't want to know about it when you go. Besides, there's a story I want to tell you.' Her eyes turn towards the coffin where a number of owls have roosted while I was away. They stare at us in silent complicity.

'Who is it this time?'

'The woman Samuel,' she says.

# 3

The woman Samuel. Strange family she married into. She was the mother of the one known as the Fat Woman of the Transvaal. Samuel was one of eighteen children, all of whom survived. Don't pull such a face, it was true. And nothing exceptional either. What made it unusual was that all eighteen children, eleven sons and seven daughters, had the same name. Samuel. And so Samuel was also called Samuel.

You may well wonder why. The reason was pretty obvious. It was the father's idea, of course. The family's surname in those days was Grobler. The father was called Bart, the first in God knows how many generations of Groblers who wasn't called Samuel. It was a disgrace to the clan, because the family name had to be Samuel Grobler, and it was to be transmitted from father to son forever, apparently in terms of a covenant made with God after the first Samuel Grobler had singlehandedly cornered a tribe of San people in a cave and wiped them all out after they had killed one of his children. His idea of an eye for an eye. That child of his must have had a hell of a lot of eyes, but that is neither here nor there. Anyway, this Samuel took an oath on the Bible that until the end of time the victory of Good over Evil – which must have been how he saw it, being only a man – would be commemorated by a Samuel in the family. But when it came to the third or fourth generation the eldest son, christened Samuel, was killed by a puffadder at the age of three.

The damage was not irreparable, for the godfearing parents duly christened their next son Samuel too in order to keep the covenant. But Samuel the Second died of croup before his first birthday. Then followed three daughters; and the father was secretly beginning to suspect God of being deliberately contrary, when at last another son was born, Samuel the Third. Blessed of the Lord, this one grew up a strong and healthy boy.

The family increased with many other sons and daughters, each with a name from the Bible, as was only good and proper, but by the time Samuel the Third was sixteen and started thinking of taking a wife, he was slaughtered in the veld by a Philistine. Heaven knows what really happened, but family tradition has it that the attacker was a Philistine, and tradition has a way of prevailing. By that time father Samuel's wife was past her fertile years and there was no opportunity of replacing the dear departed. God refused to hearken unto their prayers as he'd done once before, in the Old Testament, with Abraham's wife Sarah. Father Samuel diligently did whatever he could, taking concubines whom he successively christened Billah and Silpah and Orpa and Hagar and what have you before going in unto them, but no new little Samuel saw the light of day. History has it that as he grew more desperate he started taking whatever came to hand, even goats and sheep and wild melons, truly a man of the faith; but none of their offspring could be christened Samuel. And at the time of his death the oldest surviving son, who was our Bart, had to take over in shame and disgrace.

His wife was Lottie, the Shadow Woman. We'll come to her later. She was perennially pregnant, because if there was one thought that possessed Bart it was to restore the covenant his ancestors had made with the Lord and to produce another Samuel to resume the line. The sort of thing a man regards as important. So every single one of those children was christened Samuel the moment it entered this stern world of blood and tears. Just to make sure. And not one of them died. Once there were four of them in a single go. There was a very experienced old midwife on duty that night, these things always happen at night, it must be part of God's design to make life difficult for a woman, to avenge the eating of that original apple that turned out to be a fig; so where was I? The midwife. She caught the first one while Bart was holding the lantern; and she was still in the process of washing it when the second made its appearance. Before she had finished with this one, Bart – still holding the lantern aloft – saw the third baby coming. And true's God, just as the midwife was slapping the first scream from number three's lungs, Bart called out, 'Oh my God, Tant Sysie, hurry up, there's another one.' As the old woman made a dash for it, just in time, she snarled at Bart, 'Take away that bloody lantern, I think they're drawn by the light.'

All of this to make you understand that the family prospered. Eighteen Samuels all told. Then Lottie couldn't take it any more; and Bart began to feel more at ease.

Nicknames had to be found to distinguish between the swarm of Samuels. There was a White Samuel and a Black Samuel (presumably some of them were throwbacks), a Stupid Samuel and a Crosseyed Samuel, a Samuel Bigarse and a Samuel Windball, there was Samuel Stone and Samuel Busy and Samuel Dew and Samuel Ribbons, and only by the grace of God was it possible to tell them apart. And foremost among them was Samuel the firstborn, our Samuel, the girl who became our ancestor.

She was exceptional from the beginning. People came from far and wide to stare at her hair. She was the only Samuel of them all who was very nearly stillborn, half-strangled by her own hair which even at birth was as long as an umbilical cord. It made one feel uneasy just to look at her. The neighbour women were wondering aloud whether it didn't amount to the same thing as being born with a caul, perhaps worse? Everybody believed that the first hair would soon fall out, but it never did. It only grew longer and denser, as blonde and golden as honey from a deep hollow in the mountains. An improbably beautiful child. Before she was six years old her hair was reaching down to her thighs, and still it grew, to her calves, her ankles.

At first the mother plaited it, making a double loop in the plaits to tie them up. When they began to touch the ground she wound it round the girl's head, an amazing sight to behold. On Saturday nights it was brushed out and then she would sleep like that, covered by the golden fleece like a kaross spread over the whole bed, down to the floor.

She was a very grave child. Her father never paid much attention to his children once they were born: provided there were enough Samuels around, the future was safe. Most of the time he ɾ as away from home, hunting, or on commando to track down game or native people, all of it part of a man's good life. He only came home in time for new births, when he availed himself of the opportunity to ensure the next harvest. Lottie submitted to his ardours; perhaps she was pleased to discover that her husband needed her so much. Even though she herself remained apprehensive of children. The moment a new baby had been weaned she would pass it on to the firstborn Samuel to look after; and then she'd either begin to hatch the next or go her own secret ways. Five singles, three pairs of twins, one set of triplets, and then of course the quadruplets. In due course they all learned to take care of one another; but Samuel was in charge until at last, God be praised, the mother dried up.

From the time Samuel was fourteen or thereabouts would-be suitors made their appearance on the farm to enquire about her health and advertise their prospects. But the Groblers quickly made it clear to them that Samuel was not available; her duties required her to remain at home. Some of the young men later married her younger sisters. Samuel couldn't care less. Wrapped in her hair, like a golden whirlwind on the veld, she went her way, looking after her parents and her siblings, hardly ever saying a word.

She spoke even less after her mother had left them, which is another story. Then father Bart died of a San arrow in the left lung, quite a common complaint in those days; but he went in peace, knowing his tribe's covenant with God was secure. It was only then that Samuel began to think of a life of her own. There was still a number of little ones to look after, but much to the consternation of her brothers and sisters she calmly informed them that she'd had enough and would henceforth leave them to their own devices.

Most of the time she just wandered about in the veld, all on her own, her loose hair trailing like a train in the dust, several metres long, an incredible sight. She was really turning into a wild creature altogether.

But not for long. Once the news got round that the older Groblers were out of the way an increasing number of men – not only from the environs but from quite far afield – began to show a renewed interest in the girl with the golden hair. They were surprisingly timid, I should add, as they weren't quite sure whether she was real, or a mirage on the plains, a walking sheaf of wheat, a column of sunlight moving across the veld, almost too beautiful to believe. But gradually, as they discovered she was human after all, they became more frank in their approach. And Samuel accepted the first one who had the courage to ask her outright.

They hadn't spoken much, just enough for Samuel to be reassured that he'd come from very far away. One can only guess that she wanted to put as much distance between herself and that noisy bunch which carried on worse than a flock of birds from early morning to well past sunset; and it is more than likely that she wished to move to a region where there was no chance of ever again encountering another person called Samuel. Only after securing this promise did she leave with the man who was called Harm Maree. They travelled all the way from the Prince Alfred region to what was to become the district of Cradock in the Eastern Cape.

Harm was totally enraptured with her hair. He preferred her to go about without tying it up in any way; and in the evenings he personally and lovingly combed out the twigs and grass and ants that had got caught in it during the day: he would comb and comb, and brush and brush and brush, moving his hands up and down to let it run through his fingers like water; he could swim in her hair as if she were a long undulating golden river. What he loved above all was to take her to the stream that ran across his farm and wash her hair in it. It took hours and hours, soaping and lathering and rinsing until it rippled like small shiny wavelets. But those were the only caresses she ever permitted him. The rest of her body was strictly out of bounds.

And he was quite happy with it. To him she wasn't a woman, but a kind of plaything, something miraculous he could care for and relish; it didn't even bother him that she hardly ever spoke. He wished for no more than to groom her hair.

This suited her perfectly. In his care she became the child she'd never been allowed to be. She played with dolls, dressing and undressing them all day long; Harm took a special pleasure in bringing her more and more new dolls every time he had to go to Algoa Bay to trade. Dolls, and mirrors. Samuel could spend hours in front of a mirror without ever getting bored. In the beginning she had only one, a broken piece, a mere shard she'd brought with her from her parents' home in the Karoo. When he discovered her infatuation he started bringing her new ones. Within a few years every single wall in the house, inside and even out, was bedecked with mirrors of all shapes and sizes. And while she would preen herself and turn this way and that to look at her reflection from every imaginable angle, Harm would stare from a distance, entranced by the cool voluptuousness of her hair.

Could it have gone on like that forever? It is an intriguing possibility. Where it went wrong is difficult to tell at this remove. One may conjecture that in the long run his male nature had no choice but to assert itself, but it may well have been her femininity that proved decisive. All that is reported in the story is that a good ten years after they were married, there was another celebratory session one night, lasting for many hours, in which Harm enfolded and enmeshed their two bodies in the endless flow of her hair, twisting and turning, tying and untying themselves, on the bed, on the floor, from room to room, rolling and tossing in a pleasure that gradually became uncontrollable. And this time he broke the rules, diving in, all the way, and fell asleep like a castaway tossed up from the sea. Samuel lay unmoving, her husband's body half-covering hers. Was she in a kind of stupor? Or was it shrewd calculation to make quite sure he was fast asleep?

Only when she had no doubt that he was beyond redemption did she cautiously disentangle herself from him; still naked, she bent over him and started winding her hair around his neck, an ever-tightening noose. He hardly stirred. And she calmly continued until his body turned slack and she knew he was dead.

Then she rose, and boiled water, and washed herself laboriously and thoroughly, as if to rinse every last memory of him from her. When she had done, she took up position in front of the tallest mirror in the house, in which she could survey herself from head to toe, and slowly and methodically, with a pair of sheep-shears, cut off her hair. She finished off the task with smaller, sharper scissors. At her feet, surrounding her in a motionless golden ripple that reached to her knees, lay the hair, a pool from which she rose, more naked than she'd ever seen herself in all her life.

For a long time she stood there inspecting herself – did she already know it was the last time in her life she'd be doing it? – and went to pick out some of her husband's clothes she could wear. He was much taller than she, but quite delicate of frame, and with some shortening of sleeves and legs the shirt and moleskin trousers and waistcoat she chose turned out to fit her reasonably well. She added a wide-brimmed hat. Now she was a man, a young man built like a boy.

She dug a hole in the back yard, in the vegetable patch where the earth was soft, and buried Harm's body in it, with the hair piled on top; and then she filled it up and covered it meticulously with leaves and manure so that it would not be conspicuous. From under their bed, which he'd made himself – he'd been skilful with his hands – she took the tin trunk in which he'd hoarded his money, a sizeable heap of gold coins, they were prosperous; this she packed into a saddlebag, added her collection of dolls, and provisions for a few days, saddled the best horse in the stable, and rode off. In the east the day had just begun to break, the stars were fading, only the morning star was still bright.

# 4

Samuel rode and rode and rode, for days, for weeks, until she reached the sea which she'd never seen before and which she found so beautiful that she decided to stay there.

In the beginning she literally lived in the bush, in a rough shelter of branches she'd stacked with the help of a few Xhosa men. They belonged to the vanguard of a black wave that had unfurled itself across the Great Fish River, occupying tracts of land vacated by anxious white farmers. Those were tense times, and there was never-ending conflict between white and black: raids to and fro across the eastern frontier, campaigns, wars and rumours of war. Only in the area where Samuel had settled, in the very eye of the storm, there was no trouble; in fact, going about her private business she wasn't even aware of anything untoward. The Xhosas were the only ones to whom she ever confided that she was a woman: and this guaranteed her safety, as their nation never harmed women or children. Throughout her pregnancy she remained there. When she needed anything the Xhosas who had befriended her would travel to Algoa Bay for provisions. She learned to speak their language. When her time came they brought their wives to assist her.

It wasn't an easy birth. Samuel nearly died, but the women pulled her through with their cures and remedies; when she was in a really bad shape they brought an *igqira*, a medicine man, who hauled her back from death with his powdered musk-cat nails and tortoise shell, acrid *gli*-roots and puffadder poison and other unspeakable brews. After that she convalesced rapidly; but she was unable to feed the baby. That proved to be no problem as one of the Xhosa women had a baby of her own, and without further ado she took the small white girl to her breast as well.

Had it depended on Samuel she might well have spent the rest of her life there. But perhaps to avoid exposing her benefactors to unnecessary danger, or because she felt a new kind of responsibility towards her daughter, she eventually decided to move. The child, Wilhelmina, must have been about four or five, Samuel in her early thirties. The year, if one has to put a date to it, was probably 1810 or thereabouts.

Samuel found work as a teacher with a farmer's family on the bank of the Riet River, right on the coast, where she could be close to the sea. She still wore her hair very short, cropping it herself – without using a mirror, because she never allowed one in her home again. One of the only hidings Wilhelmina received in her life was when she came running home from an itinerant trader's wagon with a small hand-mirror the man had given her as a present. Samuel pounded it to smithereens with a hammer, then ground the shards to a fine powder in a crucible and force-fed it, mixed with bitter aloe juice, to the girl. That did it.

They were then living with the Steenkamp family on the Riet River, as I said. Samuel received no wages as a teacher; she was content with a room and some basic provisions in exchange for the rudimentary lessons she offered the children of the neighbourhood. Whenever she found herself in company Samuel spoke in a whisper in order to keep her sex a secret; wearing men's clothing and smoking a pipe did the rest. The child, she explained, was her own, the mother having died in childbirth. She would gesture to her throat to explain that the loss of her voice was somehow related to the tragedy in the family.

The Steenkamps only had sons, a lot of them; and from an early age Wilhelmina had a tough time holding her own. Samuel was, as she'd always been, a distant, unworldly person, who paid no attention when Wilhelmina came running for help; so it was only a furious instinct for survival that helped the girl prevail against that savage band of boys.

It lasted for a few years only. The Steenkamps' farm, less than an hour on horseback from the frontier, suffered heavily from Xhosa raids. Being an unruly lot, the farmer and his oldest sons would then defy all laws and regulations, crossing the frontier to reclaim their stolen cattle as well as what they regarded as fair compensation. As a result they soon ran into trouble, not only with the Xhosa but with the British troops stationed in the forts along the Great Fish River. At the same time their harsh treatment of servants and labourers resulted in a summons to appear in court; and in the so-called Black Circuit they were heavily fined. Within days of their return to the farm a new tide of angry Xhosa washed across the frontier, taking with them every hoof and horn in veld and kraal. On horses borrowed from kindly neighbours the Steenkamps set out in pursuit; but the Xhosa must have been lying in wait for them for the little commando was ambushed in the thickets beyond the Great Fish and three of the Steenkamp sons were killed. It was the last straw. The father loaded his family on a rented wagon and trekked away, deeper into the colony, as far as possible from the border. It took all Samuel's powers of persuasion to convince him not to set fire to the homestead, the outbuildings and the fields before they left. She took over.

As before, she talked a few Xhosa into joining her, not as labourers but as partners on the farm. And while most of the other farmers in the Suurveld region were staggering under their repeated losses, Samuel flourished. Nothing spectacular, to be sure; but she made enough for a comfortable existence. If she was lonely, it suited her; but little Wilhelmina had a hard time and on more than one occasion she tried to run away. However, as time passed it turned out that she had no choice but to adjust her life to the curious rhythms of her mother's in that small dark house without mirrors. At night Samuel would play with her dolls (Wilhelmina was much too robust for that); during the day, leaving most of the work to her Xhosa partners, she roamed about, spied on meerkats, broke open anthills to see what was happening inside.

It is strange to think how untouched she was by all that was happening around her in those turbulent times. Not a day went by without drama or violence of one kind or another. Yet Samuel's life reflected none of it. She simply went her unobserved way beyond the reach of history. And if she hadn't told Wilhelmina, during the last years before her death, her secret story, nothing of it all would have been preserved.

# 5

There was one last important disruption in her later life, soon after a wave of British Settlers had moved into the area. A young woman made her appearance on the farm. No one knew anything about her. Wilhelmina, the only person who might have recorded something, left only a garbled account. As a result all kinds of wonderful tales were woven around the stranger. Some said she'd come from a ship that had been wrecked on the coast; others that she'd come all the way through Africa on foot; or that she'd been the unwanted, illegitimate child of an important gentleman from the Cape who'd tried to dump her in the wilderness; or that a herd of elephants, relentlessly following her family's trek through the interior after her father had shot a calf, systematically killed every living soul on the wagons, leaving her the only survivor; or even that she was a Water Woman who'd come from a deep pool in the river and then lost her way when she tried to turn back. The most likely explanation was that her family had been massacred by marauders, that in her attempts to find help she'd lost her way and gone mad from suffering and deprivation in the wild, assailed by hunger and thirst and predators; until Samuel found her in the veld, close to death, and brought her home, where she was saved with Xhosa remedies.

What difference does it make? The girl, Marga, about five years older than Wilhelmina, but much more fragile, strange and absent in her ways, much like Samuel herself, moved in with them, and stayed on. One could turn it into quite a romantic story: Marga falling in love with Samuel and trying to communicate her emotions through all manner of subtle and not so subtle hints; Samuel developing similar feelings towards the girl, but never daring to let on, resorting instead to more and more curt rebuffs. Then the unavoidable discovery: how? where? when? Did Marga unexpectedly come upon her as she waded through the rushes after a swim? Or on the white beach as she emerged naked from the sea? Or was it more mundane? – Samuel undressing in her room, or washing in a tub in the kitchen, and Marga entering absently to discover that her host was not a man but a woman?

More silences than words surround this part of the story. We have to make do with the scant clues we have; they are significant. It would have been understandable if Marga had left after the scene of discovery, as mysteriously as she had arrived. But she didn't. Not only did she remain with Samuel, but one day the two women set out, with Wilhelmina, on a borrowed wagon: to Cape Town, they explained to whoever enquired. And six or seven months later they returned with the news that they were now married. But much later, after Samuel's death, Wilhelmina revealed that they'd never been to Cape Town at all: they hadn't even gone as far as the Knysna forest. It had all been an elaborate hoax to prevent gossip, because everybody in the region still thought of Samuel as a man, the man who whispered. Not that they had many visitors, and the few who did turn up, from time to time, were not received very hospitably; no one was ever invited to stay over. Still, one couldn't be too careful, hence the laborious planning.

To make their isolation even more secure they moved away from the farm on the Riet River and settled far away, on the other side of the border, among the Xhosa, in a sharp elbow of the Keiskamma River, near the sea. It must have been in the mid-Twenties.

There is so much one would like to know. Why should one not make allowance, in a friendship between two women, for the body in the same way as one would make allowance for death in a relationship between the aged? Only a single image from the child Wilhelmina's youthful observations has come down to us. Something she saw one night through a chink in the bedroom door. And in the final analysis the image says nothing. Or does it say everything that can possibly be said? Samuel and Marga in bed, the gentle orange glare of the lamp, and Marga stroking the close-cropped head beside her own: stroking it for hours, deep into the night, the way Harm had stroked her hair so many years ago. Then Samuel would close her eyes and drift off into dreams, moving far away from that little hovel on the bank of the Keiskamma washed by the sound of the sea, following in her mind the strands of hair meandering in all directions, ever more distant, beyond all horizons, covering the whole earth in their gentle golden pleasure, rippling with light, hair without end, world without end. And when she woke up again in the dark predawn, the lamp still burning, now low and smoking, she would find Marga's head beside hers on the pillow and begin to weep; and she would slide from the bed without waking Marga, and wander aimlessly through the house, along the bare blind walls, until the daylight came raging through the windows and she ended up in front of the coffee mill to start grinding, grinding away like someone possessed.

It must have been hard on Wilhelmina. She was fiercely loyal to her mother. She couldn't stand Marga. How to handle their relationship, in the closed world in which they lived, defies enquiry. But it's no use speculating; no use pitying her, or anybody else for that matter. All that concerns us is that she withdrew more and more into her own life. By the time she was twenty she was so independent from her mother that she joined an old German trader on his travels to and fro between Cape Town and the most distant reaches of the land of the Xhosa. Soon afterwards she met a pious turd who changed her life. Isn't it outrageous, the way we are made to depend on men for these decisive moments? But I'm keeping that for later.

Samuel accepted it with resignation. One gives birth, then the child grows up, and leaves the nest. In many ways we too are a species of bird. A rare one at that.

# 6

Samuel had decided long ago that she didn't want to grow old. It was a carefully considered decision, the kind one takes about getting married, or buying a horse, or building a house. She would have liked to go at thirty, but that was the heyday of her hair, and Harm was so passionate about it that for his sake she postponed her death. Soon afterwards came the unplanned child, and when Samuel was forty Wilhelmina was still too young to leave behind. At fifty there was Marga. But fifty-five seemed a suitable age, and this was how she explained it to Marga and Wilhelmina. Neither was disposed to take it seriously; and Wilhelmina's pious husband tried his best to preach her out of it. No one, he argued, knew in advance the day or the hour, and one shouldn't try to interfere with God's will.

All the hectic arguments around her made little impression on Samuel. Marga's tears and threats and pleading were more difficult to handle. But just as resolute as Samuel had once been about lopping off her hair, she now was about dying at the appointed time. And in a way the two events were related. Cutting off her hair had been a sin with which to expiate another sin. Now it was time to get her hair back. To do so openly was out of the question, given her relationship with Marga. (Can you imagine how Wilhelmina's husband would have reacted?) There was only one way out: to die. Because she'd heard that after death one's hair continues to grow unchecked. When Judgement Day came round she should at last be in a fit state again to meet her Maker unembarrassed.

Marga was to lay out the body, to ensure that her secret went into the grave with her. All she needed was a respectable coffin. This was Wilhelmina's responsibility. Through her trading she had established the necessary contacts. It had to be a special coffin, not one of those yellowwood-and-stinkwood boxes any handyman in the Border region could nail together. It had to come from Cape Town, a place Samuel had never seen in her life but which in her reckoning ranked with the new Jerusalem.

Leendert Pretorius, Wilhelmina's husband, became more and more insistent in his attempts to dissuade Samuel from her sinful resolve, but she would not be moved. She reminded Leendert that he'd never been officially ordained, which was quite a sore point; and she was not taking orders from a layman. With infinite patience Wilhelmina persuaded her husband, for God's sake, to undertake the journey to the Cape, and as he thought he could use a new black linen suit he finally consented.

It had been agreed that the coffin could bide its time in Samuel's voorhuis until it was required. The date elected for her death, Samuel reminded them, was 6 March 1831. They preferred not to start a new argument, but it was plain for all to see that she had many good years left in her yet.

Marga was the only one who continued to rebel. 'If you go,' she threatened, 'then I go too.'

'Don't be ridiculous, you're a mere child,' Samuel reprimanded her.

'And you're only fifty-four. You can live another twenty years.'

'We've already been through all that, Marga.'

'You perhaps, not I.'

'A person's death is a private matter,' Samuel said calmly. 'I'd prefer you to go on living. You can look after my grave. You'll have more than enough to do. But if you decide otherwise, it's your choice. I have as little say in that as you have over my affairs.'

Four months before the due date the coffin was delivered, quite an achievement given the route it had to follow, all the way from the Cape along the South-east coast, then inland from Algoa Bay. The only problem was that Samuel was still in exceptionally good health. In fact, from the day the coffin was deposited in her voorhuis she seemed more energetic and happy than ever before.

'You're not going to commit suicide, are you?' Marga asked, horrified.

'Of course not, that would be a sin.'

Marga felt slightly more reassured: anyone could see that Samuel still had a great reserve of life left in her, and if she wasn't planning to kill herself they could look forward to many more years together. The coffin in the voorhuis, polished daily and bedecked with fresh flowers, became a piece of furniture.

On the evening of 5 March Samuel performed her ablutions in the kitchen with an inordinate amount of hot water, trimmed her hair so that it would grow out evenly, opened the coffin, slid inside and made herself comfortable, and then called Marga to secure the lid with the brass bolts that came with it.

Marga refused, of course. She wouldn't be a party to suffocation. But when Samuel pointed out that the small hatch above her face could fold open, the young woman reluctantly obeyed: it was the only way to keep the peace. She was convinced that after spending a night in those cramped conditions, surely Samuel would see the folly of it all, and the whole outrageous business would come to a tidy end.

Samuel folded her hands on her chest and said, 'Good-bye, Marga.'

Marga bent over and kissed her. 'Good night, Samuel.' She was in tears, but fought them back.

It was a bright, still night. The stars in the sky were shining like fireflies.

Shortly before midnight, with unbelievable suddenness, a storm came up. The kind of storm one experiences perhaps once in a lifetime. The rains came down as if the heavens had been rent. The rumbling of the thunder caused the walls to shudder. Lightning hit the house. Everything went up in flames. Then the river behind the house broke its banks. In the flood the coffin was swept away. The whole lie of the land was changed so drastically that it was almost impossible to discover the site of the house again.

How Wilhelmina and her husband came to hear the news, no one knew. Perhaps some of Samuel's black neighbours went to their farm, which was a long way from the Keiskamma. Two days later they arrived. Their first child had been born by then, and a second was under way. They began to scour the surroundings, but it was a full week before the coffin was found where the waves had washed it up, surprisingly unscathed, high and dry on the beach. Of Samuel there was no sign. Not then; not afterwards.

Marga's body was found in the driftwood along the far bank of the river.

# 7

'And then came an elephant,' says Ouma, 'and blew the story away.'

Her eyes are closed; the effort has sapped her strength. I revive her with oxygen. She recovers surprisingly soon.

'Is it really this coffin you were talking about?' I ask her.

'Yes, of course. You can still see the marks of the flood, can't you?'

'And you think Samuel's daughter Wilhelmina carted it along the length and breadth of the country in the Great Trek?'

'What does it matter what I think? The coffin is here, isn't it?'

'I'd like to know more about this Wilhelmina. She seems to be a crucial person.'

'They're all crucial.' Her eyes flutter shut. 'We'll talk about her when the time is right.'

'But how did the coffin ever get here?'

'Wilhelmina's daughter Petronella, of course.'

'But you said her ark was shipwrecked. Then how was the coffin salvaged?'

She shrugs. Her single useful hand lies on the sheet like some poor discarded object on a beach. 'O ye of little faith.'

'It takes a lot of believing,' I remark cautiously.

'Yes,' she says. 'That's what it is all about.'

There is a purring, gently coughing sound from the coffin where the owls are roosting. In the half-dark of the room – the curtains are drawn – their eyes glow like phosphor. But their presence is reassuring rather than ominous.

Ouma Kristina looks at me again.

'Do you understand why I'm telling you all this?' she asks. Her eyes, too, seem to have acquired a kind of phosphorescence.

Wily old desert woman!

'If I say yes, you won't tell me; if I say no, you'll tell me to figure it out, right?'

Her head moves; it may have been a nod. She looks content. Without any transition she is asleep.

# 8

Behind the picture of the Broad and Narrow Ways, exactly as she said, in the top right-hand corner of the heavy frame, there is a narrow lid sliding in two almost invisible grooves and in the cavity behind it, a tight fit indeed, is a small weirdly shaped key. It slides easily into the serrated slit of the lock, and I cannot suppress the light thrill that runs down my spine. It is like entering a story, something by Grimm, Bluebeard's Castle. The door creaks, as it should, on its hinges. It is dark inside, there is no bulb in the bare light-fitting suspended from the stained ceiling, so I go over to the window to open the shutters. But it is obvious that they haven't been touched in years and they will not budge. All I can make out beyond any doubt are the piles of bulky objects I once spied as a child; for all I know they haven't been touched since then. No furniture; nothing. Only those shapes, covered, like the floor, in inches of dust and drab festoons of cobwebs.

I have no choice but to lock up and go downstairs, skulking like a guilty child, to collect a paraffin lamp from the pantry. Armed with this, at last, I am ready for the Lord Carnarvon act. Scraping the mounds of dust from the objects I bring to light a collection of carrier bags, mostly brown paper, stacked in rows upon rows, hefty as washerwomen. They turn out not to be heavy at all, only bulky; and my first thought as I plunge a hand into the nearest is that they're filled with nothing but crumpled newsprint. But each ball of paper contains something, a wad, a pad, something very old and dry and stained with what at first sight appears to be dark paint but then turns out to be, so help me God, browned and blackened blood. For they are all sanitary rags and towels, used, and gathered, and stowed. What on earth for? Ouma won't ever tell. A silent witness to – what? Her life, she said. Her femininity? Her rejection or affirmation of it? God knows; and he is unlikely to tell. Bags and bags and bags of them, years and years of bleeding, of 'the curse', of moving with the cycles of time, once every twenty-eight or so days, thirteen times a year, how many years? Should I cry, or laugh, or shrug it off? No, it is not to be shrugged off. It is – nothing. It is a life.

This, I think, is worse – both more eloquent and more dauntingly mute – than that embroidered name and date on a piece of cloth left by a great-great-aunt from the Boer War. In its silence it becomes the testimony, not of the century marked by one woman's life, but of all women, all of us, since Eve first got the blame for seducing Adam. This is myth still; yet different. All those ancient myths of the frontier woman in the frontier country; all of them conceived and perpetuated by men. So what was there left for Ouma Kristina except to spit the pips of her forbidden fruit into the faces of the myth-makers?

How curious she should have chosen today to ask me, what with my own period starting. Or has she guessed? Nothing has ever escaped her.

I wish I could tell Anna about this. But I don't think she would understand. And Ouma asked me to destroy it, privately.

Why now? Why after all these years? There can be no embarrassment attached to it, not for Ouma, and not now. Something else to figure out. And I will; I promise myself I shall. Right now there is something to be done, a pledge to fulfil.

It is Sunday now – the hour of the idiots? – and there is no one abroad; I can start now. But I shall have to bide my time; I cannot risk

Trui or the nurse or whoever else finding out. This is between Ouma Kristina and me.

# 9

I had to borrow tampons from Anna when I went there for lunch. I'd driven in to town first – having scored a victory over Jeremiah, who finally, mellowed presumably by a Sunday mood, granted me the freedom of the hearse – but of course there was no chemist open. These pious folk, I presume, don't bleed on Sunday; all natural processes are interrupted in the name of that stern threesome, Father, Son and Holy Ghost. At the Greek café where in my childhood we used to buy ostrich biltong (they still stock it, I discovered with satisfaction) I stopped to buy sweets for Anna's children, a reckless assortment of Smarties, Chocolate Logs and Peppermint Crisps for each – three, four, five, I counted in my mind, plus one extra in case I'd miscalculated – and a huge Easter egg to share: this was courting disaster, I knew, but it was on special offer (and probably whitened with heat or crumbled with weevils), it being a full three weeks after the event, and what the hell. I was in a mood for atonement and peace offerings. And even if it didn't sit all that well with the solemnity of the hearse – which I drove, for the sheer incongruity of it, at a hundred and forty kilometres per hour on that open stretch of road to the farm, singing Beethoven's Fifth at the top of my voice and glancing in glee at the oncoming cars that nearly wrecked themselves in clouds of dust at the awesome sight – I hoped they would accept it in the spirit of generosity that had inspired it. Which wasn't exactly what happened, as the children appeared highly suspicious of a non-Greek woman bearing gifts; and Casper complicated matters by issuing dire instructions that not a bite or a lick could be assayed before lunch.

The fare, carried in by a safari of servants in pink overalls and white kopdoeke, was as extravagant as anything I remembered from family Sunday dinners in the past: chicken, roast leg of lamb dripping with fat, potatoes, yellow rice with raisins, sweet potatoes in honey and cinnamon, pumpkin fritters, peas, a sweet-and-sour tomato salad, beetroot; rounded off with a baked vinegar pudding with custard and ice cream. The meal was preceded and closed with prayer, and I was aware of indeed needing some divine assistance to cope. There was little sign of enjoyment. For one thing, everybody appeared force-fed into their tightest-fitting Sunday best; I found my heart going out to the two girls, twelvish and eightish, in whom I recognised my earlier self, eyes squinting with the tightness of their plaits, narrow chests moulded in suffocatingly taut bodices. It was painfully obvious from the hunched shoulders of the elder one that she was desperately trying to minimise, to no avail, the visibility of what seemed like two small protruding crab's eyes; and a minor catastrophe erupted when Casper instructed her halfway through the meal to sit up straight, which resulted in an outburst of tears, a chair overturned, and a gawky rush to a bedroom. I promised myself that at the earliest opportunity I would take her to Shapiro's fashion emporium to do unto her what Ouma had once done to me.

'That one's been asking for it, and she's going to get it,' said Casper, half-rising from his chair, dropping his serviette, preparing for hot pursuit.

'Let her be,' I said.

'Look – !'

'Please,' said Anna.

A precarious pause, all the other children waiting in suspense, the younger girl pale with trepidation, the boys with barely concealed eagerness. Then Casper changed his mind, bent down to retrieve his serviette, and banged the back of his head against the edge of the table as he rose. A titter from the youngest boy.

'Who was that?' thundered Casper.

The two older boys responded as if they'd been rehearsing for an act: 'It was Cassie, Pa!' 'Cassie, Pa!' Whereupon the aforesaid Cassie subsided in a wretched wail.

Violence seemed unavoidable.

I had a bitchy remark ready on the tip of my tongue (something like, 'Right, now that we all know who's the strongest, how about finishing our meal?') but managed to suppress it. 'Please!' I said. 'Why don't we just try to enjoy Anna's great food?'

He glowered for a moment, then took up his knife and fork again. The rest of the meal was rather strained, but without further eruptions. And over coffee, afterwards, the children out of sight if not entirely out of mind, Casper actually appeared to mellow.

'I suppose you're sleeping a bit easier now?' he asked.

Another prompt retort ('Easier than those kids they arrested') was suppressed in favour of blandness. 'Yes. You too, I imagine?'

'Ja. But of course one never knows. For every one they arrest there's five new ones to take their places.'

'Only two more days.'

'You still believe that shit?'

'If there's no unnecessary provocation –'

'You can't trust those bastards.'

'How peaceful are *your* intentions?'

'*My* men have never looked for trouble.'

'Come again.'

'It's that bunch of terrorists –'

'They want peace.'

'What makes you so sure about it?'

'They're sending a peace commission down here tomorrow.' Sandile.

'We'll see about that.'

'What kind of welcome are you going to give them?'

'What do you mean?'

'You try to stop them with force, you may just get what you're looking for. But if you're prepared to sit down and talk you may be in for a surprise.'

'Like hell.'

'Are you scared?'

'What the fuck should I be scared of?'

'Casper, please,' said Anna.

He didn't even look at her.

'Of your own ghosts, perhaps,' I replied. He looked at me; I met his stare. 'I'm prepared to take a bet on it. If you can persuade your men to sit down with them tomorrow you may just be able to return this district to peace. If not, you'll have to live with the blame.'

'*I'll* have to live with it? That's rich.'

'Are you willing to give it a chance?' There was nothing very lofty about my intervention; it was strictly personal. It was Sandile I was pleading for, I realised. But at that moment I believed passionately that it would be worth it.

He shrugged and took a swallow from the glass he'd brought from the table. He didn't look at me.

'Don't underestimate our power,' he said at last.

'I don't. But it seems to me that if you're really sure of your power there's no need to flaunt it.'

He finished his wine in one last gulp. He looked at me again. 'We'll see.'

'Promise?'

His upper lip wrinkled in a sneer. 'I don't have to promise *you* anything, Sis.'

'You're right. You don't owe me anything. But perhaps for the sake of your family ... If they really mean anything to you, it may be worthwhile giving peace a chance.'

He grunted and got up. 'Time for a nap,' he said brusquely. 'I want to get out of these clothes.'

'I must be going too,' I said, rising.

'Please,' said Anna, almost panicky. 'Stay.'

'Ouma may need me.'

She bit her lip. 'All right.'

I waited until Casper had gone to the bedroom before I asked her for the tampons. Afterwards, she went outside with me to the hearse. There was no sign of the children. In our childhood, too, we'd been confined indoors on Sunday afternoons. In principle, at least; if only the grownups had had the faintest inkling of what we were really up to.

'You going to have a nap too?' I asked her as I got into the black monster.

'Perhaps. I'll wait until Casper is asleep.'

'Self-defence?'

She looked down, then back at me. 'There's no way out,' she whispered. 'I'm a prisoner. I always have been. I don't think I've realised it as acutely as this last week, since you came. Always waiting for something to happen. Even at university: "When will he notice me?" "Is he going to ask me tonight?" "Am I going to get this job?" "Will I have more time after this baby – ?" Waiting and waiting, from one event to the next. Until one day you discover that all that's happened is that you've grown old. And then there's nothing left to hope for.'

'Why did you try to make your life so safe?' I asked.

'What has safety got to do with it?'

'Because nothing is as safe as destiny. And once you've convinced yourself that what happens to you has nothing to do with you at all but is controlled by something you call destiny, you're as safe as any corpse in any coffin. There's no possibility of adventure left.'

'Adventure is a romantic concept,' she said sharply.

'Is it? I'm not so sure. It can be bloody painful, I've found out. It's confusing, unsettling, trying, dangerous. But it's either that – or nothing at all.'

'You've always dramatised extremes, Kristien.'

'And I always get caught out by my periods.'

'Because you know you have a big sister to run to?'

I smiled slowly and turned the ignition key. 'Perhaps I should swap some of my adventure for some of your safety.'

'Shall we try?'

I drove off, more prudently this time.

## 10

Later in the afternoon, as the farm begins to emerge from its Sunday somnolence, a very dilapidated old car drives into the yard. Watching from my upstairs window I stare, flabbergasted, at the astounding number of people that spill out once the doors are opened (one door comes off entirely). They lounge about under the trees, abandoning the jalopy like a fowl roosting in the sand with wings outstretched, while a single corpulent woman goes round to the back. She shuffles along with difficulty, rowing with hefty arms against an invisible current. Soon afterwards Trui comes to call me, and I follow her downstairs.

It takes us at least half an hour to extract from the visitor who she is and what she wants. Her name is Happiness Tsabalala. Her son, she explains at length, in a mixture of Xhosa, English and Afrikaans, interspersed with deep sighs (she seems to be suffering from a heart condition) and fits of crying, is the Karate Kid. Which does not take us very far, until at last Trui makes the connection: he is the youngest of the boys detained by the police for trying to blow up Ouma's palace — that pitiful spindly little creature who wept most of the time he was here, yesterday morning.

After we have led her indoors, and made her sit down, and helped her gulp down a glass of water (she turns down the offer of tea), she laboriously digs under her many layers of clothing to loosen her stays; only then does she become more coherent. She has come to see Ouma. I explain that she is in a bad state, and asleep; but she insists. She will not rest, she says, before she has seen the burnt woman.

We help her upstairs. It takes several minutes, as she has to catch her breath at every step. But at last we are there.

The nurse rises briskly as we enter, clearly disapproving of the intrusion, but I motion to her that it is all right, which she accepts with bad grace, standing aside with the stiff movements of the mantis she so alarmingly resembles. (Were the resemblance to go any further I might entertain fears of her devouring her patient.) Happiness Tsabalala, belying her name, freezes in shock when she sees the coffin, pressing an ample fist to her mouth.

'She is dead?' she asks, followed by a stream of exclamations in Xhosa.

'No, no,' I interject hurriedly. 'She is just sleeping.'

'Why you put that box there?'

'That is what she wants.' I try to explain, feeling more than a little foolish.

Although Happiness appears to draw some comfort from my explanation, it is with great diffidence that she approaches, brushing Ouma's forehead with a hand, presumably to make sure she is still alive.

'Au,' says Happiness in a low voice. 'She burn. She is bad. She will die.'

'She is very old,' I try to comfort her.

'The Karate Kid do it,' she adds. Another long discourse in Xhosa follows, of which I understand only odd phrases here and there; in Sandile's time I knew it reasonably well, but I have lapsed in this as in so many other respects. 'Now they kill him too,' she says.

For a moment I misunderstand and feel my heart contract; then I realise she is speaking in the future tense.

'He's only a little boy,' I tell her, putting an arm round her shoulders as far as it will go. 'I have already spoken to the police. And to a lawyer. Tomorrow I'm going to speak to the ANC. We will try to arrange bail for him.'

'What is this bail thing?' she asks, deeply suspicious.

I try my best to explain. She bursts into tears again, such a wailing that Ouma starts in her sleep and briefly opens her eyes; but from her dazed look it is obvious that she has no idea of what is happening.

'All this death, death, death,' laments Happiness.

'We must stop it now,' says Trui unexpectedly. 'We are the mothers. We must stop it.'

'Your boy kill too?' asks Happiness.

'No. But I'm worried about him.'

'We all worry,' says Happiness. 'Mandela must end it.'

'He is only human,' I try to reason, but I realise that I am out of place here.

'The mothers. The children.' Happiness is following a train of her own thought, not readily accessible to outsiders. 'This old woman too. We all getting kill, we all suffering, it's bad, it's bad. So when to change? To do what?'

'Where do you live?' asks Trui.

Happiness Tsabalala explains. In the black township at the far side of Outeniqua.

'I'll come to see you there,' says Trui. 'You give me your address, hey?'

'Bad place,' says the big woman. 'We live small shack only, black plastic, no water, much shit. Bad place for little child to growing up in, Karate Kid. I try, I try, I try, what can I do? The lots other children, much children, bad children, they make tsotsi gangs, he small still, what can I do?' She turns to me, suddenly engulfs me in her arms. 'Ag, Madam, I'm so sorry, about the house, about the old madam, everything, everything, but I love my child, I cannot help, Madam, they so bad for him.'

Ouma whines and cringes in her sleep. The nurse, having dithered in the background with increasingly evident annoyance, now makes up her mind and interposes herself between us and the patient.

'I'm sorry,' she says, 'but I really cannot allow this any longer.'

Happiness Tsabalala composes herself. With huge dignity she bends over and kisses Ouma on the forehead, then turns and shuffles out.

As we leave in her wake I see the nurse officiously wiping Ouma's forehead with a cloth.

Downstairs, leaving the two mothers together for a while, I go outside to enquire whether the other visitors would like some refreshment, but they decline, avoiding my eyes or looking back with studied neutrality. Perhaps they do not approve of the visit; but if so, why did they come along? Once again there is a depressing realisation of understanding very little. Encamped below the blackened skeleton of the once proud palace, I realise in a wave of nausea, they must see this as the ultimate embodiment of what they abhor more deeply than anything else in the world.

I'd like to plead with them, tell them that it was for them I left my comfortable life in this country and plunged into the risks and dangers and uncertainties of a struggle waged from afar; but how would they react? At best, they would look back with those neutral shallow stares. They did not go away: even that basic choice was a luxury they couldn't afford. They were here. That is the crux of it. They were here. They saw it all. They lived through it all. Now this palace is on the verge of tumbling down. A boy from their midst has done it, and may die for it.

I return to the two women, just in time to help Happiness Tsabalala shuffle across the threshold, back into the diminishing glare of the afternoon sun. Trui is clutching a piece of paper; she has taken down the address. We walk back, a female threesome, but I am not really acknowledged by them. They are the mothers; I have turned away from that, as from so much else. I feel an ache in my womb.


## I I


In the late afternoon I go for a walk. For a splendid hour, around sunset, no one needs me in the proud old ruin. I've left my shoes behind. My feet have become tender – those blessed childhood days when shoes were a confinement and a torture! – and to be honest I regret the decision after a while; yet the rediscovery of a peculiar kind of freedom is exhilarating in itself. To feel, again, the earth, its secret vibrations, the closeness of its seasons, a kind of peasant joy perhaps, an awareness of the gathering of time in the pressure of my soles. A painful and necessary intimacy. And the prickling in my nose. The smell of dust, as real as the intensity of the light on my arrival. Yes, Africa. I follow the dirt road past the ostrich camps, past the lucerne fields, until there is only space around me. For once there is something which hasn't shrunk, or changed, since my childhood. A space impervious to chronology – or, rather, tuned in to a different kind of time, not that of days or weeks or years, appointments or contingencies, but a cyclic motion, summers that blend and merge, that repeat one another without ever being exactly the same, the kind of time that sculpts contours and moulds hills and gnaws away at ridges. Ouma Kristina's landscape. This expanse, this spare beauty, this deceptive emptiness. I gaze at nothingness; nothingness gazes back. In an inexplicable atavistic reaction I go down on my haunches, find a twig, start scratching haphazardly on the hard, bare soil. It comes from the guts; it is all I can think of doing. To exorcise that emptiness. A dialogue beyond, or far below, language. And with a sense of reassurance I return to the clump of trees in the distance, against the gaudy sky, and to the phantasm of the palace which once was the centre of our universe, the spot from which all maps of the world took their bearing, the place where history began.

# FIVE

---

## *Shit-storm*

# I

I return from sleep with the memory of sex, but it is confused. There is the afterglow of an erotic dream, but whether it was Michael who was involved in it or a more distant shadow – Sandile perhaps – I can no longer tell. And the images behind my eyes, withdrawing like the small wavelets of a larger tide, are mingled with others, trailing the long hair of a woman submerged in water, streams of hair, then blurring into other images again, faint as the faded stains of a painting on a wall or an imprint in a mirror, the slight figure of a girl moving across the landscape like the shadow of a cloud, carrying memories to and fro, the sparks of fireflies exploding in a night. There is a remembered weight on my body, not that of a lover but perhaps of God, a nightly visitor; but his revelations, if revelations there were, have vanished, I grasp at them but there is nothing in my hand, only once again a smooth gliding movement as of hair, running through my fingers like water.

I sit up and the world returns. And with the world, the memory of last night. It takes time to realise that it was not part of the night's dreams, but something that really happened, so crude, so violent, I'd like to exclude it from this day; but that is impossible. Hugging my knees, the blankets drawn up protectively around me, I try to grasp the whole improbable event, no longer sure of time or sequence, only of the nausea brought on by it.

I must have dropped off during my watch beside Ouma's bed. She lay snoring beside me. In the room next door, when I went to investigate, Trui and Jeremiah were also fast asleep. Yet something must have awakened me, that much I knew. A sound of birds perhaps? More than likely. That was why, stupidly, I didn't take anything with me, only a torch, as I tiptoed along the passage, then down the staircase.

All seemed quiet, but I had the uneasy feeling of a foreign presence;

233

in my ears was still the confused memory of the sound that had awakened me, the sound of an object overturned, a glass or something broken. Perhaps it had been Jacob Bonthuys, I suddenly thought. He might have felt ill and gone in search of help, or of something to drink. Anxious now, I hurried down the stone stairs to the cellar.

As I touched the door there was another sound, behind me. I swung round quickly, still expecting to see Bonthuys returning from the kitchen or wherever he might have gone. But it wasn't. It was Casper.

For a moment I was petrified. Then I relaxed; but I was annoyed.

'What the hell are you doing here?' I asked.

'Just checking up that everything is all right.'

'I told you this afternoon there was nothing to worry about any more. How did you get in?'

'I've got a key.'

'Since when?'

'I had a duplicate made when they put in the new back door. It's for your own safety'

'Very considerate of you.' I couldn't quite keep the sneer out of my voice. 'What time is it?'

He made no reply to that.

'Casper, I've told you before I don't need you and your cowboys to look after me.' An uneasy thought struck me. 'Where are they?'

'They've gone home. I came alone.'

'That's exactly where you should be going too. Anna will be waiting.'

'I need a wife, not a mother.'

'It's my sister you're talking about.'

'You really don't seem to appreciate all the trouble I'm taking to make sure you're safe.' He shielded his eyes against the beam from the torch. 'Please turn that thing away.'

I kept it shining in his eyes. 'Go home,' I said.

'How about some coffee?'

'No.'

'Come on. What's happened to Boer hospitality?'

'I'm a Brit now,' I said. 'Besides, I have work to do. I'm looking after Ouma. And your place is with your family.'

He changed his tone. 'Ag, don't be difficult, man. Good heavens, it's not as if we're strangers.'

He came down a few steps. A waft of his breath betrayed that he'd been drinking.

'We've been through all of this before,' I said brusquely. 'On these very steps, if you remember. I hope I needn't remind you what happened then.'

'We've both come a long way,' he cajoled. 'We know what goes for what in the world, don't we?'

'You make me sick,' I said, taking a step up, trying to move past him. But he caught my arm.

'Not so quick,' he said. Jesus, I thought, this is like a cheap thriller. We're caught in some time warp. 'Don't pretend you haven't had the hots for me from the moment you stepped into our house again. Everything you've said, everything you've done. Think I can't see through it?'

'If you think this is the hots there's a surprise or two waiting for you in hell,' I flared. 'Now let go of me.'

This is where the sequence has gone haywire in my mind. He was grabbing at me, I struck at him with the torch, we both lost our balance and stumbled down the steps, falling against the bottom door, where we continued struggling fiercely. The torch had fallen and rolled out of reach, its beam uselessly stabbing the darkness in the wrong direction, at an angle away from us. He was too strong for me, of course. In a moment he had my arms pinned behind my back and was tearing at the front of my shirt. And then the door behind me swung open and we both fell, Casper heavily on top of me; and I heard somebody shouting, and a heavy object – a chair, I discovered subsequently – came crashing down on Casper's head. In the light coming from the room I could see Jacob Bonthuys. There was an expression of fear and pain on his face; how he'd managed to wield the heavy chair with his wounded arm I still don't know.

With the kind of movement I suppose one is trained to perform in the army, Casper rolled out of reach and staggered to his feet again. He was bleeding from a cut on the forehead, but he wasn't out of action yet; and there was a murderous gleam in his eyes. But he was in a panic too. He obviously hadn't expected anybody there, and shock at being discovered must have outweighed even his dumb rage.

To make doubly sure I called out at Bonthuys, 'There are guns upstairs.'

He hesitated, then made a move towards the door.

'Don't be stupid!' cried Casper, quickly cutting him off.

He could easily have overpowered both of us; perhaps even Trui and Jeremiah, had I shouted for help, which I only now thought of doing. But of course Casper's whole design had presumed privacy; there could be no satisfaction in beating up the lot of us.

'You're bloody overreacting,' he growled, tucking in his shirt, sweeping back his hair and in the process plastering most of his face with blood. 'For God's sake, I only came round for a chat and a cup of coffee.'

'Next time wait till you're invited. And knock first.' I was breathing heavily.

Studiously avoiding Jacob Bonthuys – and just as well too – Casper scrambled past me to the door, let fly with a kick at the torch, and started feeling his way up the stairs, stumbling once or twice.

'And don't think you can fool me!' he shouted from the floor above. 'I know a bitch on heat when I see one!'

He might well have worked himself up into enough of a rage again to return to me, but just then Trui's voice came calling from above, 'Miss Kristien, are you all right?'

An ornament or a vase was smashed to the ground as Casper bumped into something; then there was a fumbling at the back door and the next moment it was slammed shut.

'It's all right, Trui,' I called.

A car pulled off outside.

I went upstairs to reassure her; there was no need to tell the whole story. Then I went down again to attend to Jacob Bonthuys. There wasn't much I could do, except to rebandage the arm and give him some tablets for the pain. It could only have taken minutes but it felt like hours before I was able to go to the kitchen and make myself a cup of tea, trembling all over by now. In most unheroinely fashion I began to cry. But I didn't want to leave Ouma alone for too long. And in the end it was the need to be vigilant and occupy my thoughts – even though she was sleeping quite deeply and required no particular care – that calmed me down again. At two o'clock I was relieved by Trui. And although I fully expected to lie awake for hours I slid into sleep almost as soon as my head struck the pillow.

2

The night now a memory as unreal, and in retrospect as ridiculous, as a nightmare, it is time to face the new day. A special day, even though it looks deceptively ordinary on the surface. I remember Christmas Days in my childhood, here in this house, playing on the stoep or in the shade of the trees with my new presents; and stopping from time to time to look up, expecting to see something out of the ordinary that would mark it as Christmas, a deeper blue in the sky, an unusual sound in the birdsong, a different texture to the trees, but there was nothing to designate it as a day somehow set apart; and that never ceased to disappoint me. Today the delegation is coming from Johannesburg. Before it is out I shall have spoken to Sandile again. (How different things would have been last night if he had been here!) Yet through the open window, to which I hasten as soon as I have recovered my senses, the sky looks the same as always.

There is a ribaldry of birds in the trees. The day is ringing with their sound.

Jeremiah is busy outside, raking leaves. I haven't realised how swiftly they have begun to fall, sifting steadily down on his head and shoulders from the deciduous trees in front of the house – the few oaks, a chestnut, a single plane tree, one or two others. Time is running out. Ouma's. My own, too, here; two weeks from now, who knows, I may be in London again. By then I will have seen Sandile; the elections will be behind us, the country may be going up in flames. Does it concern me? Until a day or two ago it didn't; now the expectation of his coming has shifted something, almost imperceptibly, and in this clear ordinary morning I acknowledge it.

It is time to cross the threshold of the day. I shower and dress, with more care than usual; three changes. I go to check on Ouma. She is sleeping fitfully; the nurse is there. Making sure that Trui is out of the way, downstairs, I return to the secret room and collect some of the bags that are patiently awaiting my arrival, like passengers huddling together in a third-class waiting room. From my bedroom I make sure that Jeremiah is no longer in the front garden before I steal downstairs with my burden.

On my way out, three doors from the kitchen, I pass the laundry where Trui is ironing sheets, her back to me. The smell of her ironing brings me to a standstill, briefly, before I tiptoe past. That clean, clean smell. And I remember a late Tuesday afternoon in there, among the piles of newly ironed laundry: one of the distant cousins, Laura, had been sent with me to collect the finished clothes and sheets and distribute them to the right relatives in their many rooms. I don't know how it began; I think she offered to show me her newly sprouting tendrils of pubic hair, 'seaweed' she called it; and somehow we got carried away and removed our clothes and began to touch and inspect and fondle and compare, each a mirror for the other, all as innocent as the smell of the ironed garments still impregnated with the summer sun in which they'd dried. It was my only vaguely lesbian experience, but it opened a door to more momentous discoveries later. It ended in upheaval. Not knowing that Ouma had already sent Laura and me to fetch the laundry, Mother came in to collect her underwear and found us among the toppled bundles of sheets and clothes. She looked as if she'd seen a ghost. It must have been minutes before she found her voice – that voice – to take control. The spanking that followed was nothing. It was her tone, her attitude; the intimation that what we'd done so far exceeded the bounds, not of the permissible but of the imaginable, that caused me for many nights to wake up in terror. The event was regarded as so serious that the two of us were summoned to a conclave of all the mothers in one of the farthest bedrooms, not so much to be berated as to be lamented over, our souls consigned to everlasting hell.

This must be why the memory itself became repressed. Those other youthful transgressions – in loquat tree, attic, basement or wherever – were remembered: they were branded sinful, but not altogether evil, irreparable. But that Tuesday had to be excised from the mind. Until this morning. It must be Ouma's story, yesterday afternoon, about Samuel and Marga, that dislodged it and brought it back to light. And I'm stunned to think it could have caused such horror at the time. Returning, now, to it, I find something sweet and innnocent and satisfying in the memory; and if it is unremarkable in itself the unexpected fusion with something else, beyond me, makes it more momentous. Even the action I am about to perform acquires more weight through it.

Almost reluctant to move away from the laundry, I venture to the kitchen door. In the distance I can see Jeremiah moving among the fruit trees near the graveyard with some of the other labourers, beyond the fowl run where turkeys gobble and chickens scratch and muscovy ducks hiss malevolently. Like a child on a guilty errand I hurry round the side of the house to the large heap of leaves he's raked; watched only by a suspicious peacock – and fuck him anyway – I dig a hollow in the heap and shake into it the contents of the brownpaper bags I have brought from upstairs. I cover up the hollow again, take out my lighter and set fire to the heap.

Overhead the birds erupt in cacophony. Within minutes, Jeremiah comes running, panting. He stops when he sees me, then remonstrates angrily.

'Miss Kristien, you can't do that. We've had enough fire around this place.'

'It's all right, Jeremiah. The trees are safe.'

'This is my job,' he says stiffly.

'I'm sorry,' I apologise, not contrite at all, 'but I can't resist a heap of leaves. Don't you remember?'

'I remember. You make trouble all the time, then, now.'

'It's not so bad, Jeremiah.' I wink at him. 'When I go to town I'll get you some Springbok tobacco. Okay?' This is unfair advantage I'm taking, I know, but I have little choice. Ouma will demand a progress report any moment now, and that musty little room is still stacked high with the barren evidence of past fertility.

'Ai, Miss Kristien, really, you making it very difficult for me.'

'I'm a big girl now, Jeremiah.'

'You?' He shakes his head, screwing up his eyes against the smoke.

'Thank you for letting me, Jeremiah.'

He hovers for a few more minutes, then goes off, mumbling angrily to himself as I turn back to supervise my bonfire. I draw in the smell of smoke. More memories: braaivleis here on summer nights, lamb ribs and ostrich steaks, Ouma in charge, disparaging about men who always scorch the meat; Namibia, that far-off visit, the confinement of space; an evening beside a suburban pool, a man erupting from the hedge and storming past, disappearing as suddenly as he has appeared. I prod the flaming leaves with a long stick, watching the sparks fly. Standing back to step out of the smoke which has changed direction I discover a small dead bird in the dry grass. Fallen from a nest? Caught by a cat? Recovering another childhood ritual I pick it up and deposit it in the flames, seeing the feathers turn to smoke. Years ago Ouma said, 'Birds are the spirits of dead women.'

'Then what happens when a bird dies?'

'It becomes something else again.'

The smoke is transformed into fire, a small flare gathered into the others. There is a sense of achievement in watching the progress of this particular little transfiguration.

The heap is still smouldering, the bags reduced to glowing bundles, when I notice a grey Mercedes approaching along the farm road, and my breath catches in my throat. It must be them, it is he! But as it swings into the yard and comes past me, heading for the back, I realise it is the doctor.

He clearly has no intention of waiting for me, but I catch up with him on the staircase. He is not a good advertisement for his trade: flabby, red-faced, out of breath.

'How is the patient?' he asks without looking at me.

'Much the same.'

'I really think . . .' But he gives up; and in silence we proceed to the room where the nurse is adjusting a new drip beside the bed. Ouma Kristina has woken up, but her head is moving to and fro on the pillow. The doctor stops when he notices the coffin still standing beside the bed. 'I had hoped not to see this thing around again,' he says, casting a reproachful look at me.

'I couldn't wait for you to come,' Ouma cuts him short. 'Today it's into the box with me. I need the rest.'

'Now look, Mrs Basson – '

'You took the Hippocratic oath,' Ouma reminds him.

'What has that got to do with it?'

'If you refuse to make me comfortable I shall die,' she says. 'It will be on your head. And I'll come back to haunt you to make sure you never forget. Besides, I'll make sure everybody knows about you and your receptionist.'

He gapes at her, his face flushing a deep granadilla purple. She watches with malicious glee.

'Let's have a look at your wounds,' he says, busying himself with his medical bag at the foot of her bed. Like yesterday, I withdraw to the window, distracted by the muffled moans that escape from her as the two of them set about attending her.

When at last they have finished the doctor comes to join me at the window.

'Her condition has weakened,' he says in a lowered voice. 'I really must urge you to let her go back to hospital.'

'What for?' asks Ouma Kristina, who must have strained to hear every word. 'I've told you so many times: I'm going to die anyway. Why won't you let me do so with a little bit of dignity?'

'You can see for yourself,' I say. 'She won't budge.'

And so, with disapproval evident in his every gesture, he helps us to ease her into the coffin (now thoroughly cleaned and disinfected), which is first stood on two chairs next to the bed to make the transfer as smooth as possible.

'This is much better,' she says, exactly as I said years ago when she fitted me with my first bra. And in spite of all the misgivings I, too, have had since yesterday, I now find it satisfactory to see her lying so serenely in the coffin – not because it confirms her imminent death, but because it restores her to her, our, lengthening past.

The doctor doesn't bother to say goodbye to her as he withdraws into the passage with the nurse, obviously to issue stern instructions.

'You're being very naughty,' I remonstrate softly with Ouma Kristina. 'What do you know about him and his receptionist anyway?'

'Nothing at all,' she says, smiling. 'Don't all doctors have affairs with their receptionists?'

Before I can vent my indignation the nurse returns, and I run out after the doctor to steer him to the cellar. It is only with the greatest reluctance that he complies. This house is clearly becoming a chamber of horrors to the poor man. Thank God Jacob Bonthuys appears stable after the exertions of last night; there has been some new bleeding, but in spite of the pain it does not appear to be serious.

As we mount the stairs again the doctor stops briefly to look at me. 'Miss Müller, I trust that what your grandmother said this morning – '

'Her mind is wandering,' I say quickly. 'Think no more of it.'

He beams with unexpected gratitude. 'I knew you would understand.'

There are large halfmoons of perspiration under his arms. And as he goes out I notice that the back of his striped blue shirt also shows a dark patch. I consider following him, then decide against it.

'Excuse me, Miss,' says our house guest behind me in the passage.

'Yes, Mr Bonthuys?'

'No, I just wanted to thank you for all the trouble, with the doctor and all.'

'It's I who must thank you,' I say. 'You really saved me from a lot of unpleasantness last night. If you hadn't been here – '

'That man . . .' He clicks his tongue. 'Why do some people cause so much trouble?'

'He's scared,' I say.

'But why must we now all pay the price?'

'He'll get his due after the elections,' I assure him grimly.

Bonthuys shakes his head. 'That will still not put it right, Miss. We can't go on paying each other back all the time, all the time. There has been too much badness already.'

Noticing the book reverently pressed against his chest, I ask, 'How are you getting on with Langenhoven?'

He beams. 'It's wonderful, Miss. He keeps me busy, only the print is very small. But I read a lot last night. After the thing that happened I couldn't sleep.'

'The days must be long down there,' I commiserate.

'How long will I still be staying here?'

'As long as you need to. As long as you wish.'

'I must go back. But I don't want to make trouble for Mr Joubert.'

'There won't be any more trouble. I told you they've caught the arsonists.'

'Yes, but many white people don't like him. They always make life difficult for him, because why, they say he cares about hotnots like us. And now he's allowed all those squatters to live at his place. You know, the people who were thrown off the farms when money got short. Some was living there for generations. Now they got nowhere to go. The white farmers are angry, but what must the people do? And Abel Joubert is the only one who cares about them.'

'What about your family?' I prod him. 'Don't you want me to send them a message?'

'My wife is dead.' For a moment he closes up. 'It'll be two years this coming June. And my children don't live on the farm no more.'

'How many of them are there?'

'Two sons and a daughter. She's a good girl, but she's married now. The sons – ' He shakes his head. 'From the time their mother died they became unruly. They gone now, one to Cape Town. The other one . . .' He half turns away, then braces himself to face me. 'He's in jail in Joh'burg, Miss. So things have gone bad for me.'

As this is the first time he's ever talked about himself I am eager to press him. 'What do you do on Abel Joubert's farm?'

'I'm his foreman, Miss. So it's ostriches, mainly. And then there's a part of the farm under irrigation, so there's vineyards. He makes a good wine. But for me, I'm more a man for the birds.'

'And for how long have you been with him?'

'How can Miss now ask a thing like this? I been there all my life mos. I was born there. Just like my father, he would have been eighty-nine this year if he lived. And my mother was also born there. It's since my grandpa's time we live on that farm together with the Jouberts, all the way. My grandpa was a fisherman first, down at Velddrif. But then things got bad, so he came upcountry. Yes, Miss. And Mr Joubert's grandfather gave him a job. Christmas-times I used to go to Velddrif, there's still family there. The Bonthuyses come a long way back there on the coast. But now that I'm on my own I stay maar at home. At night I look at the stars and think of my grandpa.'

'Did he know them well?'

'They were like his friends, Miss. They were tame to him. When I was small he always spoke to me about them, how they showed him the way on the sea when he was out there fishing. He told me all their names and where to find them. The Southern Cross. The Big Hunter with his bow. The Seven Sisters. The Plough. The Morning Star. And all the stories he told me about them and about the old days. Those were good times, Miss.' Again the shy gap-toothed smile. 'After I read

Langenhoven's *Loeloeraai* and the other things he wrote about the stars, a whole book full, I began to understand a little better. Everything falling, falling all the time. It's a hell of a mystery, Miss. Later, when I was grown up, I often spoke to Abel Joubert about it. He told me all kinds of new stories, about White Dwarfs and Black Holes and suchlike things. They weren't around in my grandpa's time. Does Miss understand anything about that?'

'Not much,' I confess. 'As far as I can make out the Black Holes are very old stars that get heavier and heavier all the time, and smaller and smaller too, so in the end they kind of collapse into themselves. Now you can't see them any more.'

'That's what I find hard to understand, Miss. If you can't see them, then how do you know they're there?'

'I read in one book that it's like a man in black clothes who dances in the dark with a girl in a white dress. You see only the girl, but from the way she dances you know the man must be there.'

He chuckles. 'And Abel Joubert tells me this Black Hole swallows everything that gets close. So there's a limit somewhere, and if you go past it, it's tickets. Is that right?'

'Yes, I believe so. There's this rim of the Black Hole, I think it's called the event horizon. Once you're through that nothing ever gets out again, not even light.' I stop, somewhat shamefaced. 'I'm afraid I'm giving you a very garbled version, Mr Bonthuys. I'll try to find a book and read up about it again.'

'Then you can explain it to me too,' he says. There is a gleam in his eyes. 'In the meantime I'll watch out not to get too close to those holes. And Miss must also maar be careful about dancing with a black man.'

Below the playful surface lurks an old-fashioned soothsayer. Is there in him, as in Trui, a hint of racism? It makes me uncomfortable. At the same time I'm intrigued by this man with his many contradictions. There's so much I'd still like to ask him, but he may find me nosey. 'I must be going now,' I announce.

'Miss is very good to me.' He inclines his head in a stiff little bow.

'Your grandfather would have been proud of you,' I say, hoping he doesn't find it patronising. 'And it does *me* good to talk to you.'

How strange, I think as I slowly go up the stone stairs again, back to the light: in the beginning, the first night I discovered him here, I felt that the possibility of his death implicated me. Now it is his life.

# 3

We're in the bakkie, Anna and I, on our way to town. The two little girls are in the back, their hair caught in the wind. We've left the boys behind. Casper is already in town, with his men, to meet the ANC. I feel miffed that he's been given precedence; but in terms of the political situation in the district I know it makes sense. Anna is looking very smart, a dress that makes her look much slimmer, elegant; her makeup is immaculate. But she's wearing dark glasses. As we left her house I started asking about it, but she made a hurried gesture with her head towards the girls. I caught on instantly. And even before she briefly took off the glasses as we got in, I knew what she was going to show me; and felt nauseous.

Blindly, in obtuse anger, I asked, 'But how could you let him do it?'

A quick movement of her mouth; more a nervous tic than a smile.

'I'm sorry,' I stammered. 'But how – why – ?'

'Nothing out of the ordinary,' she said in a dry, bitter voice. 'Just another argument – about his extracurricular interests.' Then the unexpected twist. 'As it happened, you also got drawn into it.'

'Me!' For a moment I'm overcome by the memory of last night; irrational feelings of guilt. But I make an effort to control it.

'Out of the blue,' says Anna. 'To change the subject, I suppose. Launched into a vicious attack. Telling me you can't keep your hands off him. That you actually – even years ago – I'm sorry, I shouldn't have told you, it makes me sick.'

'You can't let this go on, Anna.'

'There's the children. I can't leave them behind. And he won't let go of the boys. In a way they're even more vulnerable than Lenie and Nannie. I don't want them to be like him when they grow up.'

'You must see a lawyer.'

She shakes her head.

I glance over my shoulder to catch a glimpse of the two girls, holding on for dear life, laughing, one blonde, one dark-haired. My stomach contracts.

'What can I do?' I ask, desperate.

'Nothing, I'm afraid. Except – perhaps you shouldn't come to the farm again, not when he's there.'

'I'd like to confront him.'

'He'll just take it out on me. And the children.'

I raise my hands from my lap; let them fall back, helpless. 'Fuck!' I mutter under my breath.

Suddenly, the day has broken loose from my grasp and is careening dangerously. I'm no longer sure we should be going in to town at all, not like this.

Does she sense my distress? For she asks, suddenly, 'Should we rather go back home?'

An atavistic sense of responsibility takes over. I hear myself saying, 'No. Actually, I have a date in town with Lenie.'

'What's that about?' There is a quizzical frown above her dark glasses.

'She doesn't know about it yet. You and Nannie can go shopping on your own for a while. Leave Lenie to me, just for half an hour.'

'If you wish.' Her tone is flat, listless, incurious.

I was helping Trui sort the laundry when the nurse came to call me to the telephone; I'd been waiting for it all morning, yet when it came it was inopportune. I needed the feeling of freedom offered me by the fragrance of that little room, the clean whiteness of the starched sheets, the warmth from the iron, the small hiss it made when Trui tested it with a middle finger; a reassurance more comforting than I could have expected; a recovery of a space in myself I'd thought I'd lost. And bolstered by this new contentment I was eager to talk. We were feeling our way back to where we'd been the previous time.

'Does Jeremiah know?' I asked her as we stood back to fold a newly ironed sheet between us. 'About what we discussed on Saturday?'

'I told him years ago when we got married,' she said calmly. 'I couldn't go into it without telling him. He said nothing. We never spoke about it again.' Suddenly raising her voice. 'Jeremiah is a good man.'

'I know. You deserve each other.' I made the jump. 'But you both deserve better than the life you've had.'

'We're old. It's too late to change anything now.'

'Jonnie is young.'

'Life is never easy, Kristien.' She had taken a risk in saying my name; I let her know that I'd noticed; she acknowledged it. 'For nobody. So Jonnie too must learn.'

'But if we can make things easier for him?'

'You tell me how.' She pressed the small folded rectangle of the sheet against her sagging breast. 'Don't tell me it's because there will be a new government in Pretoria, or Cape Town, or wherever. Our life is in this place. Jonnie is here. We are all here.'

'I want to arrange something with Ouma.'

'You want to take my life in your hands,' she said quietly. 'Do I have no say in it?'

That was when the nurse interrupted us; and a minute later there was Abel Joubert's voice in my ear, saying, 'How are you today?'

'Have they come? Are they with you?' I was aware of the nurse listening behind her magazine.

'I'm phoning from Sam's office. Yes, they're here. Would you like to join us for an early lunch – about twelve?'

'Of course. Who – ' I checked myself. 'How many of them came down?'

'Five.'

No names. It wasn't necessary, really; but it would have been good to hear him name them. I wouldn't push him; or my luck. My hand was moist when I put the receiver down. I needed a cup of tea. In the kitchen I put on the kettle; Trui came through from the laundry, which was in a way regrettable, because the kitchen was less conducive to intimacy. In fact, as I was pouring our tea Jonnie came in from outside, so we couldn't resume our conversation.

'Morning,' he mumbled, stopping in the doorway.

'Hi, Jonnie. Would you like some tea?'

'No. I came to see Ma.' The hostility was no longer overt, as on the first day; but there was no mistaking the distance he was keeping between us.

'All yours,' I said, taking my cup to go, then stopping to add, 'By the way, I'll be meeting the ANC people today. I'll see if I can set up something for you.'

There was more than enough to do, not only in the house but outside too; at some stage I should try to find out what was happening in the lucerne lands, in the ostrich camps – not to breathe down Jeremiah's neck but to show solidarity. I'd hardly spoken to the other labourers. But not today. I felt cornered there. It was only nine o'clock, but there was an itch, a restlessness in me that was aggravated by the space and silence of the farm. On an impulse I telephoned Anna; I was too preoccupied with my own thoughts to catch, before it was too late, the hesitation in her voice before she said, 'Okay, but give me half an hour, I'm not dressed yet.' She must have exaggerated, or otherwise she was incredibly efficient, because there was not a hair out of place when she arrived from the neighbouring farm. Only those telltale dark glasses.

And now we're in town, turning into the main street with its scraggly end-of-season trees, old stone buildings, haphazardly modernised façades.

'Would you like to come with me?' I ask Lenie when the two girls come jumping down from the back.

She looks at me suspiciously. 'What for?' Her hair is tousled. In her shorts and T-shirt she has a tomboy look, but it is belied by the incipient femininity of her movements. Instinctively – has she caught my look? – she hunches her shoulders and half-turns away.

'We're going to do some shopping, you and I. We'll meet Nannie and your mother in an hour, in the café over there. Right, Anna?'

Ignoring Anna's quizzical dark-eyed stare I reach out for Lenie's hand. It brushes mine, then pulls away. But she falls in next to me and we go round the corner towards Shapiro's.

'Where are we going?' she asks.

'How old are you, Lenie?'

'I'll be thirteen in November.'

'When I was your age, almost exactly your age, Ouma Kristina brought me here to buy me my first bra. No one else believed I needed it, but *she* understood.'

Lenie blushes scarlet. But I can see her eyes shining. Quite a pretty child, I discover.

'Would you like one?'

She nods eagerly, then mumbles in embarrassment, 'But Mummy says it's stupid.'

'That's what my mother thought too, at the time. But Ouma Kristina always knew what one needed, and when.'

In the dusky shop we are surrounded by eager, ancient little women. I explain our needs. Very seriously, they nod and hop about like bobtails on a lawn, and within minutes we have a whole pile of garments to choose from, most of them ludicrously oversized for Lenie's modest requirements. But I sweep the whole pile from the counter and accompany her to one of the floral-curtained cubicles at the back.

'I'll wait for you,' I say prudently as I let her go in and draw the curtain between us. She darts me a grateful look, showing for the first time the hint of a smile. I can hear the rustling of her disrobing below the bare globe overhead. At last her flushed face peeps round the curtain.

'I need your help, please. If you don't mind.'

The biggest of the bras is draped round her rib cage in two limp crumpled pockets suspended from her fragile pointed shoulders, sitting

247

on her chest like blinkers on a horse. I keep a straight face, make her turn round, adjust as far as possible the straps over the small bony wings of her shoulder blades. Then I leave her for a moment to fetch a hand mirror and we both study, very gravely, the reflection of her torso.

'I think,' she says after a while, 'this one is not quite so comfortable.'

'You may be right. Let's try the next one.'

She takes off the first and I hand her the second; our hands touch in the exchange; she smiles, with an unselfconscious frankness that stabs me as acutely as a knife. It is a remarkable moment: not because it repeats so precisely what happened years before, but because so much experience is caught in it. It is not that I am looking at myself through Ouma's eyes; it is not that this blithe, busy child – each movement she executes a statement of awkward grace – has taken a place once occupied by me. It is not even a question of discovering behind the two of us the long line of others (a girl delivered, at this age, into the hands of a wild rapist farmer; a child-woman with impossibly long hair playing with a rag doll; an infant on a beach watching from among her sandcastles a ship in full sail go by; an adolescent playing games with a gardener and invoking through her thoughtless involvement an avalanche of horrors, rape, incarceration in a dark cellar, death; a young woman dancing among the shrubs and trees like some moonstruck bird of night – ). It is much more complicated and more fluid than mere linearity. It is recovering, briefly, the child I lost; experiencing myself, my many selves, seeing through the multiple eye of a fly the two of us involved, involuted, implacated in each other, the girl child eternally on the threshold of womanhood, surveyed by the older woman, innocence and experience, faith and knowledge; and in us, so briefly, in the series of small gestures and actions that connect us, in the covering and uncovering of her not-yet-breasts, there is a gathering of past and future.

So much at stake; while on the surface it seems so trivial, amusing, insignificant, as we work our way, resolute and unhurried, through the whole collection of bras until we finally agree on what I've known from the beginning is the only possible choice.

'To start with, you can fill them out with hankies or tissues,' I suggest. 'I'll show you how.' There is so much, I realise with an ache of inexplicable lack, I'd love to show this child. And quite irresponsibly I say, 'When I'm back in London you must come and visit me. Will you?'

'Do you really mean it, Auntie Kristien?'

'Don't call me Auntie, it makes me feel ancient.'

'But Mummy wouldn't like it.'

'Then you can call me Auntie when she's present.'

I leave the cubicle with her, painfully conscious of time and the sweetness of its illusions – the almost tangible quality of time spilled like water, time irretrievably lost.

We choose a dress as well, and sandals; and, for Nannie, a T-shirt. I casually enquire about menstruation and Lenie swallows and nods eagerly; and although I have an idea that it's more wishful thinking than truth, we provide her with some small pads too. Hand in hand we take a long roundabout way back so that I can improvise on what Ouma once told me, not about shame and hygiene and the curse of woman-hood, but about discovery and fun and the nature of nature.

The excursion has offered me escape from the urgency of anticipa-tion, but now it comes back in a sudden wave. On an impulse I take Lenie with me to Sam Ndzuta's office. The waiting room is full of people, black and white. But the secretary recognises me and approaches, a flustered look in her eyes. 'I'm afraid we're running late,' she says. 'They started an hour behind schedule. Do you think you could come back at one?'

This is a blow. Will the morning never end? I feel a touch of panic as Lenie and I return to the café where we have arranged to meet the others. But I fight it back. The girl's small hand is warm and sticky in mine. For her sake, for Anna's too, I must see this through.

For the next half-hour I pretend to be deeply interested in the children's chatter while I struggle through the milkshake I ordered in a moment of false enthusiasm. Opposite me, Anna's face is inscrutable, and she makes little attempt at conversation. I try to read her eyes through the dark glasses, but she seems disturbingly remote. After-wards we go through the motions of perfunctory window-shopping. Anna also accompanies me to the library; after my last conversation with Jacob Bonthuys I'm intrigued to read something about the stars. Unfortunately they have almost nothing on astrology. With some misgivings I take out Stephen Hawking.

The children are running wild among the shelves; from time to time I surreptitiously check my watch. At a quarter to one we return to the glare of the sun outside. The girls are skipping ahead, chattering away, clutching their parcels. Anna and I follow in silence. Neither of us really has anything to say; the discovery of this morning lies too heavily on us.

'I must go to Ouma's lawyer,' I tell her. 'Why don't you go with me and make an appointment to see him?'

'No!' she exclaims in panic, catching hold of my arm.

'Anna, sooner or later – '

'Not now. Please. Please don't talk about it any more. Anyway, it's time to go home, I must make lunch.' She avoids my accusing stare, her mouth again twitching nervously. 'I'll be all right, I promise. Are you sure you can get back on your own?'

'Of course. There'll be several people. I'll bum a lift.'

And then they go. It is both a release and an anguish to see her drive off. The girls wave eagerly from the back.

Ouma's lawyer is a doddering, kind old man. I explain her need to see him. He will go this afternoon, he says.

Now it is time. This is the place.

As I enter the building a group of men come out, preceded by their loud voices. They're all in khaki, some in shorts, a few wearing hats. It is Casper and his gang. I recognise him too late to take avoiding action. He stops; the others move in. For a moment we are left alone, face to face. I see his expression change, but not in the way I would have expected: instead of becoming aggressive he looks guarded, then ingratiating, like a guilty dog wagging his tail.

'And how are you this morning?' he asks, aiming to kiss me.

I sidestep him. Without meaning to, knowing that in fact it is the last thing I should do, I hiss at him, 'You fucking shit.' And hurry into the building.

And now the outside world is stripped from me like a covering sheet, and I am left naked.

This time there are no other people in the waiting room. Sam Ndzuta must have given instructions to his secretary. She greets me with a brisk smile. She knocks on the door. A voice replies. She enters, then comes out again and stands aside to let me past. It is unbelievable that Sandile should be here.

As it turns out, he isn't.

# 4

For some time I can only stare at them, from one to the other, trying to impose his face on those looking at me. My mouth begins to form a question, 'Where – ?' But I don't actually utter it. Perhaps he has gone out for a minute. He'll be back. Then Sam places a heavy hand on my shoulder and ushers me towards them; in a daze I hear his voice as he breezily proceeds with the introductions, but there is an unreality about the scene, I feel very remote from them. There is a tall middle-aged woman in an elaborate outfit, Nomaza Debe. A man in an immaculate suit and striped shirt, fortyish, Vusi Mabena. And a portly old man whose white hair is starkly offset against the shining blackness of his skin, Thando Kumalo, a legendary name from the years of exile. I remember meeting him a few times, one of the grand old men, always beaming, his eyes filled with distances and spaces far beyond the present; he won't remember me, I was small fry.

But I'm wrong. He pulls me against him, hugging me. And the remoteness I've been feeling begins to dissolve. 'My child,' he says contentedly. 'What a long time it's been.' He gently pats my cheek. 'I'm so sorry about this terrible thing that's happened to your family.'

I feel the childish need to remain snuggled in his embrace, comforted by his bulk, the expanse of his belly, the deep rumbling tones of his voice; and to be reassured by his fatherly presence. But this is no time to disgrace myself in front of strangers. I must recover some semblance of composure.

Sam takes over again. And suddenly the questions are answered: the group has had to split to catch up with some of the morning's unfinished business. Mongane Yaya and Sandile are at a meeting in the township, the rest of us are going to a guest house on the outskirts of the town for lunch; the other two may join us there afterwards. I don't know whether I should laugh or burst into tears with relief. At the same time I feel furious with Sandile: why the hell didn't he send one of the others to the meeting? How could he do this to me? But of course, he didn't know; he wasn't expecting me here. I must pull myself together. I must be patient. Having waited for five years I can get through another hour or so.

I take a deep breath, but I can feel the tension throbbing behind my eyes. The feeling of remoteness seeps back. I follow the others as they troop downstairs. Whatever happens is filtered through a screen, distanced by a telescope.

On the pavement outside an old woman in rags and tatters, her legs stretched out before her like two broomsticks, is selling bruised grapes, blackened bananas, apples, wilting carrots and beans and lettuces.

In a flush of demonstrative benevolence Vusi Mabena bends over her. 'How are you, mother?' he asks.

She stares vaguely up at him through her cataracts; a fume of methylated spirits wafts over us.

'What do you think about the elections?' he persists. 'This is going to be a new place, I tell you.'

'I'll still have trouble selling my vegetables,' she says.

It is old Thando Kumalo who takes some money from his pocket and buys a bunch of bananas, a plastic bag of apples, a wretched lettuce. 'Keep the change, Sisi,' he tells her. Bewildered, she stares after him, shaking her head. This man is bloody mad, she must be thinking.

Behind the building, where Sam's car is waiting, Thando offers the wares to a boy begging under the pepper trees. I get into the car, squeezed between Thando and Vusi. The splendid woman Nomaza sits in front, her bottle-green head-dress blocking out the view. Not that I'm seeing much anyway. I'm thinking: Sandile, Sandile . . .

Thando puts a large hand on my knee. 'It's so very good to see you, Kristien. All of us together again. I almost can't believe it.'

'I'm not really back yet,' I remind him, feeling inexpressibly guilty. 'I only came back – because of my grandmother.'

'All this violence. And it's so unnecessary.' He shakes his grizzled head. 'You know, I went to see those kids in prison this morning.'

'This is not a place for humans!' I say impulsively, angrily.

Thando raises a bushy white eyebrow. 'That's where you're wrong, if you don't mind my saying so. It *is* a place for humans. It's our place. Human beings are full of shit and misery and violence. But don't forget, they're also full of compassion and hope and courage. I've seen a lot of both since I came back. You can't have one without the other.'

I know I must direct this conversation away from me. And I ask him the first hackneyed question that springs to my mind. 'Thando, did you ever expect – while you were over there – that you'd really come back one day?'

'One doesn't think of things like that,' he says, almost sternly. This is not what I expected. 'If you do,' he continues, 'you'll fall to pieces. So you just do what you've got to do. Because when you live in exile you're struggling every day of your life against both the possible and the impossible.'

'Now it's happened?'

'No, it hasn't happened yet. It's still happening. It started off badly when I just came back, I must tell you. After thirty-four years of exile.' For a while his eyes cloud over. 'Thirty-four years, right?' And then he wades in. 'You know, I grew up in this great old family house in

Natal, on a green hill, overlooking the Indian ocean. I remember it so well. It was huge, huge.' A smile. 'Of course, everything was huge in those days. My father's Black Australorps came up to my waist. Now, when I came back, it was all gone. Not just changed. Gone. As in *nothing*.' He draws me the picture of the day he went back. Not a brick or a stone was left. Except the tree, of course. The old bluegum he'd planted himself was still there. The oleander, the syringa, the dark squat tree whose name Thando can't remember, once enormous, now small and stunted. But the house was gone. There were a few shacks on the property, squatters who'd moved in. A patch of mealies, a straggling pumpkin, scrawny chickens scratching in the long grass, a litter of kittens. He turns his deep round eyes to me. 'But I have my memories, you see. So I can go on. And our little family graveyard was still there when I went to look for it. It was a windy day. There were insects in the grass. And a fine sun overhead. And I visited all the people who'd died while I was gone. My mother. My father. My two brothers. Some cousins. And the old people too, generations of them. Some of them killed way back by the Voortrekkers. All those hills are inhabited by the ancestors now, they never go away. And while they're there I can always go back. Just to sit there and look out over the sea. So I know I belong here, it's my place.' He pats my knee again. 'We'll make it work.' Adding more softly, 'My God, we've got to.'

We reach the guest house, an old manor newly restored, in green and white, with rambling roses on trellises and a wave of lawns. Inside we are joined by a handful of other guests, the town's VIPs and their spouses ('spice', Sandile used to joke): mayor, magistrate, a few local party leaders, all bursting with goodwill, flashing large mouthfuls of teeth, real and false. The women are dressed to kill, not swiftly and efficiently but hacking away with a blunt knife.

It begins, for me, on an unfortunate note when the starters are served, smoked salmon, and Vusi Mabena cracks a hoary chestnut. 'Good. All the true delicacies in life are raw, aren't they? Salmon, oysters, power.'

If Sandile had been here I might have taken it as a joke; now – from sheer spite, I suspect – I react viciously: 'So power is still the name of the game?'

A silence descends.

Then, with a slightly forced laugh, and winking in my direction, Nomaza comments, 'Don't pay any attention to him, Kristien. It's the death-rattle of a chauvinist.'

'He doesn't seem close to death to me,' I say, trying to keep it light, but aware of the tension below which I find hard to suppress.

'Don't get me wrong,' says Vusi, directing his most seductive smile at me. 'I'm the first to admit that throughout the struggle women fought side by side with the men.'

'But now that it's over,' Nomaza reminds him, 'you think you can send us back to the kitchen, don't you?'

'I don't think it's a good thing for women to meddle with politics,' says the mayor's wife, the sort of woman who gives pretentiousness a bad name. 'We can't forsake our God-given role, can we? I mean, look at what happened to Winnie Mandela – '

'This country has had many courageous women, black and white,' says Thando in his deep voice. 'We needed them in the past and we need them now.'

'Behind every man you still find a woman,' says the mayor's wife as if she has just thought it up herself.

'Isn't that the problem?' I ask, heedless. 'Why must we always be behind them?'

'Oh, but we hold the real power,' says the magistrate's wife. 'It's the woman who makes or breaks the man.'

'And is that the only criterion?' I ask. 'To measure yourself in terms of what you can or cannot do to a man?'

'We women have already achieved a lot,' she retorts. 'I'm thinking of Afrikaner women in particular.'

I raise my eyebrows.

She takes up the challenge: 'We were right beside the men on the Great Trek, were we not? Every inch of the way. And when they were ready to give up it was the women who kept them going.' She is on a roll now. 'Even in our own century it was women who proof-read the translation of the Bible, wasn't it?'

'And who did the translation?' I ask.

'Anyway,' says Vusi, 'we were really talking about large political issues, about democracy, not about purely female matters.'

Swiftly, calmly, efficiently, Nomaza moves in. 'If you deny women their self-esteem, you end up with a crippled democracy.'

'How come?'

'Because the whole Western model for democracy is the nuclear family.'

'Nothing wrong with family values, is there?' interrupts the mayor's wife.

There is, as so often in such conversations, a feeling of *déjà vu* about it all; yet the fire with which Nomaza speaks lends new conviction to the familiar arguments. 'You have a father who exercises all the authority,' she says, 'and a mother who's expected to fulfil herself by living through the others, while the children are treated as their possessions. So how do you expect to arrive at democratic values if your every point of departure is inequality?'

'I'm not sure I understand what you mean,' says the mayor's wife.

'Don't worry, dear,' her husband consoles her. 'I'll explain it to you later.'

'I think we should drink a toast to the women,' Thando intervenes diplomatically. 'Past and present.' He raises his glass of mineral water.

'To the women,' says Nomaza. '*A luta continua.*'

And the dust settles, temporarily. Which requires a deliberate change of subject; as always.

(Will Sandile be late? Will he come at all?)

'Are you satisfied with your visit so far?' enquires the magistrate without focusing on anyone in particular.

It is again the smooth – the too smooth – Vusi who provides a synopsis of their morning's discussions. After a briefing session with the mayor, the magistrate and the district commander of police, and a visit to the detainees, they interviewed a group of black community leaders, followed by a discussion with Casper and a hand-picked delegation from his commando.

'We're deeply worried about that element in our midst,' says the mayor. 'Personally, I've always held that apartheid is wrong.'

'That is very reassuring,' says Vusi. It is hard to make out whether he is serious or taking the mickey. 'It's astonishing how many people say that nowadays. Don't you agree, Miss Müller?'

Caught unawares, I blurt out, 'I'm afraid I have more faith in a right-winger who frankly admits that he hates blacks than in all these white males who suddenly try to persuade everybody that they've always been against apartheid.'

It is the wives who dart at me their most poisonous glances. But the mayor, no doubt used to handling difficult situations, smiles indulgently. 'We realise you are obliged to say so, Miss Müller, being related to Casper Louw.'

'By marriage only,' I remind him. 'I'm sure I can't be blamed for that.'

'There are some lunatic fringes to my family too,' Thando comes to my rescue, chuckling. 'I think it makes us both archetypal South Africans.'

'This district is certainly no exception,' says Nomaza. The flashpoint has been passed. 'We've already met some of all persuasions. Those who live in fear of an apocalypse, those who just quietly go about their usual business, those who are praying, those who have lost faith. You name it.'

'I can tell you one thing,' says Vusi, 'I'm just very, very glad that the unfortunate incident that started it all wasn't caused, as many people first thought, by disaffected MKs. That would have been very bad for the ANC.'

'I don't think that is a consideration at all,' says Thando, more sharply than I have yet heard him speak. (This, I am sure, is exactly how Sandile would have reacted.) 'Surely there are more important things than political harm. As politicians we should be prepared to live with that. What concerns me is human lives. The point is that people should feel safe in their homes.'

'The point,' says Nomaza, 'is that people should have homes to feel safe in.'

Thando smiles broadly. 'The woman has spoken. And she is right.' Then he becomes serious again. 'The point is that there should be reason to hope, for everybody. All the suffering that has gone before, for years, for decades, my God, for centuries, should not be in vain. There was a very good, brave friend of mine who died before he could come back: he died, after fifteen years, from the effects of the torture he'd gone through before he escaped. And before he died he said something I'll never forget. He said, 'All that suffering has taught me is the uselessness of suffering.' But that's not true. I tell you, it's not true. We can *make* suffering worthwhile. It's up to us to make that choice. And if there's something we've earned by now, I think, it is the right to dare to hope.'

'Hope for what?' asks the magistrate, who clearly requires more facts.

'For all of us to discover the simple truth that we're in this together,' says Thando. 'That from now on, even if there's still struggling and suffering ahead, we'll be struggling and suffering together.'

The conversation continues to swirl past me; I no longer pay attention. This is not what I have come for. Perhaps, suggests what remains of my Calvinist conscience, it serves me right; my expectations were too personal.

Lunch draws to a close. My headache has turned into a migraine. I resign myself to the fact that Sandile won't come any more; it is too late.

As we move through the glass door to the outside an elderly man emerges from the bar, taking very delicate, small steps, doing his utmost not to let on that he is well sozzled. In the process, not without considerable effort, he puts on his hat; but it is the wrong way round.

From behind the counter the barman, keeping a poker face, calls, 'Oom Lammie, you've put your hat on back to front, man!'

The old man stops, teeters, looks round, and replies with withering dignity, 'How the hell do you know which way I'm going?' And goes out.

# 5

And then he is there. A car stops beside a flower-bed – the brazen yellows and oranges of Cape marigolds – and two men come across the lawn towards us. One is a stranger, a trim, relaxed man with a scar on his forehead and white-rimmed spectacles. It must be Mongane Yaya. The other is Sandile. Thinner than I remembered him, and older, quite alarmingly so. His jacket is draped over one shoulder and he has loosened his tie.

Halfway across the lawn he stops. How well I know that perplexed little frown between his eyes,

'Kristien!' he exclaims.

My face has gone numb. I mouth something as Sam introduces me to Mongane. When he turns to Sandile and says, 'You two know each other, I believe?' I start laughing uncontrollably. He embraces me. And all I can think of saying is, 'You still use the same aftershave.'

The next ten minutes or so is a senseless jumble. We agree – that much I gather – that the group, or at least some of them, will pay a visit to the farm in the late afternoon to see Ouma, if she is strong enough to receive them. The rest is a blur. It is only Sandile's face I am conscious of – so much older, stamped with a weariness that shows through the vivaciousness on the surface, his hair speckled curiously with grey.

And then the others drive off and we are left alone. It seems they have agreed that Sandile would drive me home.

'Is it really you?' he asks as he gets in next to me.

'I thought you'd never come,' I say stupidly. 'I've been waiting and waiting.'

'Did you know I was coming?'

'Yes. But I told them to keep it a surprise. Now we've lost two hours.'

'You should have let me know.'

'I always do the wrong thing.'

'Don't say that.' He puts his hand on mine. An electrical current thrills through my body. 'I didn't know you were back too,' he says.

'I'm not.' I try to explain; the effort helps me to compose myself.

'I never realised the injured woman was your grandmother,' he says. 'If I'd known – '

'No need to apologise.' As he turns the ignition key I lean my head against his shoulder. 'How much time do we have?'

'Not much. We have meetings and consultations all day. But perhaps you can come to the meeting tonight? In the city hall, at eight. And afterwards, maybe – '

'Of course. I'll be there.' I start giving him directions to get out of town, on the road to The Bird Place.

'All these years,' he says.

I suddenly feel like shaking him. Jesus, we have so little time; can't we break through the small-talk, the obvious little nothings – *sweet nothing, my Lord* – the tussle with inanities?

'You've aged,' I tell him, which is not at all what I meant to say. 'You look exhausted.'

'It's not been easy, being back.' A tense smile; behind the lines I briefly recognise the face I loved. 'But it's worth while. Every moment of it. And next week – '

'Let's not talk about politics now.'

'You forget that my life is politics.'

I'm stung by the gentle reprimand; but of course he's right. 'Even so,' I say, 'you have to look after yourself. In an attempt at lightheartedness – or is it a disingenuous move to go straight to what really matters? – I say, 'I'll have to tell Nozipho to keep a tighter rein on you.'

A shadow moves across his face. 'She's no longer with me, Kristien.'

I stare at him.

'We've split up.'

'But why – ? when – ? You were so . . .'

'Coming back is not for free, you know. There's a price-tag.' He stares fixedly ahead. I can see the tension in his knuckles on the steering-wheel.

'But the two of you were so close,' I protest. 'I thought nothing could ever . . .'

It is a while before he says, without looking at me, 'One lives in exile for years and years. The thing that keeps you going is this place. The memories, the hopes, the expectations. And then you come back and nothing is really like you thought it would be.'

'But you were always so realistic about it. You used to warn everybody not to expect too much . . .'

'It's the small things that catch you unprepared. The big issues one can cope with.'

'I don't understand.'

'I'm not sure I do either.' He glances at me. 'To begin with, Nozipho had to give up her job to come back. A very good job she'd just settled into. She tried her best to cover up but I knew how hard it was. So all the feelings of guilt and resentment began. And then the kids – '

'Weren't they glad to come home?'

'To them this isn't home, remember. They were used to living in the States, they're young Americans, they have no roots here.' A wry smile. 'They can't even speak Xhosa. Soon everything just got out of hand. Choosing a school. We couldn't face the idea of exposing them to the horrors of black education. But a posh private school didn't seem right either. I mean, we *are* supposed to be freedom fighters. And then we had to buy a house. Where? In a black township with the ordinary, deprived people I'd come back to be with – or in a white suburb where Nozipho could lead a better life and the kids would feel at home? Before we knew where we were we'd drifted so far apart that it became irreparable. And even while I saw it happening I couldn't really do anything to save us: there were so many other urgent things to attend to, every hour of every day; so many people who needed help and advice and God knows what else.'

'I think I can understand,' I say. 'Even if I don't approve.' I touch his elbow. 'Turn right here.'

'And those gates?' he exclaims. 'Jesus, where are you taking me?'

'Aren't they something?' I laugh. 'When I was a child I always thought they were the gates of paradise.'

'Of hell, more likely,' he mocks. 'Abandon ye all hope.'

A single barn-owl descends on the bonnet, staring straight at us through drooping yellow eyelids.

Sandile slams on the brakes. 'What's this?' he exclaims.

'One of my grandmother's pets.'

'In broad daylight?'

'One gets used to it.'

He looks at me suspiciously, and drives on, pulls in under the trees and stares at the half-obscured palace in utter disbelief. 'You *live* here?' he asks.

'Would you like to come in?'

'Sorry, Kristien. They'll be waiting for me.' The engine is still running.

I can't believe it. I think: I haven't seen him for five years. I look in his eyes. I try to keep my voice steady. 'This is why you lost Nozipho,' I say quietly.

He looks back at me. For a long time he is silent. At last he says, 'I've paid the price. Now I've got to make it work. Otherwise it would have been all in vain. You do understand that, don't you?'

Isn't this exactly what Thando said an hour ago?

'I suppose I can,' I say. 'But I'm not sure I want to.' His face is so close our noses almost touch. For the moment, all feeling is suspended. I know it will hit me later. Right now I am almost relieved.

'I'll see you tonight,' he says.

I shake my head slowly. 'I'm sorry. Actually I can't. I have to look after Ouma.'

'Surely you can arrange for a sitter?'

'No. She counts on me. We have an arrangement.'

He comes round to open my door. For a moment we stand together. He hugs me quietly and kisses me. I know he is crying, but pretend not to notice.

Moments later he drives off. The owl is still perched on the bonnet, as if to make sure he won't turn back.

# 6

Ouma is sleeping, restless, her mouth open, making a gargling sound. It remains unsettling to see her like that, in the coffin. The nurse looks up briefly, shrugs, resumes reading. Trui, it seems, has gone home. I have the house to myself. It is the hour of the idiots again.

I need to think. I also need to be busy. I must not think about Sandile now. There is the rest of Ouma's life to dispose of; it should occupy the hands if not the mind. Relieved at having found something to do, I go to the secret room and collect as many of the bundles as I can manage. I carry them to a clearing behind the graveyard, well out of sight of both the palace and the labourers' houses. What I'll do is to pile them all in one big heap, then cover them with firewood from the neat stack behind the house, and set fire to everything at once. From the whitewashed wall of the graveyard the peacock keeps watch; it must be his favourite perch, this bird of death bearing the evil eye on his tail. Four, five, six times I make the journey to and fro. Then I stack the wood. I light a cigarette. I prepare to light the fire, but am stopped by the dire shriek uttered by the peacock from its observation post.

'Shut up!' I shout at it, and immediately feel foolish.

In response it fans out its magical tail and begins to strut along the wall.

As I bend over to resume my pyrotechnics there is a whirring sound, as if in response to the peacock's shriek, and when I look up I see a great multicoloured cloud descending. It's the birds, even more of them than I have seen before, covering the sky; then, like the funnel of a tornado, diving down towards me. I hunch down to protect myself. This is pure Hitchcock. But as it turns out they have no interest in me. They swish right past me, mere centimetres from my body, hurling themselves at the pyre. There are so many of them that it takes a while before I realise what has been happening. The chopped chunks of wood lie scattered all around me. Some shreds of the paper bags remain, stirring in the wake of the unfurling wave of birds; the rest has disappeared. They have picked up every pad and rag there was. High above, very high, already far away, and travelling farther at it seems ever-increasing speed, the great cloud disappears, dissolving into air, into thin air.

On the graveyard wall the peacock has drawn in its tail. Emitting once more its eerie cry it begins to flap its wings, gathering momentum before it, too, flies up, past the house, beyond the surrounding trees, gone. An uncanny silence descends upon the place.

Meticulous, like a nun at her devotions, I gather the scattered lengths of wood and return them to their original pile. I heave myself on to the graveyard wall and settle on the peacock's perch. It is very still; one can almost hear the sun. In an inexplicable way my mind feels cleared.

I think: At last I have seen Sandile. For the last few days everything in me has been directed towards seeing him again; it has blocked out everything else from this day, even the shock of what has happened to Anna; even, temporarily, Ouma. Now he has come, and left again. An anticlimax? Then why am I relieved? What was I expecting anyway? We made our decision very long ago. Our separate lives have continued. That he is now free is ironical, but immaterial; one cannot go back to bodies one has loved and believe all will be the same. He has to lead his life, I mine. If our ways happen to cross, as in this shrinking world it may well happen, it cannot change our courses. I am thirty-three, not twenty-five any more. There are, I hope, many years ahead of me; but the course of my life has changed. I cannot go back. What I need is another kind of freedom, for another kind of choice. Not a revisiting of what has already been decided long ago. He has come; he has gone: that is as it should be.

I go back to the house across the quiet yard; there seems more space now, even if it isn't empty. And the palace sits on the ground like a huge ship on an unmoving sea, waiting for a current to loosen its moorings, to launch itself, to explore the space ahead.

From a distance I see Trui approaching, tying her apron as she walks. Labourers are spreading out from their homes towards the ostrich camps. Life is resuming where it left off. A car draws up as I reach the kitchen door. It is Mr Jansen, the lawyer; he has brought, he says, his secretary. I take them upstairs to where Ouma has just woken up.

The visitors are taken aback by what they see: I haven't thought of warning them. But perhaps they are used to the idiosyncracies of the old. Ouma's evident pleasure at seeing them dispels whatever misgivings they may have had.

The phone rings. I pick it up and take it to my room, indicating to Mr Jansen and his twin-set suited secretary that I'll be back soon, but Ouma motions me out; she can cope, she says drily.

I hear Michael's voice. This is unexpected; I am really not prepared for it, not now. After the feeling of release I have just experienced there is, suddenly, an impression of being drawn back into some confinement.

'You don't sound glad to hear me,' he says testily; perhaps we've come to know each other too well.

'It's not a good day,' I say.

'Well, it hasn't been too good for me either. I lost a footnote and I can't seem to find it.'

'Have you looked under the bed?'

'Don't be facetious,' he snarls.

'Jesus Christ, Michael, there are more important things in the world than a lost fucking footnote.'

'Have you any idea of what my life is like right now?'

'Have you any idea of mine?'

'When are you coming back?'

'Why should you care?'

Nothing is going right, nothing at all. We should have hung up after the first exchange; but being pigheaded, both of us, we blunder on, getting more and more annoyed, more and more vicious – to an eavesdropper like the nurse, I suppose, more and more childish, ridiculous, absurd – until, with perfect synchronisation, we both slam the receivers down. Regretting it instantly; at least I am. But now neither will take the first step for quite a while; it has been the pattern of our relationship. Eventually we'll make up. I hope. Do I?

I need air. At the same time I am not ready to face the infinity surrounding the house, so I start winding my way through the labyrinth of its passages and byways and dead-ends again, its broken landings and abandoned rooms. Only much later do I remember about our visitors.

They are already leaving. 'You should have sent for me,' I tell Ouma.

'Why? I'm perfectly capable of handling my own business.'

'Wasn't there anything to sign, to witness, whatever?'

'The secretary was here, and the nurse.'

'What have you decided to do?'

'It's a great relief,' she says. 'I've been worrying about this. Now I can look forward to dying.'

I look hard at her. 'Ouma Kristina, are you not afraid to die?'

'Why should I be? I've lived among the dead so long.'

'You are so old,' I say gently.

'Age is not a matter of years but of style,' she says.

I lean over the coffin and take her hand. 'I've done as you asked me,' I tell her. 'I've destroyed all the evidence.'

The nurse looks up sharply, accusingly.

'Good. It's all going exactly as planned.'

'I must tell you about the birds,' I say.

'They helped you, did they? I knew they would.'

Even the owls that used to roost in here, I notice now, have gone.

A car stops outside.

I hurry over to the window. 'You have more visitors,' I say. 'Do you think you can handle it?'

'Who are they?'

'Friends of mine.' (Will Sandile be with them?)

'Then it's all right. I've never met your friends, you know.'

# 7

The group, explains Sam Ndzuta when I arrive outside, has had to split once again to catch up with their telescoped programme before tonight's meeting, so Vusi and Sandile have gone elsewhere with Abel. I feel a brief twinge of – what? Pique, anger, regret? This time he *chose* to stay away. But after a moment I nod to myself. It was the right decision – for both of us. Composed, I face the guests. Only Nomaza and old Thando have come out with Sam; also Mongane Yaya, who stands a few yards away from the others, staring at the palace in total amazement.

'I've heard of these places before,' he says after a while, 'but I never expected anything like this.'

'You can understand why people would want to burn it down,' I comment wryly.

'You may as well try to burn a dream,' he answers. 'Or a nightmare. It won't go away.'

'My house was not so fanciful,' says Thando, 'but the size must have been the same. Unbelievable. You must have had room for scores of relatives, like us.'

'It's empty now,' I say. 'We only have ghosts now.'

'Why the tall foundations?' he asks.

'To keep cool in summer, I suppose. And to have a place for the idiots.' I tell them about the legend of the Little Karoo.

'Any idiots down there today?'

For a moment I wonder whether he is clairvoyant; but I keep up the banter. 'I'm afraid nowadays they're all on the streets, all the time.'

'That's the price of democracy,' says Sam with a straight face.

The front door is still blocked up. I take them round to the back.

'Very quiet here,' remarks Thando. 'No birds in this place?'

'Not at the moment,' I say. 'We're preparing for a death.'

They look at me, but I don't answer, invaded suddenly by a grief so profound that my whole body contracts. For two weeks now I've been living in the shadow of this impending death, yet somehow it has remained unbelievable. Now, shaken by all that has happened today, it unfurls itself like a wave and I have no defence. Without saying a word Thando puts an arm round my shoulders. I press myself against him and burst into tears, wholly letting go, in a passion and a desolation such as I haven't felt in years.

'That's right, my child,' he says in a low soothing voice. 'That's right. Don't hold it back. You need this. We all do.'

I don't know where the others are. It doesn't matter. This is where I want to be, have had to be, for so long. Weeping – not hysterically, but in a steady uncontrollable flood – I hold on to him as if I'm drowning, enveloped by his large good body, encouraged by his voice and the hands stroking my hair. I weep for Ouma Kristina, for my dead parents, for all the women behind me and around me, resuscitated in Ouma's stories and accepted now as part of myself; I weep for my dead child, and for the lovers I have lost, for Michael; I weep for Anna and her misery, for Lenie with her new bra and the blithe ignorance of little Nannie; I weep for Sandile and for Nozipho and those like them; I weep for the children who set fire to this place, for Jacob Bonthuys down in the cellar among the stars, for Langenhoven and the girl who lived with the monster Brolloks, and for Loeloeraai, for Trui and her family: I weep for the living and the dead, for the mess we have made of this land, for the immeasurable sadness of the world, for the birds that have gone, for the spilt blood of women through all the ages, I weep, I weep.

When at last the flood spills me on a dry bank, I look at Thando through dishevelled hair – like a moth, I suspect, peering through the broken silk of its cocoon as it approaches the blinding light of day – and shake my head. 'I don't know what's come over me.' With the back of my hand I wipe my face, too exhausted, too relieved, to feel embarrassed.

'Here.' He shakes out a handkerchief which through the prism of tears seems as big as a tablecloth – the sudden smell, again, of freshly laundered, ironed linen – and offers it to me. 'I did the same when I visited my parents' graves for the first time.'

'I messed up your waistcoat.'

'Good. We can all do with some messing up.'

'Don't we have enough of a mess already in this place?'

'Not the right kind. We still need the mess of forgiveness.'

'I always thought forgiveness was a tidying up.'

'It depends. True forgiveness opens you up to all the darkness in yourself. It must be something like this house, don't you think, when it suffered the forgiveness of fire.'

'I wish you were my grandfather.' I smile, thrusting the crumpled handkerchief into his hand. 'Why don't we two just adopt each other?'

'I must warn you I'm a very difficult old man.'

'I think I'm a difficult young woman. I'm sure it will be a good match. Then you can come and live here with me. Happily ever after.'

'No. Happily ever after sounds too much like heaven. And that, I think, must be unbearable to old sinners like us.'

'Do you have children, Thando?'

He shakes his head slowly. 'I had two sons. Both died. One here in the country, in detention. The other in a raid in Lusaka.' He squeezes my hand. 'That was what I cried for, you know, the day I went to our graveyard. For the graves that were there, yes, but especially for the graves that were missing.' He takes me by the elbow. 'And now we must go in. If you are ready?'

We find Sam and Mongane in the kitchen with Trui.

'Where is Nomaza?' I ask.

Trui motions upstairs. 'You all right?' she asks, clearly worried by my looks.

'I'm better than I've been for a long time, Trui.'

'Mongane and I are going to have a word with her son,' says Sam. 'You two go upstairs.'

We find Nomaza beside the coffin, talking eagerly. I haven't had time to warn Thando about the coffin, but he shows no surprise.

He bends over and gently raises Ouma's hand to his lips.

'What is this?' asks Ouma. 'A wake?'

'I've been wanting very much to meet you,' says Thando.

'I hope you haven't come to commiserate,' says Ouma. She winks mischievously at me. 'This woman can't stop talking about what a terrible thing it is that's happened to me. I keep telling her it's nonsense. If it took an explosion to bring you back home then it was a stroke of luck.'

'It's not a stroke of luck if it kills you, Ouma!' I protest.

She pretends not to have heard me. 'Who are these people, Kristien?' she asks. 'You said they were friends.'

'They're from the ANC, Ouma. They've come to try and calm the district down after all that's happened since the bomb.'

'ANC?' She looks from one to the other. 'You don't look like terrorists to me.'

'No more than you are,' I tell her.

'If they're like me they must be dangerous.' She nods slowly. 'So you're here to close the old books and write the new chapter.'

'Write a new chapter, yes,' says Thando. 'Close the old books, no. We can't imagine the future by pretending to forget the past.'

266

'That's what I've been trying to tell Kristien,' says Ouma. 'I'm not sure she understands. I'm telling her stories. Giving her back her memory.' She shakes her head slowly. 'But there's been such a lot of blood in this country. Sometimes I wonder whether it's not going to prove too much for us.' She corrects herself, 'For you, I mean: I'll be out of it.'

'That's what we'll be working on,' says Thando. 'We owe it to people like yourself, you see.'

Ouma turns her pale eyes to Nomaza. 'Will you be in the new government too?'

'I hope so.'

'Good. We need the women. So much of the blood could have been avoided if we'd been there, you know.'

'That's why I'm here,' says Nomaza. 'Many others too.'

'It will be tough. It will be painful.'

'I think I can take it,' Nomaza says quietly. 'I've had my share of pain. But that's beside the point.'

'That's *not* beside the point,' says Ouma firmly. 'Tell me.'

'I've been in exile. I've lost my husband. And a child. And many friends of course.' She seems impatient. 'But we're not here to talk about my life. It's *you* we've come to see.'

But Ouma will not be discouraged so easily. 'What work have you been doing?'

'Since I came back I've been working with the wives of migrant workers.' She hesitates, still reluctant to accept the spotlight Ouma has turned on her; then decides it's worth it. 'They're the ones who hold the whole community together, Mrs Basson. Yet no one takes them seriously. It's always expected of us black women to honour our men more than ourselves, to regard their sacrifices as more important than our own.'

'What else is new?' asks Ouma in a modish turn of phrase that makes me smile.

'Unless we are taken seriously now, we can't hope for a better deal later. And since no one's going to do it for us, we have to do it ourselves.'

Ouma slowly turns her head to look at me. 'And what are *you* going to do, Kristien?'

I try to move out of her field of vision, but she has her eyes fixed on me. 'I still have decisions to make, Ouma.'

'Don't wait too long,' she says crisply.

'She'll be all right,' Thando comes to my defence. 'I've taken a good look at this one. She comes from the right stock.'

'I should hope so.' An impish smile. 'I wish we had the time, I'd have liked to tell you the stories I've been subjecting her to.'

'I'd like to trade stories with you,' he says.

'We'll do that when we're dead. We'll have all the time in the world.'

'That's a date then,' says Thando.

Soon after that they take their leave. Ouma is almost regretful to see them go. I accompany them downstairs.

Sam and Mongane are waiting in the kitchen, with Trui and her family. 'I want you to meet my husband and my son too,' she says, nudging the two forward. 'And this,' she tells them, quite unnecessarily, 'is now the other people from the ANC.' As if she's been hobnobbing all her life.

'Have you had your talk?' I ask Jonnie.

He smiles with new confidence. 'Ja, we'll be seeing each other just after the elections.'

'All set up,' confirms Mongane.

We make small talk for a while; Trui and Nomaza immediately hit it off, and when Nomaza compliments her on her son Trui becomes an ally for life. Jonnie appears embarrassed but flattered; even Jeremiah emerges briefly from his inherent solemnity.

Then it is time for the visitors to go. Mongane smiles brightly as he takes his leave. His double handshake is easy and relaxed. I decide that I like the man – unlike Vusi he has nothing to prove. Thando puts his arm around me and turns to Trui. 'You look after this one,' he tells her, hugging me. 'She's now my granddaughter.'

As Sam opens the car doors for them, I kiss Nomaza goodbye on the cheek. 'It was good of you to come. For the town, and for Ouma.'

'I wouldn't have missed her for anything. Now about that question she asked you – ' Somehow I knew she wasn't going to let this pass. 'What are you going to do?'

'I wish I could tell you. That's about as much as I can say. I'm confused.'

'About what?'

'About myself. About the country. About you.'

'Me?'

'Not you personally. I trust you.' Why should I not make a clean breast? 'But the whole new government. Not all of them will be like you and Thando and Sandile and Mongane.'

'Of course not,' she says. 'You've seen enough of the struggle to realise it takes all kinds. You of all people should know.'

'There will be many like Vusi around.'

'You don't like him?'

'I cannot trust him. He is too smooth. He can't wait to lay his hands on power. And he dislikes women.'

'He couldn't keep his eyes off you,' she says.

'You know very well that's not what I'm talking about.'

She looks relieved; smiles her generous knowing woman's smile. 'I wanted to hear you say that.'

'Perhaps I have an answer for you,' says Thando, taking my arm. 'In one of Boccaccio's stories a Jew thinks of becoming a Catholic and he asks the priests what he should do. "Go to Rome," they tell him. So he goes. And comes back a Christian. "Good," they say, "the devotion of our people in Rome must have persuaded you." No, he replies. When he came to Rome he saw the Church in all its debauchery and corruption and worldliness. Priests living in sin, nuns with children, the Holy Father himself a miscreant. And so he thought, a church which commits all these wrongs and yet has managed to survive a thousand years must have something going for it.' Thando smiles and enfolds me in his huge embrace. 'Think about it. By the way, are you going to vote on Wednesday?'

'I haven't even thought about it. I'm a British citizen now.'

'You're a born South African, you qualify,' says Sam. 'If you need documents, let me know.'

'Go well,' I tell them all.

'*Salani kahle*,' says Thando. 'Stay well.'

'Why do you greet me in the plural?' I ask, intrigued.

'Because you're not alone. You have all your ghosts with you.'

A minute later they are gone. Without the customary din of birds bedding down, the farm sinks into a deep silence.

Waiting for me at the kitchen door, Jonnie still wears his new smile like something he has taken on appro; Jeremiah looks more subdued, pensive; Trui puts a conspiratorial hand on my shoulder and steers me away from the others, into the house.

'Now which one is he? I hope it's Mongane, the others are too old for you.'

'Which one is who?' I ask.

'The one you said you wanted to marry when you were over there.'

I close my eyes for a moment. 'He didn't come.'

'But you said – '

269

'It's all right. I saw him earlier today. But he had other business in the district this afternoon.'

'Ag, shame, man.' She takes me in her arms. 'But I'm sure you will see him again.'

'Perhaps.' I struggle free and put on a smile. 'Actually it all went very well, Trui. It's better this way.'

'Tsk.' She grins wryly. 'And now I was so friendly with them and all, just because I thought one of them was your man.'

'What did you think of them?'

'They're very nice,' she says. 'Not what I expected at all. They're just like white people, only they're black.'

# 8

Ouma is waiting for me when I enter. It is dark already. It has been a momentous day; and it is not yet over. I have had a walk, I've taken a shower to revive myself. What has happened still clings to my skin, dry and insidious as dust, entering through my pores. But it is time now for my hour, my several hours, with Ouma. The nurse has made her comfortable for the night. Even though I should by now be used to her lying in the coffin, I still find it disturbing. Yet she seems serene, hands folded on her sunken chest, one swathed in bandages, the other free. She is barely breathing, but her eyes are open. And when she notices me, she gives the happiest little smile I have seen on her face this past week.

'Come in, Kristien,' she says. 'I've been waiting for you. We have a guest.'

I stop to inspect the room, surprised, a bit annoyed. But I see nobody.

'On the bed,' she says. 'It's Wilhelmina, can't you see? You've asked to meet her.'

'Ouma, really – ' But I am conscious of a tingling feeling on my face.

'I know you think I tend to exaggerate. So I've asked her to tell you her own story.'

'She isn't here, Ouma,' I say as gently as possible. 'I don't see anyone.'

'Those are two quite different things.' She sighs. 'All right, I'll do it then. Sit down where I can see you. But not on the bed, Wilhelmina needs all the space she can get.'

270

I pull over the nurse's low chair. In spite of myself I glance at the empty bed; to my dismay it does seem to be sagging, as if straining under a heavy weight. I turn the chair sideways to shut out the bed from my field of vision, and yield to the swell of Ouma's new tale.

Wilhelmina was the only woman in our family who actually played a part in recorded history. Not because she went on the Great Trek, many others did the same; but because she was not content to remain in the shadows and allow the men to make their habitual mess of things. She intervened. She became involved. She took charge. For some time at least. And then – but let me not get ahead of my story.

You already know something about her childhood with her mother Samuel. Not an easy way to grow up: a time of almost incessant war along the frontier: thousands of Xhosa expelled from the Suurveld on the Colony side to make room for white colonists with their cattle; massive reprisals; even more massive counterattacks; murder and mayhem, large tracts of land and many homesteads going up in flames; one Cape governor after the other blundering straight into the confusion and conflict to sow even greater confusion and conflict; the arrival of a few thousand British settlers in 1820, poor unsuspecting victims dumped in the wilderness to populate a buffer zone between the warring nations; thousands of uprooted Khoikhoi vagrants swarming across the eastern districts, denied a right to the land, and turning to arson and plunder to avenge themselves; all of this exacerbated by the attempts, alternately visionary and misguided, of missionaries to reconcile the work of God and the shortsightedness or the greed of man. Representatives of most of these fractious peoples, at one time or another, turned up on the farms where Wilhelmina lived with her mother – first among the rowdy crowd of Steenkamps on the bank of the Riet River; later, after Marga had joined them, beyond the Great Fish River in what to the colonists was 'enemy territory'. But their farm was a neutral zone, and quite remarkably acknowledged as such by the warring groups. If they had any real allies these came from among the Xhosa, who treated the household of females with great respect, even with affection; at the same time, through ties of blood and language, the women got along with the frontier boers. The real, and ultimately the only, enemy was the English – not so much the wretched Settlers who were engaged in much the same struggle for survival as their Dutch counterparts, but the faceless rulers in Cape Town who dictated from afar and whose representatives in that remote part of the country were officious magistrates and high-handed public servants.

But Wilhelmina's successive ordeals occurred on a much more personal level: the wars and raids and rampages happened on the periphery of their existence, occasionally spilling briefly across their private territory but always moving on again to more distant destinations. What Wilhelmina had to contend with was, initially, the loneliness of an existence in the bush, with only her mother Samuel, herself lost in her own thoughts and guilts and yearnings; afterwards the rough and tumble of the uncouth crowd of Steenkamp boys, among whom she was forced to hold her own through feats of physical strength and prowess; still later the much more subtle threat of another woman vying for her mother's love.

Of these tests those of strength and agility were the easiest: Wilhelmina was a sturdy lass who'd been initiated by her early Xhosa mentors into the mysteries of the veld; and among the battering, bullying boys an indomitable will to survive, linked to the skill and strength of her body, soon taught her to outrun, outwrestle, outfight and outshoot the best of them. Even as a child her explosions of temper were legendary. Through bloodied noses, plucked-out hair, pulverised toes, bruised groins, twisted ears and dislocated joints they soon learned to respect the young lady in their midst. It was to stand her in good stead through the rest of her life.

By far the most agonising problem of her youth was her relationship with Samuel. Wilhelmina's mother was a difficult man. This was presumably the crux of the matter. I doubt whether the girl ever really grasped the full extent of the intricate territory inhabited by her mother. She was taught to address Samuel as 'Father'; she was never allowed to divulge the secret of her sex to others; yet in the unavoidable bodily contact she had with Samuel there must have been an intimation of a different kind of presence altogether, physical, emotional, spiritual. No wonder she was confused. And all the more so after Marga became part of their joint and several lives.

On the whole Wilhelmina treated Marga with suspicion. But this was never an uncomplicated emotion. Because Marga also brought the greater immediacy of an acknowledged female presence; even more important, perhaps, Marga taught her to read from the Bible and the odd copy of the *Gazette* or the *Commercial Advertiser* that found its way into the interior on the wagon of some trader. And her feelings of gratitude were hard to reconcile with resentment. Situations arose which could not be resolved through physical confrontation.

Whenever life became too complicated the girl would run away, rather than face what she later termed, in a characteristic turn of phrase, a shit-storm. Such a natural impulse: the whole saga of the Great Trek may be seen, at least in part, as a collective escape. But for a young girl to run into the wilderness still infested by predators of all kinds, and snakes and scorpions and other venomous creatures, in a country ravaged almost incessantly by war, can be a hazardous recourse. However, the same instinct for self-preservation that helped Wilhelmina overcome the violence of the Steenkamp tribe prompted her to survive in the dense bush of the Kei territory.

But below the surface of her comings and goings the crisis in her relationship with her mother was growing. If Wilhelmina had not loved Samuel so much – in all respects the opposite of herself – it would not have been so painful; but it was obvious that they could not go on living together. Her disappearances into the wilderness, where no one could follow her, became more frequent, more prolonged. But she needed human company too. Unlike her mother who'd always been something of a stranger to the world – an inevitable consequence, perhaps, of growing up as one of seventeen children all named Samuel – Wilhelmina craved intercourse with people.

That was why she struck the deal with the old German trader. Her mother, perhaps in an attempt to buy off her own conscience, gave Wilhelmina the hoard of gold coins she'd taken, years and years earlier, from the house of her strangled husband, and with these Wilhelmina bought herself into what could easily have turned out a very reckless venture. They travelled to Algoa Bay, newly named Port Elizabeth; once even to Cape Town, in Wilhelmina's eyes one of the splendours of the world; and then returned into the deep interior to barter their copper wire and iron pots and cloths and jugs and barrels of rot-gut brandy and rolls of tobacco. And, hidden in a false bottom of the middle wagon, guns and ammunition.

For a year or two their trade flourished. An excellent partnership. But in the long run the old German, given to epic bouts of drinking followed by wild outbursts of ranting and raving, became too difficult to handle. *This* was not the company she desired. These were the circumstances in which, in the vicinity of Somerset East, on one of their trading trips, Wilhelmina met and promptly married Leendert Pretorius, in every respect the most unlikely choice. He was twice her age, a sickly whining creature with myopic watery eyes, obsessed with the Scriptures, and possessed by the dream of becoming a minister of religion. He was also, if the truth must be told, a randy old goat.

It is difficult to single out the consideration that clinched the matter. Did he, with his clumsy fumblings, unleash a latent passion that had lain in wait in her? Did she fall for his extensive library of almost a dozen books? Or was she attracted by his amazing store of ailments and complaints? If this sounds strange, bear in mind that Wilhelmina was a healer. Among the many things she'd brought back from her excursions into the wilderness was a treasury of knowledge about herbal medicines and natural remedies; and among the marvels she discovered on her trips with the German smous were the potions and powders and balsams of a well-stocked apothecary's chest. Even without these aids, people said, she would have been a healer of repute: a mere laying-on of hands communicated to her the sources of an illness, and to the patient the powers of recuperation. A malicious mind might argue that she could not have been any good at all as Leendert Pretorius remained ailing to the day of his death; but then the man was a walking hospital who could invent three new complaints for every one cured. At the very least he posed a challenge a woman like Wilhelmina found difficult to resist.

She brought him home with her and together they settled on a huge abandoned farm right on the Great Fish River – far enough away from her mother to guarantee independence, close enough for comfort. And promptly she began to direct all her energies towards the enthusiastic exploitation of the three main attractions between them: they had long sessions of reading from his books; she started working on his multifarious complaints; and she set about contributing her bit towards the survival of the species. By the time they left on the Great Trek, a few years after Samuel's calamitous end, they had four small children.

Leendert's main motive for joining the Trek was the prospect of becoming a religious leader among the emigrants, something denied him in the Colony because he lacked the qualifications prescribed for such a vocation and had been too sickly ever to attain them. Wilhelmina's motives were more obscure (another reason why she should have been allowed to tell her own story): they had to do, of course, with a wish to get away from what she must by then have come to regard as a place of evil; but also, no doubt, with the urge to put behind her an unfulfilling life in a remote wilderness and become part of a larger community. She could be of use to them as a healer; her skills in reading might win her some general respect; but above all, as the wife of a religious leader she might at last become part of something great and meaningful, a people's movement, instead of simply seeing life pass her by in an unpredictable flood. She had too much energy to waste on purely personal pursuits. A larger operational area was beckoning, and she was ready to answer the call of history.

# 9

It did not work out quite as expected, mainly because poor Leendert did not measure up to his own confident predictions. He turned out not to be the only man among the Voortrekkers with aspirations to a position of religious authority. There was no ordained preacher among them, as the Dutch Reformed Church had distanced itself from an enterprise it regarded as foolhardy; this should have put all the contenders on an equal footing, but they were not. In the Potgieter group there was Sarel Cilliers, an impressive man by most standards, supported quite openly by his fiery trek leader. In the Graaff-Reinet trek there was the lachrymose sod Erasmus Smit whose claims would have been ludicrous had not his wife Susanna been the sister of the leader Maritz. Leendert Pretorius could count only on the support of his wife, and formidable as she was in her own right she was only a woman. Ironically, she probably derived more authority in the Voortrekker community from her husband's limited – and ultimately failed – potential than he did from all her qualities as a born leader.

All the candidates' hopes of further advancement in the field of religion were further thwarted by the discovery that several of the black settlements in the interior were already serviced by fully ordained missionaries, which meant that when it came to the administration of the sacraments, particularly Holy Communion, the trekkers overcame even their ingrained distaste of anything English and preferred to invite these priests rather than risk the wrath of God by allowing unordained hands to defile the bread and wine.

Not that they were entirely sidelined. There was always the odd sermon to be preached of a Sunday (several, in fact, as the incessant bickering among the different factions of trekkers caused each group to cluster round its own preacher); most especially there were the sick and dying to be comforted (or scared out of their wits, as the case might be); and before and after military expeditions against allegedly hostile black communities to avenge real or imaginary depredations, there were invariably services of exhortation or thanksgiving to perform. Few could match Leendert Pretorius when it came to implanting the fear of the living God and of eternal wailing and gnashing of teeth in the bosoms of the unworthy. And unworthy, by God, they were. At least in Leendert's eyes; he had as much of a vested interest in the damnation of the trekkers as Jonah had had in the annihilation of Nineveh.

The problem was that Leendert himself was not all that worthy a man either. For someone with his weak constitution the Trek was a journey through unmitigated hell. He needed more and more sustenance even beyond the remedies Wilhelmina could provide (it is perhaps not unthinkable that the remedies themselves sometimes aggravated rather than improved his condition); the obvious recourse was drink. And when brandy in the form of the notorious Cape Smoke ran out, as happened all too often, he acquired a taste for indigenous brews, some of which were reputed to be roughly equivalent to a bolt of lightning. On some of the ever more rare occasions when he was called upon to preach a sermon the congregation had to be informed at the last minute that Leendert was unable to officiate; and to learn afterwards how effectively some mere elder or deacon had stepped into the breach did not do much to bolster the man's already shaky self-confidence.

Still, Wilhelmina supported him with an animal ferocity that cowed most of his detractors. From the outset she had been the driving spirit in their union. She was the one who, through her contact with the old German smous, had first learned about the planned migration; and having on her earlier forays met the bearded giant Hendrik Potgieter in the Tarka region, she decided that this was the group to join. When no buyer could be found for their huge farm on the Great Fish River, she decided quite simply to abandon it; they still had enough money to equip two wagons, and late in 1835 she and Leendert joined the Potgieter trek at an appointed place and slowly meandered with the others to the Great River, which was in flood. That was the first real shit-storm − and it became an opportunity of demonstrating her prowess, not only in organising the felling of scores of trees to build floats on which the wagons could be transported across the muddy waters, but in carrying in her two arms or on her shoulders logs most of the men couldn't budge. She was five months pregnant at the time. When one of her wagons threatened to capsize in the flood she was the one who tied one end of a long riem to the frame and jumped into the swirling water with the other end to steady the unwieldy float and its cargo. And when several of the women and children fell ill after the travail of the crossing, some of them ending up with pneumonia, it was Wilhelmina whose remedies, not only potent but downright vile, pulled them through.

Ironically, the only life lost in the crossing was that of her own youngest child but one, aged two, who fell off the float tended by

Leendert and was swept away. This was a blow that stunned her, probably because it was reminiscent of her mother's death four years earlier. And as it turned out it was only the first; near the Vet River her oldest was killed by a leopard; and the first baby she gave birth to during the Trek, in the vicinity of Thaba Nchu, was stillborn. But such setbacks could not permanently dampen her spirits; she even used them as occasions for some strong-armed religious politicking by insisting that Leendert lead the funeral services. As it turned out, those ceremonies were the only ones where the poor man ever approached inspired oratory.

Wilhelmina, it should be clear by now, remained undaunted by challenges and tribulations that disheartened most lesser mortals; but what turned her arse-hairs grey (her own expression: she was no mincer of words) was the ceaseless infighting among the Voortrekkers. We were talking about it again just before you came in. 'What a joke,' she said, 'the way people nowadays think of that lot as a bunch of pious pioneers who sacrificed their all for the noble cause of freedom. Never seen such viciousness and pettiness in my life.' You must imagine the scene in the Thaba Nchu region. By 1837 there must have been over a thousand wagons outspanned across the plains and valleys, representing at least five thousand people, three thousand whites, the rest coloured or black (because obviously, even in the wretched circumstances of the Trek, those farmers had to cart their servants with them). They'd all trickled into those parts in small family groups or larger clans, five or ten wagons at a time – Potgieter had about fifty; the smart-arse Maritz, the most affluent of the lot, a hundred. They'd all been fired by the same urge to get away from the English and become independent, but each group wanted to be independent on its own terms and governed by its own leader. Gradually some of the smaller groups merged, but in the end there were at least four major factions, those of Potgieter, of Maritz, of Retief, and of Uys, each of them conniving against the others. And not only the leaders were bickering, but everybody else joined in. There were quarrels about grazing and water and camping sites and firewood; arguments about religious sects and denominations and about which route to follow to get where; fisticuffs about ammunition and strayed cattle and missing kegs of brandy and lost axes or grease barrels or yokes or God knows what. Only when there was a sudden threat of violence from outside, usually by the Matabele from across the Vaal River, did they temporarily suspend the infighting. Then they'd all scramble to pull the wagons into a circular laager to fight off the enemy; or the men would ride out in a commando to spread death and destruction in retaliation. But the moment the threat subsided everybody was at everybody else's throat again.

The preachers played an active part in all this: Cilliers by endorsing Potgieter after the latter had been left out of the first government; old Erasmus Smit invoking, in his sober moments, the example of Israel to promote his own cause as a visionary; Leendert Pretorius, frustrated very early by the presence of Cilliers in the same group as himself, floating from one faction to the next trying to incite them against each other, in the hope of emerging as the great peacemaker, but achieving exactly the opposite.

But in a way Wilhelmina flourished. In between her pregnancies, and even right through them, she became the most trusted healer of the Trek, practically plucking the already departed back from death through the fervent administration of unnameable potions and direct appeals to God. These tended at times to be lacking in tact, to say the least: she was reported by eyewitnesses as addressing God as if he were an ordinary obstreperous male: 'Now you listen to me, God, if this child hasn't come out of her fever by tomorrow morning, I'm holding you responsible'; or, 'How many more times do you expect me to go on my knees to ask you for this woman to get better? She's got a family of seven to look after, we need her down here much more than you do up there, so don't you think it's time you pulled finger and did something?' In one celebrated instance, at what seemed to be the deathbed of a young girl, Sarie Kruger, she was reported to have told the Almighty, 'This is going too far, God. You're just not making sense any more. If you really have some grudge against the Krugers, why must you take Sarie? Why don't you take one of her brothers, there are five of them and they're a good-for-nothing lot. Here she is, twelve years old, ready to become a woman. How do you expect us to survive on this continent if you don't allow us to obey your own commandment by being fruitful and multiplying and filling the earth? Are you now getting forgetful in your old age? We need every woman and girl. So don't make it necessary for me to raise this with you again.' The remarkable thing about this incident was not only that the girl recovered, but that one of her brothers was killed in a hunting accident the very next day.

Wilhelmina was active in many other ways too. In the first pitched battle of the Trek, in the laager at Vegkop late in 1836, only a fortnight or so after losing her stillborn baby, she wielded a gun with the best of the men while Leendert was bedridden with a mysterious fever; but while her male companions were assisted by women and children to measure and sort lead and powder and handle the guns passed on to them for firing, she had to make do on her own. This slowed her down considerably, and as increasing numbers of the attacking Ndebele were by that time so close that they started crawling under and over the wagons armed with assegais she grabbed an axe and began to hack away at anybody who came too close. There were enough severed limbs in that part of the laager, she said afterwards, to set up a butcher's shop.

But those were exceptional circumstances. After the battle, when the trekkers were stranded for months without sheep or cattle, unable to move, she resumed her old habit of going off into the veld on her own, unarmed, on foot if necessary, on horseback when possible, to return hours or days later with a sheep or a milking cow. As the men had already scoured the environs in all directions as far as the horizon and beyond, no one knew how she could possibly have rounded up these stray animals; but she had a habit of brushing off all enquiries and going about her own business, feeding newborn infants with the milk she'd brought home, or slaughtering the sheep to distribute meat among the most needy.

In due course some new cattle and sheep were acquired, largely through the intercession of Archbell, the English missionary stationed in the settlement of the Barolong chief from whom the trekkers had acquired the territory between the Vet and the Vaal; and Wilhelmina could turn her energies towards other occupations.

It is known that on at least one occasion, while most of the men were off on a punitive expedition and reports came of an imminent Ndebele attack on one of the most vulnerable outposts where Wilhelmina happened to be residing for the time being, she took her two remaining children by the hands, one of them six, the other three, and strode off in the direction from which the Ndebele were reported to be approaching. About a mile from the camp she came upon them, a group of about two hundred armed men, and approached without hesitation. Bemused, they halted their advance.

'Where do you think you're going?' she asked in Xhosa, which they understood.

'This is not your business,' a spokesman answered. 'Stand aside, white woman, let us pass.'

'You will have to kill me and my children first,' she said. 'Where I come from, men do not kill women and children. Perhaps you are different.'

'Your people are invading our land,' said the man.

'This land belongs to the Barolong,' she pointed out, 'not the

Ndebele. We have chief Makwana's permission to be here. And anyway, we are just on our way through to the sea.'

'Then why did you kill so many of our people?'

'We defended ourselves when you attacked us.'

'Before that. Some of your men came across the river into our land and took cattle. When we tried to stop them they shot us.'

She must have had a sinking feeling: how many times had this happened back in the frontier territory? Was there no getting away from it, ever?

'That is bad,' she said. 'I shall talk to our men.'

'You are a woman,' he reminded her.

'That is why I am prepared to talk. If I were a man I would have killed you already. Do you want to see your wives live without a husband and your children grow up without a father?'

'Men are not scared to die.'

'I'm not scared to die either. But what about the others who remain behind? Don't you care about their suffering? And isn't it better to live in peace than to make war?'

'You are wasting my time.'

'War wastes time, not I. I'm trying to save time. And lives.'

'You are trying to cheat me. You want to hold us up here while your men prepare to attack us.'

'Most of our men are away,' she said calmly. 'You can overrun the camp if you wish, there won't be much resistance. You can take all the sheep and cattle we bartered from the Barolong. You can kill most of us. And then, when our men come back, they will send a commando to your place and kill all your people and take all your cattle. And then another army of the Ndebele will come against us to revenge it. And another commando will take the field. For how long? Won't you men ever learn?'

'That is woman's talk.'

'Thank God, yes. Because why should we go on bringing children into the world only so that you can kill them? Don't you think that is nonsense?'

Was there a hint of wavering in his attitude? Or was he merely getting impatient?

'Why don't you bring some of your womenfolk to come and talk to us?' she proposed.

'We keep the women out of such things. They stay at home.'

'Are you scared of sending them to talk to us?'

'I am not scared of anything.'

280

'If you're not scared you will send them.'

And a few days later a delegation of Ndebele women arrived, escorted by some men. Wilhelmina had great trouble persuading her own people – women, a number of old or ailing men, and particularly the handful of able-bodied youngsters left behind to protect the camp – that the visitors had come at her bidding and meant no harm. It was even more difficult to talk them into leaving this matter to the women; and in this respect the women turned out to be far more diffident than the men. How could they embark on such weighty matters without their husbands at their side to take the final decisions?

'Because this concerns us,' said Wilhelmina. 'It is a matter of our bodies and our children and our future.'

In the end three women, out of the forty or so in the camp, volunteered to risk it. Two of them were elderly widows, the third a hunchbacked spinster with no marriage prospects that could be ruined by the venture. With Wilhelmina herself as interpreter, they sat down with the dozen Ndebele women in the shade of some thorn-trees, watched suspiciously from a distance, the inhabitants of the camp on one side, the Ndebele men on the other.

There were no dramatic decisions, no spectacular outcome. But both sides did agree to 'talk to their men'. For the moment that was that. Might there have been any significant results in the long term? One would dearly like to know, but all this would be conjecture. Only when the trekker men returned did Wilhelmina learn, with shock, the extent of the vengeance they had meted out on the chief Ndebele settlement, where they'd left behind hundreds of enemy dead (no losses on the Boer side, apart from a few coloured attendants; invariably, in battles of this kind, only enemies are killed), bringing back several thousand sheep and cattle. This must have sent shock waves throughout the Ndebele territory beyond the Vaal, bringing a premature end to whatever beneficial effects Wilhelmina's peace initiative might yet have had.

Within the ranks of the trekkers, however, there were repercussions of a different kind. Several families let it be known publicly that they would no longer accept any services from a person who consorted with kaffirs. An attempt was made to set her cooking quarters alight; one man, whose child had been cured by Wilhelmina a month before, sent his son to ask back the wether he'd offered her in payment; when she arrived at the deathbed of one of the old widows who had joined her in her talks with the Ndebele, she was chased away by relatives, who called her a witch and accused her of being responsible for the old woman's imminent death; soon afterwards a message arrived from Hendrik Potgieter himself formally to expel the Pretorius family from his party.

This she could shrug off: by that time it had become obvious that Potgieter was set on continuing his trek to the north, beyond the Vaal, into the territory of the Ndebele (which would require either their annihilation or their forcible eviction), and Wilhelmina had no stomach for the deep interior. The sea was where she wanted to be, even if this meant joining one of the other groups. Maritz was ruled out, as far as she was concerned, by his family ties with that wretched squint-eyed creature Erasmus Smit, Leendert's adversary. Piet Uys was too aggressive for her liking. But Piet Retief appeared a dependable leader, in spite of a rather shady past as a speculator in Graham's Town (but as most of his opponents and victims had been English, that was pardonable, even commendable).

Late in 1837, two months after Wilhelmina had given birth to a new son, their trek started crossing the daunting Drakensberg range. A couple of wagons were lost down the precipitous cliffs on the Natal side, but the rest managed the descent in a breathtaking demonstration of strength, skill and sheer bloody-mindedness. Once again Wilhelmina contributed more than her share, on one occasion stepping in under a precariously poised wagon and hoisting the back up on one massive shoulder so that it could be steadied on a rock. This was not far from the sheer cliff on which she proudly painted, with a tin of dark green paint borrowed from Retief's daughter Deborah, her husband's name and the date of their passing:

LEENDERT PRETORIUS PASSED HERE 28 NOVEMBER 1837

Which must be the only example of her writing extant. How ironical that she herself should not feature on the inscription. But apart from – literally – pulling her weight during the trek, Wilhelmina was by now intent on playing a much more subdued role than before. She felt guilty, she explained to me (and would have to you if you'd let her), about the negative repercussions her negotiations with the Ndebele had had, not for herself, but for Leendert; she wouldn't do anything that could further harm his chances of becoming an officially recognised religious leader of the trek. Stubbornly refusing to acknowledge that he was his own greatest enemy, she was resolved to move heaven and earth on his behalf. In a manner of speaking.

# 10

The years Wilhelmina and her family spent in Natal represented what one might call the 'public' period of her life, but it began most inauspiciously. While Retief and a select commando of men rode off to make history at Ngungundhlovu, the Place of the Elephant, where they negotiated with the Zulu king Dingane to acquire land for the settlement of the immigrant Boers, the rest of his company provisionally camped in a multitude of small groups along the fertile fingers of the Tugela. And there, after the negotiations had unexpectedly resulted in the massacre of Retief and his men, they were attacked by wave upon wave of Dingane's impis sent out to rid the country of what the Zulus not unjustifiably regarded as the invaders. That was the infamous night of 16 February 1838.

Wilhelmina had been awakened just after midnight by her baby and she was sitting propped up against a wagon wheel feeding the child when the impi swept into their camping site. The child was killed in her arms with an assegai driven with such force that after penetrating the baby's body the point struck the mother in the left breast. Plucking the weapon from her body and flinging aside the dead child she grabbed a three-legged iron pot from the dying embers of the camp fire and charged the attackers. She killed three of them, splitting open their skulls, before they retreated. By that time Leendert and both her older boys had received stab wounds, one of the children in the buttock, the other in the shoulder, Leendert more seriously in the lung. Wilhelmina herself had suffered most, looking, as she put it, like a bloody porcupine by the time she could start plucking the assegais from her body: there were no fewer than nineteen, not counting the first one that had been driven into her breast.

She first cleaned and dressed her family's wounds. Then, recklessly ignoring her own, she grabbed a gun, found a horse (that in itself was a minor miracle as the Zulus had absconded with all the animals they could round up – over twenty-five thousand cattle, apart from horses, sheep and goats) and galloped off to see whether she could lend a hand at any of the neighbouring camps. It was only at the fifth or sixth outspan, along the Bushmans River, that she fainted from loss of blood – an event she regarded as an eternal disgrace. And within hours she was on her way again. Throughout the following days she was something of a huge angel of mercy, bursting into one outspan after the other to seek out the wounded and the dying, applying poultices and balsams, administering herbal potions, killing hares and meerkats to stick the still-warm skins to wounds where inflammation had set in; only exhaustion and the combined efforts of several of the strongest men restrained her from helping the teams of grave-diggers to prepare graves for the more than five hundred people who had been slaughtered. As in previous incidents, about half of these were servants who'd been brought along from the Cape colony to ease their masters' lives.

She must have been in something of a daze during those first few days when only her massive strength and amazing energy carried her through; not until she was finally strapped down in her own wagon with thongs cut from rhinoceros hide did the effect of her own wounds finally overtake her. It was a miracle that she survived. There had been others who pulled through with multiple wounds, Catharina Prinsloo with seventeen, Johanna van der Merwe with twenty-two; but the strenuous demands to which she submitted her body after the initial shock would have been enough to finish off most other people. Even the horse she had commandeered almost succumbed.

Had Wilhelmina not worried so much about Leendert's single but extremely serious wound she might well have given up. But she knew he needed her; even though by now, for the first time in her life, she'd begun to despise him for his weakness. At the very least, she said, he should have sat up that night with her when she had to feed the baby; they might have stood a better chance against the attackers. Although, in her more disparaging moments, she admitted that he might have compounded things by shooting either her or himself in the consternation.

She recovered. She set about scouring the surrounding wilderness for new herbs. The most remarkable of her exploits in this time was making friends with a Zulu community among the foothills of the Drakensberg. When Leendert objected, she argued that they couldn't be blamed for what the others had done. 'Those were all half-crazed men obeying orders from a mad king,' she said, 'these are peaceful country people like ourselves.' In any case she sought out the old women, not the men; and, finding once again that she could make herself sufficiently understood in Xhosa, learned from them a wealth of remedies that would have cured the most stubborn ox. It certainly cured her. But not Leendert. Which was probably why she also resorted to arsenic to keep his festering wound in check. She bought a fair supply from an Italian smous, Alberto Viglione, who found himself among the trekkers at the time (his wife Teresa had in fact played quite a heroic part in riding about on the night of 16 February to warn various outspans of the approaching danger); and when the paste she concocted from it did not work as speedily as it should, she began administering small doses orally as well. This may well have been what finally carried Leendert off a year later; but one hopes it was unintentional.

By that time they were living on a small farm at the mouth of the Umgeni. In the beginning they were plagued, not only by the usual predators, but by crocodiles. But Wilhelmina had always had a way with animals. Lions, leopards and lynxes soon learned to respect her territory. The crocodiles took somewhat longer and more drastic measures were required. She kept a peeled eye on them until one day, on a sandbank near the river mouth, she came upon one of monstrous size that had just caught a sheep. Without hesitation she rushed to the reptile, belaboured it with a hefty kierie, then grabbed it by the jaws and actually pulled them apart, stopping only, she told me herself, when the whole reptile had been torn in two. After that episode they were so tame that, as you already know, she regularly left the children to their care when they were playing on the beach.

A new baby, a girl, had been born to her a week after the battle of Blood River which temporarily concluded the hostilities between Boers and Zulus. This meant that the child must have been conceived not much more than a month after the attack on the Tugela: which says something, either about Leendert's shameless appetite or Wilhelmina's determination or both. And by the time he died Wilhelmina, clearly eager to replace the stock lost in the war, was pregnant again; six months after the funeral – a particularly beautiful service, everybody said, by Erasmus Smit, who clearly felt inspired to celebrate the demise of an arch-rival – the baby was born. This, as you may have guessed, was Petronella.

# II

Soon afterwards Wilhelmina's real troubles began: the Zulus had by then been subdued through the elimination of Dingane and the recognition, by the trekkers, of Mpande as 'ruling prince'; but the English were beginning to emit ominous rumblings about annexing the territory of Natal in order once again to lay their greedy hands on the recalcitrant Boers. And after all they had gone through you can imagine they were in no mood just to give up meekly the freedom and independence they had finally won.

For several years the uncertainty and confusion continued. By the time it came to a head, in 1843, Wilhelmina, in no mind to put an end to her productive life when numbers were needed, had already remarried. The innocent man was Hansie Nel, ten years younger than herself; he'd lost his wife in the Tugela massacre, and as it happened he'd also made the coffin for Leendert's funeral, a meek and mild-mannered man who bowed to Wilhelmina's every wish. The union was a blessed one, up to a point at least. Their first child was duly born a year after the wedding, followed by twins a year later. One of these was the boy Benjamin who later accompanied Petronella on her wanderings.

Unfortunately Hansie did not survive the event. Don't ask me what happened. All Wilhelmina has ever said was that 'the bloody clod made me very angry'. By that time her temper had acquired epic proportions, mainly as a result of conflict with peripatetic representatives of the British Empire. It was also a time when she was known to have taken to exterminating vermin on the farm through the indiscriminate use of strychnine.

Before the twins were a month old the long-expected trouble broke out. In Wilhelmina's terminology this was the worst shit-storm in her life so far. Boers and English had been glaring at each other in Port Natal for some time; the English had brought in more and more reinforcements; then the Boers struck at Congella, one moonlit night when a group of old men standing guard in the bushes on the beach noticed a company of English advancing with a cannon. The English were besieged, but one young gallant galloped all the way to Graham's Town, a thousand kilometres away, and then a large force was sent by sea to annex the territory. To add insult to injury, this force was commanded by a man from one of the foremost Cape Dutch families, Josias Cloete, who'd now turned against his own kin. Hard on his heels came his brother Henry, appointed commissioner of the new colony. The Boer forces retreated to the place with more letters to its name than it had inhabitants, Pietermaritzburg, and there Henry Cloete met them to negotiate their formal surrender to Her Majesty.

The moment Wilhelmina heard about these developments she left the care of her farm to a trusted Zulu foreman and her older children to the crocodiles that had become 'the best watchdogs I ever had', and hurried to Pietermaritzburg, taking with her only the twin babies. She wouldn't miss the looming confrontation for all the world. She arrived in time to learn that the Boer assembly was actually considering capitulation. That was in May; by early August most of the men had been won over. But not the women. With a baby on each breast, Wilhelmina made the rounds from wagon to wagon and house to house, exhorting the sisterhood to stand up for the rights and the freedom of the threatened trekkers. If the men were too dastardly then the women should take over. And while they were about it they might just as well demand the vote too, the first women in the world to do so. At first the sisters were hesitant. Then a few broke ranks, among them the hunchbacked spinster and the single remaining widow who had supported her before. And then, one evening, Susanna, the usually demure young wife of the whining preacher Erasmus Smit, came to see Wilhelmina in the small mud house of the old widow she was staying with.

What came out in the course of that long conversation, which lasted almost until daybreak, was quite astounding. Susanna had reached breaking point; she couldn't take any more. Forced into marriage with Erasmus when she'd been only thirteen, she'd submitted all these years to his emotional extortion, his bouts of drinking, his delirious ravings, his endless depressions, his visions of hell, his sickening physical demands. 'He keeps me as if he's a dragon who has bound and robbed me and holds me prisoner,' she told Wilhelmina. 'I've never been allowed a life of my own. He has a large room all to himself; there he can write his sermons or sleep off his stupors or entertain his visions or abuse his own flesh as he wishes – I've found the stains all over the floor and over his papers, and then he expects me to clean up. While I – look at me, Aunt Wilhelmina, I'm still young, I want to *live*! – I don't even have the smallest corner I can call my own. I'm no better than a bloody pumpkin, unmoving and unwieldy, waiting to be harvested by someone else.'

She had dreams too, she confided. Sometimes nightmares in which she was assailed by an army of ghosts, small grey-black dogs, cats, monkeys, mice, and swift red beetles, settling on her sinful body in such numbers that she could hardly move, hitting her in the face with their paws, their tails, their wings, flying into her ears, blowing thick smoke into her eyes; at other times there would be visions of heavenly visitors – things that would make people shudder or marvel were they to know about it. But she was not allowed to breathe a word to anyone. When she told Erasmus about it he would shout abuse at her, then blatantly appropriate her dreams and use them in his more inspired sermons. While she, frail and sickly as she was, was expected to do all the housework, with nobody to help her; cleaning up his messes was in itself a full-time occupation. And now she'd had enough. The last straw was seeing him – all the men – meekly submitting to the English and surrendering their freedom: how was it possible? She could not bear to be excluded from what she called 'working in God's vineyard'.

'If only I'd been a man,' she lamented, 'not a woman. To put a knapsack on my back and stride through the land and be witness to the wilderness blossoming like a rose!' There was a tone of hysteria in her voice as she spoke; a woman possessed. And now, she finally came to the point, she'd heard about Wilhelmina's exhortations; and leaving Erasmus at home crying in his own vomit she'd come to offer Wilhelmina whatever help she could give.

Wilhelmina was no fool. She immediately saw the advantage of having this woman – hysterical, perhaps, but powerful in her rage – on her side. She'd always loathed the creepy Smit; and because Susanna had never spoken a word, keeping herself at her husband's side like a cringing mouse, no one had ever suspected such depths of anger and energy in her frail body. But now it was different. And with the increasing status her husband had acquired, in spite of himself, since Retief's death, with Maritz in a position of high authority, Susanna could act as a powerful magnet among the restive women of Natal.

That was exactly what happened. Led by Susanna Smit, with Wilhelmina and her twins right at her heels in formidable support, nearly four hundred women marched on the hall where Henry Cloete was waiting to hear the outcome of the Assembly's decisive vote. They had with them a petition, drawn up the previous evening by Wilhelmina and her new protégé (Erasmus being once again, most usefully, incapacitated), in which they argued that no decision taken by the Assembly could be regarded as final as it would have been taken by men only; and in consideration of the battles in which they had been engaged they were now entitled to a voice in all matters concerning the state of their country. This right they now claimed, and in ringing phrases – in which one recognises both the visionary inspiration of Susanna and the rage of the more practically minded Wilhelmina – they announced their 'fixed determination never to yield to British authority'. They were painfully aware, they said, that resistance might be of no avail; but they wanted to make it clear 'that they were ready to walk across the Drakensberg barefoot, to die in freedom, as death was dearer to them than the loss of liberty'.

In the beginning Cloete, robed and bearing the insignia of his office, treated the irruption as an amusing diversion, but as the time went by and the women became more frenzied, he was getting nervous; if they succeeded in imparting that rage to their menfolk, the whole enterprise might yet founder. He broke into a long speech, inspired by his own eloquence ('I must impress upon you that such a liberty as you seem to dream of has never been recognised in any civil society, and I sincerely regret that as married ladies you claim a freedom which even in a social state would be unthinkable; and however much I may sympathise with your feelings I must tell you that I consider it a disgrace on your husbands to use this kind of language'); but they soon cut him short. 'We're not here to listen to you,' Wilhelmina told him in a tone of voice that left no doubt about the state of her mind, 'but to make you listen to us!'

He continued to offer what was subsequently described as 'a vigorous and manly protest', but this was drowned by a volley of jeers. By this time a number of men had also begun to drift into the hall, among them Erasmus Smit himself, hauled from his cups by a well-meaning neighbour; and hearing 'the vulgar and most abusive epithets' hurled at Cloete (as a male correspondent of *The Graham's Town Journal* reported subsequently), the man of God, shaken almost out of his senses, started expostulating at his wife over the heads of the crowd that separated them. In the beginning it was a mere mumbling, but gradually it rose in volume as he began to sob in distress:

'Quiet, Susanna, for God's sake, my child, be quiet, come now, my child – '

To which she shouted back, 'You shut up, you squint-eyed dragon! All these years you've done nothing, so don't try to stop me now. I'm not your child. Today *I* am putting on the breeches!'

By this time Cloete was so exasperated that he tried to break up the meeting. But the women would net let him go. To save face, for a while at least, he placed himself in what the paper described as 'an easy attitude', taking up some documents and affecting 'to beguile the time occupied by his tormentors in their continued narration'. But then it became too much for him – 'The plain truth,' Wilhelmina said, 'was that he shat in his breeches' – and suddenly he jumped up and tried to make a quick escape. This was prevented by a surge of women all around him. Some threw their aprons over his head so that he couldn't see where he was going; others started tearing at his clothes, while Susanna Smit, 'that small specimen of humanity' (the paper's words again), attacked him with her fists. It was only by the exertion of great physical strength that he finally made his escape through the side door, nearly choking from lack of air and no doubt from fear.

Later the same day the Assembly announced its decision to capitulate to Great Britain on Cloete's terms. The women had been stabbed in the back by their own menfolk. Humiliated and dejected, most of them crept back into the seclusion of their domestic existence; Susanna Smit never appeared in public again, at least not without her husband (and that only after several weeks had elapsed, presumably the time the bruises on her face required to heal); whatever else she had to say in future she would confide only to her diary.

Wilhelmina felt betrayed. Two days after the event, as she was preparing to return to her farm at the mouth of the Umgeni, she heard a wagon rumbling past in the wide street. She recognised Cloete on the front kist, beside the driver. Suddenly she was seized by what she herself described as a fit of madness. She ran out into the street, in front of the wagon, pushed aside the boy leading the oxen and pulled the team to a standstill. Cloete rose in protest. When he saw who it was, he became pale. Perspiration broke out on his clean-shaven upper lip.

Wilhelmina went up to the front seat and shouted at Cloete, in terms that would make a fish-wife's curses sound like a sermon, to come down; he declined, inviting her up to his level instead. She complied, fuming.

'Madam,' said Cloete, 'I am sure we can come to an amicable understanding – '

Wilhelmina did not deign to answer. With a single right hook she dislodged him from the wagon. He thudded into the dust like a shot vulture.

Regrettably, the confrontation made no difference at all to the course of history. It was not even recorded.

From that day, she withdrew from the public eye, returning to the isolation of her farm, where she gathered her remaining children and possessions (including the coffin of her dear departed mother, which she'd lugged all the way through the wilderness) loaded everything on three wagons, herded together the cattle she had been given in compensation for her losses and in recognition of services rendered to the now defunct republic, and joined one of several groups of trekkers, back across the Drakensberg, towards a new wilderness where, even if it could boast no sea, she knew she would at least end her life beyond the reach of the British Empire.

Wilhelmina turned to eating. She had always had a hearty appetite, but that was because her impressive constitution needed sustenance; now, on the intricate meanderings that took her, with one group of trekkers after another, across the Drakensberg into what would today be the North-Eastern Free State, and from there to the remote Northern Transvaal, there was a compulsion about her eating which at first amused, then astounded, her family. At her peak she could start a meal with a dozen eggs and a loaf of pot-bread before proceeding to the enthusiastic consumption of half a fat sheep; she didn't care much for vegetables, except for pumpkin, of which she could down a fair-sized one at a time on a sideplate; and she might add a chicken or two by way of a salad if she felt peckish.

She began to put on weight at an alarming rate. At ten Wilhelmina was sturdy; at twenty-four, when she married Leendert Pretorius, she was hefty; by the time she went on the Great Trek, at thirty, one might call her solid; and when she left Natal at just under forty she was massive. But this was nothing compared to what she became in the course of that long journey which only came to a halt, two years after leaving Natal, among a group of wild religious fundamentalist visionaries who had set out in search of Jerusalem. By the time she and her family settled beside what they took to be the river Nile, she was the size of a young hippo, and still expanding. Initially, the rigours of travelling might have restricted her gain in weight, but what to her was the sedentary existence of a settled farmer boosted an almost daily expansion of her girth.

Within a few months of reaching the Nylstroom region she took to husband a puny man, Bertus Lingenfeld, one of the zealots who had offered her family shelter. He was possessed by a religious fervour that outdid by a long chalk the devotion of the late Leendert Pretorius. A real mouse on a sugarloaf, people sniggered; but he could read beautifully, and that must have clinched what otherwise would have been an incomprehensible mismatch. When it came to matrimonial embraces he had to content himself with doing it in instalments; it was, he once confided to a friend, who in turn reported it to Petronella, like wallowing in mud. Very much, one imagines, a matter of hit or miss; but from time to time he must indeed have scored a palpable hit, because they had three children, in 1846, 1847 and 1849. Sadly, all three were wiped out, within months of their birth, by the fever that raged in those regions, as were two of the offspring engendered by the late Hansie Nel, leaving alive, from that union, only the retarded Benjamin.

In 1851 Bertus Lingenfeld himself succumbed, not to the fever, but to the ardours of love. He died in the act, which was quite embarrassing for the children (two remaining sons and two daughters – including Petronella – from the marriage with Leendert Pretorius; Benjamin from the second marriage) as they had to be summoned to help. The problem, Petronella reported years later, was retrieving the body, which was more or less embedded in the bulk and the folds of his wife's flesh.

There was little to occupy Wilhelmina. The tribulations of the Great Trek were over; the exhilaration of those heady days when she led the women against the English had dwindled to a memory that should be constantly reinvented in the telling, except that apart from her daughter Petronella no one was really interested in listening. There was no call for her services as a healer any more, because the sect in whose midst they had settled already had a medicine woman, the inspired and widely feared Tante Mieta Gous who had taken Petronella under her wing. As a woman Wilhelmina's role was played out. At most she'd become the Fat Woman, a freak at whom visitors, attracted by the growing fame of her daughter Petronella as a seer, might sometimes stare, from a safe distance, in awe. The discovery that her command of Xhosa and Zulu was worthless among the blacks of this remote region deprived her even of the easy intercourse with the indigenous peoples which previously had come naturally to her. Her only response to all these disappointments and frustrations was to eat more; and then still more.

Had Wilhelmina settled into the placidity and ease one would imagine in a person of those dimensions life might have been more bearable. But even though she withdrew increasingly from the outside world, she also became more and more irascible and violent, something of a terror in the neighbourhood; and visitors had to keep a safe distance. Her eruptions were vesuvian, and in spite of the explicit warnings issued to the curious, several too intrepid souls were maimed, and, it was rumoured, two killed, by heavy missiles hurled at them when they ventured too close.

At the time of constructing their house of timber and rough-hewn stone, Wilhelmina, who did most of the building single-handed, took the precaution of installing a front door large enough to let a wagon through; and for quite a while this sufficed to allow her access and egress. But as she steadily grew more and more voluminous, reaching elephantine proportions during the last five or six years of her life, her body could no longer squeeze through the opening. To widen it would not be prudent as the wall supported much of the weight of the house. This meant that Wilhelmina was now confined indoors. In many respects this was a boon to her children, and on one or two occasions it might well have saved their lives as it allowed easy escape from her legendary eruptions of fury. But it also created headaches, the most important – and embarrassing – of which had to do with sanitation.

The series of longdrop outhouses erected over the years, solid constructions of stone and ironwood over huge pits, and moved along a circular path around the house as one pit after the other was filled, had been built to accommodate an elephant; but now she could no longer go out. No commode would carry that weight. The only solution, which must have been a first in the country's history, was to move the facility indoors.

The problem, to phrase it as delicately as possible, was that Wilhelmina's output was directly commensurate with her intake. And as she would have nothing to do with malodorous buckets or barrels carried in and out all day, she insisted on the digging of an indoor pit. Vacating, first, a room at the back near the kitchen, a gigantic hole was dug in the floor and a sturdy seat constructed over it. In a matter of months it was full.

The hole was covered up with beams and plastered with dung, and the whole process was repeated in the adjacent room. Then the next; and so on, until they'd completed the round and were back, quite literally, at square one. By that time, according to their calculations, the first hole would have properly 'settled', allowing them to begin another round. Not a fragrant business, but it worked.

Wilhelmina spent more and more time on the massive stone-carved seat of the longdrop. Why bother to move to and fro if motion was so difficult? During her last year or two she even took to sleeping there, leaning over sideways, propped up against the wall. The only visitors allowed inside were selected members of the sect: Mieta Gous, one of the Enslins, a Greyling, and Petronella's fellow student in the art of prophecy, the young Petrus Landman, people so transported by their faith that they didn't mind sitting, one or two at a time, on the floor of the room where Wilhelmina now permanently held court.

And from there, too, she continued to rule her household with a

293

hand of iron. The sons were forbidden to marry; suitors for the daughters were turned away. The primary obligation of her children was towards her, the great queen bee ensconced on her solid seat. It was the centre of their little universe, and from there ripples and reverberations, both literal and figurative, spread through their lives, through the region, through the length and breadth of the new-fledged republic of the Transvaal.

Petronella's visitors were received in a shed converted into a kind of consulting room, because Wilhelmina would not allow them into the house. Perhaps she begrudged her daughter the fame (although in between violent flare-ups the two remained surprisingly close). Perhaps she simply did not wish to be gawked at by strangers in the state to which she had been reduced, as she slowly made the rounds from room to room, huddled above one pit after the other.

Early in 1859 they started on the third round of excavations. And perhaps it would have succeeded had it not been for the torrential rains that struck the region that late summer. The farmyard was one soggy swamp. The water filtered in under the walls which had already been weakened by the continual digging. Below the surface of beams supporting the dung floor a morass developed. The foundations were literally resting on effluent. One night, in the midst of a thunderstorm, Wilhelmina responded to a call of nature. Slowly, as she sat enthroned, she saw the floor beginning to move and sway and gently rock, heaving and subsiding like a sea. She stared, unable to stir, thinking at first that it was a dizziness which would soon pass. Then she discovered that the sturdy seat itself was trembling, juddering like a ship that had struck a rock. As it capsized, the walls too began to shudder and prepare to fold in on her. In slow motion the whole house crumbled below her, around her, on top of her. The children, awakened by what they took to be an earthquake, ran out into the pouring rain. But Wilhelmina was buried under the rubble, sinking down, down into a seemingly bottomless pit, like a whale returning to the deep. It was her final shit-storm.

# 13

It has been a long spell, interrupted many times, as Ouma grew too weak and faltering, to revive her with a sip of glucose water, a breath or two of oxygen. Sometimes she simply remained silent for up to half an hour at a time, breathing erratically through her open mouth. But the moment I tried to rise and tiptoe away, there would be ominous creakings from the bed where the invisible woman reclined, and Ouma would open her eyes. 'It's not finished yet.' And then resume.

Now she sleeps, and the bed no longer sags, leaving me to pick my way through the maze of her narrative as once I crept through the corridors and dead-ends of this fantastic house, exploring its treasures and banalities; and again I have the impression that the more secrets are disclosed the more impenetrable the mystery becomes.

'Kristien?'

It is Trui, in her petticoat and curlers, come to relieve me. I should be glad to abandon myself to sleep. Yet once again I find that the moment I lie down and turn off the light I am wide awake. How intense the life below the surface of these days. And, as on other nights, everything runs together: Anna's dark glasses that cannot hide their secret, Lenie behind the floral curtain, a baby girl tended on a beach by crocodiles, Michael tracking down his footnote, Thando's belly a cushion for my tears, a woman bristling with assegais like a porcupine in rage, Nomaza in her green head-dress: 'To the women. A luta continua', a white girl dancing with a black man at the edge of the abyss, a whale buried in a sea of shit, the birds taking flight with the leftovers of Ouma's life, her fables scattered in the wind, a handful of feathers – a whole day revolving around the emptiness of Sandile.

I put on the light and pick up the book from my bedside table; the Stephen Hawking from the library. A spell of reading should gather the footloose thoughts. But it is heavy going at this time of the night. I admire Jacob Bonthuys for his dedication. I try to concentrate. Relativity. It seems that in the mysterious region of space-time one can travel into the future or into the past, and through the journey change what has been or may yet be. One can go back there and kill one's parents before one is even born, cancel oneself, switch roles, try out other possibilities. O brave new world. But somewhere must be that limit Jacob Bonthuys spoke about. No, not a limit, the book explains, it's more of a membrane, a one-way membrane, the event horizon that surrounds a Black Hole and which means that you can fall into it but not come out, ever. *Abandon all hope, ye who enter*. Says Hawking; said Sandile.

Can it really be so bad?

# SIX

*Event Horizon*

# I

Not the best way of starting a day; and such a day. It is the nurse who tells me, when I look in to see how Ouma is doing, 'They said on the radio there's been a big bomb at Jan Smuts airport, Miss.'

'How serious was it?'

'Oh, very bad, Miss. Lots of people killed, many of them seriously.'

'You must be sorry you're not there. To help, I mean.'

'Well, actually, Miss – ' She stops to look at me suspiciously; but the news is too hot to suppress, and she launches into an account of the bloody event.

And this, I think wryly, is supposed to be the day everything is going to change. After all the last-minute accords, the appeals from the leaders of warring factions, the efforts to heal the wounds, the oil on troubled waters, after every cliché in the book, this is Election Day. Even here in our own out-of-the-way district there has been no lack of excitement. On Monday night there was the meeting called by Mongane Yaya and his delegation – Abel Joubert came round yesterday to give me an eyewitness account – with fiery speeches from all parties, followed by quite spectacular shaking of hands and embracing of erstwhile opponents (Casper, I learned, did not attend, although several of his commando members did; I presume he had more pressing business at home); yesterday, Tuesday, following dramatic appeals by Thando and by Sam Ndzuta, the youngsters arrested for setting fire to this house were granted bail. In the afternoon Trui went to the black township to visit Happiness Tsabalala: I offered to take her, but she refused to go in the hearse; and besides, she said, it wouldn't be safe for me, a white woman, to go there. But there's peace now, I argued. She shook her head. What she really meant, I knew, was that this was a matter between mothers.

I was left behind with Ouma. She was having a bad day. There was a brief flicker of life when the doctor visited her in the morning with the news that old Piet Malan the undertaker had died suddenly of a stroke in the night. She reacted with an extraordinary show of delight. 'That'll teach him,' she exclaimed, her glee untempered by the merest hint of guilt or remorse; but what, exactly, the lesson involved I could not quite make out. The very excitement soon proved bad for her, and she had to be kept under sedation for most of the day.

Later in the afternoon I was surprised, where I sat at the big dining table bringing my notes up to date, by Jacob Bonthuys. I heard what sounded like a polite cough, and looked up, and there he was in the doorway, clutching the Langenhoven.

'Is something wrong?' I asked, alarmed to see him about.

'No, no,' he assured me. 'If Miss doesn't mind I just thought I'd come out for a while. I need to stretch my legs a bit. It's good to get some air again. And daylight. It's hard on the eyes reading down there all the time.'

'How are you getting on?'

'It's good to read it all again. This *Loeloeraai* gets better every time one reads it. I mean, not only going to the moon, but going right inside it.'

With a touch of mischief I asked, 'Do you think it is all true?'

'It's hard to say, Miss,' he says seriously. 'At the end Mr Langenhoven says it's just a story, but then he describes everything that happened to him and his own wife and daughter. If it wasn't true, do you think his wife would have let him write it?'

'Perhaps she understood what he meant. Women know about such things.'

He smiled with what might have been relief. 'Even if it isn't true it's a blarry good story, isn't it?'

'I suppose it is.'

'It's like that other one of his. When Mr Langenhoven gets fed up with all the nasty, ordinary people in his little town and he just goes off with his family in a tram drawn by an elephant. Herrie. There, too, I wasn't always sure whether he was telling the truth or just lies. But in the end I decided it didn't matter, you know. Because in a way it *is* true. You can say I also went away on that tram with that elephant. It's like another life Mr Langenhoven gave me. Many other lives.'

Almost in a reflex I said, '"He who lives more lives than one, More deaths than one must die."'

He frowned. 'What was that, Miss?'

'Sorry. Just something written by another man who told good stories.'

He shrugged, and smiled again. 'Anyway, now I've also been to the moon.' His smile broadened. 'It's good to go to the moon when life gets hard.'

'You've had a hard time in this place, haven't you?'

'I suppose so, Miss. But it gives one time to think.'

'You know, you really needn't stay down there any more, Mr Bonthuys. There are many other rooms you can move into.'

'Ag, I'm sort of used to the place now,' he said. 'And what's a few days more or less? I mean, a man like Mandela was in jail for – how long? – twenty-seven years, and look at the man. It makes one ashamed to complain, is that not so, Miss?'

'Do you think the elections are going to turn out all right?' I asked.

'Ai, Miss. We must maar hope for the best. Anyway, we'll know soon, won't we? And if it works out all right, Miss can then tell Abel Joubert and I can go home. But I must first make sure.' Adding hastily, 'If Miss doesn't mind? Miss has already done so much for me.'

'I'm sure you've helped me more than I could ever help you, Mr Bonthuys.'

'Ag, that's mos nothing.' He seemed embarrassed.

'Are you going to vote tomorrow?'

'I'm not sure yet, Miss. I feel a bit scared. What if those people recognise me?'

'I don't think you need to worry about them any more, Mr Bonthuys.' I told him about Casper's meeting with the ANC delegation.

'Then I'll think about it, Miss,' he said. And soon returned to his dark quarters, once again clasping his book to his chicken chest.

Today we shall start finding out. By tomorrow – what will we know then? Will there be, after all, some lost little ray of light escaping from our own confining horizon?

Almost inevitably, as the day drew to its close, I sought comfort in Ouma's presence. How quickly this had become a habit, an act of contrition, a necessary resolution of whatever had gone before.

## 2

She looked at me when I came in: that special look she has, neither accusing nor questioning, simply to acknowledge that I am there; a look that makes me conscious of my own presence, a look which can be both reassuring and disconcerting. I took up my seat. She began to speak. It was a story I had heard before, in one form or another, when it had still been a story, a diversion, not yet gathered into our history. It was shorter than most of the others, but not any less disturbing. She spoke. I wrote. And the following was gathered into my past:

After their mother had been changed into a tree, and carried off by the birds, Kamma's children remained with their tribe for some time. I'm not sure how many there were of them, four or five as far as I could make out, most of them indistinguishable from the Khoikhoi around them. But there was one, the oldest, a girl, who looked quite different, tall and slender, with long fair hair. She certainly did not take after her father, Adam Oosthuizen, the red-bearded giant; but perhaps she was a throwback to his mother's family. Or perhaps, some of the Khoikhoi speculated, she was the result of a union between her mother and some exotic bird. Whatever the reason for her outlandishly beautiful looks, if these were initially the cause of veneration among the members of her adopted tribe, they also brought about her downfall; some might say her salvation, but that depends on one's point of view. Certainly they were the cause of the tragedy that befell the tribe, commencing with a visit by a small party of boers from the further reaches of the Dutch colonial settlement at the Cape. More and more of these trekking groups were by then moving into the interior like packs of scavenging dogs spreading civilisation and the gospel; the country was shrinking, it seemed, its space contested, penetrated, appropriated, tamed, the whole shameful story.

Whether this handful of boers, led by an impressive and respected man called David Hartman, had arrived in the deep interior, like others before and after, on a hunting or bartering expedition, or on a journey of reconnaissance, whether they were one of the last desperate groups lured by the legend of an ever-receding fantastic empire of gold in the heart of Africa, or whether perhaps they had heard specific rumours, passing through concentric circles of outlying settlements, about the presence of a white girl in the wilderness, no one can say for sure. What matters is that they arrived at the spot where the tribe was then living, near a magic pool of black water so deep it was said to have no bottom, and there saw the girl.

Some attempt was made to find out who she was and how she'd got there. But although she was fluent in Dutch, having learned it from her mother Kamma, she was very reticent; and the members of the tribe, scared of being found in the wrong no matter what they said, preferred not to discuss the business at all. So the godfearing strangers rapidly concluded that the girl must have been abducted from her parents in her infancy; and before anyone in the settlement could prevent it, she was simply swept up and carried off on one of the galloping horses. It was all so sudden that it appeared, in retrospect, like a dust devil that had descended on them from the sky at great speed, and withdrawn again, whirling her away in its dizzying current. Not even the guardian spirit of the tribe, a huge she-snake that lived in the black pool, carrying a diamond on its forehead – a gem that shone so brightly that whoever looked at it was turned to stone on the spot – could intervene.

The tribe sent out men and women in search of the girl, ever further, but they could not find her. And deeply troubled, because ever since Kamma had been carried off by the birds, they'd felt a grave responsibility towards her remaining family, they now resolved to leave the spot they had come to regard as cursed.

But this was not to be. Because just as the tribe was preparing to break up their huts, the boers returned, led by the same David Hartman; this time they were no mere handful but a huge commando, a righteous crusade sent to wreak vengeance on a tribe of miscreants that had dared to hold captive in their midst a girl from the master race. There was nothing left of the settlement when at last the boers withdrew: not a man or a woman or a child, not even a long-tailed sheep, a goat, or a long-horned ox. Contrary to their habit of driving off whatever cattle they could lay their hands on, this time their fury was so great that everything in their way had to be annihilated. All trace of the settlement had to be obliterated from the earth, to make sure that no one among the Khoikhoi would ever again have the temerity to lay hands on a white girl.

This was the story with which the girl was brought up by the Hartmans. As yet she had no name; if she had, it would of course have been a Khoikhoi name, but she never divulged it to anyone – except perhaps much later to her long-haired daughter Samuel, to whom she entrusted her story and her mother's; but if so, Samuel forgot what it was, or else it was lost further along the line of mothers and daughters – and the name by which she came to be known in the white community that had rescued her, as they insisted, was Lottie.

From her mother she had heard accounts of the lifestyle of the frontier farmers – the roughly built houses overrun by chickens and snorting pigs, the open hearths, the crude handmade furniture, the copious meals, the stone or thornwood kraals filled with cattle, the domestic occupations of the women, the hunting and roaming habits of the men – and with her rudimentary knowledge of Dutch (proof, to her rescuers, that she had been nurtured by civilised people) she soon adapted to their ways. What she enjoyed most was the single shard of mirror cherished by David Hartman's wife Hermina. And when asked about this fascination she told Hermina of her mother's magic mirror in which she'd seen, as a small child, the captured reflections Kamma had brought back from her sojourns on the Oosthuizen farm – although she was careful never to divulge any names or further particulars. Amused, Hermina treated the confidences like the imaginings of a too original young mind; and from the description of the ornate mirror she deduced that Lottie must have belonged to an affluent family of some social standing. Constant efforts were made to enquire in the environs of Cape Town (the part of the colony where such a wealthy clan was likely to have resided), but no trace could ever be found of a family who had lost a daughter in a raid by marauding Hottentots. The only conclusion to be drawn from this was that at the time of the abduction all her people must have been massacred; which served to justify, even more than before, the total revenge meted out to the heathen villains.

Lottie, always a secretive girl – whose strangeness and otherworldliness was readily explained by the tribulations and deprivations she must have suffered in captivity – never tried to correct the speculations about her origins; she owed it to her mother's memory, she confided later to Samuel, to guard as a secret what Kamma herself had obviously chosen to keep from others. And after the initial attempts to probe the darkness so evidently concealed within her, she was left in peace, to the generous if almost smothering ministrations of Hermina Hartman who, having lost all her own children through miscarriage or other more obscure causes, cared for her with all the possessiveness of a mother animal.

As a result the girl never wanted for anything. About twelve or fourteen at the time of her rescue, she soon began to grow into womanhood; but her figure remained slight, and she retained her waif-like appearance, a child of the wind, fleet-footed and shy. She was extremely bright and soon was taught to read and write by Hermina, whose mother had originally come from a prosperous Batavian family – merchants who'd prided themselves on their refinement and culture. The difference between Hermina's love and the diffidence with which her husband treated the foundling must have confused Lottie; but she never enquired into other people's affairs or histories, so what Hermina did not volunteer Lottie never discovered. In return, she found her own secretiveness duly respected.

There was one curious trait about her that never ceased to perturb her foster family. It was in fact the only thing she ever complained about: that she'd been swept away by the commando on their horses so swiftly that her shadow had remained behind. It wasn't just something she'd made up. Hermina herself discovered, one late afternoon when she went out to call Lottie in from the veld, that the child had no shadow: she was coming home with the setting sun right behind her – from even the slightest shrub a long black shadow stretched across the earth – but Lottie walked as if her feet did not really touch the ground, and her slight body cast no shadow at all.

It was eerie, and Hermina preferred to keep the knowledge to herself. But from that day there was a shift in her concern for the child: she became more cautious, almost timorous, as she had to deal with the knowledge that this one lived on borrowed time. There were other discoveries, too, the Hartmans found unnerving, most of which had to do with Lottie's habit of roaming about in the veld on her own. It was wild country, high up in the Cold Bokkeveld region, and predators were not uncommon; stray sheep or goats were regularly killed by foxes, lynxes, leopards, occasionally even by a lion. Yet nothing could restrain Lottie; and David Hartman's dire mutterings about God's wrath were very effectively smothered by his wife's protective instincts.

Hermina was the only one in whom the girl confided her reason for these wanderings. Very simple, she explained: she was looking for her shadow. She could never come to rest before she'd found it, so she had to leave messages everywhere. What kind of messages? Just messages, said Lottie. And when Hermina insisted, the girl reluctantly showed her: at first sight it seemed like writing, but it was no ordinary human script. The codes she used sometimes resembled the trails of snakes or lizards on the sand, or at other times the tiny tracks of ants, or birds, or fieldmice, or meerkats. All day long she would write these messages for the small creatures of the wild to convey to her shadow: signs inscribed on the leaves of succulents, the bark of trees, the mottled surfaces of rocks, or on tracts of sand.

It didn't bother her that these were invariably effaced again – by the wind, by the rarity of rain, by the fierce alternations of heat and cold, by the slow curve of the seasons, the migrations of the creatures of the veld. She would always return, her patience as inexhaustible as her resourcefulness, attempting every time to contrive new languages in the hope that sometime someone would understand and would transmit the messages. And if no one ever understood? asked Hermina. Even then, said Lottie, smiling, it wouldn't ultimately matter. As she had no shadow *any* sign she could leave of herself, of her whereabouts, of having been there, would do.

# 3

One day a man arrived in search of a bride. From the depths of the Great Karoo he came, driven by the need to perpetuate the family name. It was, of course, Bart Grobler. He was not very particular, as long as the prospective bride was of the female sex. Given his fixed purpose he might have done better by choosing a woman from more sturdy stock, who would make better breeding material; but most of the farmers in the outlying districts required sons-in-law to settle in the neighbourhood where they could help consolidate the godfearing civilised population; alternatively they expected a useful bride-price, which was about all a female child could provide in recompense for the unforgiveable lapse of not being a son. But Bart Grobler declined to do the former and couldn't offer the latter – he was already settled on a farm of his own in the shadow of the Swartberge, the Black Mountains, where a wagon took seven weeks to negotiate the forbidding kloofs – and so his choice was limited.

Hermina Hartman clung like lichen to her adopted child, the only creature, since her own overhasty elopement with the boer from the hinterland, on whom she could lavish her frustrated generosity of mind, refinement of spirit, and delusions of civilised behaviour; but David was rather eager to be rid of the disquieting presence he had in so ill-advised a manner brought into his own home. He somehow believed that she represented an ungodly influence, considering the environment from which he'd rescued her (for which, to be honest, she had never shown much gratitude). Hermina was confident that the little girl had come to them intact, having satisfied herself through frank examination, within the first few days of her arrival, that Lottie had not been 'interfered with' by her rude captors; but it seems that, perhaps feeling guilty at having initially entertained the same suspicion, she derived some perverse satisfaction from never communicating her finding to her husband.

All in all, what to Hermina was an irrecoverable loss (one can't be

306

sure, but rumour has it that she died within the year, of grief), to David Hartman seemed deliverance. Some hurried, secret transaction was concluded between the men, and before Hermina had an inkling of how far the arrangements had already proceeded, Lottie was carried off into the deepest interior on the wagon of her latest, surly, saviour. By the time they reached his farm below the Swartberge she was already pregnant; and it is doubtful whether her pregnancies through the following years ever allowed them the leisure of travelling to a drostdy to enter into legal marriage.

The rest you know. In ones and twos and threes, even that famous foursome, Lottie brought into the world her eighteen children all named Samuel. She seemed to form no attachment, ever, to any of them, except possibly the first girl, the long-haired one. It is arguable whether she ever really knew, or cared, what was happening to her body or why it was so regularly put to such curious and uncomfortable use. In the succession of pregnancies and births she lost her looks, her figure sagged, she grew bulbous and unwieldy as if dragged down by the heaviness of the earth. Even then she cast no shadow.

As her brood grew more and more numerous, the house more noisy and unruly, she became more lonely. Apart from, sometimes, the wise oldest child Samuel, there was no one she could confide in. In her desperation she spoke to whatever she came across, a mouse in the kitchen, a spider in the yard, birds in the trees, stones, brittle grasses. But in the end she stopped speaking altogether, even to herself. Her only remaining language lay in the signs she entered on the silent world.

When she could, she continued to retreat into the veld, that semi-desert of barren undulating breast-shaped hills and outcrops interspersed with wide tracts of flatland bearing encrusted in its rocks the remains of antedeluvian seas – shells and ammonites, crustaceans, backbones as delicate as the outline of ferns, the later bones of dinosaurs and the shapes of plant or animal life. Leaving her motley brood – some white, some off-white, some unambiguously brown, but all blessed by the redeeming name of Samuel – to the care of her equally strange, absent-minded eldest daughter, Lottie continued inscribing on the landscape her indecipherable scrawls, her birdlike, reptilian or insect tracks, sending her futile messages to that shadow which remained forever lost, and which she missed as she missed the distant past.

Until, in the end, barely thirty years old but worn out before her time and recognising in her bones the intimations of death (that much she confided to the girl Samuel before she left), one day she did not come back. All that could be recovered of her were the inscriptions she had left on bark and sand and stone; her own tracks no one could follow, they were invisible, as if her body, hulking as it was, had had no weight of its own, not even the weight of a shadow on the land.

# 4

That was last night. Short as the story was it took hours to tell, and Ouma was exhausted when she finished. I am concerned about her; it weighs heavily on me. Yet the nurse has told me this morning that Ouma seems 'more chirpy'; and even the doctor appeared more satisfied with her condition than before.

Trui has been hassling me since I sat down to breakfast. 'When are we going to vote, Kristien?' Ever since she's agreed to call me by my name she has slid into a role of maternal authority which both amuses me and makes me feel wary; I've never taken kindly to management and control. Ouma has been the only exception.

'They said on the radio the queues are very long,' I told her, quite honestly. 'Let's give them some time to drain off the rush.'

The way she rattled and banged the dishes as she put them away was comment enough.

Shortly afterwards Jeremiah appeared in the door. He had put on his Sunday best, a shiny black suit with leather patches on the elbows. 'I have washed the car,' he announced solemnly. 'We can go any time.'

'Kristien says to wait,' Trui replied, casting me a look of silent reproach.

Then it was Jonnie. He must have bought a whole new outfit for the occasion: windbreaker, baggy pants, red shirt, floral tie; his head gleamed with Brylcreem. 'Right, right, right,' he said, rubbing his hands. 'Today we're giving those boytjies in town a lesson in democracy. We're all ready.' And behind him in the yard I saw a small crowd of labourers, all decked up for the occasion, men with hats worn at angles that ranged from rakish to downright reckless, women with elaborate floral decorations on their heads, and carrying babes in arms.

'Kristien says to wait,' repeated Trui in announcement to the world in general.

I could feel my resistance caving in. Yesterday, when Sam Ndzuta had telephoned again to sound me out, I'd succumbed; I now had the necessary documents. But I was still not committed to voting; it was just a precaution.

Then came Jacob Bonthuys, appearing unannounced from the dark hole he'd turned into his home. He had no change of clothing; but he'd obviously gone to great lengths in the bathroom upstairs to make himself as fragrant as possible; and even his crumpled clothes had a new devil-may-care look about them.

'I thought about it all night, Miss,' he said, his earlier apologetic attitude replaced by a new buoyancy, 'and I just can't miss a day like this. I feel a bit like Loeloeraai. It is a strange planet. But I think if I go with you it will be all right.'

'Who is this?' asked Jonnie, his eyes narrow with suspicion.

'A visitor,' I said quickly, and then shoved away the silver I was polishing. 'All right, we can go now. I'll just make sure Ouma is all right.'

She was. And now we're on our way to town. How we all fit into the hearse – there must be at least twenty of us – can only be explained by an adept of Chinese puzzles; yet no one complains. On the contrary, this vehicle could never in its long exemplary life have transported a more exuberant load. Jeremiah having assumed his rightful place behind the wheel, we progress at a more dignified speed than the last few times I drove; even so we pass many other vehicles on the road, most of them donkey carts and horse-drawn buggies; one rickshaw-like contraption, a sight I have never seen before, is even drawn by ostriches and greeted with a huge explosion of shouting and encouragement from my passengers. There are several groups of people on foot too; from their looks some of them may have been walking through the night. Twice Jeremiah stops to invite pedestrians aboard, but after that – even if it makes me feel a heel – I persuade him that we cannot possibly accommodate more bodies. Even Stephen Hawking would have problems here.

I've never seen the town like this before. Within a radius of a kilometre or more around the city hall there is no room at all to park; even the sidewalks are jam-packed with cars. Yet when I propose to Jeremiah that we drop off the passengers at the hall before setting out to find a spot for the car, it is turned down vociferously.

'We're in this together,' says Trui emphatically, and it is endorsed with a cheer.

Fully half an hour later – a quarter to twelve by the clock on the church tower which arrogantly surveys the whole town from its divine height – we join the end of the queue. My expectations of a diminished crowd evaporate: the queue, four or five deep, stretches the length of almost three blocks. The mood is festive, even if the first news imparted to us, almost gleefully, is that the polling station has run out of voting papers. Not that there seems to be anything extraordinary about it, as several ghetto-blasters in the queue proclaim in running commentary that all over the country there is chaos at the polls. Some stations have received no material at all, at others the electoral officers haven't pitched up, still others have run out of ballot papers, boxes, or the magic invisible ink with which our hands are to be marked to distinguish the already-voted from the still-to-vote.

I can imagine the indignation this would cause among the placid British; but here there is no sign of anger or protest. It is not even a matter of resigning oneself to the inevitable: the crowd is in high spirits, irrepressible, exuberant. What difference does a hitch here or there make? Who minds waiting another hour, or two, or three, if one has already waited a lifetime? I, too, find the excitement contagious. I've never voted before. From the one election in which I could have voted after my eighteenth birthday I abstained to demonstrate my rebellion against the system that to me represented Father and his band of brothers, the men in suits, the men with the paunches, the men with the balding heads and the hairy nostrils and the signet rings and the old-boy ties and the Hush Puppies. In England I never bothered to vote, even when I could; I remained an outsider, I could never take its social issues seriously. Now, suddenly, it has become an adventure. What for individuals in the West is a small formality, something so obvious as not to require a second thought, has here become a momentous undertaking. For me – and even more so for most of those around me in the boisterous queue – this is the first opportunity ever of making my little cross for something I believe in. Perhaps I am finally to be vindicated for the vehemence with which I once responded to my faraway disparaging lover, 'I *am* a believer, only I haven't found something to believe in yet.' I feel giddy as the thoughts, so many of them, tumble through my mind: these past two weeks, the years stretching behind them, the time of my life, the long chain from Ouma's reminiscences that reaches back into the shadows, to the first woman who emerged from the waters driving her cow before her and carrying her baby on her back. Yes, I think (I write, now): yes: this is what I wish to believe in. Not merely a new political system, not democracy, not ideology, nothing as tenuous as 'victory' or 'freedom', all the great easy slogans that blacken so rapidly, like photographic paper once it has been exposed to light. No, not those abstractions: but these people around me, here, now, today; and those women behind me, all of us in search of our lost shadows. The shadow isn't there, ahead of us, in that unimaginative box in which we'll thrust our folded multicoloured papers: yet without the box we cannot reach it.

Each of the many people around me on this dazzling day, so unnaturally hot for late April, has brought a whole history along: thousands of histories are gathered in this queue, most of them, I'm sure, more fascinating than my own – with more discoveries, more joys, certainly more suffering, perhaps more spectacle than mine – but this is what moves me, here where I am standing in the spot where I have now been for the past hour, this simple and awesome discovery that I have my own history. It may be paltry; or it may be outrageous; most of it may even be invented. *But it is mine.* And all of it, the whole accumulated wave of it, will be involved in the small cross I am to trace.

They, too, must be sensing it. Relegated to the sidelines, silenced, scoffed at, ignored or degraded, today each one will mark the paper, and each mark will be equivalent to any other. I've waited for thirty-three years. There are others around me who must have been waiting for sixty, seventy, eighty. The country has waited for centuries. Is it any wonder then that a few more hours seem like nothing?

Another hour. There are enterprising individuals around, most of them young, moving up and down the queue with tins of Coke and trays of food for sale: hot dogs, samosas, boerewors, ostrich biltong, bananas. Those who have money buy, unasked, for those who don't. We all share. We all talk, and laugh, and speculate together. In our midst are businessmen in suits, labourers in overalls, youngsters in jeans, the destitute in rags, the social climbers in outfits from Cape Town and Johannesburg, or from Shapiro's. All colours, all ages, all shapes and sizes. An old woman leans against the shoulder of a young man she has never seen before. I hold for some time the dribbling baby of a young mother who looks worn out; it pees on my hip, but somehow it doesn't bother me. A young woman turns her back to brace that of a white-haired old man whose hand is shaking on his stick.

I survey my own little crowd. Trui in red pill-box hat with veil, and a purple cardigan that must be intolerable in the heat, and pleated skirt; Jeremiah as black and solemn as any undertaker; Jacob Bonthuys, arm in sling, standing very straight; Jonnie swaggering up and down the line, chatting up girls; the farm labourers and their families, the people we picked up on the road while we still had room. We take turns to wander off, to stretch our legs and ease our backs in motion.

Much further to the front I find the mayor and his wife; they seem to have no qualms today about waiting with a group of municipal workers in orange overalls. They greet me like old friends. There is the dominee, now smiling by the grace of God as if he's just received authority to forgive me all my sins. The Shapiro sisters, eager and twittering. The chemist, the women from the Home Industries, the tellers from the bank, each white face framed in a wreath of browns and blacks.

Abel Joubert is there too, with his wife Winnie. She looks more tense than the last time I saw her; beside his tanned, eager, active face hers looks much older, as if she were his mother or his aunt.

'I didn't expect to find you here so late,' I say. 'I thought you'd have been among the first to vote.'

'Oh, I deposited my first load at six this morning,' he says, his face creasing in a smile.

'Load?'

'There are so many people living on my farm – '

'Squatting,' reminds his wife, with the merest suggestion of reproach.

'Well, they have nowhere else to go,' he brushes her aside. 'And the farm is big enough, so I've invited them to stay until some more permanent arrangement can be made. But it means I've had to bring in four truckloads of people who wanted to vote. Just as well I had some help, otherwise I'd still have been on the road.'

'Who was the helper?'

'You can ask that again. Could have knocked me over with a feather. Dirk Otto, one of Casper's lieutenants.'

'Covering his back,' I say.

'Sure. And it's mixed with a lot of old-fashioned hypocrisy. But the main thing is that he turned up. As if it was the most natural thing in the world to do. If you ask me, it's catching.'

'If optimism was a disease Abel would have been in intensive care by now,' says his wife. Below the good-natured pleasantry there is an edge of stress; I can imagine how much she has been going through. Yet Abel, for all his generosity of mind, seems unaware of it. Unless he thinks it's unimportant, a woman's quirkiness, to be dealt with later, not now.

'Can you blame me?' he asks. 'Just look at this' – pointing at the crowd – 'this is as much a miracle as the multiplying of the loaves and the fishes, don't you think? All those prophets of doom – all those people who hoarded up supplies expecting the apocalypse . . .' A broad smile as he puts his arm round his wife. 'For the next year there's going to be a heavy cloud of farting hanging over the district. All those tins of baked beans. Let's hope it's good for the crops.'

There is merriment all round.

When it subsides, I take Abel by the arm. 'There is someone I'd like you to meet,' I say.

'I'll be back in a moment,' he tells his wife. She nods, resigned. I accompany him back to my place in the queue.

From a distance he recognises Jacob Bonthuys and stops in disbelief.

'I thought he was – I had no idea of what happened to him!'

'He's been on a trip with Langenhoven,' I tell Abel.

It is good to see them embrace.

Then I leave them to resume my leisurely inspection of the long queue ahead. The old, the young, the decrepit, the blooming. Everybody is ready to strike up a conversation, crack a joke, offer a sweet, a piece of biltong, a swipe from a lukewarm can of Coke. I hesitate briefly when I recognise Anna and Casper, but they've already spotted me and I cannot escape. Lenie is with them, from sheer curiosity, I imagine; although at the rate we're moving she may be old enough to vote by the time we reach the booths. She smiles up at me, her small triangular face frank and untroubled. She winks. She's wearing the bra. Casper and Anna are the only ones in the line whose faces look strained to me, but it may be only because I can see through them. He mumbles something and moves off; his buddies must be elsewhere.

'I didn't expect to see him here?' I say, bemused.

Anna shrugs. Her face looks very pale. She is still – or again? – wearing her dark glasses. She fumbles in her handbag, takes out her purse and thrusts it into Lenie's hand. 'Won't you go and get us some cool drinks?' When the girl has gone, Anna lowers her voice. 'I must talk to you,' she says. Her tone is strained.

'Of course. I'll come over.'

'No. I'd rather come to see you at Ouma's.'

'Anything happened?'

She nods and angrily wipes at a tear that trickles from behind her glasses.

'Any time this afternoon,' I say, and lean over to kiss her on the cheek.

Lenie reappears. I sip up half my Fanta through the multicoloured straw, then say goodbye to return to my place so that one of the others can take a stroll. There is something muted in the day now; Anna has cast a shadow over my earlier excitement. But it dissipates again, as a ripple runs through the crowd. 'We're moving!' comes the message from ahead. 'The papers have arrived.'

The progress is still not fast, but at least we can now shuffle along. A metre or two, then a pause, another metre, a pause, an unexpected surge of five, six metres, then a longer pause. Two blocks to go. One. A half. It's three o'clock, Dutch Reformed time.

At half-past three Trui and I cross the threshold of the hall together. In a brief panic she grabs my hand. I wink at her. She takes courage, lets go again, walks very straight to the nearest official, presents her ID, thrusts her hand under the scanner, offers it to be stained with the invisible ink, takes her floral ballot papers, goes to the nearest booth, now taking it all in her stride as if she's been doing it all her life. Drawing comfort from her assurance I follow in her wake, make a mess of the inking – it smells of orange blossoms, flavour of the month – drop one of my papers, start giggling, and scuttle into my booth.

It is very quiet in here. It's like entering a shower cubicle. I feel like throwing back my head to catch the stream on my upturned face, to feel my whole body laved by it. The water of history, I think, a little preciously: but I've always had the urge to find a word for important occasions; one small step for a man.

This is a woman's step. Out of space comes the recollection of Anna's story about Mother: how in that last election of their unhappy lives, when Father was the candidate, she cast her vote against him. The only act of defiance available to her. She's here with me now, I think. How lucky I am to be able, at last, to vote *for* something, not just against.

Almost without my noticing it the booth has become very crowded. We're all here together, as cramped as the crowd in the hearse, but just as joyous, all our bodies exposed to the exuberant stream that splashes over us, cleansing us, confirming us even as we make our cryptic crosses, as surely as a Boer woman who once embroidered her name and the date of her death on a cloth. Mother; Ouma, preserving for posterity the menstrual blood of a lifetime; Rachel, who splashed the walls of her prison with erotic paintings; Petronella, the prophet; Wilhelmina, whose sole articulation was her growing weight; Samuel, growing her hair, cutting her hair; Lottie, who wrote on bark and leaves and earth; Kamma, who unleashed the fireflies. And a host of others, shadows whose names I don't even know, but who are here. Here is my cross. Kristien Müller her mark. And damn the rest.

# 5

In the late afternoon, from my bedroom window, I see Anna stop outside under the loquat tree. She has the two girls with her. I turn off the radio. I have been listening to the news, something I haven't bothered doing since my arrival. But today is different. And we haven't gone up in flames after all. After the early-morning news about the bomb at the airport there have been no further outbursts. The great tide of violence that has been engulfing the country these last months seems to have been arrested, like the photograph of a rearing wave caught in mid-swell. Only temporarily suspended? Or has something miraculous occurred to change its course? Too soon, of course, to tell. But in the afterglow of what we've been living through today, anything is credible. The impossible has happened. Now we can face the possible.

I meet them at the back door.

'I was wondering whether you were still going to make it,' I say, briefly hugging Anna. Normally she would tense up, I know she doesn't like being touched; but she even presses her forehead against my shoulder.

'It wasn't so easy to get away.' She hesitates, looking at the children. 'Scoot, you girls,' she says.

'Can we climb trees, Mom?' asks Nannie.

'That's for monkeys,' Lenie remarks haughtily.

'You're not much fun to be with any more, you know,' complains Nannie. She has a new idea and sets off. 'Let's go and chase the peacocks.'

Lenie makes a face, then follows her at a more dignified pace.

'The birds have all gone,' I tell her.

'It's that time of the year,' says Anna, not very interested; the way she might have said, 'It's that time of the month.'

'What a day,' I say. 'I'm afraid I've become rather cynical lately, but this morning made me think that change is possible after all. I can't believe the high spirits I've seen everywhere.'

'It will subside again, don't worry,' she says. 'It's a kind of mass hysteria, that's all.'

'I think you're wrong. Look, I'm not so naïve as to think everything will suddenly be moonlight and roses. But what we've seen today – not just here, but all over, throughout the country – cannot just dissipate again. People will remember it. Surely that will help us through bad patches.'

'Why should it?'

'Because the one thing we know now is that we're all in it together.' I was still doubtful when Thando Kumalo said it yesterday, Trui this morning; now I'm prepared to believe it. 'We're in it for better or for worse. I feel a sense of complicity. It's like a marriage.'

'Marriages break up too.'

'Anna, I'm sorry! I got carried away.' I take one of her hands in both of mine. 'It was hard not to. Are things very bad?'

She nods. 'I don't want to dampen your spirits. But frankly, even if the country does change, what difference can it make to me? I live on a different level, I'm afraid it's very basic. Man and woman. And that's not going to change.' A sudden surge of urgency. 'Or is it?'

'It must. We've got to make it work for *us*.'

'You may be free to decide to make it work for you, Kristien.' There is a hard, still bitterness in her voice. 'I'm living on a kind of subhuman level. I'm not even a woman any more. I'm just somebody's wife, somebody's sister, somebody's mother.'

'And now you're blaming all the "somebodies"? Isn't that a cop-out?'

She turns on me. 'What joy can there be in kicking someone that's down?'

For once I'm not stung into tartness, cleverness. Instead, I'm surprised by the understanding I feel for her. And I reply almost gently, 'There are two mistakes in your reasoning, Sis. I'm not kicking. And you're far from down.'

'Don't be so sure.' She takes me by the shoulders and shakes me; for a moment she is uncontrollable. 'Kristien, I'm desperate.'

'The very fact you've come here tells me that you're not down and out yet.'

'Coming here was the final straw, I think.' She is more controlled now, but I sense in her a rage and a desolation that is frightening. 'He tried to stop me. He told me – he practically ordered me – to stay away from here. He can't stand the idea of the two of us conspiring behind his back.'

We go inside; I take her up to my room. She sits down on the bed. I remain standing, leaning against the window-sill.

'I'm leaving him,' she says, like a straight jab to the chin; but in a matter-of-fact tone as if announcing that she's bought a dress.

'That's the best news I've heard since I came back,' I exclaim. Her expression makes me check myself. 'Is it really true?'

'It's the only way. But I don't know how I'm going to make it work.' Unasked, she picks up my packet of cigarettes from the bed. 'Do you mind?'

'Be my guest.' I watch her closely while she holds the lighter to her cigarette, inhales, exhales; her hand is trembling. 'Would you like a drink?'

She hesitates. 'I suppose I can do with something.'

'There isn't much, but I think I can find some brandy.'

'Anything will do.'

When I return from the dining-room downstairs, ice-cubes gently tinkling in the two glasses, she hasn't moved; but the cigarette is stubbed out on the bedside table. She gulps down a large mouthful, closes her eyes, throws back her head; at last she looks at me again, a wan smile on her pale mouth.

'Thanks, Sis.'

'Have you told him?' I ask.

'I tried to, last night. That was the first time I've had the guts.'

'And?' I ask when she remains silent.

'At first he didn't take it seriously. He thought I was just putting on an act. I tried to stand my ground. I told him my mind was made up. Then he suddenly changed and became all contrite. Said he couldn't live without me, he loved me. I tried my best to be unmoved. But he knows me so well. In the end – '

'I don't believe it,' I say, more to myself than to her; and yet I do believe her. I have seen glimpses of his male wizardry.

She takes another swallow. 'In the end we made love. If that's the word for what we did. Do you think I'm kinky?'

'Does it matter what I think? Why did you do it?'

'It just happened. I became too tired to resist. One keeps hoping against hope. Still, at the back of my mind there was something like a small, angry, lucid spot. I thought: all right, afterwards we'll talk, he'll be more understanding. But when it was over he turned away and fell asleep. He thought it was all resolved.'

'What about you?'

'I was awake all night. In the beginning I just felt hurt, used, miserable. But as the night went on I became angry. I don't think I've ever been so angry in my life. I felt filthy. Like an old rag. Like a piece of toilet-paper he'd wiped his backside on. I could have killed him in

his sleep. But I restrained myself. I waited until he woke up this
morning. And then I told him again.'

'Did he pay attention?'

'He was in a hurry. He's always in a hurry in the morning. But I
told him I was serious. I literally jumped up and cut him off when he
tried to go out. He tried to shove me aside, but I told him he wasn't
going to get out before he'd listened to me.'

'Did he get violent?'

'He didn't . . . beat me, if that is what you mean. For once he didn't.
But he was furious. I could fuck off, he said, the sooner the better. But
he won't let the children go. Not even the girls.'

'And that is where it's at?'

'I'll have to see a lawyer of course.' A trembling smile. 'Just like you
told me.'

I take a cigarette and move the packet towards her, but she declines.
'You can count on me,' I promise her; but it sounds so disgustingly
inadequate, so trite.

'It's like . . .' Another pause. 'It's taken such a long time. Now I
can't go back.' Her composure suddenly cracks up. She drains her
glass. 'But what am I going to do, Kristien? If I give up the children
there's no point in going on any more. But if I take them, even if he
lets me, how am I going to cope? I have no money. I have nothing, I
*am* nothing. It's all his. I have nowhere to go. I'm forty-two. How does
one start a new life?'

'You're still in your prime. You have qualifications.'

'They're all useless now. I have no confidence. I'm not sure about
anything at all any more. Except that I've got to leave.'

'Move in here,' I say. 'At least to begin with.'

'It's too close. He'll – I'm scared, Kristien. I'm more scared than
I've ever thought possible.'

'I've often wondered,' I say on an impulse, without any idea of where
this may take me, 'why we put up with it all. It shouldn't be necessary.
It's not logical, it isn't normal. For all the thousands of years we've
been on this earth: why is it always *they* who decide, we who follow
meekly? Why does everything happen on their terms? Whether they
drag us across the Drakensberg, or declare war, or wreck the planet,
we always let them have their way. And we can put a stop to it. We
must, or else – '

'There's always the children.' She narrows her eyes. 'Perhaps you
won't understand that. You don't like children.'

'It's not that. I know I've been a shit to your kids. Although I've been trying, the last few days – '

'I've noticed.'

'I can't explain. Perhaps the abortion had something to do with it. I've never been able to face children again. Stupid, isn't it? Guilt is a very corrosive thing.'

'I wish we'd known each other better, sooner,' she says.

'We'll make up for it.' I consider for a while, then look at her. 'And I do understand what you mean about children. I mean, why we let the men get away with so much.'

'They've got us exactly where they want us,' she says quietly.

I flare up again. 'We shouldn't let them, for fuck's sake. It's not necessary. We can say no. That's the one thing I truly believe. It's up to us.'

She raises her glass, discovers that it is empty and reaches for another cigarette. She inhales deeply, then chokes briefly on the smoke. 'The problem is that it comes at a price. But you were prepared to pay it. So I thought why not I? Only it's so terribly difficult, Kristien.'

'Is there anything I can do?'

'Just be here.' There is desperation in her voice. 'Don't go away. Stay here. I'm going to need you very much.' She smiles through shimmering eyes. 'I know I shouldn't say this. I've got to stand on my own two feet. But that's the problem, isn't it? If one's never done that before. I don't even have a name of my own. I started life with Father's. Then he passed me on to Casper. Like some object of barter. So where does one begin?'

'You've already made a beginning.'

'I don't know. I'm trying to act very brave right now. But tonight, when I'm back there . . .'

In a rush of concern I ask, 'He won't try to – ?'

She shakes her head wearily. 'But it may be even worse if he turns on the charm. He knows me so well.'

'You dare not let him, Anna!'

She looks hard at me, her eyes now steady and focused. 'Tell me what to do,' she says at last.

'Oh no,' I stop her. 'You know very well what I think. But I'm not going to tell you anything. I won't take the blame for it afterwards. You *must* decide for yourself.'

She shrewdly shifts her position. 'Be honest with me,' she says. 'What would you do if you were me?'

It is a very precarious moment; she is grossly unfair. At the same time it would be irresponsible to duck out of it. Even so: dare I tell her this or not? God knows I derive no satisfaction from it; but yielding to the blind belief that it is necessary, for both of us, I say, 'Do you know that he was here on Sunday night?'

'Who?'

'Casper. It was very late, past midnight. He had a spare key. When I found him he was already inside.'

She stares at me, her eyes vacant with shock.

'He tried to force me.' Now I must go all the way. 'It wasn't the first time either.'

'When – ?' she asks mechanically.

'The day of your wedding.'

'Jesus.' She covers her face in her hands. From between her fingers a thin line of smoke curls up. After a while she looks up again. 'And did he – ?'

'No. Someone helped me. He was very pissed off.'

'And afterwards he came home to me.'

'Yes. I'm sorry. I'm so sorry.'

She leans over to stub out the cigarette. 'Well, I'm glad you told me. It does make it easier. At least for the moment.'

'Please stay here tonight. It's always more manageable in the daytime.'

'One's got to do what one's got to do, not so?' she asks with a bitter smile.

'Let me go back with you. He won't dare to do anything if there's company.'

'You can't be there all the time. I can take it. I think I can. Anyway, the sooner I learn to cope on my own, the better.' She gets up. 'I want to wash my face. And I must say hello to Ouma.'

She goes to the bathroom; afterwards I accompany her to Ouma Kristina's room. She stops in the doorway; I hear the sharp intake of her breath. I should have warned her about the coffin. Now I can only offer her a shrug by way of apology, if not of explanation. Leaving her alone with Ouma I go downstairs, feeling as if I'm walking in my sleep.

The girls are just coming into the kitchen with untidy little bunches of flowers they have picked in the garden.

'It's for Ouma,' announces Nannie.

Before I can waylay them they dart upstairs. I remain in the kitchen door. The sun has set. The last blood is draining from the sky; with its characteristic African suddenness the dark comes down. In the distance, through the trees, I see the lights from the labourers' houses.

Ten minutes later I hear Anna and the children descending the stairs. The girls are chattering away. Lenie has dropped her dignity as she comes sliding down the banister, crash-landing in the passage. They rush past me in a race to reach the car first.

Anna and I follow much more slowly.

'Look after yourself.'

'That's the one thing I intend to do.'

'If there's any need at all, phone.'

'I'll be all right. You've been a brick.'

In spite of the lightness on the surface I am only too conscious of the turbulence she is trying to cover up. And when they drive off and the red tail-lights disappear along the farm road I feel something contract in myself as a soundless voice cries out, Come back, come back!

It is a long time before I turn round to face Ouma and the night.

# 6

We are in our ark again, just the two of us, like so many times before; and more than ever it feels as if we're drifting on a slowly moving sea, sailing through endless space, a darkness without end. Ouma is lying with her eyes closed. Her breath is very shallow, I can barely see her rib-cage move. The eyeballs have sunk into the skull so deep that they are lost in shadow. As usual, only the bedside lamp is on: it is more gentle, more forgiving. The house itself is breathing quietly around us. It feels more penetrable than ever; the night is moving in on us from all sides. It seems possible that the moon, if it rises higher – it is still low, caught in the black branches of the trees outside – may proceed right through the house, skimming the empty bed.

Her fingers clasp and unclasp on her chest. The eyelids flutter without opening. Her mouth is twitching.

'Are you sleeping?' I whisper.

'I'm awake. I'm tired. It's been a long day.'

'It's over now.'

'Almost. Not quite.'

Involuntarily I glance at my watch; it has stopped. A brief consternation besets me, then passes. What does it matter anyway?

'Anna came to see me today,' she says.

'I know.'

321

'She's very unhappy. She should divorce that man.'

'Has she spoken to you about it?' I ask cautiously.

'No. But I could see. You must speak to her.'

'I shall. I have already.'

'There haven't been many happy marriages in our family,' she says after a moment. 'I must have been one of the lucky ones, don't you think?'

'But Ouma . . .' My protest peters out.

'Nine children your Oupa and I had. We were so happy.'

Again I feel the need to talk, then let it pass.

Her eyes open, with difficulty it seems. 'You don't believe me?'

'It's not that. But you said – '

'I remember what I said. There's never been anything wrong with my memory.' Slowly, as in all the nights that have gone before, the very process of talking seems to generate the strength to continue. But sometime, surely, she will have nothing left? A hundred and three years; then the bomb; and still she goes on, quietly, a small flame flickering, flickering.

I hesitate for a long time; but it must come into the open. So I ask, 'What about Jethro?'

'What about him?'

'You loved him.'

'Of course I loved him.'

'You went away together.'

Her face relaxes, invaded by a strange happiness; as on some rare occasions before I realise how beautiful she must have been when she was young. Almost effortlessly – but very softly, so that I have to keep my ear against her lips – she lets herself be carried along by her words.

'There comes a time when one has to break away, otherwise you suffocate. It's like Samuel who set out on her coffin, this very one, to look for her shadow – '

'But Ouma – '

'Or like Wilhelmina who kept with her the mirror from her mother's house, in which she could see, at night, the ghosts of the dead.'

'But Ouma – '

'My own mother, too, you remember, the girl Rachel, who ran away to the sea and never came back; which was such a disgrace to her parents that they had to dig a grave for her, and organise a funeral, coffin and everything, so that people would think she'd died.'

'But Ouma – '

'That's how it was with me too, when Jethro came and we ran away to Paris.'

'To Paris?'

'Paris,' she says, savouring the name. 'Yes. That was where we went. Old Moishe arranged it all, he knew people everywhere, he said this was his wedding gift to us. Even though we weren't married yet.'

'And it was wonderful?'

'Yes, it was wonderful.' A pause. 'In the beginning at least. In the beginning we did all the bohemian things. It was summer. I believed it would last for ever. Again, through old Moishe's contacts, we found a place to stay, a little garret in the Jewish quarter, in the Rue Vieille du Temple. He wrote. I painted. We made love. We went hungry. We sang in the streets and he played a second-hand flute in the Métro and I sketched portraits of tourists. We did odd jobs in Les Halles. We drank red wine. We'd lie about in the Jardin du Luxembourg, in the Bois de Boulogne, it was like walking hand in hand through the Seurats and the Monets we'd seen, pictures which were becoming very fashionable just then.' She begins to hum a tune, but very off-key, and very low, so that I do not recognise it at all, but it may be something from the Twenties, it sounds like vaudeville. In the middle of it she stops. 'Or we'd take a train into the country and spend days and nights under the sun, under the stars. It was impossibly romantic. It was impossible.

'Jethro had all these incredible plans for the future. I would be the first great female painter. He would be an immortal writer. Many years later it occurred to me that in some respects, in spite of all their differences, he was just like your Oupa Cornelis. Men. Brimming with plans and projects, visions, schemes, all day long. But when night falls they sit on the toilet and read the newspaper.

'It took a while for us to come down to earth again. Summer was running out. In the Luxembourg the first leaves were turning yellow and beginning to fall. The first hints of cold sent shivers through the city. I've never known a city — but then, what other cities have I known? — that lives so closely tuned to the changes in the seasons. All of a sudden our garret was no longer so hospitable. All of a sudden our love no longer seemed altogether adequate. I suppose we'd made the old mistake of confusing being in love with our capacity for living together. I hadn't reckoned with the fragility of the male ego. Perhaps I simply was unmarriable. Still, we tried our best to cheat. We borrowed money and went south, to Italy, to Greece, in search of what warmth there was. We survived the winter. With the coming of spring we returned to Paris and our spirits revived. I was beginning to be obsessed with my painting. Jethro started complaining, feeling a bit left out; he was making demands I no longer felt so enthusiastic to comply with. A new autumn came down on us, like a blight, like darkness. We had no money left. We were turned out of the garret. I discovered that Jethro had begun to see other girls, more beautiful than I was, and not nagging so much. He still had his dreams, but I was no longer altogether part of them, nor did I really want to be.

'One day I took one of the small paintings I'd done of him, the one you know; and I stole the money he'd been secretly hoarding under a floor-board in the smelly squat-down toilet on the landing of the place in Clichy where we were then living. There was just about enough to get back home on. I left him my other paintings in exchange. I'm sure he would have got something for them, he'd already sold a few behind my back, pocketing the money for his more personal needs. I didn't leave a note. I decided a clean break was preferable.'

There is a very long silence.

'And you were pregnant when you came back?' I ask.

'Who says I was pregnant?'

'You did.'

'Oh.' The hint of a smile which, eighty years ago, might have been saucy. 'I can't remember.'

'Please tell me, Ouma.'

'The memory is yours now,' she says. 'Do with it what you wish. You understand that now, don't you?'

'I'm not sure. There is so much I still need to know . . .'

But she is paying no attention to me; perhaps she really cannot hear me. 'I had to tell you everything,' she says. 'If you don't know our history it becomes tempting to see everything that happens as your private fate. But once you know it you also realise you have a choice.'

As I gaze down at her I feel my anxiety subside. It is not really all that important after all to sort out the details of her history, of mine. She has made her choices, so can I. She has lived for so very long. When she was born there were no cars in this country yet, no telephones, barely a railway. She has seen the whole world change from the age of the horse to that of space travel. At her birth Sarah Bernhardt was in her heyday, Einstein was a boy, Victoria ruled the waves. Her stepbrothers, or uncles, depending on one's point of view, fought in Paul Kruger's war, her stepsister chose to die in a concentration camp; when she was in Paris, if she was there, she might have known the young Picasso, the young Modigliani, Gertrude Stein. In her lifetime two world wars and countless other conflicts have scarred the face of the earth. She was already old when the Berlin Wall was built: she also saw it fall. Men have come and men have gone, she is still here, she has survived, nothing can surprise her. Through all their sophistry and power games, their explanations of the world and why it has to be the mess it is, she has calmly persisted with her own inventions. Behind and below history she has continued to spin her secret stories of endurance and suffering and survival, of women and mirrors and shadows and coffins and flood and shit and divine messengers and rape and incest and suicide and murder and love. The configurations may be interchangeable; the myths persist, she has lived them into being. Why demand the truth, whatever that may be, if you can have imagination? I've tried the real, and I know now it doesn't work. The universe, somebody said, and I know now it is true, is made of stories, not particles; they are the wave functions of our existence. If they constitute the event horizon of our particular black hole they are also our only means of escape.

'Forgive me,' I whisper impulsively, without understanding why, or what has so suddenly prompted me; knowing only that it has to be asked and that she is the only person in the world I can ask it of, the only one who can grant it to me without expecting me to deserve it. 'Forgive me.'

You are the only one who can do so; yet you are the only one in whose eyes I have never been guilty. You are perhaps the only person I've ever loved wholly, unconditionally, unquestioningly.

And yes, you are right, of course you are right: you have given me back a memory, something to make it worthwhile to have gone away, and to have suffered, and to have lost my meaning, and now to have come back. I used to think only other people had histories. History belonged to Father. Or to those in the Struggle: it was a train that came past, and I boarded it, and got off, it was never mine. Now something is happening to me. I'm not sure I understand it yet; but I can feel it. This was what it felt like when I discovered I was pregnant, that time. And then I lost it. This time I must hold on. I love you.

'I disapprove of death,' she says, very softly, but very distinctly.

Around us the house is alternately expanding and shrinking, a breathing in and a breathing out. The moon is high now. The walls have become transparent. They are translucent. There is space inside, infinite space.

'Poor old Piet Malan,' she says again.

I see her sinking slowly, see the flickering ghost-images of many faces passing through hers as if she tries them on and merges with them; see her falling from body to shadow to ever-changing names, cascading through time in a present that never ends; and the unreality of all she makes me see lends reality only to the seeing itself.

So many lives. Yet Oscar Wilde was wrong, I think: 'He who lives more lives than one – ' A single death suffices.

Her voice ebbs to a mere whisper. 'Do you believe in God, Kristien?'

I honestly do not know what to say.

Her lips move again. I press my ear to her mouth.

'If there is a God,' she says, 'why am I allergic to feathers?'

It is quiet now. But in the silence I become aware of a sound emerging from it, barely a sound, a mere rustle, a sigh, very low, almost inaudible, but enormous, moving through the night. Birds. They can only be birds, but they are invisible, filling the air with the soft grey whirring of their wings.

SEVEN

---

*Not the End*

# I

The funeral is today. It is Wednesday, exactly a week after the main election day. It must be the biggest funeral the district has ever known, even in the heyday of the ostrich feathers. People have come from everywhere. There are even representatives of the new government. The television is here too. I would have liked to stay away and avoid the crowds that trample everything in their way. But I suppose I am the central figure here, much as I hate it. Abel Joubert and Jacob Bonthuys are trying to deflect some of the glare, shielding me from the overtly staring eyes, the greedy media people; but it isn't much use.

For a week the gossips and newspapers have run amok. Abel Joubert has arranged to post guards at the entrance to the farm; Jacob Bonthuys has come back as an official doorman. Jonnie has joined his parents in the house to ward off intruders. No strategy was too devious for those who came in search of a story. A family magazine sent a combi loaded with flowers, among which a female journalist and a male photographer lay concealed to jump out at the crucial moment for an impromptu interview; God knows what they were up to in their floral hide-out, for they looked suspiciously crumpled when they did emerge. Faced with Jacob Bonthuys's gun they made an undignified departure.

The vulgarity of it all has taken my breath away. Even as I watch the funeral ceremony unfold around me I cannot quite believe what has happened. Surely it is too crude, too extreme, too melodramatic. But we as a people – and a family – have never shied away from the crude or the melodramatic; so how could I expect to be spared it?

I must try to catch hold of it all; to grasp it before it totally eludes me and recedes into nightmare. If only it were that.

When did I have the first intimation, on the night of Ouma's death, that something was wrong? Initially there was no sense of doom or danger. There was, at most, an urge to reach out and touch someone, tell someone. I was still sitting on the bed, all notion of time lost, gazing at the coffin before me, at her changed face now set in death, the insignificance of her little bundle of bones that seemed to be turning to dust in front of my eyes: and then the feeling of unease, a curious anxiety, began to stir in me. I ascribed it, then, to the dawning consciousness of myself there, alone, in the night, with Ouma's dead body. The need to be reassured by knowing someone else was close to share it with. Trui was the obvious person, and yet I was reluctant to disturb her. There would be enough commotion around her soon, in the days to come. That was when I thought of Anna. There was no logic for it, and no hindsight to illuminate it later. I simply knew I had to telephone her; and in that same instant I was beset with fear at the very thought that she might not answer.

In a kind of numbness I dialled her number. My hand was trembling. In my mind I was urging her on: Answer! Answer! It rang and rang and rang. I could imagine the sound at the other end, that hollow desolate sound of a telephone ringing at some ungodly hour of the night. But there was no answer. That was when I knew it had been no mere urge but a premonition.

Again I considered waking Trui and Jeremiah. I went to their room. They were fast asleep. No, I couldn't. I knew now, with absolute certainty, that something had happened. But for that very reason I couldn't face them. As yet there was nothing to tell. I was the only one who could do what had to be done – whatever that might turn out to be. Without making a sound I went downstairs, and outside to the shed, and slid into the hearse and drove off.

From afar, across the emptiness of the plains, I could see the lights of the neighbouring farmhouse. It seemed as if every single light in the house was on, looking like a great festive passenger ship passing in the night.

But there was nothing festive about the scene that met me when I went to look through the lounge window after there had been no response to my furious knocking. I went on automatic pilot; I became an actor in a barely credible, badly scripted TV play. I found a stone and hurled it through the large plate-glass window, then chopped open a hole large enough to let me through – even so I cut my arm – and clambered inside. Now, even in my bleeding, I was part of the scene I had witnessed from outside. One wouldn't think that ordinary human beings could have so much blood in them. The carnage stretched from the front room, where the television was still on – CNN bringing news of the elections; a new beacon of hope for the strife-torn world, the female announcer said in a voice that twanged like an electric guitar – down the passage, into the bedrooms and the kitchen.

An intruder. That was my first thought. It was so obvious. All the enemies Casper had made in the district; somebody, in the elation of the day's events, deciding to revenge all the accumulated bitterness of so many years. But I realised very soon that this could not be what had happened. The fact that nothing in the house was out of place or, as far as I could make out, missing. That all the doors were locked, the keys on the inside. (Outside, I'd noticed on my arrival, both the bakkie and the Land Cruiser were undisturbed in their usual spots.)

There was only one logical alternative. The bastard, I thought, too numb to impose any order on my mind; looking, from very far away, at my own thoughts as they came and went. I wasn't there. I couldn't possibly be there. The fucking goddamned bastard. So he'd done it after all. She had feared this all along. Why hadn't she listened to me and spent the night at Ouma's place? Why couldn't somebody have stopped him in time? All my pretty chickens and their dam. Almost clinically, my mind still remote from what I was witnessing, I worked my way through the house, registered what had happened. Two of the boys in the passage, one shot in the chest, the second in the head. Nannie in the bedroom she'd shared with Lenie, toppled over as if she'd just sat up, awakened by the commotion, when she was struck by the bullet. The smallest boy shot in the left temple in his bed where he'd possibly – hopefully – been sleeping through it all. Crumpled against the kitchen door, brought down presumably as she was trying to get out and run off into the night, Lenie. In her shortie pyjamas, through which, like a spelling mistake on a tidy manuscript, the new bra was visible.

Back in the lounge, Casper spreadeagled on the carpet, on his back. Three shots, as far as I could make out. In the stomach, in the left shoulder, in the forehead. And slumped over him, Anna. The hole in her right temple ringed in a blackish scorch-mark.

And then the final realisation. The thought I couldn't possibly admit. It was too outrageous. It made no sense. It made every sense. It was Anna who had done it. Shooting him first; then the children; then returning to him to kill herself. The way her body was positioned over his, her fingers still touching the pistol.

My wrist was still bleeding.

# 2

I didn't flap or run about. I didn't get hysterical. I didn't scream. I
could not cry. I sat down in a chair opposite the TV, an eye glaring
insistently at me, not looking but demanding to be looked at. What was
happening on the screen passed me by; it came from another world
altogether. For how long I remained there I cannot tell. Just sat quietly,
too numb to be horrified. It is almost impossible, now, a week later, to
recall my thoughts; whatever I try to say about it may be confusing the
blankness of that night with the jumble that came afterwards. But if
there was anything in my mind I could grasp it was that this was the
worst I was likely to see in my life. Nothing else could ever again be
compared to this. Others may have lived through experiences more
extreme; this was *my* limit. And there was a curious serenity about the
discovery. I could now relax, I might even go to sleep, there was
nothing more to fear. Nothing I could imagine could outdo this. Reality
had cancelled itself. That surge within the real towards the unreal,
which had fascinated me for so long, had fulfilled itself. There was no
temptation to betray what I couldn't change.

A woman came from the desert of death to ask, 'Do you know what
I've come to tell you?' The answer, I now knew, was neither yes nor
no. The only possible answer was before me, inside me. It was silence.

I think I thought: This is the inevitable consequence of Ouma's
stories. To transform oneself into a tree, to drown in shit, to await a
flood in a coffin, to paint on the walls of a prison, to scribble on a surface: nothing, nothing is innocent. Below it lurks the shadow, that little
investment in darkness we can call our own; one day it must break out.

Centuries and centuries of struggling and suffering blindly, our
voices smothered in our throats, trying to find other shapes in which to
utter our silent screams. Dragged across plains and mountains – just
like those others, the nameless dark servants – barefoot, helping to
preserve the tribe, loading the guns, healing the sick and wounded,
fighting and dying alongside the men, then returned to the shadows
while the men assumed what glory there was. In every crisis we were
granted, by special dispensation, our brief moment in the light: then
back to the familiar domestic obscurity of our predestined 'place'. To
suffer, to cry, to die. Theirs the monuments for the ages; ours, at most,
the imaginings of sand. And again I thought: Why have we borne it?

332

Why have we never, collectively, rebelled? For the sake of the brief ecstasy of sex? The survival of the species? A pathetic sense of security? But surely we could have done it on our terms, not always, exclusively, on theirs?

For all the fertile years of her long life Ouma stored her bloodstained towels as a silent testimony – proud, defiant, shocking, but silent – of her womanhood. But then it dried up. No longer fecund, she broke out in stories. These are mine now. I can, if it is not yet too late, assume my history. But for Anna it was too late.

Her only power was the power to destroy herself; and from that she didn't flinch. If it had to be done – I'm trying to persuade myself – then she wouldn't flinch from it. It was her only, ultimate, accomplishment; the least I can hope for is that she did it lucidly, courageously. If your tongue is cut out you have to tell your story in another language altogether. This carnage is the only sign she can leave behind, her diary, her work of art. She couldn't have done it alone. Countless others have converged in her to do this, to articulate this. There were many women in my sister, as in me: and I knew only one or two or three of them. She was a multitude. I am. We are. It is a very basic arithmetic I am learning.

At some stage I got up – the television was still on, that uninterrupted flow of images, even more absurd with the sound turned down (when had I done that?) – and went to the telephone in the passage. It was from here she must have called me, God knows how long ago, to say, 'It's Ouma. You must come.' Michael sniggering. 'Somebody called Ah-na, frightful South African accent.' How our accents do inform against us. It wasn't Ouma after all, it was Anna herself, only neither of us knew it at the time. I dialled the police, the doctor. I went back to my chair. There was blood on the arm-rest. Mine, hers, his? Ours. I sat down. I was still there when they came.

# 3

The doctor was finished first. There wasn't much he could do. On his instructions the police allowed me to go as soon as the most obvious questions had been asked (I no longer remember what I replied); it was the same officer I'd met here the first time, fortunately not the one who had brought the detained children round to Sinai. The doctor wanted to drive me home, but I insisted on returning in the hearse; for once it was appropriate to the occasion. Even so he followed me to the neighbouring farm in his car. Just as well, because it was only when we stopped in the yard under the black trees that I remembered there was another body inside for him to deal with.

Trui came running from the back door as we approached.

'Kristien, where have you been? Something terrible has happened.'

'I know, Trui,' I said perfunctorily. 'I've brought the doctor.'

'Why didn't you wake me?' she scolded me. 'When I got up you were just gone and there was Jeremiah and I alone in the house with a corpse.'

The doctor patted her on the shoulder. He went on ahead with her. I presume he told her about what had happened on the other farm, because she suddenly gasped and started wailing very loudly. Breaking from his grasp she ran back to me, threw her arms around me, nearly throttling me, and broke into incoherent snatches of speech. It was almost a relief to have her to deal with.

Jeremiah was waiting upstairs, wide-eyed but resigned. He escorted the doctor with the stiff formality of an usher at an important function, while I attended to Trui. A few minutes later the doctor came back to us.

'I'll arrange for somebody to collect the body,' he said briskly.

'There's no need. I think Trui and I can cope.'

'But – '

'It will be something to do.'

'I'd like you to know that I really don't approve,' he said. 'But if you insist – '

'I do.'

But he was adamant about giving me an injection and ordering me to bed. I objected blindly. He paid no attention, accompanying me to my room and pressing me down on the bed.

'I'd prefer to take you back with me to town to keep an eye on you,' he said.

I shook my head.

'Jeremiah and I are here, we'll look after her,' Trui intervened, calmer now, her sense of practicality restored.

It hadn't occurred to the doctor to offer them sedation; they hadn't thought of it either.

I was still trying to resist when the drug, whatever it was, took effect. And it was almost midday before I opened my eyes again, to be flooded, the moment I sat up, with all I could remember of the night before. Even then there was no violence in the recollection; the feeling of being wholly distanced from the world persisted. In a calm that must have struck Trui as unnatural I went through the motions of my morning ablutions, put on the first clothes I could lay hold of, which were the very ones I'd slept in and worn the day before.

On my way down to breakfast the phone rang. It was Michael. I took almost a minute to place the voice; by that time he'd already started repeating my name, believing we'd been cut off.

'Kristien? I just *had* to talk to you, to hear it all first hand. It sounds too good to be true. Tell me all.'

'What are you talking about?' I asked.

'The elections, of course,' he said, as if explaining to a child. 'The press is going overboard. Sounds like a miracle. After the violent run-up, the dire predictions, everybody expecting the absolute worst, and now this. Were you there? Did you vote?'

'Michael, listen – '

'Tell me, blow by blow.'

'Michael,' I said, 'I'm trying to cope with eight deaths in the family.'

'Oh, don't be absurd,' he said.

'Look, I'm trying to tell you – '

'How's your gran?'

'She's dead.'

'Really?'

'That's about the daftest question you could have asked, Michael. What do you expect me to say? That I'm lying? That I'm playing the fool? That it's all been a gas?'

'I'm sorry. But you're in such a strange mood.'

'Women are like that,' I said frostily. 'We have our moods. And now you must excuse me. I have bodies to attend to.'

It was getting out of hand. Our telephone conversations had been skirting disaster for a while: but this was the closest we had yet come to breaking point. Then why could I not feel anything? I loved the man, didn't I? More than geographical distance lay between us. But all I felt like saying – to whom, I didn't know – was, Please, please: not now. Whatever you expect of me, not now.

I had just put the receiver down when the phone rang again. It was a journalist from Cape Town. I couldn't believe it. The news had been on the radio, he said. Would I mind telling him – I pulled the jack out of its socket before he'd finished his sentence. This was a consequence I hadn't even thought about. And it made me feel sick. I literally started retching and had to run to the bathroom to throw up on my empty stomach. It was a while before the blackness receded. I knew I had to catch hold of myself. Seriously. Urgently. Something had to be done to prevent the farm from being overrun by the curious. For the first time I now began to feel threatened. The world was closing in alarmingly. Yet I was so cut off from my own thought processes that the most elementary arithmetic was beyond me – two and two make seven? make a camel? make an ark on the river Nile? – and the very last thing I could manage was precisely what mattered most: practical decisions.

Two visits, telescoped together, imposed some semblance of order on the day that had begun to slip from under my feet. The police in a yellow van; then Abel Joubert in a bakkie so similar to Anna's that I felt my breath catch in my throat.

My first impulse when the police arrived was to run away and hide; in the cellar, behind the graveyard, anywhere. For a moment I couldn't even think what they could have come for: all I knew was that I had to get away. But, curiously, when they began to question me – with commendable patience; with fatherly concern – I found that the effort to remember collected my mind, helped me to regain something of the grip I'd lost. We spoke outside, right there, under the trees: for some inexplicable reason I felt I had to keep them out of the house; they shouldn't invade Ouma's space; I had to protect her. After a while I heard the other vehicle approach, and backed away defensively; then recognised Abel Joubert, and ran to him.

He held me against him for a moment. Still keeping a protective arm round my shoulders he turned to the police. He was very brusque with them. But I assured him I was all right. His support made it easier to tell them the little bit I knew – which was even less than I would have thought beforehand. A life, seven lives, reduced to a few facts of circumstance, position, place, time, no more. Was there anything else I could tell them? Had Anna given any indications of impending disaster? Was there a history of depression, perhaps? Anything in the family? Anything whatsoever?

'That's enough,' said Abel firmly. 'What Kristien needs now is to be left alone.' He took over. He arranged with them for guards to be posted, to keep out the seekers of sensation. And he'd brought Jacob Bonthuys – now for the first time I saw him in the bakkie, his face stricken; bringing with him the reassuring smell of tobacco when he approached – in case I needed assistance of some kind. It was the most reassuring thing he could have done.

And within hours there was a smooth system running on the farm: two police guards at the gate to intercept all visitors (that first day's trickle became a veritable flood as the weekend drew closer and magazines and Sunday papers had to cope with deadlines), communicating by two-way radio with Jeremiah and Jonnie, taking turns; whatever seemed plausible to them was relayed to Trui, who did a deft filtering job before allowing me – in those rare cases where she was persuaded I should have a say – the final choice. Jacob Bonthuys manned the telephone and here, too, Trui made the real decisions. This left me free to sort out my own priorities.

# 4

First, Ouma. There was no need to plan anything beforehand: the moment I broached the subject with Trui she indicated with a brief efficient gesture the kitchen table which she had already scrubbed and covered with black plastic sheets produced by tearing open refuse bags. In matters of death, as I presume of birth, Trui assumed a natural authority. And once we had established our common purpose she issued a few curt orders that sent Jeremiah and Jacob Bonthuys hurrying upstairs to bring down the body wrapped in a sheet.

All available space on the two stoves – the regular electric stove, as well as the old black Dover which had been specially and ceremonially stacked and lit – was taken up by huge pots and cauldrons of boiling water. The kind of scene one has come to expect in popular stories about scenes of birth in some backwater community in the rather distant past.

On the kitchen table the body was laid out. The men withdrew: it didn't take much to send them scurrying. They had strict orders to make sure we were not interrupted, not even by an act of God should such occur. Sun slanted through the window, its progress still marked by Ouma's patterns on the floor, but now unheeded. It was very quiet. Neither of us spoke. Swiftly and professionally Trui denuded the body, like a narrow pale fruit peeled from its skin. I was struck by how diminutive she was, how hard, how dry, like a small plucked chicken. The large patches of burnt skin looked fearsome, yet curiously dessicated. I watched Trui washing her with great care, as if it were a baby's body, very fragile; but she did it with a thoroughness that was impressive. I could imagine Wilhelmina setting about this kind of task in the same manner, practical in the extreme, yet drawing on a formidable store of accumulated knowledge, female and arcane. And I

337

followed her example. There was no feeling of revulsion in me, nor hesitation; but it was no merely perfunctory chore either. It was, if I now think of it, a kind of atonement, a different way of asking forgiveness; in this ritual ablution I was seeking to fulfil a need in myself, if not of absolution, at least of understanding. It was a necessary function to perform before I could think of going on. And she was, as before, the only one who could possibly accord it to me. No, there were no tears; this was beyond their reach. But a sense of mourning, yes; a leavetaking; an assumption, too, of all she had left me. She was no longer Ouma Kristina. She had detached herself from this frail flesh and bone. She was the summary of all those others who had been given life through her; in cleansing her I was cleansing them, I was cleansing the abused, poor, indestructible body of woman.

Another of my small steps, I thought. Illumination need not come by itself, in a great flood of light: it can be the accumulation of small moments, gradually adding up to finality. I'd thought, years ago, before I'd left the country, that this was what had happened to me; but it had been at most a negative illumination, if such a thing exists: it had been the discovery of what was wrong in the country, what I had to escape from. Now, standing over Ouma's body, helping Trui to dress it in the long white flannel gown Ouma had designated for the purpose, I knew I had to go further. A discovery of my need of others, perhaps. How imperceptibly it had been happening: Anna, Trui, Jeremiah, Jonnie, Jacob Bonthuys, Sam Ndzuta, Thando Kumalo, Abel Joubert. I had to do something to help make it worthwhile for Sandile, for myself, all of us. Had I ever really loved? Even what I'd felt for Sandile: had that been love? Perhaps the painful experience of finally renouncing him, three days before, had opened a breach in myself. What I'd first thought of as an emptiness, a lack, might have been the accommodation of a new space inside, a capacity perhaps for love. And love goes beyond a person, an individual: it involves what I was now beginning to discover. This fatal, miraculous involvement with others; all of them, the good and the bad and the indifferent, the living and the dead. The dead, now that she has joined them, entrusted to my hands, to mould them to my needs, to be moulded by them to their inevitability. I can no longer be detached, apart. I am not simply the result of those who have gone before: if I need them, as I need Ouma, they also need me. History is not an impersonal force that sweeps us along like a flood; it is as real and physical as this body, which so serenely enfolds all its past selves. Hers, mine; ours.

Our work was done. Soon afterwards, as if summoned, the doctor arrived at the gate; his presence was relayed through all the intermediaries; he was permitted entry. He seemed taken aback when he discovered the body on the kitchen table, decently dressed by now; but after a token protest, resigned it seemed in advance to defeat, he shrugged and left her to our care. But he would be neglecting his duty, he said, if he did not warn us about certain natural stages of deterioration a body might be expected to undergo when not refrigerated and/or embalmed; if at any stage we felt – he paused to find a word suitable to the occasion – incommoded by its presence we should not hesitate to approach him. We were not incommoded. Ouma's coffin was placed in the basement, temporarily transformed into *chapelle ardente*; both Trui and I paid her regular visits, Trui I suspect for eminently practical reasons, I for more emotional, less readily definable ones, but there was no sign of deterioration. Perhaps she'd been so thoroughly dried out by the time she died, like an old apricot in the sun in summertime, that there was nothing left to pass through those natural stages. A lesson to the old Egyptians. She looked no different from the sleeping old woman I'd tended the last few weeks of her life. Except, naturally, she was no longer breathing.

There she lay, as present in her absence as in life. Until the night she disappeared.

# 5

Sequence, during the days that followed, was of no importance. An alternation of light and dark, of comings and goings, of people and silence; all contained in the stillness of that small body lying in state among the mouldy walls of the cellar.

In the daytime one's attention was dispersed. Even in spite of the human screens surrounding me there was so much to attend to: running the house with Trui, attending to Jeremiah's needs outside on the farm, keeping an eye on the comings and goings of gravediggers, meeting the few visitors I could not avoid – the dominee, the sexton, the undertaker (no relative of the old Piet Malan so abhorred by Ouma, but a pleasant, clean-shaven young man), Ouma's banker, two of Casper's relatives: his mother, a pitiful old woman who was sobbing too much to speak; and a sister, a large and severe woman, who made it clear that it was only a sense of 'Christian duty' that had prompted this visit to the sibling of a mass murderer who had slaughtered in cold blood a man in the prime of his life, the pride of his family, and a pillar of his community. She would be praying for me, she said, making the promise sound like a threat; she was even prepared to go down on her knees right there, with me, to present my case to the Lord of Hosts. However, this prospect was nipped in the bud by the old woman going into convulsions – and which of us, the sister or I, was more relieved was difficult to tell.

Other visitors, too, had to be admitted. Abel, from time to time, with trays of food prepared by his wife. The doctor, more and more rarely. A man from some funeral company who proposed to inscribe the date of Ouma's demise on her tombstone: I told him it wasn't necessary, the space might be left open. Sam Ndzuta, to report that the boys let out on bail were looked after. The old lawyer with Ouma's testament. I received him civilly, of course, but I'm afraid I did not pay much attention. I shall have to go back to him; there will be enough time for it. All I remember is that she has left me a fair amount. The farm goes to Trui; and money to keep it going. She reacted with consternation at first, but finally accepted with good grace: one doesn't argue with the dead. And Jeremiah was pleased.

Even when there were no daytime visitors to contend with, or trips to be made into town, there was a constant awareness of outside events invading our enclave. Trui had taken to keeping the radio on, full blast, throughout the day. Two, in fact: one downstairs in the kitchen, the other upstairs in the room which she and Jeremiah had begun to convert into a more permanent abode, gradually taking possession, insinuating themselves into its space – initially with small indispensable items like an alarm clock, a Bible, a torch, a change of clothing, combs and toothbrushes, the mug in which Jeremiah kept his teeth overnight (and for a large part of the day as well, as he preferred to 'save' them by wearing them only when required for eating, lengthy conversation, or the presentation of a passable front in the execution of his duties); later with more emphatic signs of occupation: clothes and shoes stowed in a cupboard, a small bedside mat, crocheted cloths, their own double bed, an old lemonwood slave chair, a framed embroidered pietà proclaiming, in High Dutch, *Great as the Sea are my Sorrows*.

These radios kept us informed of the steady progress of the election and its aftermath, a noisy accompaniment to the silent persistence of our private drama: increasing chaos as all systems of counting, checking and announcing results broke down, to be met with no more than token protest while the whole country continued to ride the crest of a wave of euphoria. The more amazing the news about the corruption or

340

inefficiency of election officials, counting errors, mislaid or stolen ballot boxes, the more ebullient everybody became in their expectation of a happy conclusion. And there was no violence. After weeks, months, years of steadily increasing 'unrest', exploding in killings on a scale that matched the atrocities from the flashpoints of the world – Northern Ireland, the Middle East, Bosnia-Herzegovina, most recently Rwanda – suddenly there was this break in the tension. A brief lull? Silence before the storm? But the stereotypes of behaviour seemed themselves to be breaking down. We had stunned the world; we were stunning ourselves. And it was borne out on the few brief excursions I had to make to town: everybody I passed in the street first stopped to exchange greetings, to shake hands. For so many years, when there had not been open animosity or suspicion, white and black had been invisible to one another, each pretending the other did not exist: now there was a sense of discovery in acknowledging our mutual presence. At the same time it was almost unbearable, as it came at the very moment I had to face this devastation of my private world. The two just did not make sense together. Or did they?

On those few occasions when I had to go into town, Jeremiah insisted on driving me. I'd never seen him flourish quite as unreservedly. The Chrysler was finally coming into its own, although I could have done without the attention it attracted wherever we went. I had the impression that he would have welcomed it if I'd resorted to small regal waves of the hand to the people lining the streets as we went by, but in this respect I failed him.

Since most of the funeral arrangements had been taken charge of by Casper's family, my chores in town were small and private. I went to the bank. I made the few purchases Trui had listed; I returned Jacob Bonthuys's book and mine to the library (the middle-aged librarian recognised me too late, and when she called my name I was already on my way out and pretended not to hear).

Only one errand I found very difficult to face, but it had to be done – not because it was forced on me or expected of me, but because I myself insisted on it as a necessary conclusion: visiting the undertaker's to view the bodies. Two large coffins, five smaller ones. Walls painted grey, a smell of formaldehyde or whatever they use in these places, plastic flowers. It was like visiting Madame Tussaud's, and that in a way made it easier. They weren't real, only waxen effigies, poor likenesses; the boys looking even more unnatural for the white robes they were wearing. I was used to seeing them covered in dust and grime, their hair unkempt, cuts and scabs and bruises on their hands and faces. They really didn't take well to being boxed, like the hampers of glazed fruit South Africans order for their friends abroad at Christmas.

Both Casper and Anna looked younger than they had been. She was too strange; and her mouth had been sewn up badly, two stitches showed. But he looked relaxed, something boyish in his face, as if given the chance he could have been a pleasant man. But the fixed expressions unnerved me, like those daguerrotypes of ancestors staring stiffly into the lens for thirty, sixty, ninety seconds, preparing for eternity. I was wishing, fervently, to feel something; but it was impossible.

It was only when I stopped to look down at Lenie that I faltered, discovering how close beneath the surface emotion really lay. The small face so heavily made up, the cheeks too blushing, the lips too red. She would have liked that, no doubt. Did they remember the bra? I could still feel the trust and eagerness of her warm sweaty hand in mine. I thought of touching it again, but didn't. Also, the undertaker's wife was hovering in the background, avidly awaiting the display of grief or horror, the breakdown, the uncontrolled sobbing she must have been confident of witnessing, and for an account of which a Sunday newspaper might well have prepaid her a fortune. So with an effort I contained my emotion and turned hurriedly away and went back to the disinterested glare of the sun outside where Jeremiah was waiting in the Chrysler.

'Take me to their farm,' I said, leaning back, closing my eyes, trying to remember, then trying to forget what I'd remembered.

The doors stood open, but the place seemed deserted. I went in through the kitchen, hesitating on the doorstep, calling out an apprehensive 'Hello?', then venturing further. Someone – servants, the good ladies of the district, Casper's relatives of whom several had arrived over the last few days – had cleaned up. If one knew where to look, which I did, there were still traces to be found, a stain on the carpet, a patch on the wall, holes where the plaster had been dislodged by bullets; but otherwise it was tidy, reduced to anonymity. Even the children's bathroom was spotless now, the signs of their boisterous evening ablutions removed. The passage with the silent telephone. The bedroom from which I'd dislodged a small resentful occupant – what was his name? Dirk? Ben? Cassie? I wish I knew – was bare; the mattress had been removed from the bed. Of course. The master bedroom. A Bible on the bedside table. How frantically one tries to reinvent the scenes no longer necessary, as if the very effort would invest them with some kind of meaning. *I am the Lord thy God.*

Back in the kitchen I found an elderly, motherly woman standing aimlessly at the sink, staring through the window at the featureless day outside. She started when she saw me, even though the imposing presence of the Chrysler in the yard should have forewarned her. I remembered her from the few days I'd spent here.

'Sanna? Where are all the others?'

'They scared of staying here, Missus. They some of them in town, other ones on farms, all over.'

'How are you keeping, Sanna?'

'Oh Jesus, Missus.' She collapsed against me, her large soft body enfolding me like a feather mattress, bursting into tears, crying out loudly in that timeless wail of grief that rips through history. 'They all dead, Missus, they all dead, my little boys, my little gels.'

For the first time I broke down. In Ouma's home I couldn't, there was too much, were too many, dependent on me. Here it was possible, with this woman, consoling and consoled, knowing what we'd lost; and crying for ourselves as much as for them.

It was that night that Ouma disappeared.

# 6

Grimly and inexorably the funeral ceremony is unfolding about me; almost literally at my feet. I would have preferred to give the church service a miss, to wait here, protected from the glare, and attend only the interment in our family graveyard (which, with eight new graves, has very little space left for further additions; the past is rapidly catching up with the future). But in the end I succumbed to the pressure – not so much to Abel Joubert's arguments about 'facing the world' and 'paying the last respects you owe your kin' as to Trui's expectations of 'proper' behaviour. So Trui, Jonnie and I squeezed in very tightly beside Jeremiah on the front seat of the Chrysler, washed and polished for three days running; and proceeded in state along the twenty kilometres to Outeniqua, with Ouma's empty coffin in the back.

I was the only one who knew it was empty. There was no need to alarm or even to alert anyone, and the men who carried it didn't find it strange that Ouma's handful of dust, as light as any feather, added almost nothing to the weight of the coffin. I am sorry I cannot give any satisfactory account of what happened: even if I hadn't fallen asleep that night while keeping my voluntary vigil in the cellar, I doubt that I

343

would have witnessed anything special to report. She was there, and then she wasn't.

Trui had tried her best to pack me off to bed early – 'Kristien, you can't go on like this, you need to get some sleep, let me make you some hot milk and brandy' – but finally gave up. There was something very special about those nights all on my own. Jacob Bonthuys would be in the upstairs room to which he'd been consigned, reading one of the books with which I'd provided him; but the others were asleep. I'd turned off all the lights. There were only the candles burning in the cellar, casting fantastic shadows on the walls from which, like nocturnal animals emerging from their hiding places in the dark, the long-lost paintings came alive: those weird copulations and carnivals and processions and celebrations. In the midst of all this, Ouma at rest in her coffin. The lid had been screwed down, only the small hatch over the face lay folded back on its hinges. Below it, her small dried-apricot face, hard and brittle and half-transparent like papyrus, inscribed with the hieroglyphs of her long life.

For her sake I wished she could be buried now so that it could be over and done with; the grave was where she'd wanted to be. But for my own sake this was preferable. There was something precious about having her around like this. Soon, all too soon, life would resume; this unnatural island in time would dissolve and the current would sweep me along again, the future was impatient to take over. But while this lasted I savoured it, and drew strength from her presence. At last, I thought, the coffin would fulfil the purpose of which it had been deprived for so long.

This is where the recollection becomes unreliable. I find it hard to believe that I could have fallen asleep. I felt so alert: and I was still sitting in the same posture, leaning forward with my chin on my palms, my elbows on my knees, when there was a sudden flickering of all four candles, as if a window had been opened somewhere. I couldn't feel a draught, yet the dancing of the flames registered a current of air. I stood up to investigate. It was then that I noticed she was no longer there.

The lid was still firmly screwed down on the coffin, leaving only the small square of the hatch open. But Ouma had gone. I went nearer. I stretched out my arm, full length, to grope inside. It was quite empty. I was bemused, but felt no fear at all. When I looked up there was a bird sitting on the back of one of the two chairs on which the coffin rested. It was so dark that I couldn't make out what kind it was, but it certainly had an unusual appearance: owl-like, but elongated, with legs like a flamingo or a crane and a peacock's tail, the feathers streaked with strange colours, like one of the figures on the wall. It might have been an effect of the candle light.

My mind was very lucid. The first thing to do was to batten down the hatch on the lid of the coffin. The old-fashioned wing-bolts were in place, large shiny brass ones which Jeremiah had polished with great care. It was only a matter of fastening them as tightly as I could. There was no telling how Trui or the others would react if they found out; it was better not to upset them. Ouma, too, I felt convinced, would have preferred me to keep this between the two of us.

Now I was conscious of being tired; and it was the first night since last Wednesday that I had a proper sleep, nine hours, a consummation more than devoutly wished.

'I had to close up the coffin last night,' I told Trui the next morning.

She gave me an understanding look. 'Perhaps you must phone them to come and take it,' she suggested.

But I shook my head. 'She belongs here, Trui.'

'We don't want a smell around.'

'No, it's all right now.'

'You sure?'

'I'm sure.'

'Then you can come and help me in the kitchen,' she said. I wondered whether she herself was conscious of how, slowly, easily, she was beginning to assume control.

Through the open kitchen door I could see Jeremiah and Jonnie moving to and fro in the distance, raking leaves, sweeping the yard. But that was not what caught my attention: what made me stop to look again was the flash of blue and green among the trees. A peacock. There were other birds about as well; I could hear them twittering and fluttering in the trees. They were coming back.

They are about us now, in the graveyard. Over the last few days they have all returned. If possible, there are even more of them now than ever before. All the way into town they accompanied the hearse; and they perched on the church when we pulled up outside, the way they'd once flocked around the hospital. It was difficult to make our way through the throng, following the empty coffin on its slow progress into the sandstone building. In front of the pulpit it was put in place at the end of the long line already settled into position. Whisperings moved through the congregation the way the wind moves through a land of wheat.

The obsequious sexton took me by the arm and steered me to the pews reserved for relatives. There were a few of the uncles and aunts I vaguely remembered from childhood. Some of them had paid a visit to the farm over the last week, formal, strange, diffident, perfunctory, offering me the wet kisses that stamped them as kin. With those solemn and mostly doddering siblings of Mother and Father had come a number of their children: some of them would have taken part in our nocturnal rampages up into the attic, down into the cellar; one or two of the cousins might have been in the loquat tree with me, hidden in the dark foliage, awaiting the right moment to pee on an unsuspecting adult passing below – but I recognised none, and was relieved not to admit into my private memories any of these stolid citizens with moustaches, with bristles between the joints on their fingers or in their ears and noses.

But by far the greater part of the reserved block was occupied by Casper's relatives, a solid phalanx of brothers and sisters with spouses and children, and uncles and aunts and cousins, and the still sobbing old mother: most of them staring at me with fixed expressions that ranged from open hostility and accusation to righteous indignation, to gawping curiosity and, thinning out towards the far end of the scale, the steadfast glare of forgiveness (in the assurance that vengeance belongs to the Lord God).

A single seat had been kept for me within this block of decent and outraged citizens. But I had Trui and Jeremiah and Jonnie with me, and I would not be separated from them.

Flustered, the sexton glanced this way and that, then argued in a strident whisper, 'Ag, I'm so sorry, Miss, but you see, these pews are for family only.'

'They are family,' I said, without bothering to keep my voice down.

If my entry had caused a wind in a wheatfield, this was a hurricane. With some luck some of Casper's relatives might have stormed out, but they had put too much effort into coming all this way, and were adamant not to miss anything; I, too, did my Luther bit, refusing to budge. I had the impression that Jeremiah, given the choice, would have preferred to withdraw. But Trui's jaw had a square set to it which announced that she was resolved to see this through with me. So was Jonnie, if for rather different reasons.

At that moment, through some miscalculation or from a sincere wish to defuse a potentially disruptive situation, the organist, suitably bedecked in black but with an aggressively purple hat, moved through a not altogether successfully improvised transition from some rather bland imitation of Bach to a powerful if heavily sentimental rendering of Handel's Funeral March. The sexton, caught between the glare of animosity from the reserved block and the imminent emergence of the dominee from the vestry, chose the lesser of two evils and, still clutching me by the elbow, scurried towards the front pew where he whispered urgently into the ear of the nearest man. The message was relayed from one to the other, and in a brief commotion four or five venerable men rose and hurried to the vestry, colliding with the dominee just as he made what he must have hoped would be a memorable entrance, and returning with rather too many straight-backed chairs upholstered in blue, which were lined up in front for us, so close to the coffins that we could have rested our chins on them.

The organist continued playing for a while longer, which clearly frustrated the dominee; but at least it reimposed some semblance of order after the disturbance. In a gesture that moved me through its very unexpectedness three of Casper's relatives came forward to take up the empty chairs beside us. One of them, a man who bore an eerie resemblance to Casper himself, briefly pressed my hand.

The service began. I tried to switch off, offended by the histrionics of the dominee who brought all the sound and fury he could muster to this crowning moment of his career. What made it easier for the mind to wander was that throughout the service there were birds flitting in through the doors and windows as if to monitor our progress, then darting out again to spread the message. I even noticed a mouse scuttling along the front of the pulpit, past the row of coffins, towards the vestry. Would there be any leftovers, I wondered. Ouma hadn't left any; she posed no eucharistic problems.

At last that, too, was over. Then came the endless procession to the farm. It looked more like a church fête or a rugby match, judging from the size of the crowd. But it won't be much longer now.

# 7

Sam Ndzuta is standing on my left beside Ouma's grave. As many of the crowd as have been able to squeeze into the graveyard are massed around the graves; overhead a vast cloud of birds hangs suspended, casting its shadow over most of the farm. Eight graves. The mind fails to come to grips with it. It's like a skyscraper: once it exceeds a certain height it can no longer tease the imagination and loses its power to fascinate.

It is also a matter of experience. If I am left dazed by the sheer extent of it, to Sam it is nothing new. 'How many times in the townships have we been to these funerals?' he says. 'Three at a time, five, thirteen, twenty-six. After a while one stops counting.'

Yet to the whites in today's crowd those funerals took place beyond the reach of history. They involved blacks. Massacred by police, by 'security forces'; or victims of 'black on black violence'. To them this is different. This turning in of the self upon the self. I wonder whether Sam understands it: whether to him this would be 'white on white'. Would he realise that he, too, is involved in this, or would he repeat our own past mistake of believing we could remain beyond it, of misreading our own terrible complicity?

Wilhelmina once said, if Ouma was to be believed, 'If it is God's will we shall stay here; and if it isn't then we'll pack our things and trek away.' But what happens when there is no further horizon beyond which one can run away? What happens when geography closes in on you, when the gravity of a black hole permits no ray of light to escape and carry the message of what has happened, is happening?

Michael telephoned again, some time this last week. His voice had gone flat with shock. 'Jesus, my love, the last time I spoke to you I thought you were making some sick joke about the deaths in your family. Can you ever forgive me?'

'I don't know, Michael,' I said. I didn't mean to be cruel; I didn't mean to be anything in particular. I was merely saying what I thought: that I didn't know, couldn't predict anything about myself.

'I've just read the papers,' he said. 'I still can't believe it.'

'I can't either. I keep thinking I'll hear a car outside and see Anna get out. I keep wishing she'll bring the children. Even the boys I couldn't stand. I keep thinking, hoping . . . But what's the use?'

'"What's done cannot be undone"?'

'Please!' I said sharply. 'This really isn't a time for being clever.'

'I wasn't meaning to sound clever. I just don't have any words of my own. A poor player. Sorry.' An awkward pause; perhaps we were both equally desperate about getting through, about feeling in touch, if only to persuade ourselves that there *were* hands out there to be clasped, and held. I remembered the early days of our love, the visit to Gough Square, Dr Johnson's famous phrase, a time when death was still a literary event; even so it excited us enough to go home and make love behind the red door. Now death has become all too real. And our earlier reflexes seem not only inadequate but obscene. I heard him saying in my ear, 'I don't suppose you've had any time to think about coming back.'

'I'm not coming back.'

It came as a shock to hear myself saying that. It was nothing I'd thought out, resolved, cleared in my mind. All of a sudden the words just came; and as I said them I knew it was true. It was the one thing that I knew for sure, now that it had been spoken.

'What do you mean?' I could hear him gasp as if he'd been hit in the stomach.

'I'll probably have to come over to sort out my things. But my life has been displaced. I have to be here now.'

'But what about us?'

For a while it was difficult to utter the words; but they had to be said, for his sake as much as for mine. 'It hasn't worked out, Michael. There's no one to blame for it. Or if there is it's me, not you. I have no idea yet what I'm going to do, but whatever it is it will be over here, not there.'

Nothing as trite, as simplistically political, as responding to a 'challenge'; nothing as private or pathological as 'proving a point' or 'proving myself'. It was both larger and more intimate than that.

And standing here among the graves, as all the coffins are lowered simultaneously to the barely restrained satisfaction of the undertaker who must see in this feat a sign of divine approval, and no doubt of excellent business in the future, I know it is the right decision. It is also the only one. But there is a difference between taking a decision because it is the only one, and doing it because you would have chosen it from any number of others had they been available. I have chosen this place, not because I was born here and feel destined to remain; but because I went away and then came back and now am here by choice. Perhaps for the first time in my life it is a decision that has not been forced on me from outside, by circumstances, but which has been shaped inside myself, like a child in the womb. This one I shall not deny. It is mine.

The birds above are breaking away from the cloud they have formed. In a great wash of sound they take off in all directions, return, swoop down low overhead, execute dizzying dives to the edge of the graves, then rush away again, a spectacular display in many colours. Most of the crowd are so intent on staring down into the graves as they fling their handfuls of petals, their handfuls of earth, on the coffins, that they do not seem to notice.

All that is still needed, it occurs to me, is old Moishe: old Moishe as a young boy, to act as mourner and to weep so extravagantly that he falls into the grave, which will earn him a pound; it would go some way towards sending his grandson and a footloose girl to Baghdad where the camels will sing hymns, in Latin, in the trees at dusk.

The crowd begins to shuffle out and disperse, trampling the flower beds; children go off in pursuit of the peacocks, oblivious of the goose or chicken shit in which they trample. I linger behind for a while. The undertaker gives a signal to his labourers to start filling up. I watch the red dust as it billows up, caught in the near-horizontal sunlight from behind.

Yes. After all, and in spite of all, this is my place.

I no longer have the wild faith of youth in my ability to change the world; but I also know that it *can* be changed, and that I want to be involved in it. It is more than a private act of commitment, a personal rebellion. For too long the women of my tribe, of all tribes, have been forced to suffer and to rebel in the small private space allotted them by the powerful males who rule the world; I do not intend to run off in search of a shadow, or to change myself into a tree, or to be buried in shit, to embroider my name on a sweet little cloth, and especially not to vent my rage by wiping out my family with myself. I understand that rage; my God, how I understand it! But it cannot be repeated, cannot go on. What I want to undertake is much less spectacular. To work with others, to bring about a world – slowly, gradually, but surely, I swear – in which it will no longer be inevitable to be only a victim. I know that the present – this small square riddled with graves – is less real than the possible.

There are points of no return that mark the beginning, not the end, of hope.

Casper's brother, the one who joined me in church, comes back to me to offer me an arm. He must think I am too overcome by grief to follow the others. But there is no need to offend him, and to explain will take too long. I accept his arm.

# 8

The moon is in its last quarter and there is very little light. But Ouma gives off a fine luminosity, not enough to see by, but sufficient to mark her position. She is sitting on her tombstone, on which the date of her death is still blank, as it will now remain. A single death clearly does not suffice; Wilde had it right. I have appropriated the peacock's roost on the wall. Some ostriches have lined up, absurd black shapes along the nearest fence. At the gate a couple of mahems, frail shadows in the dark, are humming. The palace among the black trees is dark. There are a few owls about, and from time to time there is a sleepy twittering of birds. They have resumed their old habits, their habitual perches. The crowd has gone, leaving devastation in its wake. We shall have to start tidying up tomorrow. Think about the future.

The dead are silent. They now depend on me.

This must be what Thando Kumalo had in mind when he said, '*Salani kahle*.'

'It has gone well,' says Ouma. 'Under the circumstances.'

'You should have been part of it.'

'No, I didn't want to spoil Anna's day. Funerals are not my scene anyway. People no longer enjoy themselves the way they used to.'

'I missed you.'

'But you have me now. I'll always be here. Of course, you may decide to run off again.'

'I won't. I've decided that if you could come back from Baghdad, I can come home too.'

'Why? Because it is easier now?'

'No!' I say in a rush of passion. 'Because it is more difficult. Because there is work to be done. As much for myself as for others.' I look hard at her; right through her. 'Will you help me?'

'We'll all be here.' She looks out across the graves, and beyond; far beyond. 'The things we'll do together – !'

'Until one day an elephant comes and blows the story away?' I ask, not without a touch of malice.

I cannot see her face, but I have an idea she is smiling. 'No,' she says. 'Not this time. I'm not going to make it easy for you.'

'Why not, Ouma?'

'Because, Kristien, you're a big girl now.'

# Glossary

*[Words not explained in the text]*

*ag* – oh
*assegai* – short spear
*biltong* – dried, salted strips of meat
*bliksem* – scoundrel (literally: lightning)
*Boer* – Afrikaner
*boer* – farmer
*bokmakierie* – onomatopoeic bird-name: species of shrike
*boytjie* – diminutive form of *boy*
*broekie lace* – wrought-iron trellis on verandah (literally: knicker-lace)
*bywoner* – poor tenant farmer
*doek* – see *kopdoek*
*dominee* – Dutch Reformed pastor
*duiker* – small antelope which runs with a characteristic bobbing motion
*gevrek* – hopeless (literally: dead)
*impi* – detachment of Zulu soldiers
*kaffir* – (here) member of a black tribe (later pejorative)
*kambro* – plant with large edible bulb
*kaross* – blanket of animal skins
*katlagter* – ground robin
*kelkiewyn* – onomatopoeic bird-name: sand-grouse
*kierie* – (walking) stick
*kiewiet* – Cape plover
*kist* – chest (usually for storing clothes)
*(kop)doek* – headscarf
*maar* – but, rather
*meerkat* – ground squirrel
*MK* – (member of) *Umkhonto weSizwe*, 'The Spear of the Nation', armed
   wing of the ANC
*moffie* – homosexual
*mos* – just, just so
*platteland* – rural regions

*pollies* – police
*pot bread* – bread baked in a cast-iron pot
*riem* – thong
*smous* – itinerant salesman, pedlar
*tambotie* – fragrant dark wood, much used for furniture
*tsamma* – wild melon
*veldskoen* – rough hand-made shoe
*voorhuis* – lounge (literally: front room)
*wors* – sausage